Alex Sapegin

THE DRAGON INSIDE

Book three
A CRUEL TALE

Translated by Elizabeth Kulikov

Cover Design by Marat Gabdrkhmanov

D1602756

ISBN: **9781980425274**

LitHunters, 2018

A BRIEF NOTE FROM ALEX SAPEGIN:

Dear reader,

Thank you for reading my book. I hope you enjoy this story and will continue the adventure.

The Dragon Inside:

Becoming the Dragon

Wings on my Back

A Cruel Tale

Crown of Horns

Home at Last

CONTENTS:

PART ONE, OUT OF THE FRYING PAN AND INTO THE FIRE.

Russia. N-ville...

"Iliya, are you coming?" Mrs. Kerimov touched her husband on the shoulder. "It's 2 a.m. Give it a rest."

Mr. Kerimov turned his attention away from the screen and rubbed his temples in exhaustion.

"Ten more minutes, hon. I'm just finishing the diagrams."

"Come on, cut it out."

"Cut what out?" he asked his wife, sincerely failing to comprehend.

"Cut it all out, please. I'm asking you. Enough... you won't find him. ...I can't go on like this anymore," his spouse cried, fell to the floor, hugged her husband's legs and started to sob. "If there were only a grave, I could cry there. I'd know he was there and wouldn't console myself with false hopes. Iliya, how can we?"

Mr. Kerimov picked up his weeping wife in his arms and brought her to the bedroom. He laid her carefully on the bed and lay down beside her.

"Don't say that. Andy didn't die. Do you hear me? He didn't die! I'll do whatever it takes to find him!" he said confidently.

"I don't know, Iliya. It's been six months since we lost him. I'm tired.... It's as if we live on different planets. You, with your work, you've stopped paying attention to us altogether. Stop blaming yourself and look around you. You have two girls. Give them a scrap of affection—they're not dead! Ira's gotten completely out of hand, and Olga... Iliya, I'm getting scared she's becoming exactly like Andy after he got struck by lightning. The same eyes.... I see her smile less and less often. Come back to us, please...."

Mr. Kerimov didn't say anything. He too had been noticing their family problems recently, but his constant barrage of work didn't leave him time to think. His wife was right. He'd stopped noticing everyone around him, giving 100% of himself to his work and his efforts to find his son. After the unfortunate event of Andy's disappearance, his company had come into quite a shower of funds. All the guards were changed, and new barriers were put up all around. They built new grounds and the entire territory was covered with masking nets. It was only possible to enter the territory by passing three control points and a biometric fingerprint test. Four months later, they received the very latest new equipment. After calibrating it, the physicists began their experiments, but so far their goal eluded them. They hadn't created a "window" to another world. He watched the surveillance video footage hundreds of times after the explosion, and one of them showed a good view of where Andy had been thrown. It was a coniferous forest made of giant trees, something like Sequoya, and the sky above them was visible too. And the sky was a whole 'nother matter. The edge of the stellar body visible over the horizon couldn't possibly be that of the moon. The moon didn't contain oceans or have cyclones. There were a ton of theories put forward. It could have been a parallel world, a far-off planet in some remote galaxy. One thing was for sure—Andy landed in another world.

"I'll try…." Mr. Kerimov hugged his wife. He couldn't find any other words of comfort for her. What could possibly comfort her? He stroked his crying wife's hair and shoulders for a long time with just his fingers, until she calmed down and fell asleep. Then, carefully, trying not to make a sound, he got out of bed and tiptoed to the kitchen.

Through the window, in the darkness of the winter night, the lights of the few cars twinkled, and snow was falling. Mr. Kerimov switched his focus to his own reflection in the glass. He saw a man with broad shoulders and sunken, unshaven cheeks, tired and beaten down by life. He opened the fridge, took out a bottle of "Gzhelka" vodka, poured himself a half a glass, and gulped it down in one swig. The drink burned his throat and flowed down into his stomach with a warming sensation, but did not at all bring the calming effect he'd hoped for. Staring into space, detached from the world around him, sat down on a stool and put his elbows on the kitchen table. What, what was he doing wrong? They'd modeled all possible and impossible options for starting the apparatus. They entered identical parameters for starting and activating the electromagnetic fields, (thank God all the control readings of the devices of that ill-fated day were recorded by the computers). They conducted experiments with the penetration of various objects into the active field. All for nothing….

"Dad?" A child's voice made Mr. Kerimov snap out of it. How long had he been sitting there? Olga was standing in the doorway to the kitchen in a light nightgown with her hand on Bon's back. After Andy disappeared, the dog stopped eating, and only Olga's tenacity, spoon-feeding him for two weeks, prevented a second family tragedy. Once he'd survived the loss of one master, Bon chose another master for himself—Olga. The dog followed the girl everywhere. When she went off to school on September 1st to start the fourth grade, he walked her all the way to the school building and, ignoring the commands of Mrs. Kerimov and Irina, remained waiting for her in front of the building. Soon the guards, students, and teachers all got used to the great big dog accompanying and waiting for his girl every day outside the building. He became a regular sight associated with the school. When it got cold, the children brought him a blanket, and he would lie on it at the far end of the hall while classes were going on. And, as a bonus, Mr. Kerimov could feel sure of the girl's safety walking to and from school. No one was stupid enough to come near her with a giant beast bodyguard like that.

"Yes, baby."

"Dad, you completely forgot about the time." Olga took her father by the hand and led him to the bedroom.

Time… They'd all completely forgotten about time!

"Olga, you're a genius! Time, it has a direction too! Yes! that's it!" He picked his daughter up and swung her in a circle around the room. "What do you want for Christmas?"

"I want you to be here to celebrate it with us, not at work," Olga answered sincerely. "Promise me."

"I promise."

***

At the last meeting of the outgoing year, the entire intellectual elite of the team headed by Kerimov had gathered at the table. "The old guys" sat next to the boss, guys he'd started working with back in the eighties. Five "Bandar-logs" (monkeys from Rudyard Kipling's *The Jungle Book*) occupied the opposite side of the long rectangular conference room table, members of the young generation of the intellectual elite of Russian sciences. Vera, the senior commercial director's administrative assistant thought of the nickname for the young scientists (the senior commercial director himself was present too. Some rich guy had to fork over the dough). As it happened, the name stuck right away.

Each person Kerimov had chosen and invited to the project was a bright and unusual star. They were constantly spouting ideas and proving that some of the best and most talented young people go into STEM (science, technology, engineering, and math). The "Bandar-logs" instantly became thick as thieves and always agreed among themselves. They always put forth Aleksandr Belov as their spokesperson for their cutting attacks, who answered only to the informal address "Alex," a genius from the field of mathematics and data analysis, who could describe any process in numbers. There was also Denis Remezov, a nuclear physicist, the main powerhouse and organizer of all the great endeavors initiated by the "Bandar-logs," as a rule, mainly in the form of jokes and small harmless pranks.

The scientists had been screaming at one another for going on three hours now. The new apparatus configuration Kerimov was suggesting brought heated debate from all sides. If the big boss weren't present, a couple of "hot heads" would have long since started a fist fight. They were that passionate. When the debate died down, Mr. Kerimov, drawing the line, said to Alex:

"Alex, your task is to create a mathematical model describing what we've discussed here at this meeting. I'd like to see what we get when we factor in multi-directional time with various formulas. Try making a model with a spiral or sinusoidal projection on a common axis of coordinates. It would be good to work out the scenario that includes the movement of my son in the active field, and how he affected the apparatus, accumulators, and metamaterial polarizers. From there we might be able to put together the algorithm for putting various blocks into operation when opening a "window" to another world. You, Maksimov. Oleg, your job is to put together a program for controlling the apparatus in accordance with the figures presented by our god and the model equations. The rest of you Bandar-logs will help with the transpositioning of the blocks. Alright, that's all for now. The next meeting will be on January 11th."

***

"Petrovich, what is this?" Kerimov kicked an empty pizza box out of his way and shoved the dried-up sushi onto the floor. A half-empty bottle of champagne, knocked down by the box, rolled around the floor, pathetically clinking on the wheel of the operator's chair. Another portion of the Italian delicacy plopped down onto a chair, face down as per the law of falling food, spattering sauce everywhere. Someone apparently had a good time in the operator's chair over the holidays.

Gennady Petrovich was a freckled man with wide palms and shifty eyes on a simple face. You couldn't tell by looking at him that he was a retired lieutenant colonel. He watched the fizzy beverage spilling over, eyes glinting with anger, and answered:

"Your guys wanted to order out. I allowed the delivery."

Kerimov wanted to puke just from alcoholic fumes in the room.

"Pizza and sushi: I get it, but how could they bring vodka and champagne here? Does this look like a playground to you? What, did they order themselves a stripper, too??"

Petrovich, head of the internal guards, looked down and guiltily shuffled his feet. The face of the boss of the research complex turned a shade of scarlet. Petrovich could see the smoke start coming out of his ears. Kerimov grabbed him by the lapels with both hands. He let out a muffled gasp.

"You good-for-nothing!" Kerimov roared. "What the hell did we hire you for? Had yourself a night out here in the lab, did you?! I'll show you a New Year's Eve party! I can't leave you alone for a week! Do you realize what could've happened?"

"I'll deal with the booze and your colleagues' bringing it here. I'll punish the guilty ones of my people." The lieutenant colonel adroitly freed himself from the boss' grasp and took a step back from Kerimov. The simple expression vanished from the head of the guards' face. Now a fit, strong-willed man with smart, penetrating eyes stood looking at the boss of sciences. He was accustomed to giving orders and strictly controlling their implementation. "I'm looking out for safety, not your crew's morals. Got it? Only your champs have access to the operator's room and the platform. Your Bandar-logs ... acted like it," he hissed through his teeth.

The door to the break room opened with a creak, revealing the sleepy mug of Alex the math genius and leader of the research group of the commercial scientific research institute with a long-winded abbreviation for a name. Turning swiftly at the sound, a livid Iliya Kerimov grabbed this one by the back of the collar and dragged him along after himself like a naughty kitten. Alex, heavily hungover, who'd left to go to the bathroom, hung on the boss' arm like a sausage, realizing that the less he moved, the longer he would live. Kerimov glanced into an office. The whole "Bandar-log" gang was gathered here. The young colleagues were lying side by side on a couch converted into a sofa bed. The whole place reeked of stale vodka. The former bunker's forced air ventilation system hadn't yet taken care of the stench.

"Have you all gotten a good rest, guys?" Mr. Kerimov grumbled, almost chuckling. He looked at Oleg Maksimov, who was laying his head on a dirty winter boot and had the tread pattern of its sole on his other cheek. Kerimov's desire to kill them all passed from the comic sight of them.

Returning to the operator's room and dragging the mathematician with him by the collar, he sat him down in one of the operator's chairs and hit him with a hard, foreboding stare.

"Alex, your gang," he began, accompanying the phrase with a sweeping gesture in the direction of the break room, "is closer than ever to leaving the walls of this interesting building forever, with the print of the boss' boot on their butts and their termination of employment documents in their pockets...." He was about to go on but was interrupted.

"No," Denis Remezov's disheveled head appeared in the doorway. He sniffed loudly and wiped his face with his hand, leaving a shiny trail on his sleeve. "Boss, you're going to give us drinks for another week." His hazy look ran across the room and stopped on an inverted champagne bottle. Seeing how Kerimov's face stretched out from such a statement, he corrected himself: "Well, maybe a week is a bit much, but we'll hang out for today at your expense."

The boss choked on his saliva and coughed.

"Boys, gotten your lines crossed, have you?"

"No, my memory serves me well; it's sober. I can't say as much for my reasoning and my body, but I'm sure I remember quite clearly that last night, we put the apparatus together according to the new scheme worked out by Alex and Oleg. Some people partied last night. But we were working hard! It all works great now. The "window" opens, not to America, of course, but even without the Yankees, we can sure impress the big bosses! It looks so beautiful there—you wouldn't believe. And..." Denis pushed his glasses up on his nose and tramped his feet over to his terminal. He typed on the keyboard for a minute, then a sublime smile spread across the operator's satisfied face. "Your attention on the main screen, please! Does the view remind you anything?" It was a familiar sight, truly. The edge of the blue planet over the horizon stood out especially brightly. A soft breeze swayed the tops of gigantic trees and drove clouds across the sky. "Alex, come here."

Denis waited for the mathematician, who'd been subject to "shipping and handling" by the boss, came over to him and, hugging him around the shoulder, said in a pompous tone:

"This genius, unjustly chastised by our higher-ups, he's the one who crunched the numbers and created the algorithm that moved Andy in the active field. Eventually, we dropped the monoblock idea and switched to a multicomponent scheme with several active fields by the alternate commissioning of metamaterial polarizers and multistage quantization. Half a year ago the equipment only fixed the level of the load and didn't take into account the resulting energizing of the external field. My hat's off to your foresight, boss, but time turned out to be really something interesting. By initiating different blocks and changing the potential of the external field, we opened "windows" to several worlds and were able to fixate the parameters. Based on the different starting pulses of different power and different load application vectors, time goes at different paces in different worlds, and I wouldn't be surprised if it goes in different directions. Although, Alex's been talking about that from the beginning. We're both just so surprised at your shameful ingratitude. After all, he's the one who set the time vector last time. It's a shame, of course, that a puncture into the world your son got lost in consumes massive amounts of energy, and the accumulators can only hold the "window" open for five seconds. But Oleg is sure he can fix this problem. We've just got to get rid of the four-step quantization and smooth the transition process. Well, now you're so happy you've let go of your tension. Come on, is there really any reason to bust our chops? And by the way, before I finish here, I want to ask about something," Denis asked his boss, who was eagerly gobbling up the image on the main screen with his frantically gleaming eyes. "Are we going to have some more to drink today to cure this wicked hangover?"

"Yes, you are." Iliya Kerimov looked away from the screen. He wanted to ask the guys a hundred questions, but the main one came to the forefront: how were they able to find the world Andy was in? But he could wait a day or two for the Q and A. "But first, clean the whole place up. Alex doesn't have to participate in the clean-up."

"Alex, 'We are great. We are free. We are wonderful. We are the most wonderful people in all the jungle! We all say so, and so it must be true,'" Denis recalled the quote from Kipling's The Jungle Book and slapped the mathematician on the shoulder as he did.

Leaving the youth alone to clean up their mess, Iliya Kerimov went to his office, looked at the phone on his desk for a long time, then entered a long series of numbers, and put the receiver to his ear. After a few hums, someone picked up.

"Hello." A strong, unmistakable feeling of irritation resounded in the person's voice through the thousands of miles of distance between them.

"Hello, Mr. Bratulev, this is Kerimov…"

"Considering what time it is, you better have a very good reason for bothering me," the unknown person interrupted the scientist. "Has your center been successful?"

"Not exactly what we were hoping for…"

"If not that, what?"

"The result we got is far more serious."

There was a pause.

"I'm waiting…" the voice said after a few seconds.

"Mr. Bratulev, I can't tell you the rest over the phone."

"It's that serious?" the irritation in the voice disappeared. Now the person just sounded surprised.

"Even more so!"

"Alright, I believe you. Step up security and make sure as few people as possible are in the know. Remind all your colleagues of the need for confidentiality. I'll send my chief of security. He'll organize and ensure a level of control appropriate for a situation like this. I don't have time to talk now; I hope to hear the details when we meet. Don't call me at this number anymore. Goodbye."

He hung up without another word.

***

Petrovich waved to the driver of the company car and went down the stairs to the underground crossing. The head of the internal guard of the institute came up on the other side of the road, grabbed his cell phone and pressed a button.

"Hello?" a soothing female voice said on the line.

"There's been a break in the dam," he said in a nonchalant tone.

"Understood."

After he hung up, something clicked in the phone. He tossed the now useless device into a trash can, where it quickly became a melted hunk of plastic....

Tantre. The middle of the Ort River...

Andy flowed down the river, giving himself up to the current of the Ort. He hadn't the strength to swim. Merchant vessels sailed by a few times, and he saw people's fingers hanging from the sides and pointing at him. He didn't care. He had been seen by one and all on the shooting range; a couple dozen more witnesses wouldn't make a difference. The important thing now was to find a quiet, deserted spot to lay low for two or three weeks until he could take on human form once again. As luck would have it, there were gardens and cultivated fields all along the banks of the river, and hiding a three-ton dragon there would be problematic.

"Ow!" Andy almost gulped down a bunch of water when he opened his mouth to cry out in pain. A piece of his wing got stuck on a snag and the dragon lost what was left of his left wing.

Orten was getting farther and farther behind him with every passing minute and the hope of finding clues about how to build interworld gates along with it. There was no way he could go back to the School of Magic now. It was forbidden. What was worse, Frida was lying on the School shooting range that had become a battlefield. Why? Why did he bring trouble and death to those he loved? What were the local gods punishing him and them for? If he could change the past, he never would have gone to the shooting range, and Frida would still be alive....

Andy floated on and felt hatred towards Wood elves growing in his chest, filling the cold emptiness left after the battle. His thirst for revenge was tearing him up inside, but he wasn't planning on getting even now. What for? It was stupid and pointless for one dragon to try to get revenge on an entire state. He had to try to find the Woodies' weak spots and find himself some reliable allies. The Rauu, for example. Now even the hypothetical possibility of a duel with the Icicles could be crossed off the list. The Snow Elves never avenged themselves on people they've fought with side by side. Oh, the look on Melima's face and the faces of his other classmates when they saw him as a dragon was incomparable. He had to think about that. *Hmm, I wonder—did Miduel ever find that box?* Only a couple of hours ago, he was thinking of how to build bridges towards relationship with the Rauu. Now he had to think about where to build them. It would be terrific to be able to meet with Miduel now, or... or with Rector Etran. The rector was like a Russian stacking doll: one thing on the surface, another a bit deeper inside, but if you keep digging, you'd come to a third or fourth entity. She'd trapped him so skillfully with the archives and the library. What do you need with one measly bookworm, grall Etran, Orlem countess? What do you have in mind for him? It wasn't a good idea to try to use her as an ally, but asking her advice... although, getting the rector's advice would be costly.

He needed to figure out what he'd used against the elvish mages. Andy wasn't very aware of what was going on at the moment, but he clearly remembered taking energy directly from the astral, without the astral dragon. But what happened next.... The lake of bubbling lava in the place where the mages had stood was a complete surprise to him. He'd only taken out a small crumb! Like it or not, he should conduct an experiment with the external barrier. The energy pumped through the little virtual dragon that served as a sort of plug and safety barrier was great, of course, but, as real-life experience showed, he had to train while connected directly to the astral. No two ways about it.

The sky stretched out above him. A hard rain began to fall. He could see hillsides lit up by flashes of lightning on the horizon. These were the spurs of the southern end of the Rocky Ridge, which separated Tantre from the Patskoi Empire. Here the Ort flowed in a little hook and turned towards the Gulf of Terium. Andy started paddling towards the bank. The territory became unpopulated and wild closer to the foothills. The next city, Ortag, was fifty leagues downstream. After that, the cities crowded one after another along the edge of the river towards the sea. The mighty Ort's mouth was covered and controlled by a port city, the impregnable fortress of Miket. Swimming up to the river bank, Andy inspected the mountain spurs, overgrown with vegetation. *Perfect! Couldn't have designed anything better for my needs! You wouldn't find a more beautiful spot and temporary hiding place for a lone dragon.* Punching his claws deep into the slippery, muddy bank, he crawled onto the shore and trotted right into the thicket without delay. The downpour erased his tracks.

***

The birds' singing woke him up as well as any alarm clock could. Andy opened his healthy eye and stared at the multicolored little bird hatching trills on an elderberry branch a couple of feet away from the dragon. He'd dreamed of Frida. They were dancing at the ball, where he was wearing a ranger's dress suit, and she was in a low-cut green silk dress with a string of emeralds around her neck. Music was playing and they were turning round and round in a waltz without noticing anyone around them. Then they kissed.... *Alright, you woody freaks. I'll make you pay for what you've done....*

Ten days had gone by since he'd taken up the little nook in the little cave. After he left the Ort's banks, he climbed up the inclines of the foothills for a couple of hours and found a cliff with a small cave near the stone foundation. By then he was wobbly with exhaustion, and as soon as he crawled under the stone arch, sleep wiped the crystal dragon off all four of his feet. He didn't give a fart in the wind that his snout was sticking out and water was pouring on it from the rocks above. He just wanted to sleep, sleep, sleep. If hunters had been anywhere near him, they probably could have tied the sleeping dragon up with no risk to themselves. His protective "spider web" could have screamed to high heaven that danger was approaching—he never would have woken up.

"Full many a glorious morning have I seen..." Andy yawned, The Bard's 33rd sonnet coming to mind. "Well, this one's not glorious anyway. What's on our agenda for today?"

On today's schedule was reading the ancient folio, memorizing the spells, and hunting. No matter which way you spin it, a big bulky guy like himself had to scarf some major grub if he were to fully recover. In ten days, his eye healed and recovered, and scales had grown back on his side where they were supposed to be. Now he just needed his wings to get back in working order. That was tougher. The membranes grew slowly, and each time they grew out, he kept tearing them again; all it took was getting them caught on a branch or twig. Only one of his several hunting excursions had been successful. On his second try, Andy found a natural salt lick, but it was the afternoon, and there were no prey around. The next day, he went out late in the evening and laid in wait fifty meters from the salt lick. He'd prepared the power construction for a fireball on the tips of his right claws. He had to wait until midnight. Sniffing the air carefully, ears perking this way and that, and constantly getting up on their hind legs, a small herd of spotted deer approached the salt lick. The dragon, who had been lying motionless for several hours on end, waved his paw. The red ball of fire was flung from his claws and hit the leader of the herd in the chest. The "earth knives" were activated by the strong blow of the fireball hitting the ground, but the small delay between the spell's activation and its actually working allowed the rest of the deer to run away. No matter what they say, stalking and catching prey from the sky was a lot easier and more interesting. In ten days, it had become very clear by his own experience: dragons aren't very well equipped for hunting on the ground. Today Andy decided to set up an ambush along the path to the watering hole.

His evening hunt was a good one. The dragon caught himself an eleraff, the animal he knew from his time in Rimm, which would feed him dinner tonight and breakfast and lunch the next day. The local people called them "barls." Tantrian barls were smaller than the ones living in the Marble Mountains and also had a different shade of fur. Andy had only just put on a scent and visual masking spell when he heard a whistling sound from the gully. Breaking through the shallow underbrush, a whole herd of the gentle giants was coming down from the mountains to the mountain stream. The dragon began to salivate, and his stomach growled in anticipation of the filling meal. Andy, unlike the sul, didn't circle the herd and strike the chosen victim with his fangs. He simply struck a young buck he'd taken a shine to with lightning. Trumpeting loudly in expectation of a second attack, the herd formed a tight defensive circle. Without waiting for another onslaught, the great big alpha male commanded them all to leave. First, the females and the young left the watering hole undercover by the males, then the males, and the leader of the pack last of all.

It didn't make sense to kill more than one barl. Andy had no way to store the four-ton body, and he wasn't about to cast and constantly maintain a preservation spell. The downside of spells like that was that the meat would be completely frozen, and he would have to wait until it thawed out.... After his kill, Andy devoured about a half a ton of the carcass on the spot, then became drowsy. Gathering his strength, he tore off a good-sized chunk of the vanquished animal and dragged it to his cave.

Now that he had some extra provisions, and in view of the fact that after his first direct trip to the astral he was famished, he could repeat the experiment. In the depth of his soul, Andy hoped his wings would heal from it, as his body had finished healing the first time. He was beyond sick and tired of feeling incomplete, Targ take it all!

Fighting off the desire to lie down and go to sleep, he closed his eyes and dove into settage. His internal space was flashing with all kinds of colors and tints. Against this backdrop, his wings looked like an ugly black blob. Quickly sizing up his mana reserves, he gently touched the astral dragon on his shoulder, swirled around the amulet from the hill which was blazing with a warm red flame (strange, the "toy" of the ancients that he had inherited had not done anything to make itself known in his few months of study), and began to plunge into the world of energy. This time he decided not to meld with the barrier, but to dive into the ocean of energy through the astral double. Once he made up his mind, it was done!

The force of the raging elements almost threw him backward. The ocean of energy rushed along the energy channels with incredible power. Raw mana, sweeping away the safety barriers, momentarily filled his internal storage container and spread throughout all parts of his body. Once he set the astral dragon into motion, and using it as a lightning rod and a diverter for letting go of unnecessary energy, Andy stubbornly kept on fighting the elements. He got an incomprehensible sense inside that the energy flowing through the astral dragon wasn't going out into the world, but was actually being transferred to someone. It seemed the being that was taking on the mana was feeling rapture, joy, pain, and a whole gamut of other emotions. Without getting bogged down in the strange reaction to the shedding of extra energy, Andy gathered up his will in his fist and formed a straight channel. At first, the energy's uncontrolled access to the world through the internal energy channels of his organism was cut off. Then he began working on building a dam inside himself, fencing off the astral with a kind of cap which, like a faucet, could be opened and shut and regulate the pressure of the flow. The secret force that had spun him around last time in a dizzying circle dance didn't interest him today. The tiredness he'd accumulated played its role: without leaving his trance, Andy fell asleep.

His wings had healed. The dragon checked them as soon as he opened his eyes. But after that, things got weird. No, the inexplicable part came a little later on. First, feeling his incredible hunger, Andy ate his entire store of leftover barl, downing one ton of meat in about twenty minutes. And then…. After lunch, he started feeling very itchy and again insanely hungry. Throwing caution to the wind, he bolted towards the watering hole. The dragon didn't notice that entire clumps of scales were falling off his body as he was running. He just wanted to get rid of the burning itch that went right down to his bones and the ends of his claws. Having driven the vultures away from the carcass and roared at a couple of mrowns, Andy began furiously tearing huge chunks of flesh from the giant herbivore. When he got to the intestines, Andy fell asleep right there by the river's edge.

The birds' chirping that had now become quite a familiar sound woke Andy. Without opening his eyes, he listened to his body and slid into settage. Everything was alright. He wasn't itching, wasn't burning! Stretching like a cat, he lifted his wings and opened his eyes. *Gee willakers, what the heck?!* The ground all around him was covered in scales. He turned his head around and looked at his back, then his sides—it was all shining with a new, golden armor. The colored design on his sides stood out more boldly. The black scales on his chest had taken on yellowish blotches in the center and the plates on his chest were wider now and thicker, real armored plates. Andy took a step towards the remains of the barl carcass and froze, stunned. Considering that there were no other dragons around, and the tracks on the ground near the carcass could only be his, it was shocking to see that the new tracks were about 1.5 times bigger than the old ones! What, he'd grown up in one night? It seemed an unplanned molting had started out of nowhere and the insane itch that came along with it… Well, this was one heck of a side effect!…

Scratching his head with the claws on his right wing, he immediately started digging a hole under the old scales. Ah, Gmar's not here. The gnome would have strangled him for such a squandering of resources. As he was digging, Andy felt an uneasiness all over inside. All his senses told of a danger but in a strange form. The danger wasn't to him. Abandoning the digging, he decided to listen to his instinct: what kind of Targ's bad joke was this?! Someone else's fear swept over him from head to toe. It was… a girl? He could feel the girl's fear through his blood. Andy thought for a moment. This was some kind of nonsense—*where would someone get some of my blood? Where?? Idiot! It's Tyigu! Master Berg's daughter!* He'd fed her the blood himself.

Andy began to pound his wings soundly and rocketed into the sky. The blood connection allowed him to determine the location of his destination and the distance thereto, just like a GPS. Ten leagues later, he looked down and saw a battle being fought below. A few warriors dressed in armor were up against two dozen armed humans and orcs. The whole forest path was strewn with bodies. The defense had sent several dozen of the attackers to Hel's judgment already, but they'd sustained losses too. A familiar female figure was protecting a small child with her body. As soon as he figured out who the good guys were and who the bad guys were, Andy folded his wings and dove downward.

***

"Stop!" Ilnyrgu lifted her left hand.

"Do you feel something?" Berg approached her, leaving his spot at the head of the short procession.

"Something very vague and unclear. I can't tell what it is," the orc answered, turning her head side to side.

"An ambush?"

"I don't know. It could be anything."

"Come on, more concrete now. We're not at a bazaar," Brig the Brick roared from behind.

"It's as if the space around us is all in a fog. I can't see anything with true vision! I suggest we all put on our armor and be ready for anything!" Ilnyrgu said. She flung the bag with their equipment in it down from the mule and was the first to start getting dressed. After the mage, the she-wolves[1] that obeyed her got changed as well, along with the few warriors Berg had hired.

"Have we still got a long ways to go?" one of the warriors asked.

"You'll go as long as it takes, got it?" Brig rebuffed him. He, too, was tormented by the same question, but he knew a little something more about the orc than the others (except Berg) did. He preferred to trust "the Wolf's" instincts and not grumble.

Ilnyrgu took up her spot near the mule with its small rider, on whom they'd also put some chain mail, and the caravan got underway. Keeping their guards up, the warriors cocked their crossbows and tensely examined the surrounding path of the undergrowth. The orc suspected that their enemies were using visual canopies and had prepared a "warm welcome" for them. Her sense of danger had never yet been wrong….

… She arrived in Orten on time. If she'd had an unexpected delay somewhere for a couple of weeks, Tyigu would certainly be dead by now. She had discovered the surveillance following the half-orc on the seventh day after the strange massacres at the School of Magic. No one knew exactly what had happened there. Various rumors went about the town,

---

[1] Sword fighters from the special division of female orc warriors.

each more ridiculous than the last, but patrols filled the streets. The School was cordoned off by Royal Informants from Kion and punishing mages. Rector Etran was arrested. Some said an attempt was made on the life of the daughter of his Lordship Ratel of the Light Forest. The Forest elves called for the blood of the guilty parties. War was in the air.... Big politics, with its heavy footstep, had stepped on the anthill called Orten. All of Tantre had been stirred up by what happened there.

Ilnyrgu found the agents and, surprised by this unpleasant discovery, followed the spy and was even more shocked to find out that the spy was an orc. The "tail" lead the Wolf to the outskirts of the city. She ran back faster than a hare. At the sound of her alarm, the military "star"[2] consisting of her loyal she-wolves (who had entered the city illegally and were constantly monitoring the fencing school master's house) quickly saddled up....

Berg had let his guard down. His distance from Orten to the Steppes—the kingdom of the "white" orcs—had had its effect. The problem was, the agents of the ruling house earned their bread. They'd managed to piece together data from many different confusing stories told by the western merchants and caravanners. As soon as one of them mentioned a new fencing school opening up in Orten, which was headed by a half-orc, these rumors quickly reached the royal palace. Ilnyrgu suspected at first there was only a lone informant in the city. Once he confirmed the rumor, he informed his superiors of it. Then a team of liquidators showed up in Tantre. The queen desired Berg's and Tyigu's heads, and four dozen "knives"[3] traversed the entire continent to get to their target. They were so close; they weren't planning on stopping now...

---

[2] A small military uniting of graduates of the school of combat training of Steppe she-wolves, consists of five rank-and-file members and a commander. Besides all "star" warriors being master swordsmen, two or three of them were also warrior mages and provided magical support.

[3] The unofficial name for the killers of the Steppes' special execution service.

They were able to slip out of town unnoticed. It was a shame they had not been able to rent a boat. All the vessels were chartered by the Royal agents and all access to Orten's port was covered by soldiers. The half-orc had also hired five professional guards in "the Plain," and the small caravan headed west. The refugees' road led to Ortag, where Berg was planning to make it to Duyal by portal....

"Aunt Il, I'm scared," Tyigu leaned in to the Wolf. "It's a bad forest."

"Don't be scared." Ilnyrgu turned to the girl and, looking with true vision, saw a glowing human silhouette twenty yards from the road. Danger! "To battle!" she cried at the top of her lungs, grabbing Berg's daughter from the saddle. An arrow flew over her head and hit a tree on the other side of the path.

One of their crossbow warriors wheezed and fell to the ground with an arrow in his neck. Berg and Ilnyrgu's warriors managed to grab their swords and fend off the arrows in time. Then a dozen fireballs attacked the caravan from the direction of the forest, but the magical attack wasn't successful. The she-wolves and other hired warriors were decked out in defense amulets just like shaman trees covered in handkerchiefs and scraps of material. They were spared.

"Quiet!" the orc whispered, covering the girl's mouth and looking into her wide, frightened eyes.

"It's the 'knives'!" Brig the Brick cried when he caught a glimpse of the killers in the service of the Steppe Crown, right before they threw a curtain of invisibility on themselves.

"Don't move!" Ilnyrgu shouted, throwing a protective dome up over herself and Tyigu. Just in time, too, because the mages on the "knives'" side were very alert. Battle spells rained down on them like dried peas from a sack with holes in it. The flashes on the surface of the dome were so bright they hurt their eyes. Beyond the invisible border of the magic shield, a battle was seething. Both sides sustained fatalities. The "knives" cut the guards down in the first few minutes, but they lost five of their own, too, who were killed by the swords of Berg and the lady orcs.

What Berg was doing was indescribable. Ilnyrgu saw for the first time ever that he was truly a master of the sword, who had earned the title A-rei—white wolf. The half-orc rushed between trees just like a whirlwind. His enemies didn't have time to react to his lightning-speed attacks and were quickly diced into ground round. In a few minutes, Berg had drawn half the attackers to himself. The other half went after the "star" of the she-wolves and Brig. A couple of mages methodically worked to destroy the protective dome over Il and Tyigu.

"What's wrong with you?" Il turned her attention away from recharging the dome for a second and glanced at her ward. Tyigu's eyes were glazed over.

"He's here," she pointed upward.

Even through the protective dome, they could feel the unbearable heat coming from the spot where the mages had been standing moments ago. Next, several powerful fireballs tore five of the "knives" to shreds. The enormous dragon that landed then, cutting off the tops of the trees with its tail, killed another two. A long tongue of flame from his open mouth turned four more into living torches. In another few moments, all was over for the attackers. Of forty "knife" orcs, not one had survived....

***

Berg covered his sleeping daughter with a blanket and walked out of the cave. A happy little fire lit the small clearing. The surviving she-wolves were cleaning their weapons a ways away from the fire. Three of five were left.... Ilnyrgu stirred their dinner, cooking in a pot, and conversed about something with the dragon that had rescued them. If the Lord of the Sky hadn't shown up just at that moment, they would all have been left lying there on the forest path, and Berg's and Tyigu's heads would occupy their intended places in the saddlebags. Ah, if the dragon had only shown up a bit sooner.... Berg was used to taking a philosophical view of other people's deaths, but Brig's death cut him to the core. The Brick didn't have to go with them, but he didn't want to leave his friend in a time of need. He gave his life so that Berg and Tyigu could remain alive....

"Why did you help us?" Ilnyrgu asked the dragon, blowing some foam off the spoon and testing the soup to see if it was ready.

She had already told him all the latest news. He listened carefully and started asking questions about the School of Magic. But Ilnyrgu couldn't help him at all. The ancient monster knew things, and it scared her to hear about it. She couldn't shake the feeling that the dragon himself used to live in the city of Orten. What nonsense! He asked about recent events in great detail, and was surprised to hear about the arrest of the School rector.... Then she got undercurrents of the sense that she knew him personally. He dropped a few sentences about the Rauu and then asked outright whether she knew anything about the fate of the Snow Elf students? He shook his head suspiciously at the news that every last Rauu student left Orten through a portal two days after the strange events at the School. Shivers ran down the orc's back—being in the ancient creature's presence caused an irrational fear. Berg was looking on, and he was willing to bet the dragon just smirked. The gigantic head turned towards the half-orc. The phosphorescent eyes sparkled with a deep blue.

"Okay, I've got a question for Berg." The dragon licked his chops and drew in a deep breath of the tantalizing smell of meat with spices. "Has anything unusual happened to your daughter in the past six months?"

"No," Berg shrugged.

"I get angry when I'm lied to!" The Lord of the Sky clamped his jaws shut. Berg could see the women's backs tighten with tension; he too felt a chill run down his spine. The dragon could kill them at any moment, but instead, he had taken them to his dwelling place and given them temporary shelter. "Remember that."

"A carriage... My student gave Tyigu dragon's blood to drink!" the half-orc exhaled, recalling the circumstances of his meeting Kerr for the first time. Il's eyes got as big as an elf's. She wasn't aware of this story. The dragon nodded and turned away. "As it happened...."

"That's right. I sensed my blood, Tyigu's fear, and I sensed her being threatened by mortal danger. Could I let them kill her after I saved her with my own blood.... I kind of blessed her, and it's customary to protect the ones you've blessed, not only among humans."

"Orcs," one of the she-wolves corrected him.

"Orcs then," the dragon answered in an easygoing tone. "I want to know why they were hunting you. These weren't simple orcs. They handled their weapons with the skill of many years of practice. And they don't teach peasants to fight like that," the Lord of the Sky revealed his knowledge of fencing. "Tell me the truth."

"Tyigu is the illegitimate daughter of Queen Lagira and… and mine. I should clarify that she was just a princess then…," Berg answered, letting his savior in on the family secret.

"That still doesn't explain why they were trying to kill you."

"Illegitimate children are a dishonor, and, what's more, according to orc law, the royal's firstborn has the right to inherit the throne, whether it's a boy or a girl," Il explained. "Tyigu is the queen's firstborn."

Wow, that's messed up. It's like a Spanish soap opera in the kingdom of the "white" orcs. He didn't want to ask anymore. It was clear Queen Lagira had an official, legitimate heir and the passions of her youth weren't letting her have peace. Considering the immutable laws on the succession of the throne, it became clear why the mother gave the order to exterminate her own daughter. And rights of inheritance weren't the only thing. The child could be used as a banner of freedom by various conspirators against her reign.

"Lagira hid her pregnancy. It's fortunate that I managed to suffocate the midwife before she managed to suffocate my daughter. Please allow me not to disclose how I knew she was giving birth or how I got into the palace. I did. And before they strangled us both, I escaped." Anticipating the next question, Berg went on: "Neither I nor Tyigu needs a throne. We want to live a quiet, peaceful life. I want to raise my grandchildren and pass my experience and knowledge on to them."

The dragon laid his head on the ground and stared at the fire. The tongues of fire were reflected in his blue eyes and the red sparks flew onto his scales.

"What is your connection to the she-wolves?" His sharp claw pointed to the women warriors. "Elite warriors like themselves don't help anyone out by the kindness of their hearts!" The dragon once again dumbfounded his company with his awareness. He recognized the orcs as the skillful killers they were. Everyone secretly began to wonder how the winged beast knew such things.

"Berg got the right to call himself A-rei—a master of the sword," Ilnyrgu said. The dragon coughed. "And, not long before he entered the palace, he married my sister. They killed her and all my family when he escaped. The queen wiped out all traces. Before she died, my sister made me swear not to let anything happen to Tyigu. So, there's no mystery here.

I made a promise, and the other she-wolves are from my clan, and they will help me avenge the queen for killing our relatives."

"One last question. How did you hide in the big city? There's a mage on every corner in Orten. Spotting a mask's as easy as 1-2-3 for them."

Ilnyrgu laughed. She tried hard to hide her fear behind that laugh. She explained that orcs used a different masking technique called shapeshifting. They used masks too, but, if they needed to blend in, they would choose the shapeshifting technique. The mages can't spot the she-wolves' secret technique because a person who's masked for a while turns into a different person—everything coincides up to the minutest traits and tactile sensations during verification. So, in fact, it was just some hired men who left Orten….

The dragon shuttered. The orc's words on the magical technique hit a raw nerve with him.

"Can this be learned?" he asked, beating his tail against the ground in excitement.

"Of course. I can teach it in one day. But why, allow me to ask, does a dragon need masking magic designed for humans and other bipeds?" Il smiled.

"Are you really so curious about that?" the dragon now laughed too. "I'm prepared to let you in on my secrets, but I need you to take a blood oath first. Can you agree to swear to me with your blood?" His blue eyes shone brighter than the light of the fire.

Berg looked at the ancient creature and couldn't shake the feeling they'd met before. There was something very familiar about the humongous beast.

"What have we got to lose?" the half-orc extended his hand and stuck his finger with the tip of his knife. The young she-wolves followed in kind, and Ilnyrgu was the last to take the oath, looking into the monster's yellow pupils.

The dragon cast a spell.

"Berg, please don't be too surprised and forgive me, but I had to. And all the more so since I want to take a few more lessons from you on the way to Ortag," the dragon said in his deep bass, then turned into a human.

"Targ!" Ilnyrgu whispered. "I knew he wasn't just a simple human boy...."

**

Andy squinted at the she-wolves. Something was amiss, again! How else could he explain their long faces? Master Berg cleared his throat behind Ilnyrgu.

"Can someone give me a mirror?" Andy asked.

No one said a word or bat an eye. The women kept on staring at him silently. Ilnyrgu walked all the way around the were-dragon, inspecting him. *Hmmm..., this is getting old fast.*

"What were you just thinking about?" Ilnyrgu asked, squatting for lack of a chair.

"About one of the Rauu. When you get angry, you look a lot like her. That's what reminded me of her," Andy answered and scratched his ear. He shouldn't have done that. His fingers felt the difference between an ordinary human's form and the size of the ears he had now. They were stupidly long and... um,... pointed. "Slaisa, dear, give me a mirror, will you?" With a sense of foreboding, Andy turned to the youngest of the three she-wolves who followed Ilnyrgu and held out his hand.

Slaisa smiled a blindingly gorgeous smile and handed him a little silver mirror with her long arm.

"As you wish, marvelous man."

"What if I get mad and cut your head off? Then I won't be so marvelous, will I?" Andy got going.

"I don't deserve that," Slaisa instantly turned serious and bowed. Joking was all good and all, but what if he really did take her head all of a sudden? Who knew what dragons were like? Killing an orc for them was probably the same as squashing a bug....

"Sorry," Andy said and took the mirror. "What are you all so shocked at?"

A Snow Elf was staring back at him from the mirror. That's probably an appropriate appearance for the son of Jagirra. His resemblance to her was striking. Only his eyes didn't want to change. Their bluish hue lent truth to the saying that eyes are the windows to the soul. His soul had long since become that of a dragon. He handed the mirror back to Slaisa, waved his hand to gesture that Berg should remain with Ilnyrgu, and went over to the other side of the forest lake where they'd set up camp. Lessons with Berg were over.

The spells based on a combination of three types of magic—visual, artifactual, and life magic—simple to use and effective as a Kalashnikov, had produced stunning results on Master Berg, who was standing in as Il's voluntary assistant in the lesson and who had been transformed (to the hilarious delight of the she-wolves and Tyigu) by the mischievous Il into a tall, pretty girl. But they simply didn't work on Andy. The orcish magical technique called shapeshifting turned out ineffective (just as masking spells were) on the dragon's nature and his strong natural resistance to magic on his external appearance.

Casting the shapeshifting spell was done in two stages: first, the person using the disguise put on himself or another person a special spell that integrated into their musculoskeletal system, by which the bones became "free artifacts," that is, artifacts with incomplete interweave structures. The second stage consisted of creating an image of the desired appearance. The image was then superimposed on the person under the influence of the artifact spell, and then the activation key (magic words) was pronounced. The spell's free magical connections would close in on the image cast on the person and bring about the physical changes. Everything would change, right down to the bones. The process was quick and, surprisingly, required very little mana. For a short time, the changes would strongly boost all life processes, and the person with the altered appearance would feel an incredible increase in strength, if just for a very short while. After a little time, the person would undergo an equal and opposite effect, a draining of energy. The downside consisted of an increased appetite (besides the mana required, the spell consumed a significant portion of a body's energy), and the temporary nature of the spell's action. It was completely impossible to detect the shapeshifting spell by ordinary means. The masking spell was cast over the skin and was intended for visual masking only, but the orcs' invention allowed you to actually change your form. The spell's action could not be detected by true vision, because the magic hidden inside the body masked the aura as well, splendidly.

During the long day of transition, Il talked about the interwoven structure in great detail, explaining the order of the runic power supply and creating a luminous three-dimensional circuit several times. She flashed the main nodes which connected the energy channels of the body and the visual image. Theoretically, it was all perfectly clear, but in practice, when the group stopped for the night, it turned out to be very far from what they'd imagined. The images didn't want to stick to the were-dragon and instead led to such changes that made everyone grab their stomachs and roll around on the floor with uproarious laughter. In order to understand what happened with Andy and what exactly the results were of the spells cast on him, it would be sufficient just to go to a fun house and look at one's reflection in the wavy, curvy mirrors. An hour later, his lower left eyelid started twitching, and the orcs were already tired of cracking up. Only Ilnyrgu didn't laugh. She took her student's failures personally. She had given her word to teach their rescuer the magic of changing one's appearance in one day, and now she was afraid she wouldn't be able to come through. The Wolf cursed her former words, got angry with herself and with the dragon she was indebted to. She reminded Andy of Jagirra very much in those moments....

Climbing a mossy boulder lying on the lake shore, Andy looked into the black, still water. Why wasn't he feeling anything unpleasant, such as a light aching in the bones and itchy skin that accompanied his last attempt to change his form? Why did he look like Jagirra, and his new face wasn't causing any rejection? This wasn't and couldn't be because of the magic they'd used on him an hour ago. On the other hand, the pointy-eared form indeed came about as a direct result of that. Sorcery had stirred up yet another dormant form of being inside him. His thoughts, swirling like heavy pebbles in his head, lead to one conclusion, however illogical: Jagirra lied. She lied about how the Incarnation works. Exactly where the lie lay, he would find out as soon as he saw her again.... It was better to ask than to be lost in the grip of vague doubts.

***

Two hours later, the dragon showed up at the fire. He popped up as if from underground. He'd just been missing, and then all of a sudden he was sitting there next to the others, looking at the fire. He was in completely human form. Ilnyrgu took her eyes off what she was doing and looked at him. She was surprised that not a single magical "spider web" had warned them of his approach.

"I can see all magical interweaves. All, not just the ones that stand out," Kerr made eye contact and answered her silent question. He didn't seem like a boy to her anymore. His blue, piercing eyes looked at her and concealed within them the gray of a thousand years.

The Wolf shook her head and removed the pot with the grub from the fire.

"Slaisa, do you have a comb and a string, or a ribbon?" Kerr turned to the young lady. "Can I see them, please?"

Berg followed Slaisa with his eyes only as she ran towards the saddlebags. At first, it seemed strange how Kerr singled the girl out from all the rest until Il noticed her resemblance to the vampire who had visited the fencing school.

"I'm sorry if I'm sticking my nose where it doesn't belong, but what happened to your girlfriend?" the half-orc couldn't resist asking.

"Frida died," Kerr said without turning his head and poked at the coals with a dry stick. A sheaf of bright sparks shot up into the sky. Against the backdrop of the sparks, Berg could see how his shoulders and back drooped in despair. "My blood couldn't save her. Nothing could."

What could have happened to the girl that dragon's blood wouldn't fix? Berg wanted to ask in more detail, but Ilnyrgu stuck her finger to her lips and shook her head as a sign to knock it off.

The sparks, just like little stars, rose upward and went out high in the sky. The refugees sitting by the fire cast fantastic shadows behind them and were afraid to utter a word. Everyone realized the dragon had undergone a grievous loss and was very upset about it. The mythical beast turned out to be the holder of a wounded soul.

"Many people died in that battle," the dragon broke the silence. He kept staring at the dancing flames. "I regret one thing: I didn't kill enough of those woody bastards on the School shooting range…."

Berg and Ilnyrgu glanced at one another. At least this was one bit of clarity on what had happened at the School of Magic. The orcs waited for a further explanation, but they didn't get it. Instead, Kerr scooped up a handful of hot coals with his bare hand and gently blew on them. Bright flames grew from the coals and turned into a red bird. It beat its fiery wings, releasing heat to all around. With a loud cry, the bird flew up into the sky. It circled around a few times, folded its wings, and dove like a meteor into the fire.

"It's a phoenix. It's born from the flames and dies in the flames," Kerr said, dropped the coals back into the fire and rubbed his palms together. "Thanks, Slaisa." He took the comb and ribbon from her and tossed the long braid he'd grown specially for lessons with Ilnyrgu forward over his shoulder. At the wolves' amicable sigh, he cut it off with a long, razor-sharp dagger that had appeared out of thin air. The severed maiden's beauty flew into the fire. The glade was enveloped in the stench of the hair. Kerr quickly combed his hair, took all stray hairs out of the comb, chucked them into the fire as well, pulled back the thick ponytail that remained, and tied it with the ribbon. An icy mask seemed to come over his face, etching away all emotion. Ilnyrgu could physically feel the otherworldly cold emanating from the dragon. "I'm going to have a look at the armor and clean it up. Tomorrow we'll be in Ortag by noon. Master Berg, would you help me please?"

After the battle on the forest path, the orc ladies had pilfered the bodies of the "knives." They took all the valuables, money, swords, and armor that was more or less in good shape. They sorted, packed, and loaded the metal onto the hasses they'd acquired as part of the spoil.

"Let's go. Maybe we'll pick something out," the half-orc answered. "Don't forget, we still have low stances and attacks to work out today. What time are we going to sleep?"

***

Their small company reached the city long after noon.

The muscled hunk of a guard from the northern Vikings who stood at the eastern gates dexterously caught the silver coin that was tossed at him and, biting it to be sure, tucked it into his purse.

"You picked the wrong moment to visit Ortag," the giant buzzed. "I wouldn't recommend a Snow Elf remove his hood in the city."

"We're just passing through," Berg answered, sitting on his horse and playing the role of a nobleman. The rest of the orcs were masked to play the part of his large family. Ilnyrgu was the wife; Tyigu and the she-wolves the daughters. Andy took the form of a Rauu and was playing the role of a bodyguard. The blue-eyed elf didn't look as provocative as a non-human of unknown origin. "Just to the portal platform, and then we'll get as far away from here as we can."

"The portal doesn't work nowadays. The guild mages have gathered for some sort of Thing today," the northerner enlightened and shocked the city visitors with the news. "You'll have to wait until tomorrow. Be very careful around the city: there's a lot of unrest here…. Things can get out of hand at any moment, and the magistrates don't give a care."

"Would you be so kind as to tell us where we might stay," Berg said, tossing another coin to him by his thumb like at a football game, sending it twirling into the air. "The best quiet, calm little nook… and somewhere they won't ask too many questions."

"Why wouldn't I tell you?" the northerner responded with a satisfied smile and shining eyes. "Go to Two Fountains street. At the third light from the magistracy, there'll be a tavern called 'the River Wolf.' It's quiet, calm, and no bedbugs."

The city was buzzing. It was buzzing like a swarm of angry bees in a hive. On the outside, everything looked fine, but as soon as you open the hatch, the angry bees would start stinging the careless lover of honey. Andy couldn't stop sensing an impending threat. Everything looked calm on the surface. Traders were trading, peddlers were calling out to the crowds to advertise their goods, clerks were leaning in to shops and stores on the city streets. But he suddenly noticed that all the inhabitants seemed tense. He would often see small groups of people whispering to one another. There were a lot of elvish mixes. The city center was crawling with guards. The Viking was right—the situation could explode at any moment.

People cast cautious glances at the dusty horsemen on the city streets, but no one attempted to pick a fight. The double swords behind Berg and Ilnyrgu's backs had a sobering effect on all who looked their way. Their bodyguard, wrapped up in a long cloak from under which the tip of a dagger made of smoky steel could be seen, out of its sheath and ready for action, made the family even less approachable.

They found the tavern quickly. The northerner had told them the right directions. The main room on the first floor was empty. It smelled pleasantly of food and pine needles, apparently from the pine walls. "The River Wolf" made a good first impression. The hardwood floor was clean, the ceiling was white, the tables were polished and shiny, there were curtains on the pointed windows that matched the carved walls, and there were starched white bonnets and aprons on two pretty, rosy-cheeked girls standing near the entrance.

They had a vacancy, too. You couldn't call it a cheap tavern. It was one of those institutions chosen by guild merchants of the second or third ranks, well-off visitors to the city and members of the nobility not concerned with showing off their title. To compare it to Earth, it would be a hotel for the middle class. They kept horses and hasses at a sturdy stable in the back.

The rooms provided to the guests also pleased the eye with cleanliness and white sheets on the beds. There were no vacant single rooms, and Andy, purposely or not, had to share his room with Slaisa, who blushed every time he even looked at her. *Surprising. A professional killer, and she blushes like a tenth grader, caught kissing a boy. It begins....*

Changing out of his cloak, Andy decided to walk to the small bookshop he saw a sign for along the road. It was just three doors down from the tavern. He remembered that Nimr Belka, one of the guys from the dorm in Orten and an Ortag native, had recommended the book shop near the "River Wolf" tavern. He bragged that you could buy books there unlike any they had even in the School archives. It would be a shame not to visit the little gem of bookstores. He pulled his hood high over his head and set out.

The bookshop smelled like all reputable business of that type do: like antiquity, dust, and mice. Although there wasn't a speck of dust on the books' jackets and spines or on the shelves. Order and cleanliness rules the whole place, but the ineradicable spirit of the archives lingered. The pages of strange folios in wooden frames and glass decorated the walls. Four magical lanterns hung from the ceiling, lighting the place evenly. At the sound of the silver bell that indicated a client had entered, the owner appeared. He was a Dawn-bringer.

"My good sir, are you looking for anything in particular?" the owner bowed slightly, his pink braid falling onto the counter. The Dawn-bringers were distinct among elves for their pink hair, which gave them their name. The Dawn-bringers were a mix of Rauu and Forest Elves which, after thousands of years, became its own race. Their pink hair called to mind a sunrise. "What are you interested in?"

Andy removed his hood. Not a muscle on the owner's face moved, but his aura flashed, giving away the fact that he wasn't very happy with this visit from a fellow tribesman from the Marble Mountains. The customer did not fail to notice this reaction, and he was pretty surprised by it. It was strange: the Viking at the city gates had warned him not to go about flaunting himself as a Snow Elf. It was worth uncovering the reasons behind this anti-Rauu sentiment before it led to a lethal outcome.

"Hello. I've only been in the city for an hour, but I've already noticed a dislike for Snow Elves here. Could you by any chance explain to me where the sentiment comes from? You know, I wouldn't like to run into difficulties just from being ignorant of the circumstances. I haven't been in populated places for two weeks, and the changes I see since then are somewhat disturbing," Andy asked, bowing his head politely.

The shop owner sized him up with a long, suspicious look.

"Are you aware of what happened in Orten?" he finally spit out.

"I've been working as a bodyguard for the second month now for Baron von Berg," Andy invoked the whole company's agreed on the cover story. "I've been unable to keep abreast of the latest news for a couple weeks."

"The Rauu made a treacherous attempt on the life of the daughter of one of the Forest Lordships of the Light Forest. Almost killed her. She had arrived for study at the School of Magic. The Icicles even went so far as to drag a dragon from the mountains for them. The Forest is now threatening Tantre with war, all because of your tribesmen. Do you think that after what they've done, people are going to love the Rauu and be glad to meet you? Personally, I don't believe the rumors, but everyone is talking about it, everywhere you go. Besides, there's always some grain of truth to the gossip."

To say that Andy was surprised to hear this would be an understatement. He couldn't have imagined such a perversion of the events of two weeks ago, even in his wildest dreams. Call him paranoid, call him what you will, but after hearing this, he couldn't fail to consider the connection between rumors like this and the Woodies. They'd knocked the ground out from under the feet of their possible allies in the kingdom by creating the idea that the Rauu were to blame for the conflict, and now people would not be willing to subject themselves to the dishonor of accepting help from the unfaithful Rauu. They had also indirectly accused the king of befriending their centuries-old enemies. You better believe that the politics of Gil the Soft Spoken were presented in a negative light. People remembered and associated the king with the invitation of the Norsemen to the coastal regions, the confiscation of lands from landowners, and other existent and non-existent sins. There had always been a strong pro-Forest undercurrent in Orten. In the neighboring cities downstream along the Ort, many of the inhabitants were elvish half-bloods and humans with some elvish blood. The government's reverence towards the north and the orcs did not suit many people. The society was divided. Some furiously supported the king; others hated him. Peace and tranquility in the kingdom were on their last legs. A barrel of discontent was filled with gunpowder and the wick was lit.

"So, are you going to purchase anything?" the pink-haired elf said after an awkward pause.

"I'm interested in ancient folios from the pre-imperial days. I would be most grateful if I could buy a book from the era of the dragons. The contents should be something like this...." Andy took a page from the ancient tome out of his cloak pocket and extended it to the Dawn-bringer.

The elf turned the list in his hand, stopped short of sniffing it, and spread his hands to the side apologetically:

"I can't help you, sorry. I don't have books that ancient," he smiled, and Andy realized he was lying. He did have the books, possibly just what the were-dragon needed, but he decided not to catch the guy in his lie. Better come back at a later, more convenient time.

"Might this help you remember?" a purse full of gold plopped down onto the counter. Although it was packed with gold coins, it did not change the situation.

"If you think conjuring up gold will make the ancient books appear, you're sorely mistaken. I do not have the books you're looking for," the elf repeated and indicated to the client that it might be better if he would leave. "I'm just being cautious. Your presence might affect my reputation." Since when were salespeople concerned with who was buying what from whom? How could one person's presence affect another's reputation? The elf was probably saving his skin, afraid he might be accused of ties with the Rauu... And books burn so well....

When he got back to the inn, Andy ordered dinner in his room and water be heated in a bath.

"Do you need help?" the woman who took his request flirtatiously asked.

"Thank you, I can manage," Andy answered. Outright come-ons like that turned him off. He washed all the dirt off himself and went upstairs.

The orcs had gathered in Berg's room and were discussing the situation that was unfolding. They made a mutual decision to leave the city the next morning. If the mages weren't going to fix the portal, no sense lying around in a place where things could go south at any minute. They decided to leave by the caravan road for Troid, a small city located in the foothills of the Rocky Ridge along a tributary of the Ort. Andy didn't wait for the conversation to end and retired to his room, kicked his boots off, attached a naked blade to the headboard, and plopped onto the bed. They would be parting ways now. He was planning to stay in Ortag for another couple of days and revisit the bookstore—in the middle of a dark night.

Half an hour later, Slaisa came in on tiptoe. The orc took all her clothes off and lay down next to Andy. He didn't have time to let her know she'd gotten the wrong bed. The window exploded from the powerful blast in the town square below. The gust of wind brought the ring of iron to the dragon's keen ear.

***

Berg leaned his back up against the wall and looked at his former student. Kerr's appearance did not betray his anxiousness over the coming battle. The dragon was sitting on the ground drawing some sort of convoluted figures with a stick. His blue eyes were like freezing mountain water. Not a single emotion was displayed on his familiar human face. Warriors wore those eyes as they went off to kill or be killed. As Kerr said, he wasn't planning on dying. He had business in Ilanta. It's worth feeling sorry for his enemies. The half-orc rested his head against the cold brick and closed his eyes....

They didn't have time to leave the city. That night, it "erupted." The lords of the coastal regions, the elvish half-bloods, and the regents of the Free Mages' Guild, taking advantage of the king's absence (he was making a voyage to Mesaniya to attend the wedding of the son of the great prince to the daughter of the Duke of Taiir) had staged a revolt throughout the country. And Ortag was by no means sitting on the sidelines. The town square, arsenal, and barracks of the guards located in the southern and northern quarters were simultaneously attacked in the city. The rebels gained ground in two places. They took the town square, and the guard in the southern barracks was butchered. The surviving servants of the regime (loyal to the king) battled their way to the arsenal. It turned out that the backbone of those who were retreating under the pressure of the rebel guards were Norse Vikings, and the side street running from the barracks ran alongside the tavern.

Berg had just laid down and turned to Ilnyrgu, who was smiling invitingly at him and rubbing her bare chest—the Wolf was prepared to play the role of his wife to a T, and the half-orc wasn't planning on neglecting his "spousal duties"—when the explosion rang out on the town square. Their playful mood evaporated instantly. Tyigu, who was sleeping behind a curtain, woke up and started crying. Berg and Il jumped up from the bed and began feverishly putting on clothes and battle equipment. They could hear the pounding of many hurried feet and cries from the street below through the broken window. Torches and magical lanterns gleamed. Bits and pieces of shouted commands reached their ears. Now they were in it up to their ears.

"That rotten Rauu is staying here!" they heard from the street below. "Break down the door. Surround the building. We mustn't let him get away!"

The tavern shook as if an earthquake were going on. Someone let out a cry on the street, apparently a cry of pain. Berg carefully looked out the window. The thick oak entrance door, which had flown back from the magical blow, maimed a couple of the night-time raiders. All the attackers were wearing light mail with white armbands on their left arms. Behind the main detachment, there was a small crowd of several archers. Apparently they hadn't yet remembered that arrows could fly from the ancient doorway. A mortal rain mowed the unsuspecting archers down in one sudden instant. A guild mage in a black camisole was the first to take a glowing arrow to the face and flew apart in small bloody pieces. Apparently, the guys with the white armbands hadn't bothered to put on defense amulets and had relied on the magical support of the guild. The unknown arrow pointed out their fatal mistake in one split second. Feathered death collected a rich harvest. Half the detachment remained lying on the pavement; the other half preferred to retreat. It was obvious that the tavern attackers were not professional warriors, otherwise they would not have allowed such childish mistakes and so foolishly put themselves in the arrows' path.

Before the half-orc's last thought had completely formed in his head, a squadron of warriors in armor entered the square. Someone barked a short command at which they raised their shields and formed tight ranks. At another command, they moved towards the building newly under siege. The men in the white armbands crowded in behind them. Kerr burst from the inn, dashed towards the dead archers, and picked up several full quivers of arrows. Arrows flew at the dragon, not harming him at all, burning out a few feet away—the were-dragon had not forgotten to put up a magical shield. Diverting the attackers towards himself, Kerr ran up the street. The warriors picked up their pace, and Berg, with the eagle-eye vision of a steppe orc, saw that the arrows in one of the quivers began to glow with a clear light. Running about a hundred feet away, the dragon then stopped and turned towards his pursuers. A bow appeared in his hands.

A short breath and the fugitive's right hand flashed from the quiver to the bowstring, from the quiver to the bowstring. *Thunk-thunk, thunk-thunk*, Berg could hear the ringing sounds. Five arrows glowing with a clear light flew in one chain and with fiery colors hit the magical shield covering the squadron and fell to the ground. At the second batch of five, the shield couldn't hold any longer and broke. A few blasts covered the squadron, after which a dozen or so mangled, barely recognizable bodies lay on the ground. Many more were wounded. They could forget about pursuing him further.

The she-wolves, fully armed and equipped, burst into Berg's room. They could hear swearing in the Norse language coming from the southern barracks. Four dozen or so Vikings spilled onto the square, fighting back no less than a hundred opponents.

"Let's go," the half-blood said to the she-wolves, "before these cretins remember whose bodyguard Kerr was. We'll join the Vikings. Slaisa, Toryg, you protect Tyigu at all costs. You'll answer with your heads if anything happens to her."

Berg jumped out the window. Ilnyrgu landed beside him. The orcs came to the Vikings' aid and with their combined forces they quickly reduced the number of attackers to an acceptable level. After they'd joined the northerners, they headed towards the arsenal. There were no further large-scale battles, only three short skirmishes along the way. Kerr disappeared who knows where. He reappeared with a squadron of hired men near the walls of the arsenal three hours later. From the exhausted faces and bloody clothes, it was clear they'd taken a real beating. A kind of tie had come about in the battle for the city. Neither side could get the upper hand. The rebels decided to retreat from the arsenal and were regrouping. A temporary lull allowed the forces loyal to the king to regroup too.

The dragon was again sitting on the ground drawing some convoluted figures with a stick, pondering something. The lull ended, and the rebels gathered their strength and prepared to once again storm the little fortress.

"I need volunteers," Kerr said, standing up and rubbing the sand from his hands. "We can't sit in the arsenal forever. In half an hour, those guys with the white armbands will storm us and all the mages that have joined them will be on their side."

"And just hoo er yee, dat yee should be leadin' the weeriers?" someone said from the crowd of soldiers gathered under the awning. "Da officers'll soon get out of der meetin' and they'll do the commandin'. Now shut yer mouth and hold yer tongue!"

The guards' laughs and insults followed:

"The boy thinks himself a general! Uh-huh, tossed on some mail and puffed up with self-importance, but can you even hold a sword?"

"Non-human, go back to your steppes and command some sheep!"

Not everyone laughed and mocked. The Norsemen were silent. They respected martial prowess. Some of them had seen Andy sword fighting from the walls of the arsenal. They were right behind the dragon and knew what he was capable of. Berg looked to the left. Behind Kerr, the ragged detachment he led arranged themselves into even lines. People pulled their mails and adjusted their equipment and sword harnesses.

"It's not a far cry from sheep to these numbskulls I see before me. My name is Kerrovitarr, and I have the right to command you by blood," Kerr answered in a calm, even tone.

Berg's blood went cold. What was he doing? They'd challenge him to a duel for deliberately insulting them. The half-orc wanted to stand up, but Ilnyrgu held him back.

"He's doing everything right. Relax. You're about to see a small presentation. Or didn't you train him well?" Il teased back at the unknown wise guy: "The 'dear officers' are quartermasters who don't know which end of a sword is the pointy end. If it weren't for the Viking, unit commander and sergeant that commanded the defense of the arsenal and our group of guards, 'da officers' would have given up without a fight. Kerr's thought of something, and now we just need to find out what he has in mind. He needs to make people listen to him, and in this environment, he's got one of the simplest and fastest ways…."

The Wolf was right. When the squadron of northerners retreating from the southern barracks reached the arsenal, it struck at the back of the besieging soldiers and fought their way through under the cover of the fortress walls. It became clear that there were practically no officers there. A skinny Norseman with many thin scars across his face was leading the defensive efforts. It's true, the northerner was leading well. He was organizing mobile archer and crossbow firing units that were shooting the approaching half-bloods with their magical ammunition. A few novice boys constantly rushed to bring new arrows from a small warehouse where the "firelights" were stored—arrows with explosive magical tips, and sets of army uniforms with armor. Cauldrons of boiling tar stood on the stadium. Several men were standing watch at a small winch near the parapet. The Viking sorcerer sat on the roof of the dungeon commanding seven mages located between the fortress and the oncoming guild members. The mages promptly put up shields, which is why all attempts to knock the walls down through magic or destroy the defenders came to naught. Bombarding the dungeon with fireballs was useless as well. The tower was so decked out with defense amulets that the shield's glow could be seen with the naked eye. Another factor working in their favor was the fact that the guild members weren't battle mages. If they had been, things would have gone sour for the defenders, even despite all their magical amulets. The sorcerer on the roof laughed mockingly and mooned the besiegers. It was unfortunate that the main warehouses were sealed with guard spells so complex that even Kerr decided not to try to touch the interweaves. The regimental mage who had cast the spells turned out to be sympathetic to the insurgents....

Other officers were lying on the square before the arsenal, chopped up into fine grig,[4] or were burnt to ashes in the guards' barracks. What idiot thought of building the barracks as a separate building from the place under guard? Only a miracle or the goddesses' intervention had allowed fifty guards to somehow survive and lock themselves in the fortlet. The southern squadron, which had been joined by another thirty people on the way, strengthened the defense, while the hired men who'd hacked their way through with Kerr liquified all attempts to take the fortress by storm without the proper training and reinforcement. Where the dragon had been these last three hours and what he was up to, Berg didn't ask. But judging by the looks the hired men gave him and the respect they showed him, the boy had really had some "fun." He got the general impression the revolt broke out spontaneously. The half-orc did not sense any sort of proper combat training in the attackers. If the mages hadn't been with them, and the militias of the coastal lords, the whole half-blood rabble in Ortag could have been chased out with just a couple hundred guards.

"Look, it's starting," Ilnyrgu whispered.

Pushing through the crowd with his broad shoulders, a huge warrior in double chain mail with a shiny breastplate on his chest stepped into a clear space.

"Who you callin' numbskulls, pup? You'll answer in blood for utterin' such as this. I wanna see what color yers is."

The warrior's friends cawed and whooped in support. The giant grabbed his sword.

Kerr, at lightning speed, slipped forward, bent his torso to the side, and dove under the armed man's arm. He delivered such a strong punch to the guy's jaw that the strap of his helmet broke, and he stumbled back a couple steps. The sword fell from his weakened hand and he crashed to the ground, more like a sack of oats than a warrior. His body twitched a couple

---

[4] Ground meat

times and fell still. A smelly puddle spread out from under him. The force of the blow was such that the neck vertebrae burst from his body.

"Does anyone else want to see what color my blood is?" the dragon asked innocently. The shameful death of this experienced warrior from an unarmed non-human made the rest of them keep silent and see the blue-eyed guy in a new light. The men Kerr hired snickered maliciously. "No one? Great. I repeat. I need volunteers for trips to the city. You have to be an archer."

Berg dusted off his pants and stood up from the wall:

"I'll go."

"No, teacher!" Kerr turned to him. The half-orc could sense all eyes on him. There was a variety of stares, from respectful to hateful. "I need you here."

"We'll go," the commander of the hired men said in a booming bass. "We can all use a bow."

Besides the hired men, a few Norsemen responded as well from among the free warriors. They weren't subject to the unit commander or the sergeant of the southern squadron. The she-wolves tried to chime in too, but Kerr scowled at them so bad, they lost all desire to argue with him.

The dragon looked over his volunteers and pointed to the ten people. All the men he'd chosen were of about the same build: thin, toned, not a drop of fat.

"I warn you, you probably won't make it. You can still say no, you don't have to go with me. But if you haven't changed your minds and you come, you have to obey all my commands exactly. I say jump, you jump. I say die, you pretend to be drowned rats."

"Don't worry, commander. Would we have come with you if we were afraid of Hel?" a blond hired man said. Il winked at Berg. The half-orc secretly smiled. A red-haired Viking, one of three northerners Kerr had chosen, spit contemptuously through his chipped teeth. The were-dragon nodded approvingly.

The unit commander, sergeant, and Norse mages finally appeared from the dungeon, along with a few quartermasters. The military command meeting was over.

"Unit commander sir, may I speak with you for a minute?" Kerr asked bolt upright.

The Norseman squinted his eyes and looked the dragon up and down. "Speak."

The thing took longer than a minute. Kerr suggested dividing up the defensive forces and secretly sending one squadron on a raid to get around behind the guild mages. Volunteers from the Vikings and hired men would go on the raid. According to his suggested plan, they would destroy the mages and disorganize the besiegers. After that, they'd give the signal, a green flare in the sky, and the warriors would leave the fortress and finish off the surviving rebels near the arsenal. Then come to the aid of the northern barracks, where battles were still raging on. Being on the defensive was precarious, because new militias from the coastal lords and groups of half-bloods from the suburbs could arrive in the city at any moment. The unit commander listened silently to Kerr's plan and then asked what he could do to help put it into action.

***

Andy looked out from behind the stove pipe and immediately hid behind it again. His predictions that they were preparing to storm the military warehouse, and that new lords' militias would show up in Ortag, had been correct. Columns of armed men marched the streets with the coat of arms of Lord Worx on their shields. The clip-clop of horses' hooves resounded against the pavement. They brought carts loaded with heavy equipment called chuckers, used to fling weapons. From under the thin gray canvas covering the carts, Andy could see the glow of the magical power supplies they carried. The battle equipment consisted of thick glass balls thirty centimeters around, with different innards: fragmentation-explosive ones, which were stuffed with metal scraps and a passive explosive spell, and highly-explosive ones, with the "all-consuming flame" spell. Power chargers for wall destruction were stacked up separately. Their task just got more challenging, but hey, they'd been in worse scrapes than this, right?

They got out of the arsenal without any dire difficulties. A thin rope, which was reinforced by magic, was attached to a crossbow's arrow. They fired and the arrow, which looked like a thick javelin, punctured deep into the wall of the building across from the fortress. Throwing curtains of invisibility over himself and his warriors, which made them invisible to prying eyes but not to one another, Andy grabbed the specially prepared clamp and slid down along the rope to the roof of the building. Next, the others followed by the same method. Andy took two dozen quivers full of magical arrows from the unit commander and ordered his archers to leave everything they didn't need in the fortress. They were allowed to take their swords, bows, and a double portion of magical arrows.

He ordered them all to don leather breastplates.

"We'll go along the rooftops," he explained briefly. "They're still free from the white armbands' arrows for now. It would be a shame not to take advantage of the muddle-headed recklessness of their commanders. Don't weigh yourselves down with unnecessary loads. You need to be able to jump far."

Andy retrieved a couple of twenty-foot boards from his spatial pocket he'd put there earlier. Laying them from one roof to another, he made his way with the men to the town square. He had thought and stressed for a long time over whether to put the wood into his "pocket," but, weighing the dry boards, he decided to risk it. *Thank you, builders of Ortag, for putting the buildings so close together.* The streets were narrow, only about fifteen feet wide. This trick wouldn't have worked in Orten, with its wide avenues and boulevards.

"Commander, what should we do?" Olaf, the red-haired Norseman asked him, pointing to the militiamen as they dragged their hefty shields as protection against arrow fire and at the shields arranged by the unit commanders like a fence as cover for a possible attack from the direction of the city.

"The same plan," Andy answered. "We'll wait until the lords begin storming the arsenal and concentrate their mages' efforts on breaking down the walls. We'll divide up into two groups of five. One'll shoot the 'firelights' at the carts with the power supplies; the other will distract the mages. You won't have time to get many shots in. The lords' archers will soon take you to the task, and boy will the mages be mad." The warriors gave a quiet laugh. "Your main job is to distract them away from me. Don't let a single one of those scumbags look my way. In order to increase the destructive effect, I'll up the power on the tips of your arrows.

Whatever you do just don't accidentally shake or hit the quivers. The blood will splatter from here to Kion."

"Commander, you're a mage, and a fine one, am I right?" Ulg spoke up, a raven-haired southerner with short spiky hair on his head and a long shaggy mustache. "Why couldn't we have struck from the fortress?"

Andy was expecting such a question.

"Ulg, when you got to fight another warrior one-on-one, do you hold your shield in front of you or hang it behind you? It's the same thing with magic. Half, if not all of our energy will go towards breaking through the mages' collective shield. I don't think they'll put up a dome. They probably won't be expecting a dirty trick from the back, from the besieged city. It's time. Quick, give me one quiver each."

The sound of horns announced that the waiting was over. The lords, under fire from the chuckers, launched an attack. The ten stirred with anticipation. While Andy pumped arrows with mana, the soldiers prayed to their gods: Olaf stroked his sword and remembered Odin. The mercenaries covered themselves with a sacred circle. Ulg asked Hel for a light afterlife. People were preparing to meet death, but their willingness did not mean that they would go to slaughter without a fight. They were going to win, and if they had to give up their lives for victory, so be it, but for their lives, they would try to take as many enemy lives as possible.

Andy handed out the quivers, threw a curtain of invisibility over his warriors and assigned them to the various rooftops free from the lords' archers. He'd just sent ten good people to their deaths; he had no great doubts that that was their fate. Without recharging, the curtains would last three or four minutes max. But this was the price he paid for trying on the role of the commander: being responsible for life and death. Not to say he didn't love the role of commander—he did. He didn't feel any prick of conscience or regrets at doing what was necessary to achieve victory. An icy calm came over him, and assurance that he was doing everything right. Even more people would die from what he was planning to do here—like the coastal lords' militias, as well as peaceful residents living near the arsenal who hadn't left their homes. Andy concentrated and went into a trance, a virtual valve opened wide, letting the astral energy flow freely….

He waved his left hand to signal "open fire." Closing his eyes, Andy counted the seconds between the sonorous clicks of the bowstrings against the leather gloves and the bone shields on the archers' wrists and the explosions in the ranks of the besiegers. The sound of the cannonade merged into one continuous rumble. While the enemies were still in shock at the unexpected attack from their rear, his archers jumped from roof to roof and sent arrows flying one after another. Someone took an unfortunate jump and got caught right in a flash of fire shooting up from below like a fountain. Thousands of bricks flew from the buildings in all directions, maiming and killing the rebel soldiers. Tiles and lumber from between the buildings' floors fell on their heads.

The half-bloods' commanders wouldn't be commanders if they didn't have the ability to make quick decisions. When they saw where the arrows were coming from, they gave the command to their archers to put down the attackers, but their soldiers had already taken the initiative and opened fire, to the destruction of their opponents. Andy came out of his trance and saw Ulg take two arrows: one to the stomach and one to the neck. As he fell, the southerner tore his quiver off himself and struck the roof tiles with it. A new sheaf of fire turned the small two-story building into smoking ruins. Over twenty people fell to the ground from the fragments that flew in all directions. One of the hired men climbed to a roof that was very close to the carts with the chargers for the chuckers, then took an arrow to the back. He dropped his bow and tumbled from the roof to the pavement. Andy went blind for a second. He went deaf for a lot longer. The soldiers who were standing next to the carts and the residents of the nearby houses died instantly, vaporized. The shockwave threw Andy to the ground, painfully flattening him against the pavement stones. He hadn't expected such a result, even in his most optimistic speculations. Two powerful blasts of fire sent two more of his men to Hel's judgment, swept from the roofs by the same shockwave. Fragments of bricks and shingles drummed over the building and along the pavement. The chargers had gone off with a bang. The enemy mages divided their strength and stopped attacking the fortress. Now it was more important to cover their men from the intensified shelling from the walls of the arsenal and dangers from the direction of the city. They regrouped and answered with a blow to the remaining archers using every magical weapon they had. *Freaks! You should have divided your ranks—at least someone would have been left alive that way. It's so awesome that there's not a single warrior among you. They wouldn't have let you crowd into one tight group. You'll pay dearly for your habit of collective, mutual efforts.* In the chaos that reigned, no one noticed a lone silhouette creeping amongst the street littered with corpses and wounded people.

The "rain of fire" was a pretty name for a multi-component spell based on a mix of the elements of Fire, Earth, and Air. It was a complex interweave, which Andy had studied for five days and spent an hour tracing outlines on the ground, recalling the order and arrangement of the runes. He decided not to retrieve the book from his "pocket." In order to destroy the mages, he considered a variety of options. But after asking the Viking sorcerer who had sat on the roof during the first storm about the tactics used by the self-indulgent guild members, he decided on that one. If everything went according to plan, as it was so far, he was guaranteed to make those mages meet their maker. That way he wouldn't have to chase them around the whole city. He spit, crossed his fingers and knocked himself on the forehead in superstition. *Let's hope this works!*

Standing up to his full height, he pumped the runes of the magical interweave he'd created on the roof with energy, and pronounced the activation key in his head. The walls of the nearest buildings instantly became steaming hot and broke into tiny pieces, which then melted into fiery puddles. A hurricane gust of burning wind caught the molten rock with red-hot stones and threw it at Lord Worx's militia. Three dozen mages put up a dome-shield by their collective effort which deflected the splinters, hurling at them at the speed of bullets. But the red-hot lava that covered the dome slowly but surely broke down their defense. The mages could not deactivate the dome; otherwise, the lava would fall on them. Their own dome prevented them from cooling the lava. They had only one choice left—keep the defensive dome up until the rock cooled. The fire shells continued to thresh the warriors who were screaming in pain and remained without magical protection. The trap had worked. Andy smiled, not noticing that his mouth filled with sharp teeth, and slapped his palms on the ground. The pavement was ripped open with "earth knives" springing up from underneath it. The dome collapsed, burying the remaining magicians. Everything took about a minute and a half. A fireball flew up into the sky and exploded in a greenish color. The gates of the arsenal opened, releasing the bloodthirsty Norsemen….

Kion, the capital of the kingdom of Tantre. Citadel...

His Highness Gil II, Gil the Soft Spoken, set down his mug of a strong, invigorating beverage called invigohol, looked at the panoramic map hanging on the wall, and counted the cities highlighted in red. The lords, elvish half-bloods, and other traitors had swung widely. The head of the Secret Chancellery, Drang, the Duke of Ruma, followed the king's gaze and went to retrieve His Highness' mug. He'd finished his own beverage a while ago already and was incredibly thirsty. Gil joked:

"Drang, I'm looking at you and I'm thinking, am I as much of a red-eyed pig as you, or worse?"

"Worse, Your Highness. The bags under your red eyes speak of incessant drunkenness and a failing liver," Drang joked back and suddenly started coughing and choking on a leaf from the drink.

General Olmar approached the head of the secret service and patted him on the back.

"I never thought I would save the life of a nark greedy enough to drink from the king's cup," the military man mumbled. He shared the eye color and bags of His Highness and the head of the Secret Chancellery on his tired, unshaven face. "Don't you think it's time?"

"Not yet, Olmar. Let them have their fun a bit. I want all the worms to come out of the woodwork. Drang's gone to such lengths to make sure the revolt broke out now, when it's quite convenient for us, and not when our most reviled 'woody' friends were planning on inciting it. My double in Mesaniya's living the high life, sipping wine, congratulating the newlyweds, and I'm stuck here in the citadel basement chugging hot grog. When will they tell him… er, me about the revolt?"

"Already have," Drang answered. "The mages are building a portal to quickly get Your Highness back to Tantre."

"I hope this dolt doesn't blurt out anything superfluous. I want to give those Woodies a really special going away present."

"Don't fret, Your Highness. Garad is with him, our brilliant chancellor. He'll make sure you can nail the wood elves once and for all."

His Highness' first advisor, the Archmage of Tantre, Sator teg grall Vidur, walked into the room. He looked just like the three sitting there already. Could have been their brother. Sator threw a leather folder on the table and dropped into a padded armchair in exhaustion.

"The latest reports. In all cities where revolt broke out, just riots and plundering. Drang, are you sure your people aren't going a little overboard in acting out the elves' atrocities?"

"It's fine," the main knight of the cloak and dagger waved his hand dismissively. "They were very diligent in spreading the rumors about the nasty Rauu, and spoke very poorly," here he glanced at the king, "of His Majesty the king. Hmm, yes… now people will speak quite flatteringly of the long-ears."

"What subjects I have!" the king waved his hands. "They create rebellions behind my back, and I support them in this with all my strength, while my principal conspirator is swiping my precious invigohol. The only thing that makes me happy is that the Woodies and the Pat Imperialists weren't expecting such antics on the part of their proteges. How are things shaping up at the borders?" he asked General Olmar.

"We're screening off the entire length of the border from the portal building. The Woodies and the Patskoi Imperialists[5] won't have time to send their forces through. Our game threw them off capitally. The army has been put on high alert. They're ready to move at any moment."

"What's the latest news from the cities?" Gil stared at the mage.

"All is finished in Orten. The Vikings, under the leadership of Rector Etran, are finishing off the last conspirators and Free Mages' Guild bosses who joined them. In the School of Magic, the senior students defeated the treacherous punishing mages. The rector commanded her people from within her prison cell. Can you imagine—the safest place to be. I hope Etran won't hold it against us that she was sent behind bars."

"Just so you know, she's the one who suggested this approach," the king said. "Moving on."

"In Ortag the combat is over. A third of the city has been burned." General Olmar whistled.

"When did they manage that, and more importantly, how? The fun began just eight hours ago. The army was brought into the summer camp, the arsenal was plundered, and the magical toys, except for one warehouse,

---

[5] A citizen of the Patskoi Empire.

were replaced with dummies. There aren't enough mages in the whole city to accomplish that."

"My agent did not report the details, but nothing is left of Lord Worx's militia. The half-bloods and mages have also been completely wiped out."

The king stood up behind the table and poked the mage and head of the Secret Chancellery with his accusative finger.

"Call your agents in Ortag this instant and order them into action. I want a fully detailed report on this table in an hour. Next."

"My mages have pinpointed several attempts to build portals in the outlying territories. The builders were not able to puncture through the screen. The Woodies are getting worried."

"Let them worry. It's a little late to get alarmed now. During the uproar, my people captured all the Forest's agents. Those they could not take alive, they killed." Drang stood up. "We're having a discussion with the surviving ones. We need misinformation agents."

"Exactly. If the Rauu hadn't presented us with information on the negotiations taking place between the Lordships and the Emperor, we would have kept swallowing the misinformation they were feeding us on 'tense relations between the Patskoi Empire and the Forest' for a long time. The Forest and the Empire have come to an agreement on joint military action against Tantre, and you, Drang, were not even aware of the negotiations! How is it possible? Pray to the Twins that the lords and the guild renegades have fallen for our ruse, and the long-ears have goofed up concerning the source of the rumors. I understand you beat them on their own territory, but I will not forgive any more failures such as with the negotiations! We should all thank the One God and the Twins that the Emperor hasn't marched his legions to our borders, and our screens have blocked the zone of near access to the mountains, while the Woodies are fending off the raid of the 'greenies' in the northern groves and failed to quickly deal with the situation. I know that this raid has cost us a pretty penny. I signed the papers myself. But that won't console me. We've come to the point where we're artificially concocting a situation where the discontent elements are revolting. If all were well, our enemies would have done the same thing there, in their lands! We know nothing of the Arians' goals, what's motivating them, and when they'll strike. What is there to talk about if we didn't even know that Miduel, the High Prince of the Rauu, was hauled up in the School archives, and a were-dragon were conducting his studies at the School. How many are there? Whose side will they be on in the coming conflict, and how powerful are they? We're blind in our decisions and conclusions." The king walked along in front of the huge map with wide steps. His eyes shone with anger. "We almost blundered the conspiracy in the Free Mages' Guild, and only Rector Etran's announcement opened some eyes. Targ, this state is preparing for the worst war in history, and it might be destroyed by a handful of dissatisfied and power-hungry mongrels. The Icicles will aid us in keeping the scum in check. What do you say, gentlemen? How are you? Having a great time?" Gil sighed and stopped. The red light blinking on the map at Orten turned into a constant green light, meaning the city was now under the complete control of the royal forces. "General Olmar."

"Yes, Your Majesty!" the general jumped up and stood at attention.

"Listen to my command. March the regiments out of the summer camp and crush the mongrels. I order you to decimate all the lords of the coastal region right down to their roots, by any means. Level their castles to the ground; they don't serve any defensive purpose anyway. I don't want my descendants to have to quell their uprisings, as my grandfather did, my great-grandfather too, and now I, in turn, have to deal with them. Drang...."

"Yes, Your Highness!"

"As much as you can, work with the Philistines. You can stop mitigating the filth you spread regarding the Forest. In the newspapers, reveal the negotiations with the Patskoi Empire. Tomorrow, or rather, later today, I will declare Penkur."

PART TWO, NORTHERN WINDS.

The Northern Sea. Red Island. Lurdberg...

A Northern wind chased heavy, low-lying clouds across the sky. Ragged clouds poured out a horrid drizzle, their pregnant, moisture-filled bodies clinging to the hilltops. A fog rose up over the sea and covered the entrance to the White Fjord.

Tyrnuv hiked up to the height of the mountains and looked down. Dozens of vessels were anchored near the steep vertical walls of the Fjord. The white blanket of fog periodically revealed the masts of another ten ships headed to Lurdberg harbor.

Strong gusts of Severan, the cold Northern wind, beat a gap in the continuous cloudy veil, and the bright rays of the sun lit up the coast, forced the mist to turn pink, and uncovered the unsightly picture of the neighboring island. Tyrnuv turned away. Billows of smoke were rising over Oskolock, as if the god of the soil had awoken and made the mountains spit fire and ash. A thick black cloud was rising over Berngrold, the city of the "gray" coastal-dwelling orcs, located on the neighboring island. If he squinted, he could make out the handmade volcanoes on the other side of the island. The orcs had burned their cities. Special teams poisoned the rivers and wells.

"Tyrnuv, what's up? You look like you are frozen to the spot." A broad-shouldered Norseman joined the orc on the mountaintop.

"I'm saying my goodbyes, Harald. I never thought I would burn my house down with my own hands."

"A Viking's home is his drekkar," the Norseman disagreed.

"A drekkar should have a harbor waiting for it," Tyrnuv responded and sat down on a big flat boulder. Harald sat down next to him, his ax resting on his knees.

"Maybe you're right, but don't forget that a wife should be waiting in a Viking's harbor. How is Brunhilde?"

"Still can't get over the fact that your sister married me?" the orc elbowed the Norseman.

"Come on, you're better than many men as far as I'm concerned," Harald looked at the orc from under his bushy eyebrows and stroked his beard. "Brunhilde didn't *want* to come back. What did she have going on here to keep her? And you already had your drekkar then. You didn't chain her up. You sent the ransom and compensation according to all the rules. You're only an orc by name. Your granddaddy was a Norseman, and granny a half-blood Dawn-bringer and orc, your mom too has roots in the Lynx clan. Those fangs aren't so orcish now, are they?" The Norseman laughed. Tyrnuv tilted his head to the side in agreement. Orcs had boarded his grandfather's snekkja, knocked him senseless, tied him up, and tossed him underfoot. A strong storm broke out on the way back, and they set the Norseman at an oar. When they arrived in the orc city, they freed him, and the granddad didn't want to go back. He collected a team of dare-devils, took the drekkar from the captain who'd captured him (they agreed to split the spoils fifty-fifty), and headed out to sea. A year later, the granddad owned five ships and commanded three hundred gray (and not so gray) Vikings. "But how then did you get here?"

"Underwater. With straws. We froze our buttocks off, but we cut the snekkja's anchor lines and led those merchant ships off during the night. We hurled black lily bulbs at the guards to make sure they didn't wake up. Who would have known your sister would be on board, or that I'd end up with her, and sorry, but I ain't givin' her back. It'd be a shame to miss out on a wife like that. Good times! We used to get after each other somethin' else...!"

"You tricky Loki's spawn," the Norseman laughed out loud. "Targ take you and Loki instead of an anchor. Thanks for the nieces. You'll raise 'em as Vikings, for sure. Look out for that Semira—they'll take her away like you took Brunhilde!" Harald slapped the orc on the shoulder and then suddenly grew quite serious. "Where are you planning to go?"

"To Key Island. King Gil declared Penkur[6] and is giving away land on the western edge of the islands. There's a nice couple of harbors there.

---

[6] A magical ritual of peacemaking and forgiveness where all sins are forgotten. In declaring Penkur to the "gray" orcs, the king of Tantre is essentially saying there is to be no enmity between the peoples, all claims are settled, and their relationship can begin with a clean slate.

I'm just afraid of one thing—that we'll get kicked out of there, too, sooner or later."

Harald cracked his knuckles, stood up from the boulder and walked back and forth, his ax clinking against his shins.

"Three weeks ago I went to Wolf archipelago…," he began. Tyrnuv gave him his full attention, listening with interest. "Again, instead of cargo, a drekkar full of mages and birds in cages." Harald stopped and looked at the city at the foot of the hills. The wind made his thick braided beard move. "I just happened to be in the tent when the mages did their sorcery and looked through the eyes of the gulls, and the crystal showed the images. Tyrnuv, you've known me a long time. How much bad blood we've created together, how many goblets of mead and sweet wine we've drunk together, and no one could call me a coward." The Norseman turned sharply on his heels and looked at the orc. Harald's pupils dilated and his pudgy cheeks got red. "I'm not afraid to die; I'm afraid I'll die in vain. You should see Gykhyborg! Hundreds of ships in the harbor and dozens of raids, warehouses, warehouses and warehouses, around the barracks of the guards…. Thousands of warriors and mages practicing. The mages noticed and destroyed the birds within two minutes. He had to move it out of there. We barely escaped. Sveiny Squid went to the bottom of the ocean. The Arians scorched his shell. Tyrnuv, they don't need islands, they need a lot of land! The Lynx and the Dragons are wasting their time building fortresses. The Arians will level them like waves level sandcastles on the beach. The orcs' islands aren't a problem for them. They'll seize anyone who doesn't leave while on the march. They're going to deepen the harbors and build walls on Wolf archipelago. They'll simply kill off anyone they don't need. The Arians have turned the island into a transfer base and are getting ready to debark on the shore. We could approach one island, but what's going on on the rest—only Odin knows."

"Why are you telling me all this? What's your point?"

"I'm telling you this because I want you to know: I'm heading south. The Arians have won. Norsemen still dwell on the Eastern Stone, but it's no longer their land. Perhaps they won't touch the western territories, but they don't allow my clan there. The Vikings continue to live singly. And living one by one like that, they'll be smeared out like butter on bread. Gil and the Rauu were right to worry…."

The sound of a large signaling horn rang out over the Fjord, cutting the Viking's words short. Above the narrow strait, squeezed in on either side by man-made latticework steles, a luminous arch appeared. A second magical construction lit up on the outskirts of the city. Far below, people began to shout and cry and animals roared. A line of refugees stretched out from the city. The closest ship to the over-water arc raised the anchor, clapped its oars in a friendly gesture, and the vessel disappeared under the arc, only to reappear on one of the Ort's numerous delta arms. Humans and orcs, going up to the platform of the above-ground teleport, came out near the walls of Miket. Tyrnuv stood up and stretched his legs.

"Let's go, Harald. We have a lot of work to do. I'll be the last to leave. Sigurd'll steer the 'Killer Whale.' I think my eldest has earned the right to drive that drekkar."

Ten hours later, Tyrnuv was standing near the above-ground teleport surrounded by fifty personal warriors. The last vessel had passed under the arc two hours ago, and the mages destroyed the construction. The city, set on fire by the orc warriors, was burning away. Black oily smoke from the houses, covered in peanut oil, rose upwards and, submitting to the wind, spread along the tops of the hills. The strong bang from the magical charges going off brought several rocks down into the waters of the Fjord, blocking the harbor. Tyrnuv waved his hand to his men and went up the wooden bridge to the boat. The homeless and abandoned dogs in the city howled heartrendingly….

Tantre. Southern Rocky Ridge. Thunderstorm Plateau. Rigaud…

"Let's go to the seventh platform!" shouted the gross-dert[7] of the wing of griffons and landed his beast. Rigaud, as adjutant to His Excellency, followed from behind on Blackie.

From above they could see the stunning view of a huge field with hundreds of griffon pens. Wide canopies were scattered here and there, with a huge tent towering in the center. At the edge of the plateau, dozens of mages and hundreds of skilled workers were mounting the framework for a gargantuan portal arc. His Excellency the gross-dert of the third independent wing of combat griffons, in his "chapel" before the flight had said that command was announcing training for pilots in order to test the general formation flying abilities of the whole crew before the start of major military operations. Rigaud was only now seeing just how major they would be. Hundreds of griffons and humans below, hundreds dissecting the sky, and beside them, riders on nimble dredgers landing on the adjacent area.

Blackie beat its wings faster and ran along the ground. Rigaud twisted his leg and removed the loop of rope that was around it. Unlike many, he didn't tie himself to the saddle. He used a rope running under the griffon's belly and around his legs. It was known as the "orcish" way of riding, was considered safer than strapping in, and was a sign of personal mastery of griffon riding. Even if the old veteran his father had hired to teach him sword fighting hadn't done a good job with that, he had certainly hammered the science of griffon riding into his skill set.

"Rigaud!" the gross-dert cried.

"Ler, yes ler!" Rigaud dashed over to his commander.

"Our tents, numbers thirty to forty: lock the griffons in the stalls and feed them, assign the men to tents and send the quartermasters for some hot grub and rations. Get it done by the time I get back from the brigade headquarters. Dismissed!"

"Yes, ler!" Rigaud saluted, turned around on his heels, and ran to his wing. He had a lot of work to do.

Once he had taken care of the griffons, he divided the men under his command into groups of fifteen and assigned them tents. Then came the

---

[7] See glossary

quartermasters' fat mugs, with which it was typically pointless to argue, but today they showed simply fantastic acumen and understanding. The quartermaster by the title of alert-dert, who was just one rank higher than he, scrupulously recorded Rigaud's request and promised to organize hot grub served in twenty minutes. He got the impression that the One God had given the base soldiers a kick in the pants. He wiped the sweat off his brow with the sleeve of his flight jacket and grinned sadly. Could he have possibly imagined a month ago that he would be a military man? If someone had said this to him, he would have made the "crazy" gesture, twirling his index finger near his temple, and spat three times as the idiot walked away.

Targ take Kerr, that pig he used to call a friend. Stole Frida—one. Started a fight with the elves—two. Turned out to be a dragon—three. The day after the memorable massacre at the shooting range, the Royal Informants who arrived from the capital arrested Rector Etran and half the teachers who participated in the battle were suspended from conducting classes. A game of "chess" began at the school. All the Icicles were asked to leave Orten within eight hours; the "punishers" and mages from the Free Mages' Guild joined the group. Half the classmates in their study group were detained and placed in a school dungeon—"pending investigation," as one of the magicians put it.

Coming late to class due to their interrogation by the Royal Informants, Timur and Rigaud looked out the window and saw their classmates in chains. They decided to make a run for it. His friends would have never guessed whose soul the guys in the gray cloaks with black trim were coming for. No one wanted to be sent to the dungeon. Perhaps the decision to flee was ill-conceived childishness—they later let everyone go anyway. But at that moment, when the world was turned upside down, and incomprehensible things were going on at the school, running for it seemed like the best option. But not everything turned out fast and smooth. The mages from the Guild complicated the exit process. They had portraits of Timur and Rigaud and compared them to everyone wishing to leave the city.

"I have an idea," Timur suggested. "We could go join the volunteer corps. None of those petty mongrels can reach us in the army. We could sign a junior contract for two years and be free from sand, dust, and punishing mages."

"I don't want to," Rigaud answered.

"Do *you* have any suggestions that don't involve prison slop?" Timur snapped.

Nothing came to mind. Even his other pair of pants was still in the dorm. At the end of Tanning Street, a guard detail appeared, reinforced by a magician. Rigaud grit his teeth, followed Timur, and with a quick step made his way between the passers-by to the nearest volunteer office. He wanted to eat prison slop even less than he wanted to eat army grub.

The clerks sitting in the office weren't in the least surprised to see new recruits from the nobility. A gray-haired veteran, all covered in scars, the commandant of hired soldiers, after asking the young people the reason that brought them to this institution, grinned with his whole mustache. The experienced campaigner didn't miss the young men's glance through the window at the guards outside. *You've done something, you little dirtbags....*

"Fill out these application forms," he said, handing them some papers. "When you're done, come back to me immediately. You may address me as 'ler.' Understood?"

"Yes."

"I said 'ler!' Yes, ler! Got that?"

"Yes, ler!" Rigaud and Timur barked.

"You're now in the army of the kingdom of Tantre, so get rid of the degenerate manners. You may as well change your attitude now, or it's going to be an uphill battle for you. Go, write."

"Yes, ler!" Rigaud practically screamed. Timur silently sat down at the small desk in the corner of the room.

Ten minutes later, the unwilling new recruits had filled out the forms and went to the commandant's table. The veteran took their papers and dove into reading, periodically grinning through his mustache and casting quick glances at the former bookworms.

"You're all-out masters!" he laughed and pressed on the paper rectangles against the tabletop with the palm of his wide hand. "If half of what you put here is true, the royal army should jump for joy to have you, and our enemies should go ahead and stab themselves so as to avoid a slow painful death." The commandant stood up and walked over to the door to the inner courtyard. "Follow me."

They hadn't taken two steps when the heavy oaken door to the courtyard burst open from a strong kick. A tall man in a white dress shirt and leather pants stormed into the room waving a short sword.

"Mert!" the guy yelled at the top of his lungs. Judging by how he acted and held himself, Rigaud suspected he was an officer. And he was right. "Who is it you're sending my way? These monkeys in the inner courtyard can't tell their backsides from their latrine! What are you sending me these peasants for? They've never even seen a griffon with their own eyes, and if they have, it was from cleaning the dung from the stables! Not only can you not trust them with a sword, I'd be wary of giving these cretins a bludgeon for fear they'd kill themselves with it! What garbage dump are you picking them out of? Crooked shushug half-breeds and trunkless barls! And who's this?" The commandant deigned to pay attention to Rigaud and Timur, who were hesitating behind him. "Come here!" the officer commanded, grabbing the applications out of the veteran's hand. "Hmm, well, worthless scum, move it," he barked at the friends after glancing at the text.

To the soundtrack of the officer's continuous obscenities, the whole group booked it to the courtyard, covered in thick oak chopping blocks, where a gigantic thug with the stripes of a sergeant on his sleeves was drilling a dozen new recruits who looked like an outright countryside bandit.

"Bill!" the officer called to the sergeant, not stopping his swearing. "Drop those pregnant swamp slugs and get over here."

"Ler, yes, ler!" the sergeant bolted upright and ran over.

"Do you see these two?" the officer poked Rigaud in the back with the tip of his sword. "Test them on the wooden swords. Start with the fat one. Don't 'kill' him right away. You can have a little fun."

The merriment didn't work out, or rather it did, but not in the way the officers were expecting. Timur, released into the circle, getting used to the sergeant's dueling style, first deliberately held back, and then, as master Berg had taught him, knocked his opponent's sword from his hand and whacked him on the head with his wooden sword, hard. The sergeant "wavered" for a second and then crashed down on his rear end. Rigaud gave his friend the heads up from behind the commandant's back. The quiet man had conquered. The unit commander and the officer would never have believed that the "fat one" had just picked up a sword for the first time in his life a few months ago.

"How about that!" the officer cried. The commandant grinned under his mustache. "And can you do that same trick again, with me?"

Timur did not repeat it. The second match was the mirror opposite of the first. A few minutes in, he took a blow to the head, fell on his bottom and began counting stars.

"Slim, get over here!" the officer yelled.

"Ler, my name is Rigaud, ler!"

"I couldn't care less what your name is. Until you throw me down, I'll call you worm!" At this, the other new recruits, left unsupervised, snickered in the shadow of the awning. They supposed Rigaud's chances at slim to none.

Rigaud picked up the wooden training sword Timur had dropped and twirled it around a few times to warm up his wrist. He wasn't planning on letting that insult slide. He stepped into the circle and immediately went on the offensive. He'd gotten a chance to observe his opponent's fighting style during Timur's duel. The haughty officer wasn't at all expecting the "worm" to immediately corner him and knock his weapon away, then give him a good kick in the buttocks to boot.

"Again!" the fire of competition sparkled in the losing man's eyes. The defeated soul required revenge. *Alright, let's go again.* The second duel was over just as quickly. The officer's wooden sword went flying in a nice half-circle and hit one of the new recruits standing in the shade. "Impressive! Who taught you?"

"Master Berg the half-orc," Rigaud answered, who now realized he was in a league above his opponent. The classes with the half-orc had not been for nothing. Rigaud, who dreamed of surpassing Kerr, had accomplished much and could rightfully be proud of himself. Berg had managed to turn the young man into a worthy duelist in just a short time. The daily morning and evening workouts in the school park had taken effect.

"Never heard of him. What else can you do?"

Rigaud and Timur said they were mages in training. Rigaud added that he could fly a griffon.

"I'll take these two," the officer said to the commandant. He then immediately addressed his new subordinates: "My name is gross-dert Ron teg Ridon. I'm a commander of the third independent wing of combat griffons, of which you two are now soldiers. Call me 'ler.' Is that clear?"

"Yes, ler!"

"Very nice, Rigaud."

"Yes, ler!" Rigaud stood at attention.

"When we get to the summer camp, you'll arrange fencing lessons for the entire wing."

"Yes, ler."

***

As soon as they got to the camp, Rigaud and Timur were sent straight to the uniform authority and barber. The former gave them a few sets of clothing and boots; the latter turned their noble locks into military brush cuts. The new recruits were assigned to the barracks. A daily drill began.

Rigaud, who already knew how to ride a griffon, was assigned to a feisty, finicky creature named Blackie for its handsome black fur and feathers. Timur was named a second-in-saddle in a feather of large golden griffons and given his own personal chucker.

Rigaud set out to fulfill the commander's order. He organized fencing lessons which became mandatory for all the officers of the unit. Teg Ridon himself did not hurry to attend. The former bookworm's personal mastery and the commander's advocating for him, as well as the lack of high-born nobles in the unit, saved Rigaud from being challenged to a duel and other unpleasantness. A few of the old guys objected to the young upstart but feared to challenge him.

Rigaud listened to the stable master's advice and ended up finding a way to manage the naughty beast. Blackie liked going for swims and loved ginger cookies. It was willing to sell its own mother for a bite of the luxury. The new rider took full advantage of his "transportation's" weak spots. The lazy griffon responded with gratitude and soon yielded great results.

Three weeks went by caught up in daily worries. Without even noticing it, Rigaud slowly became immersed in the army lifestyle. He began to appreciate the discipline and prefer the strict daily schedule, planned out down to the minute. The indefatigable gossip didn't change his ways here either, and quickly became the center of the group of young riders and officers. The gross-dert noticed his subordinate's ability to collect tidbits of information and organize people (under the influence of the army, Rigaud's leadership abilities awoke), attributed to his noble roots and unfinished magical education. He deemed him his adjutant and gave the order to promote him to the rank of roi-dert. Timur, for his success shooting a chucker, received the rank of unit commander.

The coastal lords' and elvish half-bloods' revolt did not come as a surprise to anybody. Rigaud read the papers and kept abreast of the situation in the city. He kept his fellow soldiers well informed of everything. One morning, the alarm sounded in the wing and they all headed to the north of the country by portal.

The army, coming in from the summer camps, brutally dealt with the rebels. Rigaud and Timur took part in the storming of three castles. Although you can't really call a massacre of innocents like that a storming. First, the whole wing attacked the castle or fortress at once. Special flexible tubes with magical chargers attached to the griffons' saddles. When the riders flew over the fortress, they would tug on special cords and dump magical treats on the defenders' heads. Hundreds of military mages stationed near the fortress prevented them from shooting the griffons down. After massive bombardment, if the defenders did not wave the white flag and did not hang a shield reverse-side out on the gates, the battle mages would take over. The army did not have to risk the lives of its soldiers. A few hundred magician "warriors" concentrated on the castle or fortress and simply wiped the unfortunate opponents from the face of the planet. After a few demonstrations of what they could do, the lords started leaving their lands, castles, and militias and hiding who knows where. The abandoned castles were razed to the ground. The half-bloods who surrendered were spared; those found with a weapon in their hands were executed on site. No trial, no trace left of them. Having been given carte blanche by the king, the Norsemen who settled on the coast drowned the rebels on their and the surrounding lands in blood. The Vikings did not have mercy on anyone. Four days later, it was all over; unpleasant memories and castles burnt to the ground were all that remained of the lords. The negotiations taking place between the Woodies and the Patskoi Empire, the fact of which had been disclosed in the newspapers, as well as the news of rebel ties to the Lordships almost lead to another war. Now the state had to defend elvish half-bloods; indeed not all of them supported the rebellion. Many fought for the king with weapons in hand.

The wing did not return to its home base. The general staff decided to organize massive training. Rumors ran through the ranks that the Patskoi Empire had declared war on Tantre, but for now, no one could confirm or deny this. Rigaud, who had a knack for analyzing different gossip, was inclined to believe it were true and considered their maneuvers well timed. The only thing that surprised him was the place—Thunderstorm Plateau in the Southern Rocky Ridge.

***

Once he had organized hot food for the men, Rigaud ran to the location of his wing and in the first tent ran face to face into Timur. The young man, who had grown up a lot in the last month and smelled blood, looked confused.

"Hey, buddy! What bug's bitten you, or did a griffon peck you, that you're wandering around the camp like a shadow?" Rigaud asked Timur, who had lost the last few extra pounds.

"I just saw Rector Etran," Timur answered, twisting the button on his sleeve nervously. "She's been given her job back, she said that they're gathering all mages except combat mages for military retraining, regardless of their name, title, or bloodline. After the training, the troops will get orders."

"What was the rector doing here?" Rigaud asked, surprised.

"I don't know. Half the teachers were with her. She said we were two full-of-ourselves bumpkins, making ourselves out to be goodness knows what, and imagining that the special forces might want us. As it turns out, goodbye army?"

"Not goodbye, just 'see you later.' I don't think they'll cancel our contracts. Probably after the retraining, they'll send us back to the military."

"Maybe so," Timur kept twisting the button. "Targ!" The threads couldn't hold out and the dark little circle, the same color as his flying uniform, came off.

"Rigaud!" the commander's roar reached the friends' ears.

"Sew the button back on. Well, gotta go," Rigaud patted Timur on the back.

"Rigaud, where are you idling around?" teg Ridon yelled at him.

"Ler, my fault, ler!"

"Your fault. Did you feed the men?" Rigaud nodded. "Alright, I'll let you off the hook. Follow me, make it snappy. The general's gathering all the wing commanders. We'll see what he has to say. Stay behind my back and don't move to the right or left."

Teg Ridon walked briskly towards the staff tent; Rigaud stomped a couple of steps behind. Why had these desk-job generals taken it into their minds to have a powwow at this time of night? When they were about a quarter mile away from the headquarters, Rigaud saw dozens of supplies coming in from an open portal. Maintenance engineers walked along beside the carts. Tubes and saddlebags full of ammunition were carefully loaded onto all the supply carts.

"Ler, I don't think they've called us here for training, ler," he told his commander.

"Keep your thoughts to yourself. We'll find out at headquarters," Ron retorted, examining the transport drivers driving all over the wing.

The officers were met with a pleasantly cool temperature and the low hum of voices upon stepping into the administrative tent. In the middle of the tent, there was a wide table with a few stands for crystals; wicker chairs were arranged in a circle. Almost all seats were occupied. Rigaud counted the number of wing commanders and quietly whistled. Seventeen people, and maybe more would arrive. But even with just those present, that would make about two thousand griffons gathered on the plateau. He was becoming more and more convinced that this was no training session.

Pulling the canopy back, a few Rauu entered the tent in summer costumes made from the skins of mountain cats. What were they doing here? Judging by the amazed expressions on people's faces all around, all officers present were asking themselves the same question.

"Respected officers!" someone called from the entrance, "His Highness Gil the Second."

Rigaud sprang upwards as if a strong spring had been unleashed in his spine. He stood at attention and devoured the king with his eyes. The others stood at attention beside him. Gil the Second was a man of average height; his wavy hair framed his handsome face and strong chin. Rigaud did not manage to note the color of the royal's eyes due to just how bloodshot His Majesty's eyes were. That, coupled with his pallor, told Rigaud His Majesty had been having a hard time lately. The Chancellor and several generals followed the king in.

"Please be seated," the king waved his hand. The crowd sat down in their chairs. "I won't take much of your time."

His Highness really did take only five minutes, but his words shocked many. The newspapers had published reports of base negotiations between the Forest and the Patskoi Empire. There was only a tiny blurb on what the accursed forest "friends" and their "kind" southern neighbors had prepared for Tantre. It turned out that according to the agreement they reached, they were going to divide Tantre into two occupied zones. Everything in the middle and southern reaches of the Ort was to come under the protectorate of the Forest; the Empire would have taken the rest. The insurgent revolt, inspired by agents of the Forest, was supposed to be the excuse for the Woodies to declare war and was funded by the Empire's money, but the quick and capable actions taken to quell it prevented the enemies from quitting the ranks in time.

"Nevertheless, despite all our diplomatic efforts, today I've been informed they have indeed declared war," the king went on. A dead silence fell upon all in the tent. "Your wings have been gathered on Thunderstorm Plateau in order to strike at Pat's legions concentrated at Ronmir. Seventeen royal wings and seven air regiments of the Rauu ally army should become the instrument of retribution which will forever repel foreign enemies' desire to attack our states… General Olmar, continue."

***

General Olmar stood up heavily and walked to the table, sighing.

"The old man's failing," Rigaud heard a quiet whisper behind him. "He's in his eighties...."

"Gentlemen, officers," Olmar coughed into his fist a few times. "His Highness (a short bow towards the king, who was now seated) has given you a general outline of the situation. I shall expound. Tantre is being threatened by a war on two fronts. We're facing the powerful fist of the Empire's northern legions and the Forest's hundred-and-fifty-thousand-strong army." A murmur of alarm rang out in the tent. "Quiet! I need quiet here!" The general put his hand up as a gesture calling for silence. His eyes flashed threateningly from under his bushy eyebrows and he coughed once again. "Over the course of twenty or more years, the Woodies have been strengthening their army with specially grown half-bloods. Our intelligence has obtained information on the purchase by the Woodies of about twenty to twenty-five thousand slaves, so we can only indicate the approximate number of our opponents' army. If you count regular units, the watchmen's squadrons and the border guards, the Lordships have no less than two hundred thousand spears at their disposal." Someone whistled loudly. "And now, about the Empire's legions. The main mass of the griffon wing forces and church knights are concentrated in the vicinity of Ronmir. According to our agents' information, the total number of troops massed by the emperor totals up to one hundred and thirty thousand people, and this without counting the auxiliary units, clerks, and mages." The general paused. A ringing, deafening silence reigned under the thin felt dome. Olmar leaned on his hands, palms down on the tabletop, and looked at all the people gathered in the tent. "No country can survive a war on two fronts unless it uses all necessary resources towards its military effort, both manpower and material resources. If we want to win, we have to act swiftly and decidedly. The main advantage of the countries of the Northern Alliance," here the commander allowed himself a barely noticeable grin, "in case you weren't aware, is the fact that the Pats' newspaper writers christened the military-political alliance between Tantre and the Rauu Principality 'the Northern Alliance.' They hit the nail on the head, so to speak. I repeat: our main advantage is the griffons and the drag wings, of which we have three times more than the Imperialists. The Empire and the Forest realized all the advantages of a strong air force too late," the commander again let out a strained cough. "We've invested a lot of effort into hiding the true state of this army from the Imperial agents. We've significantly reduced the number of griffons on paper. It's time to reveal what we've really got. Please." Olmar gestured to his adjutant. A box of several rock crystals appeared on the table instantly. The agile fellow secured one of them in the rack and pressed the metal plate that activated the illusion spell. A picture of Ronmir and the surrounding area unfolded before the audience from the height of a bird's flight.

Ronmir, from its very origin, served as a trans-shipment base for the Imperial troops. Two thousand years ago, the Empire of Alatar required a reference point for further advance to the north. A small border village, located on the right bank of the Rhone River, was best for this purpose. From the nameless village to the Rocky Ridge there were convenient trails right up to the passes. In just a short time, the village turned into a city of thirty thousand, surrounded by military camps. After the conquest of the northern lands, convenient roads were built through the mountains, and Ronmir became a trade and transport hub, connecting the growing Empire to the far-away barbarian provinces. When the Empire fell, so did Ronmir's prosperity. The trade routes were cut off; the legions withdrawn from the north did not stop but continued southward and burned up in the fire of civil war. The city was desolated. The population shrunk ten times over. Four hundred years ago, Pat captured the southern foothills, declaring themselves the successors of the bygone Empire. The large town in which the once blossoming city was reborn once again took on a strategic importance. The barracks and military camps were rebuilt. From there the Pat legions headed north several times and returned to where they came from, empty-handed. The barbarous province turned into a strong kingdom. Strong fortresses appeared on the passes; the foreign army locked down the mountain passages. The Emperor of Pat was preparing to attack from there yet again.

"Ronmir," the general said in his wheezy voice. The end of his long pointer touched the illusion and rested on a clump of rectangles from the northern side of the city. The image immediately got larger and all present could see clearly a fortress standing apart from the city, dozens of barracks inside and thousands of tents laid out in straight rows outside the walls. The commander's tone and manner of presentation changed. He moved from lengthy sentences to short, stopping phrases. "The barracks are our main target. Our agents report mages were in the fortress last night. Our intelligence says the number of Imperial 'warriors' is over fifteen hundred. They housed the mages in the barracks of the eastern fort." The pointer moved a little to the left. "The western fort. The rooms here are divided up, some to the 'pure ones' and some to the 'lasso brigade.' The Emperor has made a deal with the official Church. Ten thousand special forces raiders were dispatched to sweep the local terrain. The 'pure ones' ordered them not to spare anyone. Another order was to destroy all temples to gods other than the One God. Your main task is to completely destroy the mages and the 'pure ones.' The raiders and sorcerers must die!" His strong fist hit the table. "Without mages, any army is just a crowd of idiots in uniform. Your second priority: capture the enemy griffins and destroy the arsenal. A separate brigade, which we will form from the best swordsmen and fencers, must capture the mana accumulators designed to 'puncture' our protective magic screen. To the commanders of the wings and Rauu regiments: I order you to allocate ten riders who can handle weapons. The 'puncture' structures and the stables are located here and here." Olmar, once he had pointed out the locations of the storage warehouses and the griffon stables, switched to presenting the plan of attack….

Patskoi Empire. Outskirts of Ronmir…

Mitku walked up to the top of the hill and looked around. Below, in the crevice between two sloping hills, Lake Nechai emanated with a dank, pre-dawn fog. Behind him, through the smoky vapor, the lights of the city and the citadel of the military camp near the walls twinkled brightly. The mountains, silent dark giants, rose to the sky, most visible at sunrise and sunset. Mitku took a step towards a trail, barely visible in the morning twilight. He tripped on a rock jutting from the ground and almost fell, stumbling forward. Gran laughed meanly at him from behind. Orweed, who was following Gran, lightly poked his friend with his fishing rod, which was cut from purple osier willow.

"What's so funny? I almost did a nose dive into the earth. It's dark as the underworld here. Targ must've pushed me, you guys, to go fishin' at such an hour." Orweed yawned contagiously and stretched his whole body; watching him, the others also yawned so big their heads almost turned inside out. "Oooh, you guys, such a thick fog's comin' from the lake. I shoulda gone restin' in a haystack instead. You fish-poops…."

"Watch where yer goin'!" Gran turned around and immediately fell flat on the ground after tripping over a long root. His old fishing rod snapped in two with a dry click; his net flipped out of his hands with a *pling*.

"Weeell, there's nothing to get all mean about, Mitku said, and he and Orweed helped their friend up.

"Eeh," Orweed looked at the fading stars and the disk of Nelita, melting into the horizon. "Soon they'll sound the alarm in the citadel to wake everyone up." He stopped and looked mournfully at the twinkling city lights. "It's too bad I'm only fourteen. I'd join the legions if I could. Oooh, what a force! They'll tromp down those Tantrians like squished roaches!"

"The hornless goats!" Mitku swore. "I hope the Tantrians crush them."

"What are you saying!" Orweed threw himself at him, chest puffed out. "Watch what words come out of your mouth! You're against the Emperor?"

"I'm serious!" Mitku answered, clenching his fists in anger. "Haven't you heard that these goats are knights? The squires and militiamen got drunk and shouted it in the tavern. Noble sirs! Argh. They yelled that they would burn the cities and all over! All the boys—the sword. All the non-believers—the sword. All the old people—the sword. Throw the men down the wells, take the women and girls and then sell them at the slave markets... and some more stuff even worse. I have an aunt and two cousins, girls, in Panme. They live on the other side of the mountains. What, should we just let packs of knights and militiamen first rob them of their honor, then sell them as slaves, or let them chop up your father's brother-in-law? They almost raped Frosta on the homestead in the evening. Mirt and dad only just managed to fend off the attack on my sister. They kicked Mirt in the legs so bad, and dad they just beat up everywhere, all on his face, the rotten scoundrels. They were shouting that we're Tantrian trash and we should kiss their boots. I went fishing with Gran... dad's not going to open the tavern today." Mitku kicked a little pebble and sat down on a dry uprooted tree. Gran, upon hearing such a confession from his friend, fell into a dazed silence.

"You... um, where were the guards?" he pushed Mitku gently in the shoulder, who waved his hand in a gesture of helplessness.

"Those guards crapped their pants." The boy spat at his feet and threw the tackle to the side. "The guards, who ran to the screaming cries, stopped at the gate and faltered at the entrance, afraid to approach the 'pure ones' militiamen. They were going crazy and making a ruckus. Someone chastised them, but a guy with a narrow face who looked like a rat, a 'pure,' just laughed out loud and said that the Vegils's hadn't the guts to argue with the servants of the Holy Church."

Gran turned towards the lake. He too dreamed of joining the legions, but after hearing that, his desire faded a little.

"Well your sister's really getting a swelled up head. Couldn't choose a man she liked, wanted a pretty boy rich boy! No husband, so here they came for her!... Ow!" Orweed toppled to the ground, kicked down by Mitku.

The teenagers weren't just fighting, they were fighting to the death. Fists and feet flew, with some teeth in the mix. The husky Orweed held Mitku in a death grip; Mitku punched his enemy in the jaw, bloodying his lip and knocking out a tooth. In response, Orweed bloodied Mitku's nose. The war had not yet begun, but it had already divided friends and neighbors into different camps. Orweed unconsciously repeated the words of his father, secretly envious of the successful innkeeper, who moved to Ronmir from Tantre a quarter of a century ago and who built the tavern from scratch. Throughout the years, it had become more and more popular, which couldn't be said for the rest of them. Willingly or not, children take in whatever is said and all that goes on in their homes by their parents, for better or for worse, and sometimes they take this out on those around them at the most inappropriate times.

"Look!" Gran cried, not even trying to separate the fighting friends. Observing a strange dark mass in the depths of the gorge tore him from reality and the fighting going on behind him. Turning around, he saw the friends rolling on the ground and pounding one another with their fists. Thinking for a moment, Gran whacked them violently with the fragments of his rod a couple of times. The adolescents jumped off from each other and, rubbing their bloody pulp all over their broken faces, looked toward the lake.

The dark shadows emerging from the gorges turned out to be thousands of griffons and their riders. The animals, tearing off the wisps of fog creeping over the lake, seemed to come in an endless stream. Many of the griffons bore two riders. Saddlebags and tubes full of ammunition were attached to the sides and saddles of the half-birds. The second rider would hold the bows loaded with magical arrows. Some of them held chuckers to the griffons' sides.

"What are they?" Mitku wheezed.

"And there…." Gran looked at the mountains hidden in the white haze in the east with wide open eyes. Yet another living river flowed towards Ronmir, resembling a dark stripe on the gray earth. "How many are there? Who is it?"

"Tantrians…." Orweed sighed, noticing the crest on the blankets spread over the griffons' bodies and under the saddles. He turned to Mitku who was standing frozen to the spot, staring at the battle griffons flying forcefully forward.

From the lower reaches of the Rhone, the third column of attackers emerged, clearing away the milky fog. Plumes of smoke and flame shot upwards over the fortress. The boys heard the rumble of explosions.

***

Timur tossed his chucker from one hand to the other and glanced behind him. His squadron of fifty quickly swept through the air behind the head griffin.

"Hold formation," he said in his first-in-saddle's ear. Nimir nodded and patted Pumpkin on its feathery neck.

The half squadron he now commanded, the rank of roi-dert… it had been a day of skyrocketing career growth for the seventeen-year-old, or rather, evening and night. Timur chuckled. Last night had been quite eventful.

Teg Ridon, coming back from the headquarters, had required a storm of activity. He gathered all the officers and sergeants into his tent and made some announcements.

First, there would be no training. The army of griffons—yes, the *army*—would be sent to strike at the Pat legions in the outskirts of Ronmir.

Second, third, fourth, and fifth wings were tasked with storming and destroying the arsenal.

Third, half the second-in-saddles would be removed from the golden griffons. Combat mages would replace them. Ridon replied to the angry murmur that came from the servicemen left on the ground by saying that it was by order of the king and anyone who required additional explanation could go ask him for it. No one did.

Fourth, the transportation would take place by portal. Mages would take down the protective screens on the border for this purpose. The attack would proceed from three different directions at the same time. Mages have been called in from the Orten School of Magic, under the direction of Rector Etran, to quickly re-orient the exit points. They've brought the crystal energy accumulators of the ancient "smoky veil" artifact, because reconfiguring the direction of the griffons will require massive amounts of mana. (That was the answer to the question about what Rector Etran was doing here.) All of them—from His Highness right down to the last stable boy—owed a bow of thanks to the idiots from the Imperial army headquarters who thought of maintaining their protective screens from ten in the evening to six in the morning. Teg Ridon himself offered them a low bow, wished them a horrible loss, and sent them all to Targ. Let the dwarf god have his fun with them.

Fifth, the third strike wing was being urgently reformed. The light-weight griffons would be transferred to the tenth wing. Instead of them, four feathers from the Rauu air regiments will be placed on duty. Additionally, the wing was sending ten of our best fencers to the disposal of a separate wing of special forces. Rigaud had to choose nine people and report for duty to his new unit in one hour.

Six, all sergeants will be given communicator amulets to organize and coordinate military actions, besides the standard defensive necklaces, of course.

Seven, they were third in line for going through the portal. And finally, in order to keep the attack a secret, seven hours ago some units of "shadows" and "invisibles" were transported onto Imperial territory, whose responsibility was to take out the Imperial soldiers at the far and near lookout posts. The commander assured them that his "boys" would break their skeletons from their bodies before they'd let even one warning message get past them.

On the organization of the storm: the wings would fly over the target in three echelons and would drop all the "presents" from the first bags and lesser tubes. After bombarding the arsenal and approaching it, the mages would get off the griffons along with the second-in-saddles, who would be armed with chuckers and would make their way to the dungeons. In order not to get in one another's way, the fourth wing would leave to storm the tent camp while the fifth would remain as a backup and go where they were needed most. Any questions? No?

All those gathered in the tent didn't have a moment to let their guards down when the commander called Timur.

"In an hour, four full Rauu feathers will get here. I appoint you..." stopping and thinking a second, the commander turned to the staff: "Um, scribe, immediately record the following: by order of the third wing, Timur teg grall Soto shall be given the rank of roi-dert. Count Soto..." A murmur ran through the tent. No one knew the young sergeant was a titled noble. Timur and Rigaud, naturally, hadn't blabbed about their origin, and the commander hadn't found it necessary to let his subordinates know. He rightfully supposed that an army was composed of commanders and soldiers, as opposed to nobles and peasants. "You are hereby responsible for coordinating efforts with our allies. I think your background will allow you to find some common ground with the Icicles. You're all dismissed. Those of you who've been ordered to leave—you have half an hour to collect your things and move your feet to the tenth wing. Rigaud's ten, report to the arms master to pick up the reinforced amulets and shells. You can leave your flight helmets; they can protect your heads from a cutting blow about as well as a cone-shaped helmet or other iron pot. Roi-dert Soto, quickly get your new stripes and get yourself in order; not so much time is left before our guests arrive."

The officers headed towards the exit. Timur was stunned at being given the rank of an officer and stayed behind. The sound of yelling and swearing came from outside. The commander darted out from behind the curtain and ran out; the young roi-dert followed. What they saw made them want to laugh and cry at the same time. Alert-dert Vard, a commander of fifty men, had slipped on a pile of griffon droppings and fallen flat on his face. But that was the end of the humor—Vard had broken his foot upon falling. The Life mage who ran over to attend him stated that he would be out of active duty for at least a week. He couldn't get him back on his feet any earlier. Teg Ridon found some choice words, glanced around and his gaze rested on Timur.

"Roi-dert Soto!"

"Ler, yes, ler!"

"Take command of these fifty men. Remember, you still have all your duties regarding interactions with the elves. Don't let me down, man."

"Yes, ler!" Timur saluted. As if he didn't have enough on his plate....

Timur understood the motives of the higher-ups who'd sent the Snow Elves to them. He understood perfectly. Serving in the military shoulder to shoulder would join them together like nothing else could. The meaning of military fraternity was not lost on the arrogant Icicles.

Surprisingly, the Rauu who arrived at the camp did not make the slightest fuss. They were very well versed in the concepts of discipline and obedience to their highest ranking officer. Timur put on a tough guy look and, flaunting his stripes, which testified to the fact that he'd seen some combat action already, and the brand new miniature feathers on his chest, and went out to meet the adjunct sergeants. He assigned the personnel to the tents that had been designated for them. He invited the sergeants to the command wing; the rest he ordered to go to bed. Only four hours were left until reveille....

At five thirty the sound of a horn blared over the wide mountain plateau. The military camp was flooded with the light of a multitude of magical lanterns. The transport drivers, who hadn't left the field kitchens all night, brought hot grub to the wings. The mechanics were putting saddlebags and tubes on the griffons, who were not happy at being woken up so early. A constant buzz hung over the camp, as over a busy birdhouse. The rush of adrenaline and the smell of the combat half-birds' droppings were in the air. At half past six, a green flame climbed high in the sky, meaning high alert. People saddled up their griffons. The first wings in line started taking flight. A gigantic portal lit up with a clear light at T minus fifteen minutes and counting. Dozens of silhouettes of mages could be seen in the low light of the magical portal, scurrying about servicing the arc. The king came out of his tent. His Highness decided to personally oversee the pilots to their combat mission; the outcome of the war was riding on this surprise attack. Two yellow fireballs exploded high over the earth. The wings, occupying different echelons of the air, began to take formation. The surface of the portal flashed so brightly it was impossible to look at. The steles on either side immediately glowed red. The first wing disappeared into the unknown. Two hundred feet back, the griffons of the second wing dove towards the ground.

"We're ready!" Timur cried into his communicator amulet. "We're at an interval of ten leagues! Nimir, follow the commander."

Nimir made the turn. The arc was getting close very fast. There was a clap, then a short blindness... and before their eyes, an incredibly beautiful landscape appeared, mountains flooded with the light of Nelita. Teg Ridon ordered everyone to "hug" the ground. Looping between the mountains, thousands of griffons flew towards Ronmir. The head dozen griffons retreated into the gorge leading to Lake Nechai. Not a single lookout post sounded the alarm. Using true vision, Timur perceived on one peak the cooling dead bodies of the Imperial soldiers killed by the "invisibles." He began to shake. This wasn't a game. The previous storms he'd taken part in when he'd had to dump fatal cargo onto the lords' soldiers, wasn't a problem for him. Maybe that's because he was far from his victims and did not perceive them as enemies. In Ronmir, everything would be different. He would have to get out of the saddle and fight with the enemy in hand-to-hand combat. He could be killed....

***

Ronmir appeared unexpectedly. The griffons hadn't yet stirred up the layer of fog over the lake when the panorama of the gigantic military camp came into view before the riders' eyes.

"Arm your chuckers! Safeties off! Open the release valves!" Teg Ridon's voice sounded through the communicator amulets. Timur repeated the order.

The legionnaires' tents and the half-naked figures dashing out of them flashed by below his griffon's belly. Caught unawares, the Imperial soldiers did not have time to organize a way to rebuff the air strike. The fifteenth, sixteenth, and seventeenth storm wings flew out over the camp. From the west to the deafening, magically-enhanced sound of the cawing of striped griffons, the second Rauu regiment dove in.

A few wings were circling over the fortress. Clumps of dirt, logs, bricks, and tile from the barracks flew up to the sky. Protective domes flashed brightly. Magicians in the barracks suffered losses, but managed to put up their defense and shoot down about a hundred griffins. The bombs dropped were absorbed by the dome. Driven by their human riders, the griffons increased their altitude and started flying in giant circles. This tactic was called "the carousel." The regiments attacking the mages hovered in a few echelons and, circling in a carousel formation, began to drop their bombs on the dome in a constant stream. At some point, it could no longer withstand the attack and popped. The officers had been waiting for this moment for a long time. The simultaneous bombardment of cursed bombs by five hundred half-birds and the magical attack by the combat mages riding in the second saddle stripped the enemy of any chance. The barracks were enveloped in a hot flame, which absorbed the delicate flesh of the people trapped in four walls… one force overcame another. The wings moved to the western fort. The "pure ones" and the lasso brigade, who had remained unnoticed for a short while, managed to install chuckers on the roofs, and burning griffons fell from the sky.

Timur finished bombing the ground targets, a task he was already accustomed to. This exhausted half the ammunition in his saddlebags and tubes. The protective dome over the warehouses pooped out.

"Begin your descent!" he heard in his ear.

A wave of the hand and the half-birds began to land. The second-in-saddles unbuckled and charged towards the arsenal. A hot battle was raging near the doors. Timur jumped onto the pavement, grabbed his chucker and couldn't manage to take even two steps before dozens of legionnaires came hurtling towards him from two half-destroyed barracks. Many of the defenders were wearing white underpants and armor on their naked torsos, but the insanity of combat and the thirst for blood made them dangerous enemies.

A couple of point-blank shots swept the first few rows of enraged soldiers away, and then the fighting began. A dozen of the parachuting mages was killed right away upon landing. Apparently, they had become "warriors" not long ago and weren't able to activate several spells at once. A short moment of hesitation was all the legionnaires needed to get close enough to cut off the heads of some Tantrians. Everyone got mixed together; those still in the air were unwilling to shoot and bomb from above, for fear they would strike their own.

Timur picked up an enormous bludgeon from the ground, and with all his formidable strength, hit one of the Imperialists on the head with it. The man's eyes rolled back and he fell onto the road like a spineless amoeba. Within a moment all signs of life left him. The battle quickly entered the phase wherein the combatants no longer paid any mind to nobility. Courteous manners were guaranteed to lead to the funeral pyre. People were cutting, chopping, and stabbing one another with knives, swords, and axes. Fallen warriors retrieved the curved daggers from their boot tops and attempted to get one last stab in before leaving this life. Valiant cries rang out over the pavement. The ancient stones flowed with hot blood.

Timur slowly but surely made his way to the arsenal. All attempts to bring him down by magic and then chop him up failed. The bludgeon shone in his hand like a white dickie bird. The fallen were killed by his subordinates following him from behind. Ten Rauu covered his rear and sides. The battle in all its inglorious gore presented itself before Timur. Under his feet were hacked limbs; intestines hanging out of stomachs stank; the wounded moaned. If the Tantrians hadn't had air support, no landing forces could have helped them reach the gates of the arsenal. Timur spun like a top, beat, bounced and dodged, slipping along the blood-stained pavement. How long the carnage lasted, he did not know. His sense of time was completely lost.

In the sky, too, a short battle broke out. Intelligence had not reported a large griffon wing stationed in the southern part of the city. Left without command, the Imperial officers couldn't think of anything better than using it to repel the attack.

Two griffons tightly grappling with one another collapsed to the ground; the ammunition in their pouches exploded. The stones, clay, and sand of the roadway flew in all directions. A deep funnel was formed at the site of the explosion. Leaving a smoky trail, a half-bird beaten down by a chucker flashed in a fiery flourish as it fell. Half a minute later another griffon fell to the ground. The earth shook and a wall fluttered from the powerful explosion, and the wall of the arsenal, which had lost its magical protection during the bombardment, collapsed. Timur simply could not imagine—he could not fit in his head—such carelessness that in the citadel, no one had bothered to enhance the magical protection of the ammunition depot.

"Timur, cover me. I'm going in," Nimir said, who had appeared out of nowhere. The tip of a crossbow arrow with a green feather stuck out of the first-in-saddle's shoulder. "I don't have much time left," he drawled and showed the black stain around the wound that was increasing in all directions. "It's poisoned. Sit down on Pumpkin and fly right away. She won't let anyone else on her. I have fifteen minutes left while my antidote magic holds off the poison."

Timur, hiding his tears of anger and sniffing, hugged his first-in-saddle awkwardly and ran to Pumpkin, near whom a striped griffon, one of the ten Rauu, crashed to the ground in a fit. Its rider lay on the stones face down. Timur looked with true vision and saw by his aura that the elf was still alive, just stunned. Grabbing his ally by the belt, he threw him over the empty second saddle. Pumpkin glared at him unhappily and clicked her beak.

"All together!" he screamed the uncertain, standard phrase into the communicator amulet, thereby giving the signal for an emergency evacuation. The sky over the fortress instantly cleared. Wings beat loudly; Pumpkin lifted up off the ground. The rest of the fifty followed.

"Soto, quickly take your men to the white hill!" the amulet spoke up. "Mages there have built a minor portal. You won't be able to get away otherwise! Make a beeline to the hills, that's an order!" the amulet vibrated with Teg Ridon's voice.

"Ler, yes, ler!"

They were a stone's throw from the hills. The three dozen griffons still alive with their riders flew down to the ground and walked on the beasts through the arc. Timur watched his people and then carefully started landing. The rider was still in bad shape. He wasn't able to get away quietly. The ground shook beneath them from a strong blast. Obscuring the rising sun, enormous flames rose into the sky. The air, which had become tight and heavy, threw the portal-building mages onto their backs; Timur and Pumpkin dove into the rippling teleport.

Tantre. Southern Rocky Ridge. Andy...

Andy snuggled up against a tree and laid his head against the rolled-up blanket, warmed by the sun. Today they didn't go into the village either but stayed on a wide field near a pure mountain stream. Slaisa shot two grouses along the road and promised to cook a rich stew for dinner. Ilnyrgu had built a fire. A slight breeze blew the smoke towards the were-dragon. Stinging his eyes, it made him think of the gigantic flame of the funeral pyre built on the deck of the snekkja headed on its last voyage along the Ort from Ortag's main dock….

…A black, caustic smoke spread over the water and, breaking into little shreds by a gusty northern wind, carried the bodies of the fallen warriors to Valhalla to Odin's feasts, to the heavenly palaces of the Twins and Khirud the lightning-armed. The mighty Ort did not wish to send the snekkja to the strong current and turned the boat in the center of the inland city harbor. Andy watched the bright flame as it consumed the bodies of the Norsemen and of Berg. Toryg—a female orc who had been given the honor by the northerners of being buried with the warriors—lay beside the half-orc's hut. The red-haired Olaf was left alive without a scratch. He laid the orc woman onto the bundles of wood beside the hut himself. The hut housed the Vikings, gone yet triumphant in battle. Some of the warriors set straves[8] or mugs of beer on the footpath. They put the personal effects[9] of each of the departed alongside his body and put chicken's eggs in their hands.[10]

"The Valkyrie…." Olaf said to the other Vikings, going down to the pier. No one asked any questions. Everyone had seen how the female orc had fought. "Kerr?" the red-haired man turned to Andy and glanced at the two bound men.

---

[8] Burial meals. The funeral feast was a necessary element of the funerary cult. Most of the Icelandic sagas contain information about funerals or funeral feasts, at which the whole region, sometimes several hundred people, gathered. The remains of funerary meals, "straves," as they were known, in the form of bones of animals and birds, eggshells, etc., are found everywhere in Viking burial mounds. It was believed that the dead were present at the feast along with the living. The dead, as can be determined from the sagas, had an uncommon appetite. Dead soldiers were given bowls of beer, believing that they drink on a par with the living.

[9] Supplying the dead with things was a common phenomenon for pagan rituals: according to "Odin's covenant," "all the dead should be burned and […] their property should be put with them in the fire."

[10] The Vikings considered eggs a symbol of rebirth and resurrection. The shells have often been found in burial mounds.

"I will." Andy sighed heavily. He knew his duty. The Norsemen formed a wide circle and untied the captive lords' warriors. The unit commander, all mottled with scars, took a step forward and threw a couple of swords at the two now free men's feet.

The soldiers grabbed the weapons. The short, elderly sergeant looked at Andy, who had stepped forward, and snarled meanly. The second man, a young guy across from him, convulsively grabbed the sword and looked around with a bewildered look. It was part of the funeral ritual. Fallen warriors should have guides and servants in the afterlife. The Vikings had preserved much of their Earthly heritage, although the form and content of some customs had changed in part. Some of them died, faced with new beliefs, and some were born at the junction of cultures and influences of other peoples. But the funeral ritual remained, even if altered somewhat by people over the course of time. Andy did not know exactly what motivated the unit commander and the other northerners, but he was not about to refuse a strange offer or honor extended to him. The new world continued to try him and test his strength. This was yet another test, and he had to pass it. The Norsemen had taken him into their circle. He wasn't about to push away a hand extended in friendship. Earning respect was challenging; losing it was easy.

Andy went to meet the doomed warriors with a heavy step. The sergeant, grinning grimly, tried to catch him in a counter-attack and got stabbed in the liver. The young soldier, with a loud shout, lowered his sword to the place where his opponent had stood just a moment ago, and died with a heart pierced by cold steel. The northerners picked up the defeated soldiers and laid them at the feet of their dead tribesmen and orcs—the very place for servants. A large male horse was led to the pier. The unit commander held the stallion's bridle as it stomped its hooves. A few minutes later, the dismembered animals[11] were laid on the deck. Nanna, the unit commander's wife, cut the heads off a rooster and a chicken and threw them on the snekkja. The Norsemen pushed the boat away from the shore with their long wooden poles. The current grabbed the ship and carried it out to the middle of the harbor. A flaming arrow lit up

---

[11] A set of sacrificial animals has been well documented by Scandinavian sources. All the sacrificial animals, primarily the horse and the cock, were equally related to death, the afterlife, and the cult of fertility. The horse was one of the most common "vehicles" that deliver the deceased to the next world.

the sky and buried itself into the bundles of wood, which had been generously covered with oil.

Andy walked up to the orc women. Tyigu let go of Ilnyrgu's hand and hugged him around the waist with her face in Andy's stomach. The girl was trembling. Andy awkwardly patted her on the head, secretly shocked that he had completely lost the ability to feel sorry for anyone. Hiding the bodies behind the clouds of smoke, the greedy flame swallowed the small craft. In thirty minutes not even a trace of the now buried warriors remained on the rippling surface of the water. The Ort's current had carried the smoking remains of the fraternal grave to the sea.

"May you have a light afterlife, brothers!" the unit commander cried and was the first to head towards the tables set up on the shore. The remembrance feast had begun.

***

…Master Berg and Toryg died in the northern barracks. It was so stupid—Andy couldn't call it anything else—and ordinary. Was it Hel, who had cut off two more spikelets as she gathered her harvest, or had Khirud wanted to change the guard at his throne? Well, who cared about the religious aspect anyway. His mentor was gone. What had motivated the half-orc? Why had he decided to go with the Vikings to free the guards who were surrounded in the barracks? Andy didn't know. The she-wolves, in response to all his questions, only answered that it was a matter of paying his debt of honor. And when had Berg managed to incur debt? Either way, Ilnyrgu and Toryg went with him, and Toryg died a few steps from her teacher. When the fighting in the city ended, Andy tried to discover the truth from primary sources and questioned the warriors and Ilnyrgu for a very long time. But they could not draw a clear picture for him of how Berg had died. No one saw the actual moment of the half-orc's death, as is often the case. In the throes of battle, each one was busy with his or her opponent. The narrow streets of Ortag did not allow them to turn around; the battle at the northern barracks took place in a crowded place, people had no time to look around.

The Norsemen bolted through the gate of the arsenal and went around the big fire they had caused. They trampled Lord Worx's militiamen in the dirt, squished the squadrons of white armbands against the walls of the buildings, and passed like an iron boot over the still living mechanics who manned the fortress chuckers. Burned by red-hot and molten stones and beaten down by the magical attack and the quick death of the mages, they practically didn't put up a fight at all. After clearing the nearby streets and rooftops, the unit commander divided the men into three squadrons. The first stayed in the fortlet; the second and third headed towards the barracks. Andy, dragging his feet heavily, got out of the volcano he had set up himself and trudged to the arsenal. He could barely walk. The applied spell drank up a fair amount of his internal reserves, which went to pumping mana from the astral, and it struck him painfully with the "recoil." Still, operating with such enormous volumes of energy in his human and dragon bodies were two different things. What was easily done in the winged hypostasis was much more difficult for the human. The internal energy that had been lost in the commotion calmed down in about twenty minutes.

Andy sat down on a pile of bricks left from the outermost building and focused completely on listening. From the north side, explosions were sometimes heard; fires blazed and flared up like morning heat lightning. A dark smog hung over the city, obscuring the stars and the Goddesses' Eyes. The soot from the houses burnt by his spell fell like fat flakes on clothes and earth. At some point, silence fell…. After a moment, a cannonade broke it. Judging by the frequent cracking sounds, Andy concluded that the Vikings had reached the barracks and were firing on the rebels with "firelights."

It would have been foolish to expect the planned operation to take place as planned. Squeezed in from both sides, the rebels resisted fiercely. Among them were magicians and swordsmiths, who took a lot of souls to Hel's court. The sheer accident or great luck for those besieged in the arsenal was that the best fighters and fencers of the besiegers were close to the magicians at the moment when Andrew brought the "fiery rain" down on them. If things had been different, the brave performance of the Norsemen and mercenaries outside the walls of the fortress could well have ended in blood gurgling forth from cut throats.

Things at the barracks turned out differently. As soon as the shelling began, the rebel commanders and the soldiers of Lord Worx, realizing that their plan to seize the strategic facilities had failed, regrouped their subordinates and tried to break through the line. Evenly dispersed over the retreating army, a few mages were covered in defensive amulets from head to toe, which more than compensated for their small numbers. They managed to hold the shield and fend off Ilnyrgu's and four mages from the arsenal's magical attacks. The offense and the defense switched sides; the massacre began.

A couple of master sword warriors and the last few mages left alive responded to the rebels' fierce attacks. The Norsemen ran out of magical arrows, so they no longer needed to defend the troops as they burst through. The mages, ready to strike at the annoying Ilnyrgu and the former bookworms from the arsenal, to the chagrin of master Berg and Toryg, had formed a compact group. A couple of orcs and archers, using Andy's technique, decided to take to the rooftops and cut off the retreating forces' escape route. One of the mages saw a human figure on the roof. To avoid coming under fire again, half the mages put up a shield, and the other half attacked the building.

Berg had time to jump from the roof of a crumbling two-story building into a narrow opening among the fighters. Toryg and the archers were under the rubble of a fallen structure at that time. A cloud of dust covered the street. In a few moments, the pavement was piled with sheaves of bodies of the guards, who were warlocks of magical interweaves. Those under guard outlived their bodyguards only by a few minutes. Under the constant attack and arrows that came with "surprises," the mages' defensive amulets lost their charge. Berg's jewelry, on the other hand, weren't drained by any kind of attack and were full of energy. He pressed right through the shield they had up and fed those mages some cold steel. They had zero chance of declining the "filling lunch." Once he was inside the tiny dome, he showed the villains what he could do. Some swordsmen unexpectedly joined the exchange; they did not save the mages, but they went at Berg with all their might. The half-orc caught one of them in a sharp transition to a low stance and dealt him a cleaving blow to the legs. The swordsman fell onto the dirty pavement, where Berg promptly cut off his head with a second swing of the sword, sending him to Hel's judgment. But here, the witnesses' stories diverged. The poofing dust blocked them from a good look at the details. Some said the half-orc's foot got caught in a deep pothole. Ilnyrgu, busy with three foes at that moment, said that a wounded lords' soldier stabbed him in the calf with a curved ankle knife. In the end, a second swordsman managed to take advantage of the half-orc's momentary troubles, stabbing him with a dagger.

From underneath the rubble of the dusty street, coughing and spitting gray spit, Toryg appeared. Her defensive amulets had saved her from dying under the weight of the heavy debris. When she saw Berg falling onto the pavement, she went insane. Flying on the killer like a whirlwind, the she-wolf carried him to the walls of the building, boxed him in, first cut through his thigh muscles on his right leg, then pierced his throat. Once she had slaughtered the swordsman, her eyes burning with rage and pain, Toryg threw herself at the Lord's soldier. There was no defense from her twin swords. They were short, no longer than twenty-five inches, but the "twins" could not be better suited for battle in a crowd and at short distances. Over ten orc women had already been killed when she butted heads with yet another master warrior and luck turned its back on her. In a battle of mastery, steel sometimes wins over steel. Upon meeting the smoky steel of her enemy's blade, forged by dwarfs, with a ringing cry of protest, the sword in the she-wolf's right hand broke. The corpses at her feet prevented her from increasing the distance between herself and her enemy. Just as hers had done moments ago, her enemy's sword cut the muscles of her right thigh. On the way back after this strike, the tip of the enemy blade struck her armor; a few rings of chainmail fell to the ground, splashing in her scarlet blood. The wounded orc got a few more swings in, but with each heartbeat she got weaker and weaker. Ilnyrgu, finishing up with her opponents, hurried to her aid, but it was too late. The lord's master swordsman's sword gleamed in the first rays of the rising sun—and the young she-wolf's soul was sent to Khirud.

***

When they had disassembled the rubble and the barricades, the guard, half consisting of those same Vikings, came out onto the streets. Things immediately got tight for the fighters. Those who had the misfortune of falling on the pavement never got up again, trampled down by their enemies and their allies alike. After finishing with Toryg and beating the hired soldiers of the second squadron of northerners, just like a cork popping from a bottle of champagne, the rebels and the swordsman burst out onto the open fighting space. Instead of the fizz of champagne, warriors and the men wearing white rags burst forth. They rushed to the southern city gates, the road to which, ironically, ran past the arsenal.

Andy sat on a pile of bricks with his eyes closed, looking like a statue from afar, had fallen into a trance. He was patching and strengthening his internal energy channels. Along the way, his muscles bulged. The astral dragon shone with all colors of the rainbow and radiated warmth, which poured forth with a pleasant languor. He had absolutely no need to take energy directly from the astral; he used the old tried and true method. The deafening sound of stomping feet broke into his quiet world of settage like thunder. His people wouldn't be that loud.... Andy fell out of his trance and looked at the street. Around the nearest bend, he saw the first bothersome folks. It was too late to run under the cover of the arsenal walls; no one would take the risk of opening the heavy gates for his sake. *What about constructing some sort of killer spell...? No time. Hmmm... been a long time since we faced impossible challenges... watch out, or life might start to seem too pure and clean.*

A tall warrior with twin swords in his hands was moving ahead of the battered crowd. His bow appeared by itself out of nowhere. He put the bowstring on the bow and his bone wrist guard on his left arm in one swift, smooth motion. It all took less than a half a minute. While the "lone warrior" prepared his bow for battle, the distance between him and the armed attackers was reduced by half.

Thunk... thunk... thunk... the bowstring's fatal song sounded. The arrows, with red-hot tips, sped towards their intended victims. There wasn't any time to "charge" them with mana. One rebel, looking in surprise at the feathered arrows sticking out of some men's chests, fell under the feet of his comrades. A second, who had managed to cover himself with a small shield with a convex umbo and a long protruding spike in the middle, cried out in pain. An arrow, fired from fifty steps away, punctured the shield, and his arm. A third, a warrior with two swords, in a careless motion of the blades, beat back both death bringers aimed at him. The next two Andy sent met the same fate. Andy let a few more fly, which met their targets, and put his bow back into his "pocket." Time to switch to a blade.

The enemy swordsman smiled, swung each sword around at his wrists and signaled for Andy to come at him. No matter how confident the guy was, his self-esteem must have fallen a bit when he saw the cold steel of the elvish blade—apparently, the sword's former owner was someone he knew. Andy didn't stop to think. In a few long jumps, he traversed the distance between them and with all his strength kicked a small pile of smoldering coals. The swordsman shielded himself instinctively from the coals flying right at his face and... lost his right arm. There was no time to play at politesse and nobility. A chopping blow to his leg made the enemy fall to the ground; the sword, held "backwards" (opposite the thumb) in his left fist finished the job. The swordsman's death brought on a sudden sigh in the ranks of the rebels. The slight hum of the sigh grew into an enraged roar. Dozens of people threw themselves at Andy at once. Things got tough fast, but one thing made him happy: the street was so narrow, no more than five armed men could fit in a row. Retreating under the pressure of the crowd, he knocked down the most zealous with short lightning bolts and thinned out the rows with occasional fireballs. Those struck down by magic and the sword fell at the feet of the attackers, who seemed not to notice the losses but continued to move forward with the force of a bulldozer. Andy decided to leave direct connection to the astral as a backup, as his most deadly last resort. He had only just gotten his energy channels in order; he had zero desire to tear them with the boundless power of the ocean of energy. If he got really desperate, he could always change hypostasis. He had already killed more than twelve people; now he was working on his second dozen. The rebels tore their way to freedom; behind them were the guards and mercenaries, who dreamed of getting even for the death of their friends and colleagues. On the streets running parallel to his, iron rang out with might and main; people shouted. Andy lost his old blade, stuck in the hackneyed shield of one of the insurgents who had pounced on him. He could have stopped, grabbed the shield from its owner, and pulled the blade out, but it seemed somehow inconvenient to do so surrounded by sharp steel. No matter how great of a warrior you are as a one-on-one opponent, standing your ground against a crowd's just not realistic. He had to walk quickly backwards, zap the most zealous ones with lightning and other magical surprises and try not to fall down on the pavement. Turning around meant taking a knife to the back or a dagger to his shoulder blade, and then they'd certainly chop him to pieces. But even now, he'd already been adorned with a few deep, bright red cuts.

Overhead, arrows whistled and swelled in the crowd with fiery explosions. On the wall of the fortress, Andy could see the silhouettes of Slaisa and Lista with light, simple bows beginning to fire deadly shots at their enemies. Ten minutes later, the battle was over. The Norsemen had broken through other side streets, surrounded the remnants of the rebels and forced them to surrender.

They still had to shake all the residents of Ortag out of their houses and send them to fight the fires. In all the hustle and hassle, they kind of didn't have time to mourn Berg….

At nine o'clock in the morning, a portal opened at the city gates that spat five hundred warriors out carrying royal banners on long staffs.

"They're a little late!" Andy thought. It seems their rousing bugle call came after the fact. The unit commander handed over full command to the military administration and got to work organizing burials. Andy, during all the ado, slipped into the bookstore. No one said anything to him about the half-orc.

"What do you want?" the owner of the store popped out from behind a curtain and stared at the door, which was torn off the hinges. No one had answered Andy's persistent knocking. "Get out of here, now, or I'll call the guard!"

"Go ahead and call," Andy leaned lazily on the shop counter. The Dawn-bringer was startled. Just like the first time they had met, he stared at Andy's blue eyes.

"You again?! Throw on a disguise so they wouldn't recognize you as a Rauu?"

"You're mistaken. This is my true form," Andy responded and squinted at the shop owner. "The books!" His fist hit the counter with a boom.

"I don't have them!" The elf's back went up against the wall.

Andy grabbed his blade from his "pocket" and laid it in front of him on the counter. The elf stared at the sword. The words on the sword's handle made his eyes open wide.

"A tribal sword of the house of Ok'late," the shopkeeper mumbled. "How did you get this? You must be quite a risk taker, or who are you? You must be completely stupid to risk incurring the wrath of one of the most powerful houses of the Forest."

"I couldn't care less about the Forest."

"Then why are you showing me this sword?" The fact that the sword had appeared out of nowhere made an impression on the long-ear.

"To show you that if I don't see those books in five minutes, Ortag's going to lose one book shopkeeper."

The shopkeeper went pale.

Andy had no intention of killing the shop owner, of course, but he had to make him part with the books somehow. By hook or by crook, he'd take the book. If you won't come along quietly….

"I'm not afraid to die," the elf said bravely. "I've lived a long life, and I don't fear Hel's judgment."

"You do fear," Andy loomed over him. "Otherwise, you wouldn't have lied and told me you don't have the books or turn white as a ghost when I threatened you."

The elf did not know what a ghost was, but judging by Andy's tone, it wasn't a very flattering comparison. He was offended. He breathed in, preparing to let loose a formidable come-back, then… breathed out through his teeth without a word. Yellow vertical pupils appeared in the sassy non-human's eyes. The Dawn-bringer made an attempt to grow into the wooden partition behind him and hide from the scary sight. However, this didn't work out for him; the magic he'd studied didn't include techniques like that. The shop owner grabbed a protective charm. He'd read of such things in one manuscript, but never seen anything like it so far in a few thousand years….

"It can't be," the elf whispered with his pale lips. The pupils disappeared. The uninvited guest grabbed his blade.

"I'm going to count to ten. Either I'll get a 'yes' from you, or I'll burn this flea-bitten dive to cinders." Andy's left hand lit up with a bright flame. (What could he do? No choice but to resort to outright extortion and threats.) "Defensive spells won't save you from me."

"A curse on you!" the elf snapped. "I'll bring the book!"

"You should have done so right away instead of trying to mess with my head." The hot flame went out.

The owner un-stuck himself from the wall and disappeared into an ancillary room. Andy put his blade back into his "pocket" and sat down on a narrow chair for customers. His sleepless night and crazy morning were starting to make themselves felt through his building exhaustion. He was tired and hungry. Sleep could wait a bit; he had to find Berg and clear up a couple of questions… but boy could he use a snack….

"Here," the Dawn-bringer slapped a few folios and two folders tied with string onto the counter near the chair.

"Thanks. Let's see what we have here…." Andy picked up the first folio.

Two of the three folios were fakes. The three-dimensional schemes in the drawings were not visible at all. The rest was not distinguishable from the original ancient book; people worked on conscience. In the third volume, there were many articles on the theory of magic, and two dozen rune schemes were given. He set the book aside. The elf watched Andy closely, how he inspected the goods he'd given him. The folders contained pieces of books and separate pages, torn out from who-knows-where. Of the whole pile of papers, Andy selected no more than ten pages and one piece of one book.

"I'll take this. How much do I owe you?"

"?!" The shop owner practically choked on his spit. Andy grabbed one purse full of gold from his "pocket" and tossed it on the counter. "The folio and the pages cost three times more!" the shocked elf overcame his momentary muteness.

"We're going to say we've agreed on my price, or do you want to bargain some more?"

The shopkeeper waved his hands to signal "negative."

"And what about this?" the ever bolder elf's palm lay on the parts of a book Andy hadn't looked at.

"Fakes. The rune schemes in them are just scribbles, unreadable. I hope you'll keep my visit a secret?" Andy spat back at the old elf on his way out. "I really wouldn't like to kill such a helpful elf."

The shopkeeper nodded a little; he too did not want Andy to kill him.

Once he left the elf's shop, Andy headed towards the arsenal, where the Norsemen and the warriors they'd selected to help had carried the bodies of the fallen guards and hired soldiers. The disarmed rebels, under the watchful eye of dozens of mages and fifty soldiers, rattling their chains, dismantled the debris and ruins in the nearby streets.

He noticed the orc women right near the gates of the fortress, kneeling over the bodies on the ground. Ilnyrgu hugged Tyigu to herself. When she saw Andy, the girl broke free of the Wolf's embrace and threw herself at him. Andy picked the crying girl up and stayed where he was. He already knew whose body was lying on the ground. The half-orc's face was peaceful. Looking at him, you might think the mentor had gone into a trance and would open his eyes at any moment. But the sickly white color of his skin ruined the picture. Not a drop of blood was left in his complexion and a deathly cold had set in. Barely noticeable dark dots showed up on the eyelids and lips. Berg's death hadn't hit him yet—he couldn't get it through his head. Like a freezing chunk of ice in his chest, it ruined all his plans. Not long ago, he had called Tyigu his goddaughter or, as they say in the local jargon, overshadowed all around. Now he was responsible for her. On Ilanta, words aren't thrown around just like that. Even less so words like that. *Master, master, what have you done, Berg?*

Ilnyrgu got up and went over to Andy. He could read an unspoken question in the Wolf's eyes.

"We're changing our route," Andy answered her without her having to ask, and hugged the girl close. "We'll leave right after the funeral. First, we'll go to Troid, as we planned, and from there by portal, we can get to Kion. We'll take the foothills to Troid. There could be elvish survivors and robbers on the caravan road."

"I don't get where we're ultimately headed?" Il interrupted him.

"To the valley, to my parents."

"Why not wait until they repair the portal in Ortag?"

"Because combat mages are rebuilding it, and they're only going to send active-duty soldiers and army cargo through. I already asked."

"Targ! Is there another reason?"

"Another reason? Olaf the red-haired whispered in my ear that the army warriors and commandant were very stubbornly asking one question: who gave the mages away, and how? A couple of them were very unrestrained in their answer. Now the guys in uniform want to meet the guy—he's a natural, they say! You know very well what close friendships with military lead to. At first, it's all flattery and chatting, then threats and a sword to your throat. Do I need that?"

"Where are you getting this from?"

"An inheritance from Alo Troi. I don't want to know, but I know. Let's go get our things together."

The orc looked at Andy in disbelief but didn't oppose him. She recognized him as the commander of the group. He had told the orcs about

Alo Troi during one of the stops along the way to Ortag. He skipped the details of how they met.

They left the funeral feast as it began to get dark and the Norsemen were pretty buzzed. Ilnyrgu and the unit commander exchanged glances; he nodded. The old veteran was as sober as a judge. The Wolf had taken him aside that day and, in a small nook hidden from the army mages, had a conversation about the possibility of quietly leaving the most hospitable city of Ortag. To the unit commander's credit, he didn't ask unnecessary questions, just looked at Andy and raised one eyebrow.

"Yes," the orc whispered in response.

"And the girl? What does she have to do with it?" the warrior let slip. A sharp dagger touched the throat of the observant and too smart for his own good northerner. "I get it. I'm not an idiot. Lower your blade, or you might cut me by accident. Half my people and I owe you our lives, and we won't talk. After the evening bells chime...." The unit commander pushed the orc's hand away, turned and walked back to his men. He stopped suddenly. "At the Thing, it was decided to bury Master Berg according to the customs of the Norsemen. Is that alright with you?"

"We'll consider it an honor," Ilnyrgu bowed.

Olaf met them as they exited the funeral house.

"Quiet. Your horses and hasses are here. Come with me."

The Viking led them through the narrow winding streets to the southern gates and knocked three times on the window of the guard house.

"Halt!" A Viking who resembled Olaf came out from the house. "Let's go. I slipped the soldiers a 'quicksleep' potion. They'll sleep more soundly than the dead for twenty minutes. Your horses." Olaf held the rein of a bay stallion in his hand; they heard the sound of horseshoes clicking on the pavement as a second horse followed.

"I'm coming with you," the northerner explained.

"The boy is mine. Aren't you a little confused?" Ilnyrgu's vicious voice sounded from the darkness.

"No," the Viking knit his brows.

Andy raised his hand in a conflict-stopping gesture and approached Olaf, who was saddling up.

"Are you certain?" A nod. "You'll have to swear an oath of loyalty and a blood oath." A second nod. "Alright, you decided yourself. He's coming with us. I have spoken."

The gatekeeper lowered the bridge and opened the wicket gate. The orc women, hidden by cloaks of invisibility and a curtain of silence, dismounted and walked through the gates single file. Outside the city military secrets lurked; it would have been very awkward to call attention to themselves.

"A good girl! Mess it up, and I'll cut off your balls myself!" Andy heard the guard's intense whisper, addressed to Olaf. "Sorry. Come back alive."

"Your brother?" Andy asked the newest red-headed member of their hodge-podge group, riding up to him by orienting himself on a special beacon and standing in the stirrups. They were all covered with invisibility cloaks, so they used the beacon to keep track of one another.

"Uncle."

"So, who is it you're pining for?" he asked directly.

The Viking's eyes sparkled from under his ruddy forelock. He bit his lip, annoyed that his secret was discovered so soon, and quietly answered:

"Slaisa's lit a fire in my heart," he said, bowing his head contritely. "I wanted to steal her, but a woman like that won't live with a husband against her will. Hit me if you like, but hear me out, I..."

"Don't worry about it," Andy interrupted him and slapped him on the shoulder. One problem solved—someone for Slaisa. The Viking stopped short, apparently digesting what this could mean—don't worry? "Slaisa's a warrior and," Andy paused for a spellbinding split second, "not indifferent to me. But don't worry, I won't get in your way. So it all depends on you. She really is a good girl." The red-head smiled. "You'll take your vow in the morning," Andy finished, suddenly serious.

***

They'd been making their way through the bald hills for five days now. Every day their path got higher and higher. The mountains on the horizon became clearer and clearer. The white snow-capped peaks were shining ever brighter in their view. For the first time, after having galloped through the night and most of the day, the small caravan arranged an overnight stay in a small village. The locals, hungry for news, provided the travelers with a hefty hayloft at their disposal. In exchange, they demanded they tell them what was happening in the kingdom. The stories were bleak. The peasants shook their heads in disbelief; the women gasped. Andy asked the local hunters about the paths.

"Keep going about one more day, but by tomorrow's twilight you'll have to either abandon your horses or sell 'em in Tront, they won't go any further. Up until Tront, em, 'bout a day's journey through the gullies and river valleys," a short, stocky peasant with a big beard right up to his most roguish eyes told Andy, rubbing his hair back as he spoke. "You gotta go huggin' to the peak of the Nose stone, then you won't get lost."

The next morning, saying goodbye to the villagers and buying freshly baked bread and fresh milk on the road, the group moved along the indicated landmarks.

"Aren't you getting off the path?" Ilnyrgu asked him when the last wooden wattle was far behind them.

"No," Andy answered. "I see a magnetic line."

"What?" Olaf butt in and got a slap on the back of the head from the Wolf. The Viking cursed mildly and drove away from the chatting couple.

"Let's just say I can see the birds' path in the sky, and they fly directly from south to north. I'm flying by that," he added, lowering his voice. "Get it?"

"I get it. Tell me, did anything happen between you and Slaisa?" Ilnyrgu turned towards him.

"Nothing happened, and nothing can happen."

"Could happen, and it would be for the best."

"What are you getting at?"

"Your red-haired friend is looking at Slaisa like a cat looks at cream, just short of licking his lips. He'll probably bore a hole in her back with that gaze."

"Olaf's a good guy. Brave when he has to be, not empty-headed, and he's a good warrior. He doesn't take hot-headed foolish risks, and he doesn't hide behind anyone's back. He wanted to kidnap Slaisa, but he realized that the warrior orc wouldn't take a liking to that approach," Andy continued his advertisement.

"He's right about that. Slaisa would have gutted him like a chicken. But about courage you overestimate him. If he likes her and loves her, he should go right up to her and say so."

"Is that the Viking way?" Andy asked, surprised.

"I don't know how Norsemen do it, but that's how we do it. Can't you see the girl's torn between the two of you? She definitely has feelings for you, and the Viking's to her liking too. You think she hasn't noticed how he looks at her? She may be a warrior—true, but Khirud created her without a spear between her legs." Andy grinned. "But the nature of Taili-Mother manifests itself in her." Ilnyrgu slapped her hass on the rump and rode away to the end of the caravan line. Andy waved his hand at the northerner and briefly filled him in on the latest development in this soap opera. The Viking blushed to his ears and cast a quick glance at the girl, who was galloping along at the head of the patrol.

In Troid, they sold the horses and spent the night in a new hayloft. That evening Olaf gathered his courage and approached the orc. Ilnyrgu turned away and hid her smile. Andy pretended he had to go to the bathroom; Lista walked away and coughed loudly into her fist; Tyigu was already sleeping like a log.

"Kerr, thanks," Olaf took him aside the next morning and bowed low at the waist. That night he and Slaisa quietly slipped away from the hayloft.

"Wipe that grin off your face, man!" Andy grumbled. "You're shining like a polished teapot on a sunny day. Hurts my eyes to look at you."

The redhead's grin widened till it was ear to ear, displaying all thirty-two teeth. Judging by the orc warrior women's laughter, Slaisa was getting a bit of friendly teasing too.

The Viking and the she-wolf left the village side by side. The northerner's shining woven silver necklace hung around the orc's neck.

"Slaisa and Olaf, sittin' in a tree!" Tyigu called, who'd learned from Andy. The young couple blushed to the color of lobsters.

The third night, they stopped in the woods. The Viking and the orc shared a horse blanket. Andy decided to show off his culinary talents and made plov, a Russian rice dish, for dinner. Rice and carrots were known in this world, but the gang was trying them with meat and spices for the first time. Tyigu, who climbed up onto her godfather's lap, asked for a story, and then another one. The storytelling ended on "The Golden Antelope," towards the end of which the girl calmly fell asleep in the arms of the small group's commander.

"How are we going to proceed?" The hasses with our things loaded on them might not get through here," Olaf said, scratching his neck, looking at their surroundings from the height of the bald hills and trying to figure out their next move.

"No problem. We'll take the loads off the animals." Andy began to undress. Lista put his clothes in one of the saddlebags without a word.

"Commander, what are you doing?" the Viking said, surprised, his lower jaw hitting a boulder on the ground. The northerner's eyes made an attempt to pop out of their sockets and go into orbit.

"Slaisa, you haven't told him?"

"What for?"

"Judging by your betrothed's reaction—you should have told him! You can pick the ants out of his teeth and shake the dust out of his beard yourself. Put all the things on me. Il, tuck this berserk's jaw back into place. He'll start collecting stones and flies in that gaping mouth. And you, young lady," Andy turned to Tyigu, "hop on me". There was no need to tell her twice.

Olaf regained his senses as a result of a group effort. However, he was stuttering and staring at the dragon right up until that night. The guy was super shocked.

They had wild goat kabobs for dinner made from the result of Lista's successful hunt. It was soaked in red wine vinegar and sprinkled with white pepper. Everything that wasn't fit for the kabobs was gobbled up by the commander in two easy bites. Instead of skewers, they used sharpened raw twigs from the wood of an everlasting tree. Despite all his apprehension, the Viking's jaw worked perfectly, a finely-tuned machine, as he gulped down the scrumptious chunks of meat. His apprehension had impressed itself upon the young man's mental health—his eyes seemed to gleam in a foreboding way. Tyigu, as usual, asked for a story. The others gathered 'round and immersed themselves in the world of Narnia. The girl had been sleeping for a while already, but the fairy tale went on. The storyteller could see by his listeners' eyes that it would be best not to stop in the middle. Otherwise, they'd torture him cruelly to find out what happened in the end.

By the evening of the fifth day, they reached the outskirts of the small village of Belogorsk, which was built on the old caravan road. The hasses, who were once again carrying their cargo, without holding back, passed by the village and stopped two leagues farther on on the bank of a mountain stream.

"Tomorrow we'll be waaay over there," Andy took the little girl by the hand and pointed to the cupola of the church that was visible twenty leagues from the stop they were at.

***

Andy didn't feel like waking up at all....

He had taken his turn standing watch during the night, thrown a "spider web" beyond the borders of the camp, and plopped down on his side. The naive lad actually dreamed of catching some z's, you see… when the sleepy Tyigu came out of the tent.

"I'm scared to be alone," the girl rubbed her eye with her little fist. "Can I sit with you?"

"Yes."

They took the sleeping things from the tent. In fifteen minutes, the fidgety little live wire was sleeping sweetly, cuddled up to the dragon's warm side on a camel blanket spread out on the floor, using a rolled up blanket as a pillow and covered with Andy's wing. The dragon was afraid to move, he so didn't want to wake her, but she kept tossing, turning, and constantly kicking in her sleep.

Olaf went out to the "dog's" watch. He tossed dry twigs into the fire, stretched and yawned contagiously; watching him Andy clicked his teeth after a big yawn. Thirty seconds later they changed places; the dragon yawned, and the man followed. After five minutes of each yawning in turn, Olaf quietly swore, spit, and went off to tour the perimeter. Lista snickered from her tent, who had been watching the alternating yawns by the males in their group from an open tent window.

"Go to sleep already," Andy barked.

"Right away," the orc answered and closed the curtain. Andy, just like a big animal trap, clicked his jaws together. A loud, uproarious laughter came from the tent.

The flame, dancing inside the circle of large rocks, made the shadows move, threw myriad blood red sparks into the sky, and created a rhythm of the crackling of the logs. The flame jumped from branch to branch, and new red petals began to curl up in the intoxicating dance. Andy fell asleep to the fire's pleasant warmth and choreographed etudes….

His internal alarm clock made him open his eyes two hours later, at six thirty in the morning. Olaf, with his hair all sticking up like a sparrow ruffling its feathers, was sitting before the fire sanding a carved wooden sword. A morning chill blew from the narrow river valley, covered in a blanket of fog. One of the orc women beat a ringing signal on the pot near the river. Andy raised his head from the ground and breathed in deeply. The wind brought the scent of Ilnyrgu. He realized Lista and Slaisa were still sawing logs. The sound of Ilnyrgu splashing and snorting happily reached the dragon's ears. Olaf, who'd heard the sound of the splashing water, awkwardly shrugged and threw a couple of fat branches into the fire.

"How are we going to make our way today?" the northerner asked Andy.

"On our legs," Andy said. The Norseman snickered.

"Seriously?"

"I'm serious." Tyigu started moving under his wing. "Half the way, up to the cliffs, we'll go the usual way: I'll carry the load, the hasses can have a break. The second half of the way, we'll switch. It's not worth frightening the people who live in the temple with the sight of a cart-pulling dragon, or even anyone who doesn't live in the temple; I don't know what buildings are there. We should ask the locals what to expect."

"Go ahead and ask them," Olaf grinned. "They'll hide in their houses and not even stick a nose out. To them, we're wild bears or mrowns. And they also say that Norsemen are barbarians...."

"I managed to learn something from the local women yesterday. There's an abandoned temple to the One God there," Ilnyrgu said, coming back from the stream. A few ice-cold drops of water fell from the orc's wet hair onto Andy's wing, still spread out on the ground; he got a shiver all over the membranes of his wings. He recoiled. "Not exactly abandoned, of course: someone lives there, whether it's priests or monks.... You won't get anything more out of the locals, not even under torture. Our redhead was right: they're wild."

"It is what it is. Too bad there's no other way. The road to the new highway starts at the monastery. Let's say two days keeping going straight, and we're in Troid," Andy mumbled pensively, raising his wing. Tyigu turned away from the beams of the rising sun and tried to catch hold of Andy's membrane. "Il, go wake the sleeping beauties." To Tyigu: "Come on, honey, time to get up." An unhappy grumble came from under the improvised blanket. "Uncle Olaf made you a new birch sword."

The grumble stopped suddenly. The girl pushed the wing away and turned to the northerner, who was holding his right hand behind his back.

"Show me!" the child's eyes shone joyfully.

***

Despite the long, difficult road, the day flew by. The monastery, visible from the camp, was not as close as it seemed. The natural hills and valleys in the landscape made the actual distance on foot a lot longer. To get on a convenient path that led to the religious abode, they had to huff and puff along for a while, moving over sharply inclined slopes and narrow valleys all overgrown with underbrush. There were a good number of rocky cliffs with debris falling down too. Andy filled the role of the ground-clearing bulldozer. He soon tired of wading through a continuous carpet of woven swampy rosemary on the slopes. Ilnyrgu came after the dragon. He'd given her all the control threads of the free tracking modules. Every other league, the group stopped for three or four minutes and the mages, with both hands and both dragon's paws, put up voluminous "spider webs" to check whether some kind of danger lay ahead. It searched for people in particular, but for the time being they'd gotten away with no adventures. There was no need for extra supervision. The second half of the day was even more fun. Andy changed hypostasis and immediately felt all the delights of the hiking trip he'd been previously spared by his scales. When you have a tail and are covered in armor from head to toe, clouds of gnats, mosquitoes, blood-sucking flies, gadflies, and ticks don't cause any particular discomfort. It's just a slight humming in the background; barely notice it. However, once he had become a human again, oh how all the above-mentioned members of the insect world rejoiced.... He got the impression that the winged blood-suckers choose the spot on your body they're planning to bite ahead of time, then stick their stingers and prickers all the way in. Scare-away spells and magical lotions didn't work on them. On the contrary—they bit and stung all them more. He was beginning to understand why the monastery was deserted. The monks were more ascetics than masochists. There were no idiots who would agree to feed the innumerable hordes of mosquitoes and other such evil pests with their own blood among the religious. Andy looked at his companions with pity. He forgot about the little villains quickly after turning into a dragon, yet they.... Olaf seemed swollen, as if he'd just come from a week-long bender. While they were making their way to the foot of the bald hills where the monastery was, they had all worked themselves into an exhausted mess. Their legs were giving out from under them from fatigue. Their rear ends and inner thighs ached, chafed in the saddles. They all wanted to crash and zonk out.

"Welcome, pilgrims, to our humble home." A monk came out through the small wicker gate to meet the tired travelers. He was wearing a baggy gray tunic with a hood. The garb of the servant of the One God reminded Andy of Catholic monks' habits that he'd seen in books and films, tied around the waist with a rope. The monk, removing his hood, was an older man with a pleasant round face and lively, kind eyes. Thin wrinkles ran from the corners of his eyes to his temples. The man, rubbing his spiky gray hair and glancing at the Wolf, asked: "what brought you to us?"

Ilnyrgu tapped the sides of her hass with her heels and rode forward. That morning, at breakfast, they had decided that the Wolf should play the role of the mistress or a lady of noble origin, traveling with her son on urgent business from Ortag to Troid. They came up with the most prosaic excuse for their traveling through the woods—actually, they didn't have to come up with anything: a revolt had occurred, and there were many bandits on the highway. The rest of them played the roles of her companions. Andy, who took on the form of a Snow Elf, kept a little to the back. After taking on the form of a bodyguard, he decided not to change form again. A Rauu-bodyguard with blue eyes with no whites would cause less questioning than a human bodyguard of that description. Keeping behind and a little to the right of the orc, he apprehensively examined the high stone walls spanning the monastery grounds. It was a real fortress that, with enough provisions, could withstand a long siege. Desolation reigned all around. The ubiquitous wormwood and birch trees had had time to put down roots in thin slits; their green tops were visible in the most unexpected places.

"We would like to stay the night with you, and we're prepared to make a substantial addition to the monastery treasury," the orc said.

The monk nodded at her words and examined the group, smiling a fatherly smile at Tyigu, who was sitting proudly in front of Lista, sharing her saddle. Andy felt as if he were burned with boiling water from the old man's gaze. *Oh, he's not looking at us just out of curiosity; we have to be extremely cautious.* He squinted at the monk: *what a kind mask, sickeningly kind.* His attempts to solve the puzzle using true vision were for naught. The monk's aura was lit up with soft colors of calm and polite interest. Why then did the guy literally reek of trouble? Andy sniffed the surrounding air. There was a strange smell hovering around the abode, a smell that was somehow familiar.

"The residents don't need money," the clergyman said, smiling with just the corners of his mouth. "Who needs it here? The mrowns or the bears? Brothers can provide everything they need for themselves. What's more, we have several excellent hunters among the brothers, whose secular skills have come in very handy in their new venture. Merchants along the highway willingly buy what they hunt. I see two of you are mages," the monk said, more stating than asking. "In exchange for your overnight stay, the monastery would kindly ask you to charge two small amulets with mana."

"I don't know whether we'll have enough energy…," the orc bargained with him.

"You will." The monk waved his hand dismissively. The crystal "amulet of accord" hanging around the man's neck lit up light green, showing that the speaker was not lying. It was very hard to fool the magical knick-knack. "I don't think you'll have to spend much strength on it. Do you agree?"

"If that's all…." Just like Il, Andy too was searching for a hidden agenda in his words, and couldn't find it. The religious was telling the truth. "We agree," the warrior orc said. The crystal flashed brightly for a split second and glowed steadily light blue.

"Please follow me." The monk went through the gate. The travelers didn't see the satisfied smile flash across his face that was met with a nod by the gate guard.

Jumping down from his hass and passing through the wicker gate, Andy found himself in a small walled-in courtyard. A real prison cell. There was a gallery for archers along the tops of the walls, from which you could fire at invaders storming the monastery. But the gallery was empty; nobody was aiming at them with bows—this inspired optimism. The scent from the street grew stronger. The wicker gate in the gates shut behind them with a bang. The hasses' hooves went clattering on the stone pavement. Andy became tired and apathetic; the scent got even stronger. At that moment, a switch went off in his brain. His memory, prompted by a bad feeling, obligingly served up the memory of a certain two-chamber cage he'd been forced to sit in, along with an old orcish shaman. The smell was the same as that from the smoke from the bulb thrown at the feet of the reckless slave by that butthole mage. Andy wanted to cry out and warn the others of danger, but instead he just quietly laid down on the ground, followed by the rest of the group.

With an ear-splitting screech, the inner gates opened up, and the courtyard was filled with a dozen mighty monks with stretchers, their faces covered with wet rags.

"Take this meat away," the "clergyman" said in a commanding voice. The assumed film of paternity fell from his eyes, turning them into sharp, cruel points. The monk, smiling a poisonous grin, eyed the orc. "Put these two in the preparation room," he pointed with his hangnail covered finger at Ilnyrgu and Andy. "The rest in the brig. What a strange family. And our second elf in two days…."

We fell for it, Andy managed to think before giving in to the dark nothingness.

***

"You awake?" Through a blurry film that covered him from all sides, Andy examined a man with a smooth bald shaven head. "You just lie there, don't struggle," the man said, and something wet and unpleasant touched the prisoner, who was constrained by metal handcuffs.

Andy blinked. The whitish blur became clearer and soon cleared up entirely. The prisoner made eye contact with the monk who'd met them at the gate, in whose gaze he could read the sentence issued to the naked elf, bound in notrium. The monk, whose spiky gray hair had been switched to a smooth-shaven head with runes drawn on it in black pencil, twirled his brush in a little bucket of ink and began to draw some sort of symbols on Andy's cheeks.

Andy jerked his head back and got a punch in the jaw.

"I said don't move!" the monk whispered, "or I'll have them fix your head in a vice."

Okay, so civility was out the window. How were the others, Andy wondered. *Tyigu? What have these beasts done with her?* Andy felt his chest literally weighed down from the onslaught of worry. *Mighty Twins, we're in a bad way!* Judging by everything, it would appear that the people who had captured them crossed their prisoners off the list of the living, and if he recalled the glance this cur in a habit had cast at the she-wolves, nothing good was awaiting them before death. *Grrr, grr, GRRRR! If only I could get loose!* Andy clenched his fists in futile anger. He could do nothing now. *Cursed notrium!* The enchanted metal reliably blocked all his access to the astral; he could only clench his teeth, clench his fists, and plot his revenge.

"Angry? That's good," the monk said, drawing the next in a series of signs on Andy's face. He turned his head towards an assistant who was holding a tray with tools on it. On the back of his head, Andy saw the symbol for Hel. Helrats! Black Servants of Death. It was a forbidden cult, pursued by law enforcement in all countries. They were scum; they'd perverted faith in the Twins. The dirtbags had come up with a very effective cover. No one would ever think of looking for priests of the accursed cult in a monastery to the One God. They were really in it up to their ears now. Excepting some sort of extraordinary occurrence, the entire group could be written off for fertilizer. Any other fate was highly unlikely. *Gosh, how could I have been clever enough to stick my head in a sul's mouth?* The helrat finished with his right cheek and started on the other side; Andy caught a whiff of a whole slew of stinky scents, one of which was most unmistakably foreign to a human. His nostrils involuntarily flared. If he wasn't mistaken, that was the scent of a dragon…. "Anger strengthens the runic connections. The madder a person, oh, I mean elf, gets, the faster his mana and life force are drained from him. We have some candidates for ascension to Hel, but they cannot meet the goddess today for a few reasons. They invaded the peaceful life of the monastery too unexpectedly for us, yes, too unexpected. And indeed the brothers outdid themselves when they greeted them. Hmm, what am I saying? My point is, we don't need just strength—we need your strength sucked out of you in a peculiar way and put into a statue of Hel."

"Shushug dung."

"Now, now, no need to get nasty. You yourself agreed to charge a couple small amulets with mana." The priest grabbed Andy by the chin. "Did anyone force you to walk through our gate? No? Excellent. The ritual and the spell require certain agreement, no matter how it's attained. Make a note of it: I didn't tell you any lies. Your friends were able to spend the night here. It's of no consequence that their chambers may not be to their liking." Andy gnashed his teeth from his contempt and boiling hatred of the man. "You're not putting any energy into charging the amulets. I'll have to work for you. What's the trick?"

"Are you saying there are different truths?" Andy interrupted the loquacious priest's rhetoric.

"Exactly! I opened the door. You did the rest yourselves. The truth is, we need sources of mana for the crystal accumulators in the image of our goddess, and your death to Hel's glory will do just the trick. The girls will be of good use too; they're pretty flowers. We just have to think what to do with the northerner and the girl."

"Slimeball, even after death I'll come find you and tear you limb from limb. Don't you lay a finger on them!" Andy almost cried from exhaustion. *The brute, the brutish beast.* He'd find a way to get to his throat and get even.

"What an expressive young elf. Young and stupid. Don't you think you're not in a position to be making threats? What do you care about humans? Think of yourself. Don't forget, after death, you'll still be serving Hel. The monastery doesn't throw away good material. We love quiet, calm zombies. It'll be fun to set you and your employer on the Viking. Interesting, I wonder how long he'll last against two living dead?" The helrat finished drawing the runes on his prisoner. "Take him away!" he called to the darkness. "I can get a lot of mana from you. We've got ourselves a cow worth milking."

From the darkness came two rag-clad human figures. Andy shuddered. Their white empty eyes showed clearly that these two had no connection to the land of the living.

The zombies easily lifted the construction that contained Andy. It was something like a stretcher and a wheelchair combined. They brought it down a long hallway with many doors on both sides. After two minutes of the "palanquin's" rocking evenly side to side, the procession, which had now been joined by new members dressed in white robes and new followers of Death carrying long black candles, entered a temple.

The temple walls were decorated with intricate frescoes illustrating the lives of saints. Thousands of candles illuminated the towering inner cupola with an even light. The scents of incense and melting wax permeated the air. Sometimes, as if an invisible giant were breathing, the candle flames suddenly leaned to one side and began to twitch and quiver. Then the shadows of the priests standing in several circle formations came alive, bending and jerking in an elaborate dance. This temple differed from regular churches to the One God in the giant pentagram on the floor. A structure in the middle of the pentagram was holding Ilnyrgu, naked and covered with runes. Crystal energy accumulators stood on stands at each of the points of the star, from which silver strings rose to a statue of Hel hanging in the center of the cupola. Zombies walked up to the center of the pentagram and installed the stretcher with Andy on a special pedestal. He wanted to call out to the orc, but she did not react. Apparently, the warrior had not yet come to.

"We've arrived." The priest who had drawn the marks on Andy stopped at the dragon's stretcher. The helrat had already changed into a white tunic that went down to his knees, tied around the waist with a belt made of multiple grinning skulls. A silver sickle bounced at the priest's right side. "Now your life's path will end and the path of your afterlife will start. Shall we begin?" he addressed his victim. "You don't mind if we take a little mana from you and your life?"

"And if it's too much mana?" the sacrificial victim wheezed.

"No such thing!" the helrat grinned. With his sickle, he made cuts on the forearms and ankles of the prisoners, then left the circle.

The priests in the white robes started an annoying chant. The servants standing in circles moved to the opposite side. If it were possible to watch from above, the observer would have seen three circles spinning towards one another. The pentagram and the markings on the victims glowed bright neon. Just then the notrium chains holding the bodies unlatched themselves. True, the magical metal not only held the prisoners, it interfered with the ritual. Andy jumped up and threw himself at the priests—in vain. A force field sprung up from the borders of the pentagram and threw him back, and almost threw him into the orc's altar. A powerful fireball he sent flying at the force field dissolved helplessly against the invisible barrier. Other spells met the same fate. Thousands of invisible needles pricked his body; Ilnyrgu moaned and went into convulsions. The invisible needles sunk in deeper. The runes on his body started to itch terribly. The priests finished their circle dance and fell prostrate; the silver strings and hanging statue of Hel lit up.

Andy felt his magical reserves draining, as if being sucked out by a vacuum cleaner. Perhaps his life really was about to end. Struggling to cut off the foreign channels, he dove into settage and began to vehemently destroy the energy-sucking tentacles that were stuck to him. The struggle ended in defeat on all fronts. Just like in the myths about Hercules and the Hydra, every time he cut off one channel, two more would appear in its place. Despair made him dive in even deeper and go into a trance; the ocean of astral energy opened up before his internal eye.

"And if it's too much mana?"

"No such thing!" he recalled the fairy tale of the golden antelope he recently told his goddaughter. The antelope asked the greedy Raja: "And if it's too much gold?" and got laughed at in return. The Raja was punished; he got buried under the golden coins flying from the antelope's hooves and begged, "Enough!" The gold immediately turned into shards of clay. Funny, or sad, but his quibble with the priest was quite conformable to the fairy tale ending. *You say there's no such thing as too much mana?* Andy let the ocean flow....

***

This wasn't Irei Ter Ars' first ceremony, and certainly not his second. Those being offered to Hel always displayed the same behavior: they struggled, let fireballs fly, cast other combat spells, tried to break the barrier. Dummies. They all, in the end, quietly laid down on the floor, drained dry, after which the necromancers had their way with them, and they continued to serve the Mistress. They could serve her in various ways. This arrogant Rauu was no different than all the rest. *It was so nice to watch his reaction when I told him of what awaited him in the near future. So much hatred and contempt, what rage and what an unconquerable will! And how long did I get to play with him? A few blows to the force field, an attempt to destroy the straps, and the elf quietly laid down on the floor.* Irei had expected more from the pointy-eared elf. But things were going the same as always.

Irei prepared to deliver the "kiss of death" to the woman, but something held him back. The lines of the pentagram and the silver strings going connecting to the statue of the Mistress suddenly glowed unbearably brightly, playfully changing colors and flashing. The protective barrier went into a low vibration. The Rauu got up and spread his arms wide. The Snow Elf's eyes shot forth blue flames. The accumulators whistled slightly, overwhelmed by the flow of energy rushing from the pentagram. The Rauu turned to Irei and smiled from ear to ear. The priest, intuitively sensing danger, put up a multi-layered shield around himself and glanced at the prisoner. Something incomprehensible was happening to the elf. He was glowing like a magical lantern. He fell on his knees and….

***

Andy felt he could no longer handle the fountain of astral energy rushing through him. He changed hypostasis. He signaled the warrior orc, who had come to, to take shelter underneath him and covered her with a protective dome. Energy flowed through him in an unending stream. So as not to burn his internal channels, he "poured" an enormous amount of mana through his tattoo and through the astral dragon. He could sense bits and pieces of other people's emotions: joy and surprise, pain and suffering. The barrier could no longer withstand the force. The white-clad figures of the priests clamored to their feet and stumbled backward towards the temple walls. The sacrifice was clearly not going as planned. Andy covered himself and the orc with a shield and curtain of darkness. The helrats didn't have time to react. The statue of Hel glowed brighter than a thousand suns and, burning the priests' eyes, exploded. The protective barrier burst. The freed energy shattered the temple cupola into tiny shards and shot upwards into the sky in a bright pillar. Dozens of servants of the accursed cult were vaporized. In the mayhem that now reigned, the dragon beat a hole in the wall with a powerful punch and ran rampant around the monastery, killing the priests who had predicted the need to flee the ceremony. The zombie servants quietly sank to the ground, free from their masters. This time, the unfortunate individuals passed away for good. Once he'd killed all the priests who came his way and burnt the guards in the barracks to a crisp, he went back to the former temple.

The main scumbag had survived. That's why he was the main guy. Commanding an animal instinct, the priest put several shields up around himself, and unlike his brothers, survived the destruction of the temple, to his own delight. Stepping away from the blast which had almost deafened and blinded him, he looked at the dark dome where the pentagram used to be, and the melted walls of the building. The temperature was so high, the bricks bubbled and melted just like wax.

"No such thing as too much mana, you say?" the gigantic dragon said, after breaking down the wall.

Andy leaned over the trembling helrat, enacted the "battering ram" spell, broke through his defense and picked up the two-legged beast by the throat with his paw. Ilnyrgu came out from under the protective dome.

"Where are my friends? Talk, slime sucker!" The priest swung freely in the angry dragon's paw like a rag doll.

"They'll die in the prison cells if I don't undo the strict staying spell," he wheezed. "I'm not afraid to die. The Mistress will accept her faithful servant."

Andy thought for a minute. The priest really could have cast a binding "harness" spell on the guys and Tyigu, in which case they would die as soon as the slippery cowardly filth did. In the powerful magic storm that occurred in the wake of his solo performance, it was impossible to tune in to the helrat's psychophone in order to determine whether he was lying or not. It was problematic to try to determine the location of the orc girls and the northerner using "spider webs" because of this same storm. There was a fifty-fifty chance either way. He'd told Berg that he would take care of the boy like an overshadowing tree, no matter what happened, so he had to find a way out of this situation. Soon he would experience the recoil, and that would not be pleasant. The consequences of letting the limitless energy flow through him were already showing up; he could feel the onset of pain and a nervous tick. No matter how you spin it, he needed this dog alive.

"I promise to let you go alive if you show me where my friends are and free them from the 'harness,'" he said to the scumbag. "Remember, if you decide to trick me, I'll kill you slowly, ve-e-ery slowly. The orcish she-wolves can make people suffer. You'll curse the day you were born."

"What she-wolves?" the priest choked.

"Il, show him." The orc took on her usual form and smiled maliciously. "Master Ilnyrgu is skilled in more than just swordplay. She can use needles and forceps like you've never imagined in your wildest dreams."

"No need to scare me, I'll do as you ask," the helrat wheezed, who had heard a lot about the elite warriors of the "white" orcs from the Steppes. People who knew what they were talking about had told him such cruel and gory stories, he was cut to the quick. "Put me down," he wheezed.

"As you wish," Andy responded, and loosened his grip.

***

"Commander, how are you?" Olaf asked Andy right away, as soon as they freed him from his shackles.

The commander did not look his best. He was trembling. His blue eyes were surrounded by dark circles and were shining as if he were feeling feverish. He was biting his lips from the intense pain of the recoil, and the were-dragon's forehead was covered in perspiration. It turned out there wasn't any staying spell on the Norseman. The helrat cringed and tucked his head into his shoulders. The elf, who had turned out to be an ancient dragon, could very well have torn his head off for the lie, and still could break his promise, if he should happen to poke his nose into the lower levels of the dungeons.... The orc standing behind the servant of Hel poked him with the tip of a silver sickle. The white tunic she'd torn from a servant in the temple flung open, revealing her tempting breasts. Unlike Andy, after the episode in the temple, Ilnyrgu looked her absolute best. She had been completely "recharged" by the free energy. You could even say she'd taken a dip in mana. The warrior's eyes sparkled; her cheeks were rosy. It seemed she was flying over rather than walking on the ground.

"Don't even think of using magic! Where is the boy and our things?"

"Yes, yes, one moment...." the priest began to nod. "They're in a different wing."

"Lead the way!" Andy turned to him. When he laid eyes on the pointy triangular teeth in the elf's mouth and his two-inch claws, the fake monk became even smaller. The dragon's yellow vertical pupils were literally nailing him to the spot. "What are you just standing there for, brute? I said lead!"

"Commander, ..." Olaf pointed to the claws.

"A result of the overload. What do you want? I'm a dragon, remember? Now it's really making me writhe. If you could imagine how hard it is for me to be in human form right now...." Andy said, who was feeling worse. He wasn't only in pain, he was now hungry too. He watched the priest out of the corner of his eye. The helrat's gaze shifted nervously from side to side; his hands were trembling. Strange, what's he so upset about? Apparently, he has something to hide in the next wing over. Something that wouldn't make a dragon pat him on the head.

"Yes, yes, right away...." the priest took small steps. "The second left."

"Step aside, mongrel!" Olaf pushed him and, taking a step forward, picked a sword up from the floor that had been dropped by one of the zombie guards. The zombie's body was lying right there and already starting to stink.

The Servant of Death darted to the side, but Andy slid forward. A sword extracted from his "pocket" appeared in his hand. The tip of the blade dug into the dip at the base of the unfortunate would-be fugitive's neck.

"One more stunt like that and I'll gut you along the tendons in your legs. Where's the boy?"

"Here," the helrat went pale, pointing to a door with metal stripes and hinges. "Remember your promise!" he said, looking pleadingly at Andy and bowing low.

Andy squinted and tried to calm down. Breathe in, breathe out. Once more. The accursed worm—shaking in his sandals. He so wanted to do away with him. Andy's knees actually trembled in his thirst for blood. He had to be more easy going, tolerant, liberal, like on Earth. He had committed an atrocity, and he was about to be served a sentence of zero years… that's the most just court in the world!

Olaf pushed the door, reinforced with iron and froze. The Viking's jaw hit his chest again and forgot to get back into place. *What's he so shocked at?* The Norseman stepped aside, and the rescuers laid eyes on a stunning sight. What the fudge, holy shamokin dam, and other such phrases…. I wonder what that's called in their local language, what the she-wolves, shackled in thin chains, were wearing, and the silver-haired Snow Elf crouching in their company. Andy, in a rage, charged into the room. The girls, dressed in something extremely scanty resembling scraps of silk that barely covered their chests and the area below the waist, fell prostrate.

"What do you wish, master?" the three prisoners said in unison.

"Uhhh… what's with them?" Andy, copying the northerner, turned helplessly to Ilnyrgu with an open mouth.

"Obedience amulets and behavior modulations," the orc answered, tearing the heart-shaped necklace from Slaisa's neck. The girl gasped and fell to the floor. A thin diadem with a tiny pattern of runes written on it flew off the young she-wolf's head and, jingling a little, went flying across the chipped boards. "Remove the other necklaces and diadems."

"What? Where am I?" the elf moaned, rubbing her temples with her palms and blinking. Coming back to reality was painful.

The sounds of thudding blows and a stifled wheeze came from the hallway. Olaf, in a fit of anger, was beating the gasping and groaning priest in the face. Then, when he had fallen to the floor, he began kicking him. Andy felt somehow relieved and less stressed just from what he was seeing.

"You promised!" the priest cried, and immediately got a punch to the nose. His lips were round like an "O" and tears were streaming from his swollen eyes like a river.

"Olaf, enough!"

The Viking stepped away from the fake monk, stood for a few seconds, growled and spat a few times.

"They didn't have time to do anything with the girls," Ilnyrgu said, placing her hands on the other she-wolves' stomachs.

"But, judging by the outfits, they were planning to!" Andy blurted out in contempt, examining the representative of the pointy-eared tribe. The elf, who was now realizing she was covered in the most minimal amount of fabric imaginable, practically shoelaces, one on top, one on bottom, quickly covered herself with her hands. Andy wasn't dressed to impress either. He was flaunting a dirty shred of cassock wrapped around an improvised belt. Olaf squatted down near Slaisa and threw his undershirt around her. The orc, forgetting her membership as a she-wolf, went ahead and cried, dropping her gorgeous head on the Viking's chest.

"It's over, it's all over now. Don't cry, my dear one," Olaf whispered, rubbing her hair with his wide palm.

The priest, forgotten by all, moaned in the hallway. Ilnyrgu took the Viking's sword and left the room. New strokes of the sword could be heard from the hall.

"Where is Tyigu?" After she had finished her exercise of putting various colored bruises on the man's body, the Wolf pressed her blade up against the throat of the servant of the forbidden cult.

"And the rest of the prisoners? I remember well what you said about other victims!" Andy leaned over him and, drawing air in through his nostrils, again caught the musky floral scent of a dragon. "And why, brute, do you smell like a dragon?" he roared.

"EEEEEEeeeek!" the priest screamed.

Ilnyrgu crossed her hands. An enormous pulsar crashed against the shield the orc put up. In the next instant, the helrat flew into the air, banged hard against the ceiling, then was turned around 180 degrees and bumped against the wall a few times.

"Levitation spells have never worked for me the first time," Andy complained to the Wolf. Having guessed beforehand that the enemy would lash out at some point, he put up a shield before the orc and struck back.

"Really? Are you telling him that?" she smiled in response to the tirade. "One request: don't use a levitation spell on me!"

"Olaf!"

"Yes, commander!" The northerner walked out of the room hugging Slaisa.

"Take my sword and go around the floor in search of notrium shackles or a chain. Something about our friend turns me off. Should have zapaged[12] him right away. You can leave Slaisa with us. I give you my word: we won't eat her.

"I'm on it." The Viking took the blade. "It's an excellent sword, a master smith must have forged it!" Olaf admired the tiny grid on the metal for a few seconds, which called to mind little men holding one another by the hands, and then ran down the hall checking every room. Ten minutes later, the Norseman came back holding a whole bundle of chains made of the gray metal. They stood the priest up and smartly wrapped him in the notrium, binding his arms tightly to his sides in the process. "And now you won't be waving them around without permission."

"Do you need him to repeat that?" Andy asked the helrat.

The priest, who had come to, turned away, proudly cocking his head, and got a strong blow which sent him rolling across the floor.

Olaf rubbed the knuckles of his right hand:

"The slime! I almost broke my hand on him!"

"Olaf? Did I ask you to?" Andy said angrily, poking the now unconscious body with his toe.

"Sorry, commander, I couldn't help it. I can't keep hold of myself when I think of what THAT guy could have done to Slaisa."

---

[12] Zapag—to tie up, capture, trap in a net.

"Il, Olaf, stay here. Get the girls out of their chains, then keep looking for our things. You," he poked the Viking's chest with his pointer finger, "carry that priest until he wakes up. If he hasn't been made an idiot by your caresses," the Norseman smiled, "I'll ask him a couple of questions. By the Twins, don't let him escape. First off, gather up some weapons—there are a lot of former zombie guards lying around here—and I'll check the basement of this dungeon.

Andy wiped the sweat from his brow and weaved some combat spells. In order to activate them, he just had to pump energy into the rune Keys. It would have been a dumb idea to go downstairs without a few "surprises" up his sleeves.

Descending from one floor to the one beneath it, he set up "spider webs" and checked all the rooms and cells—neither a cursory nor a thorough examination revealed any living soul. Fearing he would be too late and Tyigu would be dead already, he enacted the "battering ram" spell on the metal door that lead to the lowest level and, jumping two steps at a time, darted on downward. He'd gotten quite attached to the girl lately, who somehow reminded him of Olga. He didn't even suspect a strange fatherly feeling would awaken in him. The fidgety little girl was like a daughter and a little sister to him at the same time. At first, he tried to figure out his feelings, what brought on that attitude towards someone else's child, and then he stopped his soul-searching. The staircase led him deeper and deeper underground. Soon he stopped counting the intervals. Sparse magical lanterns and the reigning gloom gave the impression of an eternal descent.

The descent stopped suddenly. The carved staircase led Andy to another door. He didn't even have time to put his hand on the knob when the door swung open itself, and a trio of zombies with bared swords jumped out to meet the uninvited guest. The short sword fight ended in the dead men's eternal repose by way of beheading, and one deep scratch on the deliverer's left hip. The zombies turned out to be a little more agile than expected. That was bad. The presence of living dead in the basement meant that their master was somewhere nearby. And what was even worse, he was clearly aware of the visitor and not at all happy about it. Apparently, he could monitor who went where through some special spell or amulet.

Andy stepped carefully over the defeated zombies, walked through the doorway and froze. This was bad, as bad as he could possibly imagine—the master of the zombies stood in the center of a large room right through the doorway and was squeezing Tyigu against himself, holding a thin blade to her neck.

"Perhaps we can talk?" Andy was the first to break the silence, examining the local version of a kidnapper. He wasn't a mage. At least, there was something good going on. He had been controlling the zombies through a communicator amulet. A ton of magical junk was hung around the guy's neck. Most of the amulets had multi-directional and mutually exclusive functions. If you were to activate them all at once, there was a hundred percent chance you could multiply yourself by zero. The guy was apparently a novice when it came to magic. And his face was somehow familiar... it was the guard at the monastery wicker gate! Now it was clear why he was holding Tyigu. It wasn't hard to put two and two together regarding the connection between the guest and the purpose of his visit.

"There'll be no talking. Now throw down your sword—or she'll die!"

"Okay! Just don't hurt her." Andy threw his blade on the ground and kicked it away. The nervous guy pressed his sword harder against Tyigu's delicate neck; a few drops of blood appeared.

"Lie down on the floor!" the man cried.

Okay, I'll make it look like I'm obeying; I'll get down. The kidnapper is a coward. You can see how his hands are trembling, and his eyes are shining. Compared to him, that priest we left with Olaf and Il looks like a hero. But this coward has to prove he's the master of the house....

"Elven spawn!" the guy howled. His nerves could no longer take it. He activated a powerful defense amulet, kicked the girl away from him and, jumping towards the elf, who was lying on the ground, brought his sword down on him. Andy quickly jumped to the side, extracted his old sword from his "pocket," which he had taken the time and effort to retrieve on the battlefield in Ortag and pull out of the shield cast off by the rebel who had used it. A short bolt of lightning shot from his left hand. The guy gasped, his eyes bulging. Andy's good old sword finished the ordeal.

The baby girl stood up from the ground and threw herself in the arms of her rescuer. The rescuer sighed in relief and hugged the girl. His stress slowly left him. He just couldn't imagine what would have happened if the fake guard hadn't fallen for his trick.

"I knew you would come to save me!" Tyigu began to chatter. "But why did you drop your sword? I would have bitten that villain's hand. He was a bad guy. The bad man threw me in a cage with Rary and Rury and told them to eat me, and Rury said he doesn't eat people. Then the villain grabbed a fiery whip and started beating the babies, and when the guy in the next cell over said he's a creep, he started whipping the guy, and I got out between the bars and shot a fireball at him! Then he really screamed! I wanted to run away, but the guys without eyes caught me, and all the other villains went upstairs." Andy was sitting on the floor playing with the girl's pitch black hair, stroking her head. Tyigu's monologue went right by Andy's consciousness; her words went in one ear and out the other without touching the cochlear nerve, then hit the wall and dissolved. *Almighty Twins, what are you punishing her like that for? In such a short time, she's seen what some adults never see in their whole lives, and yet remains a wonderful kid. What did she ever do to deserve this?* "...smelly zombies. And then I was locked in a small cage where I couldn't slip between the bars, and then, boy, did I cry. I told Rary it's you and that you were coming to save us, but she didn't believe me, but I wasn't worried for a minute. Rury said humans don't save dragons, only kill them, but I said, you were a dragon too...."

Catching something about dragons, Andy, who'd been zoning out for a minute, gently shut the girl's mouth with his finger.

"Tyigu, what dragons are you talking about?"

"Well, I just said, Rary and Rury, they're little, the villain beat them."

"Stop—wait! Rary and Rury are dragons?!" Andy sniffed. It certainly did smell musky in there.

"Of course! Let's go—I'll show you!" the girl jumped to her feet and set off, pulling Andy behind her by the hand.

Andy didn't feel like going anywhere. The "recoil" and his fatigue were beginning to take their toll. He had to go through the whole "I can't" routine and swearing in Russian. Even though he had almost forgotten his native language by now, he remembered these words well.

Tyigu led him through a suite of rooms. He stopped near a pair of them—*holy mackerel*—there were two real, fully equipped alchemy labs set up in the basement! What's more, someone had been working with ingredients extracted from dragons in one of them. There were vials of blood, ground and whole scales, some sort of extract, and flasks closed with corks. *Now I know why the monastery didn't need money, and why the merchants readily bought the hunters' goods, and what kind of hunters they were, whose worldly experience came in handy.* Andy clenched his fists in rage. *I'll let the priest go—let him go over the edge of a mile-long cliff! I remember that slimy piece of scum was nervous about going downstairs—he knew he'd be killed on the spot as soon as I saw this.* In the second laboratory, he discovered golden lily bulbs and distillation devices. *Drugs.... These brutes didn't shy away from making money that way either.... That might be why this nest of helrats hasn't yet been discovered. The "monastery" probably had its agents in Ortag and Troid and was bribing the right officials with their plentiful gold, and maybe, with dragon's blood. The "monks" have been making a fantastic profit from this. Ten or twenty thousand pounds on a few "administrative" costs was no skin off their nose. Someone's going to pay dearly for this. I'll make them!*

"We're here," Tyigu said and tugged the massive metal ring on the door. Andy guessed they were right in the vicinity somewhere. The smell was leading him to them no worse than it would a hound dog. He moved the girl away and opened the door.

Before the tired were-dragon's eyes was a natural cave about forty by seventy yards in size, turned into a prison and a corral. The prison was lit by three dingy magical lanterns hanging from stalagmites. A small stream flowed along the length of the cave. The air down there was cold and damp.

Andy filled the lanterns with energy. The room got brighter right away. Tyigu let go of his hand and ran along the front of the cages.

"Rary! Rury! I told you Uncle Kerr would save us, and you didn't believe me! He's here with me now, and he'll help you and your mom!"

Andy stepped forward and broke the locks off the cage doors, setting a few prisoners free. A few of them no longer had any need for freedom. Merciful Hel had accepted them into her arms. Andy came to two enormous cages. One of them held two small dragonlings with reddish scales; they were no bigger than oxen. The other held an adult dragon whose coloring was no longer discernible. They were all half dead! Reduced to skin and bones, among other issues. The mother dragon was missing whole patches of scales. Her face and paws were bound in thick chains fastened to anchors. There wasn't a healthy spot anywhere on her back and wings. The little dragons were not fettered, because before a certain age, they cannot spit fire. The dragonlings hurried to the farthest possible corner from Andy. Rury opened his wings and hid his sister behind them, stuck out his neck and breathed in through his nostrils trying to determine through scents who it was standing before him. His whole back was covered in stripes from the fiery whip; the scales that had been hit were darker. There were a few tears in the membranes of his wings. *Those brutal helrats—they're just children! Those helrats aren't human, they're sub-human, they're….*

"Uncle Kerr, are you crying?" Tyigu dashed over to Andy and extended a handkerchief to him, by some miracle still intact.

"Yes, hon. Stand back. I'm going to break the cages."

Andy changed hypostasis. The mother dragon stared at him. Her tail began to thrash against the ground. Rury stopped hissing and curled up into a ball even more, not taking his wing from in front of his sister. The appearance of a grown dragon instead of a human was totally unexpected for the prisoners.

"Oh man, have they scared you so bad?" Andy said shaking his head and broke the cages. Then he broke the chains and opened the metal fetters around the dragon's legs. She then took the chain off her snout herself.

"Thank you," she wheezed.

"Uncle Kerr, there's another cage here, you missed it. It's the guy who stood up for Rury and Rary," Tyigu cried.

Apart from the other cages, Andy saw another, made of gray metal. Notrium again. They must've found a mage they were planning to sacrifice.

Andy tossed the cages in his way to the side and walked over the mage's confinement.

"Hello, Kerr," the mage said, holding the bar with his right hand. His left arm was dangling limp at his side, swollen and blue on the forearm. His face was covered with many scabs; his eyes were puffed and bruised. His shoulders and back were striped from the fiery whip.

Andy froze.

"Timur, is that you?!" he gasped, barely recognizing the familiar face.

***

Timur stirred the coals, which immediately flickered with a lazy red flame. He breathed in the appetizing smell of barbeque and looked at the chef with a questioning look. This was the first time he'd seen a dish like this. He couldn't wait to try it. Ilnyrgu was the cook today, because one member of their collective refused to accept the job of cooking due to reasonable winged circumstances. She had to take the time to cook herself. The orc, grinning, glanced at Andy, who felt like a babysitter/mother hen. Rary and Tyigu settled comfortably under his left wing, and Rury under his right. Boys on the right, girls on the left. Tyigu flatly refused to sleep in the tent. Of the travelers' things that were found still intact, she brought over a blanket and a big sheet used to wrap the items in for carrying. She made Rury, who was feeling very sleepy from the meaty meal, move over, and gladly snuggled up against the dragon's warm side. The girl was desperately jealous of the dragonlings' relationship with Andy. The "mother hen" laid his head down on the warm stones and rolled his eyes. Timur and the Wolf snickered from the sight of it. The dragon heaved a sigh.

"In three minutes take 'em off the flame," Andy told the orc. He, the dragonlings and Lanirra, their mom, gorged themselves on venison from an icebox that they found under the house. The local adherents to the forbidden religion did not suffer from asceticism. They had a lot of money, so the "monks" did not skimp on food. The stores and the icebox were stuffed with tied packages of groceries and food stuffs.

Whole bodies of bulls and deer, enormous fish that looked like the sturgeons found on Earth, baskets of frozen trout, wine and vegetables. In a separate container, they kept jerky and dried fish, dried fruits, pickles, and jams. The full warehouse said that the helrats had settled here seriously and for a long time, but one angry dragon spoiled all their fun, cut them to the quick and turned out to be a fly in the ointment.

While Ilnyrgu was conjuring over the improvised grill, Andy was listening to Timur's story, starting from fleeing the School and ending with the battle of Ronmir. He didn't hold it against his friend that he'd set him up like that. He lamented at first that a certain tailed individual might have been somewhat franker with his friends, but he did not develop the topic. He had no news of Frida. According to Timur (and Andy readily believed him), after the battle on the shooting range, there was so much chaos at the School that even the number one songbird of their class opened his beak wide, dumbfounded at the abundance of rumors, gossip, and untrue stories and could hardly discern a crumb of truth as to who started the battle. When arrests began in their group, they decided that army grub was better than prison slop and quickly flew the coop. For the last month, they'd been chowing down not only army grub. The soldiers, loyal to the crown, had managed to "bite off" other "delicacies" they got to taste while putting down the rebels and the bombardment of Ronmir. And, apparently, they would be "enjoying" this cuisine for a long time to come. The Empire had declared war on Tantre; it seemed the Woodies would soon join in, and there was no end in sight....

"How did you get here?" Andy asked Timur.

"If you hadn't blown up the arsenal, I wouldn't have wound up here. The explosion creamed the portal settings and coordinate binding. When we were flung into the frame, I noticed a ripple, and in the next second, we flew right to the priests. The helrats, not being idiots, flew at me with swords straight away. I had to fight a little, and it sucks that it was just a little: a whole crowd of zombies ran up and really scared the pants off me. While I was 'relaxing' behind bars, I had time to chat up my neighbors. It turns out the priests would build a 'needle-like' portal once every two weeks that allowed them to pierce the screen. A human can't go through a portal like that, but a small portion of cargo certainly could. They had a transfer point set up around Ronmir. On the day of the storming of the military camp, the priests were planning to transfer the next portion of their product. Probably what happened was a short-term overlapping of vectors, and a counter channel is what they got. At the moment of the blast, the channels overlapped and sent me and a wounded elf I'd picked up—who actually turned out to be a girl—straight to the priests. And there you have it. So, you got to me just in time. If you'd gotten to the priests a week later, I wouldn't be any different than the rest of the prisoners."

Half the prisoners freed by Andy were indeed a sorry sight: thin, with burning eyes, grimy, and screwed up. Many of them were covered in fresh scabs and shining with whip wounds. Timur didn't have time to get lice from them, but he was in a bad state. The "monks" had welcomed him in a most unfriendly way: the encounter ended with his left arm broken, which turned black in twenty-four hours, and three broken ribs…. And of course there was no need to mention the cuts, abrasions, and bruises—the young man was one big bruise. Andy remembered the laboratory, asked the dragoness for permission to give the half-dead humans her blood to drink, changed hypostasis, and ran to fetch some vials. Coming back to the basement, he was met by Lanirra, who started reciting some sort of spell over the vials. When he asked what she was doing, she answered that she had performed the cleansing ritual, separating her blood from herself, and therefore ridding herself and humans of the possibility of mutual mental influence. That was nearly impossible already, but it was worth taking precautions, all the more so when they weren't aware how much her blood had been distributed across the world. Half an hour later, Timur was pretty healthy (if you don't count his emotional scars, which could not be healed by dragon's blood). He was back on his feet. Andy broke the wall down and thereby blocking the exit from the cave with the debris, then helped the dragons climb to the monastery. Everyone exited through the door.

***

Andy was aware what "business" they had going on. When the priest saw Andy come back from the lowest levels of the dungeons, he started sweet-talking him. He told him where the treasury was hidden, the accompanying documents, promissory notes, and property deeds. He informed him of other "monasteries." Andy and Ilnyrgu, dissecting the bookmarks, began to study the contents of the papers. They were especially interested in maps of the kingdom with incomprehensible symbols on them. The helrat, realizing they had him by the… udder… communicated to them that the symbols were the locations of dragons' nests, discovered by their search squadrons. Those that no longer contained anything to catch were circled. The dragons who used to live there were already captured and prepared as specimens. The income and expenses books they found showed, in neat handwriting, to whom, when, and for how much each "product" had been sold. The geography of the "monks'" economic activity spread from the Light Forest to the south of the Empire. A large portion of the sales took place in Tantre; there were descriptions of transactions with Rauu.

"Can you remember all the nests?" Andy asked the priest.

"I can. I myself added them to the map. Only I have that paper," he responded and added: "the map shows all the places we know about where dragons dwell."

"Very good. None of your other priests knew about the map?"

"The hunters knew, but you slaughtered them in the temple."

Andy nodded to Ilnyrgu and dragged the priest out of the office.

"Wrong answer to my question," he told the helrat as he dragged him to the eastern wall built near a high chasm. "It would have been better for you if you didn't know about the map and the preparations. You would have lived longer. I'll let you go. But as you say, there are different truths. Did I lie to you? You'll fly over the cliff alive...."

The priest, screaming and howling, flew down from the hundred-foot-high cliff and landed on the sharp stones below. His notrium chains prevented him from using a levitation spell.

No one can know about the dragons' nests. Ilnyrgu's one of us. She's proven that many times over. She can be trusted, Andy thought, but he did not believe in the slimy guy's goodwill....

***

Andy grew pensive. The declaration of war was bad news, if not horrible news. Just like that, all his plans had gone to a hot place in a hurry. His idea to get home to the valley through Kion were out the window, and now war. As if that weren't enough to worry about. Tell me, where's a convenient place to hide three large-tailed creatures and a dozen former basement prisoners? Let's say the people can live for a while at least in the former monastery. They can eat their fill, and then get on with their lives, all the more so now that they're no longer just riff-raff, but people of means, faithful to His Majesty. Andy, having found the helrats' treasury, had dished out a nice portion of gold and silver coins to each one. He'd gotten his hands on the financing papers and communications of the "abbot" along with the treasury, who had other communities, the movers and shakers as well as the lesser riff-raff. They were interesting documents and also smelly ones; they stunk like a skunk or a muskrat for miles around. And what was he to do with the dragons? Where was the purse he could pour gold into for them? Lanirra wouldn't be able to walk for three more days yet, let alone fly. Could he leave her alone here? Why did he bother saving them if that's what he planned to do? His problems seemed to be growing from a molehill into a mountain....

Il removed the kabobs from the coals and whistled to Slaisa and Lista, who were practicing with swords. The girls were on fire. They were dishing out such a whirlwind of cold deadly steel that Andy was surprised they hadn't taken each other's heads off yet. Olaf freely collapsed on an armful of fragrant hay brought in from the stables and, with passionate eyes, gobbled up the sight of his "lady." From time to time, in the heat of the moment, he would knock with his right fist on the open palm of his left hand and spit off to the side, but the Viking didn't make any comments. Lista had taught him not to. At their first stop, he had had the carelessness to (the Viking wasn't thinking, mind you) step on the orc women's "calluses," criticizing their manner of conducting a duel. It goes without saying that the orcs paid too much attention to stabbing the enemy.... Lista nodded and invited the Norseman to join them. The referee, Ilnyrgu, snidely inquired of the critic—perhaps he should turn down the effect of his pain spell, the spell that signals conditional death or injury ("game over" in their training exercises)? The critic grinned condescendingly and somewhat haughtily..., and in a couple of minutes, was writhing on the ground from an arbitrarily arresting blow to the liver. Lista hadn't left him a chance. Catching his breath, Olaf wanted satisfaction. The warrior smiled blindingly and agreed to a match, giving Olaf the chance at revenge, then another one, and then she tired of proving her superiority in fencing. The last stabbing blow fell in the right sirloin part of the enemy's "organism." Naturally, the northerner's rear end went numb. The Viking raised his hands, admitting that he was wrong. The orc laughed contagiously and kissed him on the shaggy cheek, earning a disapproving glance from Slaisa. After the severe, showy reprimand he'd earned, the Norseman asked if he too could study with them, explaining himself by saying it's never too late to learn what you don't know or can't yet do. In life, everything you know would come in handy. Ilnyrgu looked at the lean but incredibly physically strong candidate skeptically, then agreed to step into the noble role of mentor.

Hearing a whistle, the opponents saluted one another with their blades and walked in an orderly and dignified manner to the fire. The travelers refused to sleep in stuffy monastery cells. They settled down on the monastery's upper rocky platform which was more like a small training ground. They built a fire in the center of the camp and pitched their tents.

A refreshing breeze was blowing at the very top, carrying all the biting and blood-sucking pests away with its gusts and imparting a pleasant coolness their way. The third floor of the residential building rose to the same level as the platform, overlooking the campground through the cells' narrow slits of windows. The people freed by the dragon were staying there too, on the first floor. They couldn't hear a peep of what was going on above. The former prisoners slept like logs....

"Where did you get those 'twins,'" Olaf asked his girlfriend.

"The swords of the master who killed Berg," Il answered instead of Slaisa. "The unit commander permitted me to take them as part of the distribution of trophies from the spoils after the battle. They're good blades, as it happens, for close combat, and the length is right for Slaisa for quickly grabbing them from behind her back. Let her get used to them. They can't be carrying everything around in bags," she said.

"Can I see?"

"Sure." Slaisa extracted one of the blades from its sheath and presented it to her betrothed handle first.

Olaf grabbed a rag from his belt and, taking the sword by the blade and the handle, examined the reddish grid left on it after etching and polishing, then tapped on the metal with his fingernail, listening to the long, clear ringing sound.

"A fine sword!" Andy nearly choked when he heard the Viking's familiar words, darn it all to.... "I just don't get what this ring on the handle is for?" Olaf rubbed the wide ring on the handle. His finger settled in a little dip. "Oh...." The ring twisted half a turn; a little needle was launched from the handle. It flew ten feet and bounced off the dragon's scales. Lista carefully picked up the unexpected find.

"Let me smell it...," Andy said. The girl held it out to him. "Poison! It smells like boiled extract of the root of swamp thorn-apple." He sniffed. "Wait, it's crap, not poison. It's hard to kill with this substance; you can only paralyze your enemies for a couple of minutes." The unexpected guess made him pause quietly. He turned and looked at Ilnyrgu. "You said...."

"Yes, these are the swords of the one who killed Berg...." Olaf gave the blade back to Slaisa. The orc grimaced as if she were being given an ugly spiked marsh viper.

"Take it," Andy hummed. "It's a fine blade, and it became a fine blade only after you picked it up. That lowlife that had it before you has nothing to do with it. A wicked master defiles an honest blade."

"May Khirud grant Berg a spot behind the throne," Ilnyrgu whispered quietly, then added loudly: "Well what are you all standing around making faces for? Let's go have our barbeque, look lively now! By the way, where's Lubayel?"

"She went to a cell. Said she doesn't want to eat and sleep outside," Timur answered, chewing his first bite of tasty meat. "Mmmm... I didn't know orcs could cook so well."

"Thank your friend. Dragons invented kabobs by scorching their prey in the fire from their mouths!" Ilnyrgu smiled. The dragon grew embarrassed. He'd never encountered such an interpretation of the origin of kabobs.

The pale oval shape of the elf woman's face appeared in the window to the cell. Yet another walking problem....

"Can I try some?" Lanirra walked up to the fire practically unnoticed, which was almost unbelievable given her size. The dragon drew in a breath of air through her nostrils noisily. "It smells so good... I think I may start drooling." Il took two appetizing pieces from the spits, laid them on a wide burdock leaf, and extended them to the dragon. It was barely a crumb to the dragon, but it was enough to let her taste it. "Thank you," Lani thanked the orc. The tip of the dragon's right wing gently touched the membrane of Andy's wing, which was strewn out on the ground. A pleasant languor ran over his body. The female dragon turned around, touching her savior a second time.

Darn, well, what's that about? Darn it all. Is Lanirra playing with me? Once, I could chock it up to coincidence, but twice? I'm not saying it's not pleasant. On the contrary! I just somehow don't feel like a... um, an alpha male, ready for action. Making a deadpan face, he pretended he hadn't felt her touches and had no clue what she was getting at. He was a winged dim-wit. He may be a dragon, true, but.... Papa Karegar, during his instruction and mentoring, had made even the possibility of meeting a dragon of the opposite sex completely impossible, so the ins and outs of interpersonal relations with other dragons remained for Andy a sealed book. It was a lot simpler with humans. He had a grandmother on Earth who was a doctor and happened to have a ton of encyclopedias and informative literature at her house. He had watched, before the fateful lightning strike, a couple of films by German cinematographers. His mother's fashion magazines had given him at least some idea what to expect. His first personal experience gave him a practical outlet for the "how" and "why." But he had yet to encounter any dragon films or magazines. There was a giant gap between the "how" and the "why," or a white spot on the map, and indeed he wasn't ready for these "interpersonal relations." If Lanirra wanted to attract the young dragon's attention, that was one thing. But if her plan was to thank him in that way for rescuing them, that was something else entirely. He didn't need any such gratitude. Honestly, he saw Lanirra as a partner for a completely different dragon—a black one, and not nearly as old as he would make himself out to be. The thought lived in his head like an annoying worm: what would Jagirra think of the dragon? It was possible the elf would disapprove of her adopted son's behavior. Her relationship with Karegar wasn't so cut and dry. She acted like the Mistress not only of the valley but of a certain cozy cave near a small waterfall. Oh yes! Brazilian soap operas were standing on the sidelines nervously smoking against the backdrop of the passions of the winged tribe. Now he just had to figure out how to realize his plans to make his father happy without getting his own butt kicked....

It was probably worth having an open talk with Lani, telling her the whole truth. He shouldn't let the situation come to hurt feelings and unnecessary ado. Andy half covered his eyes with a protective membrane and cast a sidelong glance at the female dragon. She looked a lot better than she had a few hours ago. A filling supper and freedom from notrium bars had worked wonders. Lani was actively pumping mana, directing it at her own healing. Her aura had gone from a dim light to a bright glow. The dark torn spots on her exterior were closed over with rainbow-colored patches. The rips in her wings were still there.

Without waiting for any kind of reaction to her provocative actions, the dragon flashed her yellow eyes, heaved a sigh, turned around in a circle a few times and lay down thirty feet away from her rescuer. Well there you go, she's offended. Andy called Timur over, asked his friend to cover Tyigu with a blanket, folded his wings and quietly got up and tip-toed over to the other side of the platform. Lani, watched by the orcs and Timur, got up from her spot and followed him.

"Lani, we need to talk…," Andy began.

"What about?" the lady dragon answered indifferently, looking at the claws on her front paws.

"About us, among other things."

"Are you kidding? You took my children under your wings, and you're ignoring me. You saved me, declared me your wife, and now you're mocking me…."

Andy sat down on his tail. Not noticing the pain in his unnaturally twisted rear end appendage, he opened his jaws in shock at the dragon's words. Several insects that were flying by just then flew in. *What an announcement! How 'bout that—where and how have I managed to cross the line between a bachelor and a happily married man? Calm down, just calm down. Let's try getting at the problem from another angle. Something tells me I should get to the bottom of this right away, or things'll only get worse from here on out.*

"Lani, don't rush with words. Please don't interrupt me. Just hear me out. Listen carefully, and then make your conclusions."

"Alright."

For the next fifteen minutes, tweaking a few of the details, Andy told her his story. Eyes shining and tail banging the ground in disbelief, Lani listened to everything he had to say. Her wings periodically lifted up off her back, giving away their owner's upset emotional state by their slight trembling.

"I'm eighteen. Please tell me when I became your husband?" he ended his narration with the question.

"When you took Rury and Rary under your wing, you declared them your children. So, according to custom, I became your wife. How can you not know simple things like that?" the dragon said as if it were obvious. Lanirra stood up and looked him over from all sides skeptically. "It can't be. When I was eighteen, I was not much bigger than Rary!"

Well darn! Trouble is here—open the gates…. I warmed the children, soft-hearted guy that I am. And look what it got me! Who knew a simple act of participation in her children's fates would lead to such a conundrum? How can I explain this to her??

"Lani, I used to be human!" Andy whispered.

"I was born three thousand years ago, ten years before the Great War. My father told me something about embodied ones. I remember well that humans can become dragons at a young age and grow slowly—like dragons! And you're full size!"

"I underwent the Ritual when I was sixteen, just under two years ago."

It was the female dragon's turn to drop her jaw. When her tongue dried out from the wind, Lani closed her mouth.

"Which means, you weren't making me your wife?" she said skeptically. "Why then did you cover Rury and Rary?"

Darn, this has got to sound crazy to her. I ought to go beat my head on that boulder over there. Which of us is three thousand years old? Well, yeah, in human years it's like a thirty-year-old woman meeting a nice man in the prime of his life, who then tells her he's three years old. Idiot! The least offensive thing a lady can say to a guy, and Lani's not showing signs of unfailing patience.

"Because I love kids."

"Then why do you look like a grown dragon?" Her yellow eyes squinted at him in skepticism. *Oooh, yeah. I'm definitely going to have to break that boulder into a million little pieces.* "You should be just a bit bigger than Rury."

"I don't know, probably because I became a dragon at such a late age for one undergoing the Ritual. My adopted mother was always worried about me growing too fast. Rary and Rury are like a little brother and sister to me."

The lady dragon thought for a long time. She closed her yellow eyes with the transparent membranes. Lani periodically removed the membranes and glanced at Andy, as if checking to see whether he was still there or if he'd decided to bail.

"Kerr, tell me, how did you get out of the Circle of Woe?"

"What circle?"

"The circle with the pentagram, where the priests placed their victims and sucked all the mana and life out of them," Lani clarified.

"I gave them so much mana, their artifacts couldn't take it," he said.

"There isn't so much mana, not in dragons or in humans, not even half as much as needed to break the artifacts on the pentagram beams," she summarized. "Unless a dragon was taking energy from external sources. Were you giving them outside energy?"

"Yes." Lanirra was thinking like the smart, logical mage she was.

"Now I understand why you look like a grown dragon. In order to work with astral energy you need a fully developed system of internal energy channels and storage accumulators." Lani fell silent again. She raised her head and looked at Andy cleverly. "And would you share mana with me? I can heal faster with your help."

"I would, but I don't know how."

"I'll create the channel. Look at my aura. Do you see a white spot on it?"

"I see it. It looks like a rose."

"Send your energy to the flower."

Andy dove into settage, touched the astral in the same familiar way, and sent energy from the ocean to the flower the other dragon had indicated. Sharing mana turned out to be such a nice feeling….

"Kerr, wake up. That's enough," he heard, as if through an insulated barrier. Andy opened his eyes and jumped away from Lanirra. It turned out he had covered her completely with his body and wings. *Geeze, man! After that, you simply must marry her!* "Thank you," the lady dragon whispered. "Now I'm quite sure you became a dragon not long ago at all," Lanirra chuckled. "I believe you, and you will be a brother to me until you grow up a bit, and then we'll see," she added, licking herself, and touched the membrane of his wing with her paw. *Heck, the sentence has not been reprieved! It's just postponed. But maybe by then, the heavenly judges will declare clemency?* "You're so funny and naive. Any female dragon could wrap you up in a tight membrane. I'm so hungry."

The old scales began to fall from the lady dragon's sides; new ones pushed through looking like little red scabs. Lanirra playfully bit Andy's neck and ran to the icebox. He knew very well that at that time, eating wasn't what a dragon wanted—scarfing was. Now they'd talked. He was a little hasty in thinking of Karegar. First, he had to avoid tying the knot himself. Today's conversation was a reprieve. It would be ten years before he would have to worry about it again for real.

"Kerr, what was that?" Timur asked him. "You glowed."

"I was healing Lanirra." What else could he say?

"Really? Is that what they call it nowadays?"

"Timur, do you want to get your face bashed it? I'll make it so bad dragon's blood won't help any more."

Timur lifted his hands defensively in a peacemaking gesture, with a slight smile still on his face.

Andy carefully laid down between the sleeping dragonlings and Tyigu, thought a little, as if he were wary of committing another snafu, and covered the kids with his wings. In fifteen minutes Lanirra flew up to the platform, after having consumed an entire bull. He looked at his "sister," who was no longer limping, who laid down cozily next to her son. *Women. Just try to figure them out.... The heavenly sculptor must have cut them all from the same cloth, whether humans or dragons!*

"Tell me about yourself," he asked.

Lanirra's story was simple and uncomplicated. She was born three thousand years ago, shortly before the Great War. The elves' spell and the death of the chiefs stirred up all the dragons. Anticipating a massacre, her father relocated his fifteen-year-old daughter to the Southern Rocky Ridge, so hated by dragons because of its proximity to the ocean and strong winter snowfalls. A lot of snow means only a little prey. The little dragon was left alone for a long time. She didn't keep track of time, but several months went by before her father returned to the cave.

Lani learned from him that the Great Forest, like the dragons, was no more.

"Soon there will be no one left at all," the old dragon said to her gloomily. "There are practically no females left. We will die out, but the elves will not outlive us for long if they can at all."

They lived together, just the two of them, for about five hundred years. Her father taught her magic, explained their customs, sometimes even brought humans, elves, and orcs in and explained the differences between them and whether it was possible to live with them peacefully. The old dragon did not let her go anywhere. She was not allowed to fly farther than ten leagues from the cave, but he himself sometimes was away for a week or two on end. The news he brought was always terrible. The dragons had taken cover in the mountains. Rangers from the Forest elves were hunting them. Their former allies were not helping the winged tribe in any way.

"The cowardly snakes are afraid," he said then, spitting fire. "No wonder the orcs from the north knocked them out. Neither the Arians nor the Rauu are helpers anymore. The yellow bellies…. The time will come when they will remember the dragons, but I don't know who would fly to their aid."

Soon Lani was left all alone. One rainy morning, her father simply did not wake up. Dragons live for a very long time, but they are mortal. She left her home cave in search of a new dwelling.

For a few days, the dragon wandered about the mountains. But she did not meet a single fellow tribe member. No one answered her inviting calls. The young lady chose a secret valley and settled in a small cave on the incline of a volcano extinct since time immemorial.

How great her surprise was when humans came to her cave and brought several rams as a gift. The dragon magnanimously accepted the offering. It didn't occur to her that hunters could have found her cave, and the offering might be poisoned, but luckily that's not what happened. By the following summer, a whole village had grown up in the valley. The humans had peacefully sown the fruitful ground, raised herds and periodically appeared at the cave with another gift. Lani did not touch the settlers. She unleashed a few free modules into the village through which she could study the bipeds' language and culture.

A few years later, cave mrowns came to the valley from the neighboring lands and began to prey on the cattle. The humans appeared at her cave and asked the "winged death" to protect them from the predators' rule by force, promising to bring a cow or a bull to her every three months, and two rams every month. Lani thought about it and agreed. She ate like a bird—a very large bird. The mrowns were chased out in three days' time, and those that refused to be chased—eaten. Meat is meat, right? Why don't humans like cat meat?

But one day the peaceful life came to an end. Thousands of armed humans came to the valley and burned the village. A large faction of mages set out towards the dragon's cave. After launching a few dozen enormous fireballs at the newcomers and leveling the remains of the village to the ground along with the conquerors, Lani flew off. She had hidden in the deep backwoods for over a thousand years until she encountered Norigar. He was a big red dragon, as big as she was, who had flown here from the Northern Rocky Ridge, where the hunters had destroyed his nest. He killed them, but it was too dangerous to stay where he was, so he headed southward.

Lanirra lived with Norigar for over two hundred years. They constantly changed caves and flew from one place to another; teams of hunters scoured the mountains in search of them. The moving continued until the female dragon realized she was in the family way. The pair decided to take up residence in a cave that seemed safe, far from human settlements.

When the time came, the twins Rary and Rury were born—Rarirra and Ruritarr. Their family happiness lasted twelve years.

What happened next in Lani's story Andy already knew from the priest he had executed.

Helrats spotted the dragon as he was out hunting. Not wasting a single day, back at the monastery they formed a squadron of dragon catchers, but their scouts brought the news that in the mountains there was a whole nest. They called in rangers from the Light Forest to take the reins. The Woodies didn't shy away from consorting with forbidden cults if it got them the chance to hunt their ancient enemy. A multitude of birds, controlled by the Woody mages, flew off into the mountains. A few days later, they knew the exact location of the cave. So as not to frighten the dragons, the Woodies resorted to cunning. For three months the birds brought hundreds of dried black lily bulbs to the cave. One fine evening (for the hunters), smoldering tinder fell on the pile of bulbs. The husband and wife were caught unawares. The black poisonous smoke put them all into a deep sleep, parents and children alike. The priest didn't know what became of the male. They had agreed to hand him over to the Woodies. But "his little woman" and the dragonlings had remained in the monastery for six months. They were witnesses to how that captivity ended.

It was 5 a.m. The sun would soon rise. After the dragon recounted her life story, the travelers retired to their tents. Silence fell on the former monastery. The long day and no shorter night had come to an end. Lani was quietly whistling through her nose in her sleep, her face tucked under her wing. Rary and Rury gave a little peep now and then. Tyigu sometimes kicked in her sleep. Andy laid his head down on the cool stones and thought. He had to sort out his thoughts and make a plan. Everything that had happened yesterday and today left nothing but greasy black ash in place of his former plans.

First. His sharp claw drew a long line on the pavement. He would leave the human prisoners here. He had zero responsibility to care for them, and they could do just fine without his help. They'd been given a good meal, gotten a good night's sleep, had the benefit of a huge amount of grub, and they could go where their spirits took them. Or stay here. He couldn't care less.

Second. He drew a second line next to the first. Timur and the conceited elf Lubayel. Andy remembered how she'd slapped him in the face when he came back from the lower levels of the dungeons in the form of a Rauu—how dare a foul mix look upon a naked high-born elf with his shameless eyes?! He lost the gift of speech and just stood there blinking stupidly, trying to figure out what just happened. He had never been slapped before in his life. He'd been tortured, burned with fire, poisoned with flies, and had his teeth knocked out, but a slap in the face…. The completely unexpected slap made him see stars and offended him. He felt unjustly humiliated. He had to save his reputation and his honor. Never mind that she had been stripped, subject to mind control, and nearly used as a sex slave. She had no right to be embarrassed or upset. Even with everything he'd been through, Andy was still a teenager and a male with a fragile ego.

"Name, title, unit number?" he yelled at the top of his lungs. "Quickly! You may address me as 'ler,' got it?"

The elf jumped bolt upright. Slaisa's clothes, taken from the luggage they'd found and given to a friend in need, didn't quite fit her in the chest. Her army instincts, now deeply ingrained in her head, had their effect. The Rauu introduced herself and barked the title of her commander and her unit number, adding that she was a griffon rider with the rank of sergeant. Timur snickered.

"Roi-dert," Andy turned to his friend (Timur had told Andy his title back in the basement). "What is the punishment in the griffon wings for offending a senior ranking officer?"

Timur listed several types of punishment—from extra on-duty hours to lashes and the brig. It all depended on the type of offense. When he was through with the punishments, he smiled and said that he was responsible for the ally he'd saved at Ronmir; therefore, he too bore a portion of the blame. Timur and the elf got two extra shifts and came under Ilnyrgu's command. After one hour, one of the orc women let it slip that the commander had no military title. The elf said nothing, finished peeling the potato she was working on, cut some meat, but decided not to have dinner and went to her cell. *Well, let her go!* Andy's own self-assessment put him at the rank of a lieutenant. Considering his firing power as a dragon, he was equal to one whole griffon wing. The elf didn't come out for dinner— she sat in her cell all evening. Pride goeth before a fall.

However, he now had to decide what to do with her and her rescuer. Neither of them had two coins to rub together—both had good hearts. Weighing all the pros and cons, Andy decided he had to send Timur to Troid. The priests had killed Pumpkin; the griffon riders were transport-less for the moment. It made sense to assign his friend a couple of hasses; Timur would get the food supplies in the morning himself. He would provide them with weapons—they would need them. He would charge the arrows with mana. They would make it to Troid. They weren't children.

Third. Andy grabbed a pebble and drew a fat third line. Himself and the "company." This was an interesting question. His thoughts rattled around in his empty skull with the rumble of an iron barrel. Not a single possibility stuck in his mind. *My people.* The orcs, Tyigu, Olaf and the dragons were firmly set as "his" people in his mind and he thought of them as nothing less than family. He would be willing to slit anyone's throat for them. Tyigu and the winged babies even more so. He knew why Lani had chuckled. He became attached to the dragonlings in an instant. Now Andy understood Karegar and Jaga very well, why they hadn't wanted to send him into the outside world. Everything Daddy had had to go through… it was awful to imagine. Dragons' parental instincts were unbelievably strong, and he was hooked like a fat fish chomping at the bait on the end of a line. On top of all that, he felt traces of Alo Troi's mental perception and his sense of fatherly love for his daughter.

No matter what the others thought, he was responsible for them. Andy tried out the word *family* and he liked the way it sounded. He wasn't planning on losing his family. He would make it to the valley, he had a notion of how he would…. And then he would fly to all the nests discovered by the helrats and gather all the dragons into one place. Enough hiding in bears' caves. Even ten winged monsters would constitute a real threat, especially when one of them could wield the energy of the astral. They would entrench themselves in the mountains so deeply and firmly that the hunters and whole armies would break their teeth on them. He just had to decide whether it was worth it to build bridges with the Rauu? In light of recent events, it appeared something was rotten in the state of Denmark. The ones who appeared white and fluffy were not always so. According to Timur, the Rauu were true heroes who sacrificed themselves at the walls of Ronmir, but a few bad apples spoil the whole batch. Take Lubayel for instance—she was an awesome girl. Knock all the arrogance out of her, and she'd be priceless. So… should he go on with it then?

There are no two ways about it—I have to go to Troid and capture the portal arc. Now there's a real thought! War has only just been declared, so, everything's in a state of upheaval with the higher-ups. The soldiers are harassing the citizens, and the citizens are doing the soldiers bad turns. It's the best time to catch fish. No one can hide in a monastery for long. You can bet your butt corrupt officials or other helrat communities will soon be here to check on them—which means we should be expecting company. But if we take the arc, we can kill two birds with one stone—get the documents, the proof, to the authorities and also travel—not to Kion, but straight to Gornbuld. I'll charge the portal with energy. No one expects us to be so bold. We can take the control amulets from the monastery to make sure the mages who control it don't squirm.

Andy rubbed his paws together. In the morning he would tell "his" people his plan. What would the orcs and Olaf think of it? Lani's opinion didn't matter—she would be a heavy artillery strike aircraft.

Disturbing the pre-dawn calm, one of the free tracking modules sounded an alarm; literally a couple of seconds later, one of his voluminous "spider webs" went off—twenty low-flying griffons were fast approaching the monastery. *Targ! Talk about timing! It's those "guests" I was expecting! Speak of the devil!*

Putting on their armor and the tack on their horses as they went, the orcs darted out of their tents. Olaf pulled back the string of his bow; "firelights" glowed from the quiver with a clear light.

The second "spider web" went off. Thirty more riders on half-birds appeared from the direction of the mountains. There could be no more doubt—the army was descending upon the monastery. Powerful magical lights suddenly burned in the sky. Andy dove into settage, connected with the astral, and prepared to destroy the enemy completely and without warning. No one could stop him. Let a whole regiment of griffons come at them.

"We're not the enemy!" A magically enhanced voice rang out over the camp. "Please don't shoot. Three griffons will land near you!"

"We're not the enemy! Please don't shoot. Three griffons will land near you!" it said again over the dragons and people.

Three half-birds carrying two riders each separated from the first group.

"Golden griffons," Timur whispered.

The griffons hovered majestically over the platform and, beating their wings quickly, carefully landed. The first griffon bore Miduel. Knocking with his carved cane on the pavement and groaning, he descended from the beast. The second one bore Melima, and, holding her hand to her forehead, Frida….

PART THREE, SHADOWS OF THE PAST.

Tantre. Ortag. Frida...

"Can you sense anything?" Melima walked up to Frida and kicked a pebble with the tip of her boot.

"Yes, it was him. I can sense his mental cast very keenly. He was standing right here." Frida took a few steps along the former street and stopped, looking around helplessly. She was very sure that several buildings had been wiped from the face of the planet by a strange magical tornado. What kind of magic had been used here? "Cold and emptiness. Kerr wasn't thinking of anything. He was weaving the spell."

"And he killed dozens of people and mages with one movement of his hand," creaked Miduel, who appeared from around the corner, surrounded by ten bodyguards. A tall, gangly Norseman with the embroidery of a unit commander strode alongside the elf.

Miduel stopped a few steps away from Frida and commanded the bodyguards:

"A frame. Quickly take a measurement of the density of the mana.

As if someone had waved a magic wand, a small suitcase appeared out of nowhere on the ground, with a rotating frame on the lid. They installed an hourglass next to the frame.

"The sample has been taken." Sand fell from the hourglass' upper bulb. The elves counted the number of times the frame made a complete rotation. "Eighteen bell! Unbelievable! The density of the magical field is higher than at Mellorny Tree Crowns, four bell higher."

Frida closed her eyes in fatigue and carefully sat down on a neat bunch of bricks. Her head was killing her. She, like a sniffing service dog, was searching for Kerr—only a dog hunts by scent, while she went by the traces left on the residual mental field. It often seemed like they were just about to catch up with him, but he constantly disappeared from the trail; then the trail would pick up again where they did not expect to find or even sense him. And now they were late again. The day before yesterday, they had spotted him that night at a funeral feast, but in the morning the hotel room was empty. No one saw how he disappeared from the city. She didn't know how much more of this fruitless running around she could take. She was tired. The vampire opened her eyes. How much time had passed since they'd left home? Two weeks, and she wasn't getting any closer to her goal....

The marble mountains. The vampire enclave. Frida, two weeks ago...

Strong gusts of north wind, clinging with their invisible bodies and grabbing with their twister arms at the trunks and branches of the flowering trees, plucked apple-tree-colored petals off and sent them spinning in a fanciful dance of intricate patterns, first lifting them up and making them execute complex ballroom steps, then letting them down and dropping them on the ground like so many oversized snowflakes. The garden trails were temporarily covered with an intoxicating white carpet, but the next mischievous gust, like a carefree kitten, once again lifted the petals and began to beat them with its soft flow paws.

The breeze invited itself into a room through an open balcony door. The airy silken curtains swayed like sails, and with a quiet rustle the white scraps of flowers laid down on the floor, a gift from an untiring restless spirit.

Frida sat on the bed and stared into space, seeing nothing, noticing neither the flowering gardens through the window, nor the white and pale blue mountaintops, nor the little white stone houses, scattered over the slope like tiny toy houses. But the happy-go-lucky north wind did not want to stop its frivolity. The curtains suddenly shook and flew up to the ceiling. The apple blossoms tore off the floor and threw themselves up in the girl's face. Frida snapped out of her reverie from the light tap of petals to the face. She stood up. One petal was stuck on her right cheek, wet from tears. The vampire was crying. For the first time in her life as far back as she could remember, she was letting tears have their way.

"Look at the city and the gardens. Look at these mountains and the Whispering Waterfall. We may very soon lose all of this forever…," her father had said before leaving her chambers. "The world is changing, daughter, and not for the better. Vampires may no longer live isolated from all the rest. I'm not telling you a big secret. You could feel it yourself in Tantre. War is on its way to us, and it's not planning on passing us by. It will come to our doorstep and wipe all the vampires out if we don't find ourselves a strong defender who needs us and who is a good match for us. We're being offered protection, the security deposit and payment for which will be your hand in marriage. I understand what you're feeling. You're not the daughter of the head of the clan or even the daughter of a member of the Council, but the Rauu chose you. Believe me, Prince Neritel's son is not at all a bad match. I won't force you. The wedding will take place only with your consent. That's what I told the Council, and that's what I'm telling you, but know this—our future, no more no less, is what depends on your answer. You'll have to make a very difficult decision. Perhaps my words sound pathetic, but I personally would not want to weigh my personal happiness against the future of an entire people. Think about it…." Her father looked at her with a sad expression, gloomily smiled and stepped out, closing the door behind him. Frida threw herself onto the bed. Her father wasn't exaggerating. It was impossible to lie to an empath. You could not tell the whole truth but never speak any falsehood. His fatherly emotions were colored with a rusty-gray tone: sadness, concern, pity, regret that things turned out this way. Somewhere way in the background, she sensed a sparkling pride in his daughter. Before the father slammed the door she caught a slight scent of vanilla. It was a feeling of love for his own child and the hope that she would be happy. Would she?

"I won't force you. The wedding will take place only with your consent. …but I personally would not want to weigh my personal happiness against the future of an entire people."

Her father was an excellent speaker. His words sounded lofty and convincing, that's for sure…. He was not lying, and because everything he said was so accurate, his words effectively stripped his daughter of any choice in the matter. No one could understand her. She couldn't understand herself and would curse herself for centuries to come if the clan should suffer because of her. That's how she was raised, that was vampire custom—the interests of the people and the clan first, then all the rest. Her father had spoken of her goodwill. In fact, the Council had already made a decision. Frida had been unobtrusively notified by his lips. She went to the balcony and closed the door. The curtains hung still, lifeless cuts of fabric. Now she too was like this lifeless cloth….

It was hard to live not remembering what happened to you in the last three months. The Life mages were powerless against her amnesia. The last, oldest mage said something to the effect of its being the result of some sort of mental trauma and external magical effect. Her memories should come back, in time. Time heals all wounds. Frida pulled the wide collar of her nightgown apart and looked at her chest. Tiny, barely noticeable scars were her living reminder of the battle she took part in but could not recall. The weight of the loss she'd incurred hung on her heart. Something familiar and warm remained just beyond the edge of memory. The mosaic of recollections was difficult to assemble into a clear picture. Frida clung to others' stories and tried them out against her feelings, caught specks of memory on the periphery of consciousness. What had happened to her that day? Her father said that the Rauu had brought her home two weeks ago, floating in a cocoon of life-giving gel. There'd been some sort of flare-up at the Orten School of Magic, and she'd been drawn into it. As a result, she was severely wounded. She couldn't get any more information out of him. He preferred to be silent. She understood by his few words and deeply buried hidden emotions that he knew more, if not everything, but he wouldn't say. Her mother looked at her with deep-seated pain and pity. Any attempts to extract information from her were also futile. She gave the same answer to all questions—you just focus on getting well. Worrying is not good for a girl who spent a week unconscious. We'll talk about your questions later. She got nothing but a conspiracy of silence. Her anger at her parents was lodged in her soul like a sharp needle. They were secretly happy about her lack of memory and could not hide their forbidden feelings from their daughter.

Three days ago, a delegation of Snow Elves arrived at the enclave. The parade of Icicles rode past her house, and Frida saw the personal standard of prince Neritel, now flapping in the breeze over the Council building. Their offer to fortify the newly formed alliance through the bonds of matrimony between the children of the two peoples came for her like a clap of thunder out of the clear blue sky….

Frida wiped the petal off her cheek, threw a silk robe on, and left the room. She had been mourning her fate. But if marrying her off to the elf could buy the vampires protection from total destruction, she was prepared to make that bargain. The past was behind her. She couldn't remember whether she loved anyone, and if so whether he was good or evil or some combination thereof. Her duty to her race forced her to think of the future.

She would give her consent, and perhaps, betray someone by doing so. But, before the newlyweds could enter under the "wings of love" in the temple of the Twins, she had to hear the truth—why had the Rauu chosen her of all people?

She found her father was in the backyard. He and her younger brother were working on how to defend oneself from a warrior armed with an ax. Frida stopped off to the side and watched Frai trying to bend away from her father, who was swinging the weapon of the dwarfs and Norsemen. Her father was provoking his son to attack by swinging the ax broadly side to side. During a wide swing, the warrior exposed himself to an enemy attack from the other side. The swings only seemed terrible. Actually, the attacker was opening himself up to a strike—easy peasy. Axes were much more threatening and dangerous when swung in short half-loops and twists at the wrist wielding the head of the ax, also low chopping and slanted strokes without swinging. The Norse call the ax the shield crusher. The dwarfs call it the king of the battle. At some point, Frai made up his mind. He took a creeping step, a short stroke of his sword, and… dodging his son's cutting blow, her father then jerked his hand. The notch of the ax hooked the shield, and in the next instant, Frai was on the ground. Her brother sat cross-eyed on his bottom, spitting Bordeaux blood from his broken lips. It wasn't very pleasant, taking the metal edge of a shield to the teeth. At fourteen, it was time to stop getting caught in those kinds of traps. Frida herself got a shield to the nose for the last time at thirteen.

"What do you say?" her father turned to her.

"I consent."

"Wonderful. I'll ride to the Council. You work with Frai on knives, then get after him with a pair of swords."

"Dad, there is one thing."

"I bet I can guess what it is." Frida sensed a wave of regret and strange longing. "I'll tell you when you get back, I promise."

He didn't come back alone. The rolling clatter of horses' hooves told the vampire that guests had arrived. Frida waved to her brother to stop the training and ran into the house. Meeting guests in armor and fully armed was considered bad form.

The young vampire went down to the basement, threw her armor and under-armor off and climbed into a barrel full of pre-heated water. What bliss... to wipe the sweat and dirt off one's self. Frida bathed, snapped her fingers to activate the warm wind spell, dried her hair and donned clean clothes.

The house was quiet. Strange, she had heard very well the clatter of hooves of several horses. Frida walked around the first floor, not seeing anyone except the cook and the old stable hand. She shrugged and went upstairs to her room. Whatever.

"Hello. May the grace of the Twins be upon you," a female elf greeted Frida from the chair by the window. "You have a lovely home."

"Melima?" Frida said in surprise, seeing her classmate from the School of Magic. "What are you doing here?"

"How can I put it," Melima stood up in one swift movement, "I came to tell you not to go crazy with grief. Miduel's so severely reprimanding the diplomats who presented his words as the literal truth in the last report, that I'm afraid they'll no longer need toilet paper, ever in their lives. There won't be anything left to wipe. Apparently, there are idiots on our side and yours, and which of them was the first to suggest a wedding as a way of sealing a military alliance, we'll soon find out. There isn't going to be any wedding. They've already signed the contract. The High Prince has another offer for you.

"What is it?"

"The High Prince would like to suggest you set out in search of a certain young non-human you're quite familiar with."

"Why?" Frida was surprised at the elf's words. Her friend was surprised that she was surprised. Melima's unusual (for a Rauu) behavior suggested the elf wasn't aware of her friend's amnesia.

"I thought you loved Kerrovitarr," the Rauu answered.

Frida froze on the spot. She went pale, even for a vampire. Just as pushing the button sends a crossbow's arrow flying, uttering the name Kerrovitarr ripped through the curtain of forgetfulness. The battle on the School firing range, back to back with Melima. Kerr with two swords, all covered in other people's blood. The fireball in front of her face. All these sharp, clear images rushed in, filling the gaping void in her memory.

"What's with you?" she heard Melima say as if from deep in a well.

"I'm fine," Frida got a hold of herself. "You're right."

The elf grabbed the vampire by the elbow compassionately and led her to the bed:

"Have a seat. You look paler than Hel. What do you mean, I'm right?"

"I loved and love Kerr."

"Then why did you agree to the wedding…," Melima didn't finish.

"Like my dad said, it sounds pathetic, but I love my land even more. And I, no matter how sad it is, had to judge my decision based on completely different categories. I am my clan, but my clan is not me!" Frida collapsed on the bed in exhaustion. Now she could see her agreement to the wedding from the position of one who had recovered her memory. It would have changed nothing. Literally, nothing. The trap had robbed her of her choice for a long time. If Kerr had been there, her decision could have been different, but he wasn't there. "Maybe you could tell me how the battle turned out?" she asked, glancing at Melima's blue eyes.

"Maybe I could. We won."

"I don't mean that!" Frida roared.

"Sorry. It's hard for me to think about. I didn't want to hurt you.

"Can I ask you one tiny question?" Frida nodded. "Did Kerr tell you anything about himself?"

"Not a thing."

"Okay…," Melima drawled.

"Stop being so cryptic. Okay—what?"

"Okay, I get that he didn't tell you anything. Kerr is a were-dragon." Melima turned away towards the window. The vampire's eyes bulged in surprise and gasped, then closed her mouth with her hand. "When a fireball exploded your chest cavity apart..." Frida's hand instinctively went to her chest, touching the small scars. The elf, through her reflection in the glass, saw the gesture and smiled wryly. "With wounds like that, even vampires don't survive. When the Woodies' little present hit you, Kerr flew into a rage and changed hypostasis. He covered you with his blood. When you didn't show any signs of life after that, he threw himself at the elves. It was a scary sight. Enemies who've been cut with a sword look a lot prettier than ones who have been half chewed up, hacked up with his tail or burnt with the fire from his mouth. Most of the Forest mages were turned into a lake of molten lava. The Woodies surrendered. He was wounded quite badly too." The elf fell silent.

"What happened then?" Frida couldn't hold back.

"Then he jumped into the Ort. I haven't heard anything more about him since. The High Prince is organizing searches. We need your help."

"Answer me one last question. Why me?"

"Were you with Kerr?" Frida blushed. "Alright, I'll take that as a yes, plus you've got dragon's blood on your wounds..."

The door quietly creaked. The old elf entered Frida's room, the end of his cane tapping against the wooden floor.

There was something in him, elusive, that brought together two representatives of different races.

"Hello, granddaughter," the greeted Frida. "May I sit down? You sit too; we're going to have a long chat." He paused. "No need to bow," the Rauu added in his creaky voice. "No formalities here. Have a seat."

Frida sat down on the very edge of the bed, ready at any moment to jump up again.

Miduel sat down in a second chair, laid the carved cane between his knees, and folded his hands together over the handle of the cane, which was cut from a solid piece of mountain crystal. He looked at the vampire for a few minutes, his ice-blue eyes sparkling from underneath his bushy eyebrows. His gaze called to mind a high mountain lake covered with a haze of mist. The silence began to weigh on Frida's psyche. She tried to figure out what she was sensing. Something was off about the ancient elf. The flood of another person's feelings—from interest, sadness and hope to a carefully hidden irrational fear—diluted the fluids of the incomprehensible bond between the old man and the young girl. The vampire couldn't help herself. She drew breath through her nostrils as if the smell could give her the answers she was looking for. Melima, sitting motionless in a chair by the window, followed the High Prince's gaze to the owner of the room and back. It seemed the old elf and the vampire were having a telepathic conversation, the kind only close relatives could have.

"Hm," the High Prince's voice broke the silence. "I didn't think you could smell it. You really have a strong gift."

"Smell what?" Frida asked. The girl was sick of people not speaking plainly, mysterious half-truths she'd been feed all day yesterday and for two weeks now.

"Blood." The old man squeezed the cane, his joints cracking. The skin on his knuckles went pale. The Snow Elf's mask of indifference was betrayed by his worry. Freezing for a couple of seconds, he lifted the head of his cane to eye level and gazed into the crystal, repeating in his creaky voice: "Blood."

What a substantive answer.

"Blood?"

"Dragon's blood. We've both drunk from the same source. You received deliverance from Hel's embrace, I—vision and thirty years of active living." Frida didn't understand at first what dragon's blood the High Prince was getting at, but, her eyes meeting Melima's, she remembered the elf's words: "Kerr is a were-dragon."

"Kerr…."

"Yes, granddaughter. Forgive me for calling you that."

"It's okay, I'm not offended."

"We've drunk the blood of the same dragon. You, of course, don't remember it, but nevertheless, it's true." The School firing range and the ball of fire that burned her chest flashed before Frida's eyes.

"Melima refreshed my memory."

"Did she tell you why I'm here?"

"Yes. You want to find Kerr. But why me?"

"Because an empath who has received a whopping dose of dragon's blood can find Kerr by using his mental cast, all the more so since you've been intimate as a man and a woman."

"What does that have to do with anything?" the blushing red to her ears Frida asked rudely. She wasn't pleased with the intrusion into her private life and digging in her underwear.

"It's relevant because being intimate with a dragon leaves its mark, and coupled with a dose of blood, it won't let you err." The Rauu wanted to go on, but he was right to stop there, flooding the space with sparks of irritation directed against himself. "It's a shame that neither you nor I are universal mages of all the elements. If one of us were, then searching for your, I don't want to call him 'your ex-boyfriend,' would be over and done with today."

"Why?" The words "ex-boyfriend" resonated to Frida with an unpleasant ring. But they hid something important.

"Eh hmm," the old elf let out a muffled cough. "Have you heard of the 'melding of the elements?" Frida nodded. "All dragon mages are complete universals, which is why they are, first of all, magical beings, and they can sense their blood in those who can wield the magic of all four elements. One caveat—a full elemental mage who has partaken in pure dragon's blood, which has not been obtained through a special 'extraction' ritual, can also sense very well whose blood he drank. A small portion of the dragon's blood remains and lives in the person, supported by the magic of all the elements. If the simple 'melding' ritual is performed, then the blood, like the little needle of a compass, will point to its originator. From a close distance, a dragon can feel 'extracted' blood as well."

The elf fell silent. Frida closed her eyes and thought about what he had said. Two things were bothering her: the word "ex," and why Melima and the old elf had zeroed in on her closeness to Kerr. At the School of Magic, she'd been taught to think logically and to understand the main points. Even before she went to the School, she picked up a blade. Her father handed her a wooden sword at four years old, and her training as a warrior and professional killer began. During her training, much time was devoted to analyzing and dissecting various situations. The clear, connecting points of the discussion stuck out. The High Prince's surge of emotions, blazing in the empath's perception like bright lights, was cause for serious concern. What were they hiding? The ancient elf said they would have a long chat, but was rather evasive with his words. He mentioned intimacy and then steered the conversation in another direction, skipping to the effect of the blood. It was a strange conversation as if the old elf were feeling out her emotions and moods.

Frida stood up from the bed and walked around the room. She did not like where this conversation was going. She would agree to help find Kerr—that went without saying. But she was tortured by a constant nagging doubt. What was she missing? Why was the old elf feeling guilt, pity, trepidation all at once, and what seemed like the desire not to participate in the events at hand? Behind the whole gamut of moods, there was a carefully hidden fear of not being in time for something and….

"Questions tormenting you?" the High Prince interrupted her projections. "I'm prepared to answer them."

"Alright…," the girl faltered, catching herself in unbecoming behavior, bowed to the elf and sat down in her previous spot. No matter how you spin it, she couldn't allow herself to ask the questions that interested her of the head of state of another country without his giving her permission. She had already allowed herself a little too much, forgetting, upset, and overwhelmed as she was, who it was she was talking to and periodically interrupting during their short interview. Violating the rules of etiquette, she had jumped up from the bed without the Prince's permission and was pacing back and forth like a sul in a cage, which was not at all befitting a warrior and a vampire.

Moreover, there was no guarantee that when she asked her questions, she would get true answers. The Rauu were masters of weaving wordy lace and piling up the uncomfortable topics in a heap of husks. However, since permission had been given, she ought to take advantage of it.

"I have a few questions." Miduel bowed his head in consent. "The first…," Frida hesitated. The old elf smiled encouragingly. His teeth were white and looked strong. "Why did you want me to marry the son of the prince, and secondly, why might Kerr be my 'ex'? Thirdly, I'd like to know the truth about the consequences of intimacy with a dragon and why you attach such great importance to it. Fourth, and last: what are you wary of?" The girl wanted to say "afraid of," but the word might be taken as an insult. The High Prince's smile faded like a spring snowfall from the mountain slopes. Melima was struck with indignation and anger at the insolent woman's words, but Frida was not going to step down. She threw her bangs back and looked straight at Miduel.

"I'll answer your questions," the elf said, setting his cane aside. Frida sensed such a rush of feelings from Melima that she realized they would probably not be friends anymore. "The first and third questions are related to one another, but I'll begin from the beginning. I expressed the desire that new blood come into the ruling house. I do sincerely apologize that certain persons took my words quite literally. Ghhm, hm. You are now a bride to be envied. Your children will almost certainly be fully universal and very strong mages. Dragon's blood and physical intimacy leave their mark. During the act of love, dragons unconsciously share their magic." Frida looked at the elf carefully and realized he was trying to confound her. Besides common blood, they both "spouted" magic foreign to elves and vampires. Only now did Frida notice Miduel was completely covered in a cocoon of "mind shields," which didn't help him much in his conversation with her. Other people's magic was that keyhole that allowed Frida to examine other people's, in this case the elf's, feelings. "Besides magic, they leave an 'imprint' of their aura on their partners. In time it fades, but before it does, it allows us to very accurately establish the owner of the mental cast, especially in places where the dragon used magic. Why might your young cavalier become your ex? It's all about blood. Blood and magic dragged you back from Hel's judgment, and it's not yet clear what effect they had on you. You had an enormous dose. A living human would die from such a dose, but you were on the brink, and it the opposite happened. You have the gift of an empath, and how it might react to Kerr now—only the Twins know." Miduel raised his gaze to the vampire, whose outward appearance gave nothing away, grinned and went on: "You wanted to ask what I'm afraid of? I fear much. As it happened, I know a lot about Kerr. Only his parents and he himself know more than I do. I don't know all his secrets, only those laying on the surface, but that's enough to draw a few conclusions. He's too independent. He won't trust anyone and, I'm afraid that after what happened on the firing range, he'll no longer trust Rauu or humans. The notrium cages he's been forced to sit in completely discourage this feeling. He tried trusting me, but I was too preoccupied with my own self…. That stupid attempt to catch him in a net did no good and much harm. He trusted you of all people, so much that he wanted to tell you his secret. I don't know whether he loved you, but his willingness to take that risk says much. I'm afraid the Forest elves will catch him and kill him. In light of recent events, that would be very difficult for them to do, but Targ loves cruel jokes. I'm afraid he'll no longer want anything to do with humans or Rauu, and he would have the right not to. What's more, I'm afraid he'll have decided to avenge himself and become our enemy. Kerr doesn't know his own strength, not yet. Seeing him in the enemy's camp would be fatally dangerous. I'm afraid I was too late in recognizing the catastrophe that threatens the entire world, too…. Our cowardice will be felt in all Ilanta. Kerr won't solve the problems alone, if he even wants to help and solve them at all…. I'm sorry, granddaughter; we need you for more than finding him. I ask you, please, I beg you, convince Kerr to help me…." Miduel didn't finish his sentence.

"I agree," Frida answered, whose soul was warmed by the elf's pleasant words about Kerr's trusting her. She was prepared to accept him as both a human and a dragon if only the scary predictions about the effect of the blood weren't true. "When do we leave?"

"Today. In five hours, the mages will build a portal to the suburbs of Orten." Miduel gestured subtly with his hand. Melima stood up and left the room. "Did you feel that?"

"What was her name?" Frida answered the question with a question, understanding what the old elf wanted from her.

"In five hours, on the arch platform." Miduel took his cane and went to Frida, who was bowing in reverence. "I'm glad I was right about you," he added, permitting the girl to stand. He stood in the doorway for a few seconds, shrugged his shoulders and left, leaving the vampire one on one with the thoughts that tormented her. Miduel hadn't mentioned the name of his lady dragon.

***

"May I?" Melima stepped into the room without waiting for permission and stared at the entire arsenal laid on the bed.

"You may since you're here anyway," Frida said, tightening a thin strap on her thigh and testing how a short dagger held up in the sheath on it. A second knife was strapped to her left shoulder. The elf was willing to wager that more than one more dagger, stiletto or stabbing blade was hiding under the ranger's outfit the vampire was wearing. Frida grabbed a sash with long combat knives attached to it which was worn across the stomach, followed by a sword. Her mail, arm shields, leggings, and a helmet with ten defensive amulets were placed in her traveling bag. She put on her combat glove, turned to Melima, and made a fist. There was a click—three long blades popped out of the glove.

"Thirty warriors are riding with us, fifteen mages with a temple accumulator, and King Gil's giving us fifty guards too. Why do you need so many weapons?"

"These are MY weapons. It's very possible I won't ever be coming back here!"

"Why not?" Melima asked the stupid question.

"Do you want to hear my confession or are you just curious?" Frida answered, not at all in the mood for a conversation. She had had her "fill" of elves for today, of weddings, and other sweet offers. There was just over a half an hour left until the appointed time, and she wasn't about to spend it gabbing.

"Sorry. Are you ready?"

"That's everything. I'm ready," the vampire said, pulling the bag's string and tossing the strap over her shoulder. "Let's go."

She wasn't able to have a heart-felt parting with her parents. One important thing had disappeared from her relationship with mom and dad—trust. They said goodbye dryly, her mother gave her the traditional tinder flint and steel, meaning may the god of fire, the protector of the family hearth, always warm my daughter while she's on the road, and wished her a stellar passage. Her father guiltily avoided eye contact, but even so, Frida could feel that his soul was very perturbed. He was constantly reproaching himself for listening to others' convincing and not telling his daughter the truth.

Frida patted Frai on his wild locks of hair, bowed to her maternal home, turned around sharply, and stepped towards the portal platform.

Tantre. Seventy leagues south of Ortag. Frida...

"Can I help you?" Rur walked up to Frida.

"Help, please," she answered calmly, stretching the hammer to him. "Nail the pegs in on that side."

"Thanks," Rur smiled, emanating warmth and a child-like joy.

The vampire looked at the dark-skinned half-blood and shook her head. Frida listened to her feelings: she ought to admit to herself that she liked Rur. He had integrity. He reminded her of Kerr more than anyone else in his behavior and attitude towards her. He was a strong warrior, an awesome rider and naive like a child. His naivete—that's what set him apart from Kerr. That was a trait completely foreign to Kerr.

"Okay, it's done. You just have to put up the tent," the half-blood's eyes glinted red in the twilight.

"Thanks, Rur."

"Of course." A satisfied smile looked like a snow-white string of pearls on the dark face. He sat down beside her, crossed his legs and held his hands to the fire. "Were you thinking about him just now?" Rur asked, picking up a large golden scale that Frida had recently been looking at and had set down. Before he spoke, she felt his sadness and regret that she was not thinking of him.... His white claw scratched at the scale.

"Yes, Rur."

"You don't look well. Should I boil you some invigohol?" Participation and care sounded in his voice.

"Sure, if it's not too much trouble." Her headache did not want to go away. Frida leaned back against the soft moss and rubbed her temples. Almighty Twins, how tired she was! A little more of this and she would be as red-eyed as the son of R'ron from the Cat clan and the elf Senima.

Targ, Kerr, where the heck are you??

Melima came out of the darkness towards the vampire's tent.

"What do you feel?" No so much as a how-do-you-do.

"They rode by here three days ago. The mental cast is very strong."

"That means the unit commander wasn't lying. We're on the right track." A pair of red eyes flashed behind the elf's back. Rur had returned. He was holding a mug with a steaming hot aromatic beverage for Frida. Melima looked at Frida suspiciously as she took the cup. Then she glanced at the guy. Her lips curved into a barely visible smile, and without another word, she disappeared into the dark night.

Ten minutes later, through their combined efforts, the tent was up. Frida tossed her blanket on the ground. Her fatigue forced her to give in, but, lying under the dark curtain, she couldn't fall asleep. Her head was splitting for the second week now. The old elf's prophetic words were coming true....

***

The portal brought a search expedition to the outskirts of Orten. A squadron of fifty royal guards met the Snow Elves. The warriors looked in surprise at the two young women, completely decked out in weapons. The sight of a purple-ish, red-eyed elf (wearing thick leather gloves that hid sharp claws) brought them no less surprise.

Not even stepping away from the arc, Miduel already got things going—everyone was busy. He formed four search parties from the mages and the guards and sent them to search up and down the Ort, on both banks. Two dozen elves set out separately along the country trails and roads. All searchers were given communicator amulets and told the times to check in. The main group headed out along the old caravan road, towards Ortag through the northern foothills. The old elf explained his actions and decisions, saying that a wounded dragon could not have swum very far. They had to find where he exited the river to the shore and go from there.

For two and a half days, the main group walked slowly along towards Ortag. The calm passing of time and mosquito feeding ended at lunch on the third day.

The old Rauu sat down by the fire on a folding stool. A pair of personal bodyguards immediately set up a makeshift table and set it with silverware. Miduel did not deny himself any material comforts. After the first course, one of the mages ran up to him and held out the communicator amulet. The High Prince, dabbing his lips with a napkin, took the device. For a couple of minutes, he listened carefully to the report.

"Let's get packed up," he quickly said.

The lunch remained uneaten. After thirty minutes, hot sand over the quenched fires was all that remained of the camp. The group set out for Prizhim—the place where the foothills met the Ort as it curved to the west.

A wounded dragon couldn't have swum pretty far. The rest of the search parties responded promptly.

The sweetish smell of decaying bodies and burnt meat made the humans and elves wrinkle their noses. Rur supported Frida in the saddle for the last few minutes up to the rendezvous point. Her headache, falling on her like snow in the summertime, zapped her of all her strength. The forest path was strewn with orc corpses partially corrupted by carrion. Some of them looked like a barl had stomped on them. Near the small pile of stone debris fallen from a cliff lay a few bodies in melted armor, charred beyond recognition.

"Granddaughter?" Miduel turned to the vampire. Frida uttered the magic words and almost collapsed from the saddle. Thank you Rur: he caught her in time. An all-consuming rage swept over the girl. Strange images clouded her vision.

"He was here," the "granddaughter" said, wiping blood from her nostril with a handkerchief.

"'Knives,' the royal killers from the Steppe." A guard, examining a corpse, wiped his hands on his pants. "Under the left armpit, there's an orcish tattoo, the symbol of the 'knives.' They're way out from the kingdom of the 'whites.'"

"How many are there?" Miduel asked, closing his eyes and running his hands over a corpse.

"We counted forty, sire," a second guard reported.

"Strange happenings under the Goddesses' Eyes. A whole combat squadron of orcs was lingering about Tantre, and from the kingdom and Rauu principalities' special forces, not a peep. Were there any survivors?"

"The survivors pillaged the bodies, burned their own dead companions and went to the bald hills. The dragon went with them. A heavy rain has washed away the tracks here, but a little further on we can see very well the dragon's footprints. There are also footprints of hasses and horses."

"We track them further."

"Your Majesty, what shall we do with the bodies?"

"Leave them there. Don't forget to record the sight in the crystal. His Highness King Gil will find it useful to have an ace up his sleeve during negotiations with the envoys from the Steppe."

A few hours later, their scouts discovered a cave. The second group found a burnt barl carcass and next to it a sea of scales, most of which were buried deep. The investigators combed every inch of the surrounding area. All clues pointed to the fact that six people were with the dragon, one of them a child. After some time, another one joined them. Judging by the breadth of his step, they supposed the seventh one to be a man. The High Prince only grunted at this news.

Frida continued to suffer from a splitting headache all day. Near the cave it became unbearable. Miduel noticed the young woman's condition.

"Try going off a ways," he suggested. At one hundred yards from the camp, her head stopped hurting. At the old Prince's command, they set up a separate camp for Frida. The scouts brought her scales an hour later. The girl took a few golden half-circles for herself.

They measured the magical background near the cave. In thirty seconds, the frame spun around twenty five times: the mages could not hold back at expressing their emotions—they gasped, gawked, whistled, patted one another on the shoulders, and spoke in superlative tones. They measured again, for good measure. The number of complete rotations was no less. It was unbelievable. The density of the magical field in one isolated place was higher than the average for Mellorny Tree Crowns by eleven bell!

The Tantrian mages immediately contacted the Royal Academy of Magic, indicating the coordinates so that they could install an amulet charging station here. The mana was draining only slowly; the station could function up to three full months.

The next day the expedition followed the trail of the small caravan. Frida hadn't yet gone to the main camp when her headache came back with a vengeance. Her unpleasant symptoms made the heart ache anxiously…. It was turning out that the whole trip, from the cave to Ortag, Rur stayed near the vampire, helped her when she was having a tough time and didn't let her spirits fall.

Kerr was not in Ortag, but they found out that he fought on the side of the king's guard during the battle with the rebel elvish half-bloods and Lord Worx's soldiers. Kerr caught the enemy mages in a fiery trap. The method by which he did away with them horrified many. All that was left of them was a small mountain of molten rock. Only a group of ten powerful combat mages could do such a thing. It was hard to believe that one single person had done it on his own.

The active search led the Rauu to the bookstore, where the pink-haired elf told them about his desire to send all the importunate guests to the halls of Targ; they could take with them the vile blue-eyed fellow tribesman from the northern mountains and never again show up near his shop. As soon as Miduel went into the shop, the second-hand bookseller's verbal diarrhea abruptly stopped. The Dawn-bringer told the High Prince, in detail and at length, what he and Kerr had spoken of and what books he bought. The old elf listened to the merchant, thanked him for the valuable information, and hinted that raising his voice at clients was not a good idea.

Miduel, Frida, and Melima, were shocked to find out what Kerr looked like when he was in the city, and who he was with. The Norseman guards were very sure that six full-blooded orcs were with the Rauu half-blood; two of them perished as heroes in the battle. At the Big Thing the Vikings decided to bury the orc master swordsman and the fanged Valkyrie with their warriors, according to the customs of the northerners.

Every description of the orc master sounded just like Berg to Frida…. Cornered by the incontestable facts, the unit commander of the guards informed them that he was the one who helped the valiant assistants of the guards to escape—where they went, he would never tell. His word of honor was before all else. They had hired Frida instead of a hound dog. Her head started hurting at the southern gates…. And once again they took to the exhausting road, accompanied by her headache.

***

The noise in the main camp made the vampire lift her head from the rolled-up blanket she was using as a pillow. She did manage to fall asleep eventually. Frida pulled on her suit and crawled out of the tent.

"What happened?" she caught Melima in the midst of the chaos.

"The mages spotted a strong magical flash, two days' travel from here. They say it lit up half the sky. I don't know; I was already snoozing by then. The maps all show an abandoned monastery there. Miduel believes it was Kerr's magic. He did not want to wait to catch up. He contacted the army and requested winged transport."

"I see. I don't understand. Why would Kerr use powerful magic in an empty monastery?" Frida straightened her jacket, pulled the lacing on her sleeves and checked the ability of the combat knives strapped around her stomach to pop out of the sheaths. Just in case. Anyone who would use magic with such a huge amount of energy sure had a reason for it. It would be stupid to spend a monstrous amount of mana to create a simple optic effect.

"I don't need griffons tomorrow morning—I need them this evening, tonight at the latest. What? I don't know how! Send them through a portal to Ortag, and from there to the camp. It's only an hour and a half's flight. The mages will set up beacons. I'm waiting." Choice words could be heard from the High Prince's tent. If some cargo loaders had been standing nearby, they would have gotten a kick out of it. Many interesting words and phrases were included in the stream of obscenities that came from the old Kauu's mouth. Frida blushed. Along with the blush, which covered her face, ears, and neck, her memory kicked in, and she recorded Miduel's most valuable verbal pearls for the archives. Who knows, they might come in handy, no—they'd be for the general edification of all the students.

The camp looked like a knocked over anthill. Humans and elves went in all different directions, each pursuing his own goals or at least trying to look busy. The mages gathered their suitcases and in whispers discussed how much energy must have flown through the chimney in the area of the monastery, and whether it were possible after such a doomsday that a localized, regional mana source might appear, something like what they discovered near the dragon's cave. The guards, in the light of magical lanterns, packed up the pavilions and tents. Separate warriors checked the equipment. Several investigator rangers looked at the mess going on in the horse tethering station and went to sleep in the forest. They'd had more than enough commotion for now. They carried all their own belongings in their backpacks on their backs and were ready to leave—a minute to relieve themselves after the ascent, and since nobody was going to go outside the guarded magical perimeter, it wasn't worth making a fuss. Frida looked at the investigators and decided to follow their example, but it didn't work out. She did not have time to lay her head on her rolled-up blanket before Melima appeared at the tent.

"Miduel summons you." Once again, not so much as a how-do-you-do.

"What does he need?" the vampire yawned.

"What am I, your messenger girl?" the elf snapped in sincere frustration.

"No, but you sure seem like one," the vampire teased the pointy-eared elf. A good portion of anger was the response to the harmless words. "Let's go, errand girl!"

The High Prince's pavilion was lit up like Orten's central boulevard. The fuss in the camp had calmed down somewhat; a good half of the expedition members had packed up their stuff and were cooking an early breakfast or a late dinner. The hasses, awakened by the hustle and bustle, occasionally snarled near the farthest tent.

"Get ready, granddaughter. You'll fly with us," the elf said to the vampire. "How many times do I have to tell you there's no need to bow?"

"You're my senior," Frida answered, curtsying again. Miduel waved his hand.

"The griffons will be here in forty minutes." *Wow, so soon?* "The combat mages will build the portal according to our beacon coordinates. It's a pity that we don't have the coordinates for the monastery, but it's alright. I think the first griffon riders will put beacons by the walls."

"I can come?"

"Hold on a second. What do you feel now?" Miduel asked.

"I'm waiting and I'm afraid," Frida answered, carefully rubbing her sweaty palms on her suit. "I'm waiting for the moment when I can see Kerr, and I'm afraid we can't be together." The High Prince took his eyes off the maps and looked at the girl.

"Let's hope everything turns out alright."

"I do hope so. May I go?"

"Go," the old Rauu said dryly.

Frida left Miduel's pavilion and in three minutes was near her tent. What was he so worried about? The whole way, she acted as a bloodhound. That whole time, he'd called her granddaughter a couple of times—no, four, twice in Ortag. She understood that she was just baggage—Kerr had been found; he no longer needed her. They had crossed her off the list. *An enviable bride—ha!* A bad feeling tormented Frida. The headache that gripped her every time she stood where her beloved had been did not allow any chance for a favorable outcome. The old elf was excellent at forwarding his hidden motives; he had figured everything out—she and Kerr could not be together. The wedding scheme was now kablooey. The High Prince wasn't going to offer her a way back. Going back on his word would be dishonorable. Frida wasn't stupid. She understood what was what and the sudden decision to cancel her wedding to the elf prince—Miduel did not want to expose himself to a possible ally. And the fact that Kerr, if hurt, could make a boo-boo, well, she'd witnessed that in Ortag. The destroyed street was a scary sight. According to the High Prince, this was nothing compared to what a dragon could do. Several hundred dragons in one hour had turned the Great Forest into a lifeless wasteland.

The Rauu had placed Melima in the line of fire, so to speak, by tasking her with advertising the prince to Frida. Melima, who had been trying for a week to establish some sort of relationship with the vampire and telling funny stories about her brother, stepped aside as soon as Frida welcomed Rur. Frida sensed a slight contempt for the idiot who preferred this purple half-blood to her brother the prince and heir creep into Melima's feelings. Alas! All she could do now was to convince her beloved Kerr to help the Icicles. The Icicles had good and noble goals. They weren't deceiving anyone. The future of the whole world really did depend on the success of their mission, but for some reason, Frida wished the elves would just go away and was going to beg Kerr to send them down that path. She understood that it was base and dishonorable, but she couldn't do anything else. She couldn't forgive them for calmly making her a victim of circumstance. And there was another little worm eating at her as well—these long-ears had really gotten on her nerves with their snobbishness. Miduel was the only one who didn't suffer from that flaw. The rest of them talked down to her. Besides the old High Prince, Melima stood out from the others, but the girls still hadn't become friends. The elf couldn't forgive Frida's rejection of her brother. Rur was yet another story, a whole 'nother story, that Rur....

The tent was packed and loaded onto a hass in ten minutes. Frida got her chainmail out from her traveling bag, along with the defensive amulets.

She considered for a long time what to put on. In the end, she put the mail back, and a bunch of amulets took their place around her neck.

The crackling and bright glow of the portal told her the wait was over. Two full feathers of golden griffons landed on the platform near Miduel's pavilion.

"Go on. I'll fly off with the second griffon and collect the rest of the things." Rur, as always, approached silently. He brought sadness and boredom with him.

"I'll get the things. You fly on the first flight out." A royal guard came out from the darkness of the night. "High Prince's orders. Mages and the top warriors will fly in the second saddles. Five minutes to take-off."

***

Frida looked out from behind the first-in-saddle's shoulder—with every flap of the griffon's wings, the monastery got closer.

"We've crossed a 'spider web' set up over the perimeter," the first-in-saddle shouted, pointing at a stone with a blinking red light. Vague shadows flashed on the upper flat area of the monastery complex. Her temples began to tingle. Miduel was right—Kerr was here.

"Holy twins, intercessor for the One God! Look!" the pilot pointed ahead. "Dragons!"

Her headache got stronger. Squinting, Frida saw two grown dragons on the platform, a red one and a gold one, and two small ones. People were standing near the dragons, seeming so small compared to the ancient monsters. The humongous dragon bowed its head. The children, as if on command, darted under its wide wings, which it spread out for cover. Interesting—was this golden handsome fellow... Kerr?

A little below the platform she could make out the main buildings of the monastery—a temple to the One God, flickering in the first rays of the rising sun. It had melted walls and a cupola that had fallen through into the interior. The girl looked with true vision. If it weren't for the safety belts, she would have fallen off the saddle. Frida never saw such a riot of energy. The great dragon wove an attack spell of such power that she was struck by a chill. Two griffon feathers and ten mages were to the ancient monster like flies to humans. He could bat them all away with one swing of his wing or strike with his paw. Her temples felt like they were squeezed in a vice....

One griffon flew ahead; its rider shouted something. Without waiting for an answer or taking the ancient beast's silence for consent, three griffons, including the vampire's, flew over and landed. Unfastening her belts, Frida jumped to the ground. She was struck by the dragons' feelings—vivid, complex... there was interest, curiosity, caution, and a readiness to kill all the newcomers if they even thought about one fast move. Swinging her head from side to side with the intense ache, the vampire stepped forward.

The emotional blow almost knocked her off her feet. Surprise, disbelief, joy, fear that what he was seeing wasn't real—all these emotions rushed over her from head to toe. A sharp ache came along with the foreign emotions. The handsome golden dragon folded his wings and took a step forward.

"Frida?!"

"Kerr?"

The dragon turned into a person. The red-headed Norseman standing next to him tossed him a long robe.

"Frida...."

Tantre. Foothills of the Southern Rocky Ridge. The former monastery...

"May the grace of the goddesses be with you, master Miduel," Andy said respectfully and bowed to the old elf without losing his own dignity, keeping his back straight. "I gather you made use of my gift."

The Rauu smiled slightly, with composure and restraint, but showing his even white teeth. Wrinkles appeared around the corners of his eyes. Looking at him, it was hard to believe this was the weak old elf from the School basement. He now appeared to be a lively old elf of about sixty.

"And greetings to you," the elf returned his greeting with a bow of the head. He glanced at Frida, who was being supported under the arms by two tall orc women with a full complex of weapons typical to the she-wolves. They led her towards the tents. They were interesting, these orcs. There was an unusual mix of attack and defensive amulets hanging around their necks. And everything was chosen so carefully: not a single extra detail or amulet mismatched with the effect of the others. You could tell that whoever put the group of artifacts together was a master of his craft—a very good master.

Turning his attention away from the she-wolves, the elf glanced at Andy and the third orc woman standing behind him. The woman seemed bored. A total indifference to everything that was happening was written on her face. But her attentive gaze, keeping their entire surroundings under its strict watch, involuntarily made him cautious. The Rauu had had dealings with the elite warriors of the Steppe who surpassed the mastery of the swordsmen of the mountains and the Forest. The orcs were warriors from age to age; their martial arts schools were legendary throughout all Alatar. True, only a small circle of people knew of these schools, but that was enough to create a certain opinion among experts. The other states do themselves a discredit to consider the orcs barbarians. The children of the Steppes were no longer the dirty animals they were three thousand years ago. The kingdom of the "white" orcs in the east was much more developed than many and had long since been creeping up on the eastern borders of the Patskoi Empire. And what of Shanyu Hygyn's infantry? The elite regiments of the "white shields" were considered the best units of all the known armies and inspired terror when they showed up in armor on the battlefield. Humans, Rauu, and dwarfs ought to give thanks to the Twins and the One God that the peaceful gray orcs also are content to simply shepherd cattle on their vast plains. The "greenies" remained barbarous, but this too was only for the time being: if someone steps up and is able to unite them under one flag, the entire north will be quaking with fear. Miduel turned his gaze away from the beautiful orc and looked at the camp Kerr's friends had set up on the platform. Mmm-hm. Yet another surprise that was putting to rest his thoughts of careless or unplanned action. Just beyond the tents, in the shade of a wide-branching tree that hid him from being spotted from above, sat a red-haired Norseman with his bow in his hands. The bowstring was armed with an arrow, glowing with a clear light, which made Miduel keep his shield spell interweave handy. He involuntarily cringed—Kerr had found himself some paranoid friends who suspected everyone of evil intent. *Hm, what about the were-dragon himself? How much has he changed since we last met, and in what way? Life hasn't been kind to the dragon, constantly tossing various trials his way. What has he become? Humans and elves are sometimes forever changed after one major battle or harsh ordeal. They become their own shadows or become proud. Who and what is Kerr now?*

There he stands. A cold look and complete calm. His aura glows with even, pure colors. Even so, the fingers of his right hand are in a certain pose. One quick movement and a magical attack will wipe all the griffons off the platform, along with their riders and the mages. The monastery is literally full of mana. The elf relaxed, calculating the density of the field. All signs indicated over thirty bell. What could have happened here that would allow the boy to splash such a quantity of mana out into the world? The decimated temple to the One God... perhaps it contains the answer?

Andy, his eyes half closed, observed the old elf. Miduel was puzzled. This wasn't the reaction or welcoming he'd expected. So what did he have in mind? Earlier, Andy was alone. He was looking for allies and a protector, and now he had eight souls in his charge. He had to step up.

"Master, perhaps we cannot stand around in the middle of the field?" Andy broke the awkward silence.

"Yes, perhaps we can find an isolated nook to calmly chat?" the Rauu responded.

"I think you need to rest from your journey. Flying on griffons drains you. I swear that I won't go anywhere without talking to you. I hope you won't disappear either?" Andy bowed shortly to Miduel. His last phrase struck a chord in the old elf's soul. The Rauu's face betrayed a hint of annoyance and regret.

"You're right, it's tiring. We're prepared to wait as long as it takes. I think you're quite anxious to speak with someone else besides me, and I completely understand you. I was young once too." The old politician transitioned the conversation to personal relationships, pointing out his opponent's youth. Andy grunted.

"Master, I do have one small request. Please remove the humans and griffons from the platform. The children are frightened." Andy pointed to the little dragons, whose faces showed no trace of worry. Their red-scaled mamma wasn't displaying any signs of fear either, lounging on a load of blankets taken from several cargo griffins. What were a few puny people to her, when she had such a protector nearby? "May the Twins constantly bless you. I'll see you this evening." Andy turned his head towards his right shoulder and with a barely noticeable gesture, signaled Olaf to stand down. He ran his glance over Melima's imperturbable face and master Miduel's vexed face, and headed towards the tents. Behind him he could hear the elf woman's boots' leather creaking, the clatter of heels mixed with the tap of a cane hitting the pavement, and various muffled commands. The elves' camp was removed.

***

"Maybe you shouldn't be so abrupt with the old elf?" Il sat down on a wide log, glancing at Andy questioningly.

"Maybe you're right. Who knows. I think it's worth keeping a little distance from the Icicles. I've thought a lot about the Rauu and rebuilding bridges with them, but now they'll only get in the way. What I have in mind, many will not like. Miduel impresses me. He's not snobby like many Rauu. But he's not the whole people. The master is a walking history of Northern Alatar. He remembers dragons."

"What's stopping you?"

"Miduel is a politician. He's used to thinking in terms of slightly different categories. For him, not just individual people are petty cash. In politics, they make bets that affect thousands, tens and hundreds of thousands of lives of humans, elves, and dwarfs. Miduel's thinking in the grandest terms, the size of whole states."

Ilnyrgu stood up, sat down next to Andy, took his hand and squeezed his hot dragon's hand between her cool palms.

"Where did you get the idea that the elf's a politician and he's got an agenda?"

Andy gratefully covered Il's hands with his right palm.

"Il, I'm not blind. Notice the humans, elves, and griffons—they're army units. The royal guards and mountain ranger investigators. Do you think they'd give command of soldiers from elite parts of various states to a simple Rauu? And how they bow before him and run to carry out his every command?? Il, I don't want to be ground in the gears of state machinery."

"I get that," the orc smiled sadly and turned away. "Are you afraid of repeating Berg's and my fate?"

Andy stood up and shook the dirt and dust from his robe, looked at the orc and shook his head. Was he afraid? He was—who wouldn't be? More than anything, he was afraid of breaking.

I've already come under the wrath of a state. The reasons for it and the consequences were somewhat different, but the outcome was the same. I'm prey in the royal hunt. I don't know the reasons that brought Miduel here, but I can say *who* he needs."

"Who?"

"Me. He needs me. I'm a dragon. The prey has gotten bigger, and the stakes in the hunt are higher."

"Aren't you taking a bit too much on yourself?"

"You know, I'm not taking anything on myself. It's all just piling up on me of its own accord, like from a cornucopia."

"A what?"

"From Hel's bottomless purse. For the first time, I have something that's valuable to me and I love, something worth fighting for, and I don't want to lose it." The orc said nothing. She realized Kerr was talking about them. And her expectations and feelings turned out to be right. He went on: "It's you: Tyigu, Olaf, even Lanirra and the kids. Miduel will try to take all that away from me, no matter what noble goal he's pursuing."

"And Frida?"

"Frida...." Andy waved his hands as if they were wings. He then caught himself doing something much more characteristic for a dragon than a person and got embarrassed. "I lost her once. I don't want to lose anyone else."

***

Lani, closing her eyes and resting her head comfortably on the soft bags the elves had unloaded from the griffons and were now afraid to take away from the dragoness who was casually lounging on them, pretended to be asleep. In fact, she kept listening carefully to Kerr's conversation with the girl and was jealous. She opened her eyes for an instant, removed the membrane, looked at the were-dragon and immediately went back to pretending to be a sleeping log who could not care less about his business. At some point, she felt sorry for both of them—no matter what, the mental connection established between them beat hard at both parties. The one good thing was that its working radius was small, about a quarter of a mile. Was Kerr completely out of his mind to use magic and intermingle himself with human blood? Or wasn't he aware of the consequences? When she thought about it, it had to be that. But geez, for a grown dragon and a mage to be so naive…. Lanirra stopped her train of thought. The old Rauu, by the look of things, knew that the little human could determine whether Kerr had been somewhere or not. He probably didn't know all the details; otherwise, he would not have allowed the girl to implement the "melding of the elements" and attach herself to the dragon. In order to follow the trail, the "blood summons" would have sufficed. It would be stupid to stir up dragon's blood and whip up changes in the aura using the "elements." The effect of the dragon's blood would wear off by itself after seven or eight weeks; in this girl's case, she'd have to wait over half a year. But what if…. Lani imperceptibly surrounded herself with a cocoon of will shields, erecting multi-layered protection for herself, and tried to stave off her trembling. Rary and Rury, who were lying under her folded wing, noticed her state and began to rub their snouts on their mother's cheek. Lani calmed down, jerked her tail, folded her other wing, which was reflecting the sun's warm rays through the membrane, yawned, and opened her eyes. Something crunched lamentably in the luggage bags….

"…That's when I felt the pain for the first time." The dragoness quietly snorted. Of course, you felt it. Blood strives towards blood; that's what causes the hyper-exaggerated sensitivity in the temples; that's what caused you to strive towards the dragon. Uhh… the Rauu! That old elf is cunning! The little human grabbed her temples. Kerr tried embracing her, but she gently pushed him away.

"I'm sorry…."

"I know. I never thought someone else's blood would tear me apart, and I wouldn't be able to tell if a feeling is mine or not...." The were-dragon's flame tried to smile, but tears came to her eyes.

"Don't cry." Kerr, taking a step forward, hugged Frida. The human girl froze in his arms just like a little bird. "Frida, I swear, I'll do everything I can to ease your pain."

The dragoness covered her eyes with the translucent membrane. *Yes, he will! I saw how his aura flashed right through the shields.* Lanirra heaved a sigh. She'd weaved such rosy plans in her head. Now her hopes were dashed. *Incredible—that strange little human only wields two elements, but she was able to obtain a mental attachment to a full mage—inconceivable! I guess she really loves him—Hel take her!*

Hmm, perhaps I should give him a hint at the solution? No, I won't say anything. If Kerr removes the bond, nothing will work out for her, and that way not all's lost. He hasn't made her his wife, but she's not planning on letting her happiness slip away. I can't kill the girl; he's too attached to her. I have to think of something else. I do have one advantage over the humans—time. A dragon can wait a couple of hundred years if necessary; humans and elves won't last that long. Lanirra was not afraid to admit to herself that she had really taken a shine to the "individual" and wasn't planning on sharing him with anyone. Trysts on the side were one thing—so what, even with the humans, but not as serious as this. He should have one wife—and not a human female! No dragoness would ever put up with a second mistress in her nest.

The little human girl is enjoying her temporary victory for now. Lani would do everything she could to turn Kerr away from her. He took in her children and would be taking care of them, and their mother would be right there for that.... The dragoness wasn't kidding when she had made her subtle marriage offer. As far as Norigar went, she'd finished mourning him a year ago. She knew that no dragon ever escaped from the clutches of the Forest elves alive. According to the stormy words of the abbot killed by Kerr, which he'd thrown in the locked-up dragoness's face, she was lucky to end up in the monastery. She would live a while at least, while the elves couldn't wait till sundown, they were so eager. And the children, Rary and Rury, they see him as a father. They might get brothers and sisters out of the deal, while the little human could never bear the were-dragon any offspring. That pair was sterile.

***

"Uncle Kerr, the little human's awake!" Frida heard the small dragonling's sonorous voice. The sleepless night in the griffon saddle brought her to her knees immediately after her conversation with Kerr. She opened her eyes, sat up to resting on her elbows and immediately fell back again. The pounding headache just wouldn't leave her alone. She gathered her strength for a minute, tried to control her condition in various ways…, but the proximity of her beloved smashed to smithereens all attempts to get rid of the drills in her temples.

Frida lay there a while with her eyes closed, steadied her breath, chased the ache drilling at her head to the edge of her consciousness, counted to one hundred, and decidedly stood up. She had to check with the winged baby—how long had she been sleeping? Judging by the tents of the stationary camp on the platform near the former temple to the One God, which she could see from her tent, a long time. That is, she could remember well that before she laid down to sleep, there were no tents in that spot.

The large golden dragon walked up to the improvised sleeping quarters. He was emanating cold, covered in the most powerful will shields as he was. Frida had read about something called the "icy silence," but she'd never seen it in real life before. It was sad that the person she loved (something strange about calling him a dragon) had to put up the most powerful and fierce magical mental defense between them. The "icy silence" froze absolutely all feelings for a while; the emotional background goes blank and it seems like there's a block of ice standing in front of you. Timur was walking along beside the dragon. Now there's the last person Frida expected to see here. It was very nice to meet her old friend. Timur was sporting a new uniform with the stripes of roi-dert on his shoulder. He'd bought the uniform for two golden pounds from one of the griffon riders. The lucky sergeant just happened to have an extra set with him. Now he'd unexpectedly come into a small fortune.

Kerr changed hypostasis and changed into the clothes he'd prepared for himself beforehand.

"Frida, can you tell me why Miduel came here? Maybe you overheard some conversations or rumors?"

"Long story short—he's here for your soul!"

Kerr nodded. This wasn't news to him.

"I guessed as much. The master probably wasn't going to pay me a visit just for kicks."

"The High Prince is the superior governor of the principalities of the Snow Elves. I thought you knew."

"Woah! So that's why the elves are running around as if they've been stung in the butt—and I'm acting towards him like he's some librarian! I almost made myself on equal footing with the highest monarch of their people! Well, I guess he really needs me, since he let my casual attitude slide. Tell me please, how did he get to your town, what did he say, who did he see?"

"I can only guess who the High Prince saw in my town. It's not every day the ruler of a neighboring state comes to a nondescript little town in the vampire's enclave. I can only tell you what I know or what I think, or what I suspect." Frida rubbed her chin and glanced at Kerr questioningly. He nodded encouragingly. There was a sincere interest written all over the were-dragon's face, but all the empath's feelings were bemoaning the deathly cold that reigned inside him. Kerr's burning cold and Timur's fiery interest were in such contrast to one another that Frida got the impression she was sitting in front of a fire on a cold winter evening—the fire warming her on one side, the frost's cold breath making the other side numb. Though it was difficult, the vampire tore her gaze away from the blue eyes boring holes in her. Her eyes fell on the tight, dusty socks sticking out of Timur's flying boots. For a few seconds, she stupidly stared at her own shoes, then a detached look came over her face, and she began telling them everything that happened to her from the moment she woke up in her parents' home. During the second half of the story, she began to include her observations or guesses regarding the elves' or Miduel's actions in particular. She did not skip the part about the wedding that never took place, or the supposed reasons it was cancelled. She indicated that they were due to the High Prince's desire not to spoil relations with a certain well-known dragon.

"Still, it's all underway," Kerr said, plopping down onto a wide boulder and leaning his back up against a pedestal sticking out of the ground. "It's getting interesting. My wish to meet with Miduel is starting to fade. I was right: he's a politician."

"You say that like it's a bad thing. You don't want to meet with him?"

"We can chat, but I realized from Melima's careful words that the High Prince is here to request aid. Helping him, granting his request means placing my life and freedom in the line of fire for some cause. I don't intend to die for someone else's cause and I will not help the Rauu."

"What do you mean?" Timur joined the conversation.

"I have a couple questions for my former allies," Kerr answered obscurely. Timur and Frida glanced at one another. "Can we be done here? My 'icy silence' spell is wearing off. I really don't feel like recharging it—it makes you feel like a wooden dummy, like everything inside's been burned out, a piece of ice has been put in place of your head, and your body's been changed to a wooden log." Once he said this, Kerr looked at Frida and the vampire drowned in the boundless blue of his eyes. "Go to sleep. I'll be nearby. Timur, please don't follow me. I need to think."

***

"To be or not to be: that is the question." Shakespeare's characters probably never faced situations like this—when your head could become at any moment as empty, white, and smooth as the skull of poor Yorick, and the whole action takes place against the backdrop of a flaring war comparable in scale to the First World War.

Andy lay on the far edge of the platform and admired the beauty of the mountains. He changed hypostasis and was catching some warm sunrays with his outspread wings. He could think easier as a dragon. The world was always brighter; the logical and not-so-logical connections between humans, objects and events were clearer. Andy stared into the distance—what a view. The mountains in the south crowded upon one another, like soldiers in the ranks, reflecting with their hills the bright rays of the star above them. Just like the words of that Russian song, "the only thing better than a mountain is mountains." The bluish-white caps of the nearest peaks, wearing their green skirts, the foothills, were surrounded by veils of gray clouds, set to the lyrical mode. The quiet whistle of the drifting snow and the drawn-out buzzing of the wind in the crowns of the mountainous trees helped him abandon the world and build a harmonious train of thought:

What do we have at our disposal here and now? We have no more, no less than the superior governor of the Snow Elves, in the flesh. He's extremely interested in a certain dragon. So interested, in fact, he left the underground library of the Orten School of Magic and, instead of letting his cheeks get numb sitting on the throne of the High Principality, rushed out in pursuit of the fleeing monster. Not just rushed—headed an expedition, disturbing the wedding of his own great great grandson to Frida along the way, who has become, thanks to dragon's blood, an enviable bride and possible mother to strong mages. Isn't that so? Yes, that's so. Why were the nuptial preparations ceased? Why would Miduel of all people, no one else, despite all the benefits of his descendant's wedding, decide not to impose upon the were-dragon and gently beat his own grandchildren in the face instead—as if to say, you're not biting? Well, that's not what I meant…. Hmmm…. So, that's it then? That's it. But what could have been so fascinating as to attract the old elf? My being able to change form? No, that's not it… something else. Why aren't the Rauu interested in Lanirra? She's a mage, she can wield all the elements, but still—not interested. How am I different than Lani? My size, my color, my strength, my magic? Stop. Magic. I'm getting warmer…. The astral. Yeah, that's it. My ability to work with the astral. Although…, the book said that astral mages weren't as uncommon as fully universal mages. One in three hundred has the ability to take mana from the astral, or something like that. Hmm, "to take from," okay, but how much? Lani was very surprised I could get out of the helrats' trap by "feeding" them mana up to their eyeballs. She may be a naive dragoness, but she's not stupid. Her father raised her for five centuries, taught her magic. I'm sure he wasn't stupid or a fool. And neither is she. The ancient winged beasts studied in the universities of Nelita and were such powerful mages, their bipedal followers had a lot to learn to catch up to their level. …So, that only leaves the astral. What does it have to do with me? What's unusual? Frida said the mages were surprised and discouraged at the density of the magical field near the cave. As I recall, she said they decided to install an amulet charging station on the spot where I entered the astral and let energy into the world…. I think I've got it! The puzzle comes together into a clear picture—that's the last piece! Wow, I'm one smart cookie! Just like my aunt Sonya from Odessa. Now they're going to chop that smart cookie up into pieces and share me, or ask me to provide mana. But do I need that? No. But just one small question left—would Miduel let the goose that lays the golden eggs go, just like that? What a heavy question…. Where in the world did that old guy get the idea that I'm special? He couldn't have just thought it up out of nowhere. Either someone told him, or I'm the one who gave it away with what I said or did. What could the elf have clung to? I remember he almost miraculously recovered his sight when I said Karegar's my dad. Miduel didn't believe I underwent the Ritual at sixteen. That's it! He didn't believe me so he checked; after checking he found that it was true, and so he sent all the warriors and bookworms he had at his disposal into battle for my sake. Well, Miduel, for that you've got my respect and major props."

Hmm, now let's see. What other trump cards do I have in my hand, besides the astral? The old elf's guilt at what he did to Frida—definitely. Is he guilty for leaving his dragon allies in the lurch, the ones who destroyed the Great Forest? Well, that idea is not fresh, no sense in dredging it up again. Lanirra's father said the elves and the Arians left what was left of the dragons just when they needed help most. There were only dozens of them left when there used to be hundreds. The elves were afraid of the winged tribe's power. They were so afraid, they preferred to forget that they'd been on the same side, and close their eyes to the squadrons of hunters ransacking through the many hidden and secluded places, in hopes of finding a dragon. Now I just have to decide whether I need Miduel at this point or not? Is it worth taking the weight of the elves' problems on my shoulders? In light of the fact that I'm planning to fly around to all the nests shown on the map, I do need the Rauu. In the long term, they can and should be lured to my side, but for now, too many people are looking at us dragons as if we were a valuable treasure, including some Rauu. What else? I'm having a brain fart… Oh yeah, I'm forgetting one small thing— monarchs really don't like it when you say no to them, especially if you're not a monarch of a neighboring country or an Archmage. I cannot directly refuse him. I'd better make up some excuse, like a pressing errand, or just direct him to the entire monastery archives. Let them clean the Augean stables themselves. Well, it's time now, isn't it? Arguing with the powers that be is a bit awkward…, but someone has to do it!

***

Miduel, setting his cane aside and folding his hands behind his back, measured the tent with his wide steps. Everything's going wrong.

Kerrovitarr... He should have changed his name to Kerrovigarr long ago—meaning a giant hulk who doesn't comply. What's happened to him that he started displaying a noticeable coldness towards elves? Miduel took the little box that contained the kran from the table. He stared at it for a long while. Finding no acceptable answer, he put the artifact in his camisole pocket. *The boy doesn't want to hear anything. He took his vampire girl and asked the elves to leave as if to imply we'd have time for a long talk later on. And I have no choice but to put up with the young dragon's whims. And where has he found a female with children? The former prisoners are saying nothing. Couldn't get a word out of them. It would be easier to speak with a stone. The warrior Rauu, the griffon rider, who was freed by the dragon and the orcs, can't say anything intelligible. However, the female dragon and the dragonlings are obviously taken under his wing. The children are one thing—okay. Dragons are always affectionate towards their own—but the female! Has he accepted her as a wife? On second thought, no; he's too human.*

Miduel stopped, turned on his heels and took another step. *His human nature's having its effect. On the other hand, he's becoming less and less human every day, and it's very hard to determine his ancestry. The ancient kran doesn't give any past memories. All images begin from the Incarnation. But if I'm to believe the word of the book shopkeeper from Ortag, Kerr visited him in the form of a Rauu, and that was not at all an active illusory mask. There's no basis to suspect the Dawn-bringer of lying. Anything is possible. Jagirra seemed to have agreed to the Ritual painfully quickly. She probably wouldn't have taken so much trouble over a simple human.*

The vampire.... Perhaps I made a mistake, taking her with me? She's a very good girl, no doubt—smart and well-read, a first-rate swordsman, and as much a top-notch warrior as a seventeen-year-old could possibly be. Right now she's up on the platform with Kerr, and I'm here, tearing my hair out wondering what they're talking about!

"Your Majesty," one of the mages guarding the High Prince's dwelling slipped into the tent. Miduel turned with eager interest. "May I present Kerrovitarr Dragon Gurd."

"Let him in!"

"Good evening, Your Majesty," Kerr stepped into the pavilion and bowed at the waist.

"Oh stop," the Rauu waved his hand dismissively and smiled warmly. "Oh, I see you've come with a whole mess of papers. May I ask what they are?"

"Of course, but in just a minute. I'll leave the papers with you. I don't need them, and you and the dwarfs will, very much so."

"I'll take your word for it. Have a seat." Miduel waved his hand towards a small furniture set made up of two light wicker chairs and a small round table with a teapot on it, steaming with hot, refreshing invigohol.

"Thank you, master."

The Rauu nodded cordially.

Obeying a subtle gesture, or some other form of command, two silent elves came forward from behind a curtain and quickly set the table with bowls of baked goods and fruits.

Andy sat down in a chair, leaning against the comfortable back, observed the precise, measured movements of improvised waiters, who were actually the High Prince's bodyguards, and wondered what direction the conversation would take.

When the bodyguards left, Miduel pronounced a curtain of silence spell over them, poured the beverage into two deep porcelain cups, and took a sip. Andy, following tradition, took the first sip of the hot broth, enjoyed the delicious taste, held it in his mouth, and did not forget to lift the cup to eye level paying tribute to the old Rauu who had prepared it; only then did he swallow.

For a few minutes, they enjoyed the superb beverage, surreptitiously observing one another.

Miduel relaxed, leaned his cane against the chair and stretched his legs. Now the person sitting before Andy was not the all-powerful ruler of one of the main states of Alatar, but an elderly Snow Elf, constantly exhausted from the responsibilities heaped upon him. The Rauu, like an old man, sipped the hot broth and munched sugar cookies, from time to time fumbling with his hand in the bowl, searching by the only known methods for the sweetest and most crispy specimens of confectionery art. In those moments, he reminded Andy of a clever old man from a fairy tale, the mushroom king, who was ready to answer any question. Andy set his cup on the table.

"More?"

"Yes, please." The High Prince poured a second helping of the invigohol.

"Thank you."

"Take some cookies. Melima baked them, and these rolls."

"It's hard to imagine her in an apron, in front of an oven."

"I agree. She's a wild woman, but even so. No one makes sugar cookies and buns better. I guess there are more sides to her personality that we give her credit for."

Behind the meaningless small talk, an icy alienation stood between the old elf and the young were-dragon.

"So, you've decided to turn me down?" Miduel said, abruptly interrupting the idle prattle.

"Hm?" Andy almost choked on the roll he was eating. What a turn-around! The High Prince suddenly took off at a gallop, pulling the rug out from under his opponent and tossing Andy's prepared words in the trash.

"Do you want to know how I knew?" Andy nodded. "I'm too old. Humans' and elves' behavior is no secret to me. You were drinking the broth, and I was mentally evaluating your body language, gestures and such. Over a thousand years, one can learn to determine without a doubt a person's mood, using those little signs that no one else notices, like the kind of pose a person assumes during a discussion. The tension of the muscles, the expression behind the eyes, the tone of voice, the level of perspiration, the body language, the color and glow of the aura. You were calm which said you'd made a decision. There wasn't the slightest sparkle of doubt in your aura, or regret, which means you thought about it good and hard and added up all the pros and cons. But why? You haven't even asked what I want to ask you or offer in exchange for your services and help?"

"Master, I really did think hard. I thought about myself and about you. It all ended with me firmly deciding who I really am. I figured out what my priorities are. I have someone to care for, someone to protect. I have no desire to place my neck on the chopping block for some lofty cause, no matter how noble it may be or what motives are included in striving towards that goal. You can call me selfish and cynical if you like."

"As far as I understand it, that's not all. As far as I've been able to study you," Miduel took the kran from his pocket and handed it to Andy, "you've never been selfish or cynical."

"Well, that's not all. You're correct. Master, you are responsible for your people and your country, while I'm responsible for those people who trust me. These people, dragons, and orcs, have become my family, and until I've lead them to a safe place, I can't turn my attention to anything else. We both bear the weight of responsibilities, and you can't say that one load is greater or lesser than the other. We each have our tasks." Andy fell silent. Miduel stared straight ahead, his face like stone. Only his bushy gray eyebrows twitched to the beat of his thoughts. "I can't take on your tasks." The elf's eyes flashed like two blue fires. "I came to you to ask many questions, but first just answer me two. Answer honestly. What I have to say next depends on it."

"Two?"

"Yes, just two."

"Alright. I'll try to be an open book," Miduel said and closed his eyes. He'd gleaned a lot from his conversations with Rector Etran, including the fact that the young dragon sitting in front of him wasn't as simple a being as he seemed. The youthful appearance hid a second essence, and this essence was extremely, to the point of paranoia, cautious. Before the Royal Informants asked all the Rauu to leave Orten and arrested Etran, the rector managed to show the old elf a selection of materials on the siege of four hundred years ago that the young man had collected, and to describe his actions, including his requirement to be provided with a way out of the Free Mages' Guild. A short excursion through the papers created more questions than it answered, both about the history of the siege itself and about the former bookworm. His stated age of eighteen did not at all correspond to the conclusions one could draw from his work putting together the folder: everything was too exact and pithy. That hardened, cunning Etran wasn't showing or telling all there was to show and tell, either. Miduel could sense she'd left a few aces up her sleeve. Saving them for a rainy day. Now all Miduel had to know was what she was hoping for? Kerr wouldn't let himself be used as a puppet. He would listen to others' advice, but he would act on his own. This the High Prince knew for sure.

The Rauu had previously examined all the details of their upcoming meeting in his mind from every angle, for a few hours. He created various models of the dragon's behavior, his own and Kerr's questions, answers and… then threw all his work in the garbage. The psychological portrait did not correspond to the boy's actions in Orten, Ortag, and on the forest trail. Why had the dragon gotten involved in someone else's fight? What were the royal killers of the Steppe doing in Tantre? Who were they after? What wasn't the Norseman, the unit commander in Ortag, telling him? And what really happened in that former monastery? What prompted Kerr to dive into the astral and pump energy into the world? Miduel involuntarily cringed. The density of the magical field in the region of the temple was fifty bell—three times higher than in the center of the Mellorny woods! The mages accompanying the elf were in shock. No one talked about the charging station. The wizards were crawling on their hands and knees from the magic of the destroyed temple, gathering crystals from some energy accumulator. The small fragments, the size of a pinky fingernail, were so saturated with energy that they could compete with the temple's lesser mana collectors. The Rauu had completely forgotten about the power of a true blood. He had time to find and meet with them, many of which were stronger than Kerr, a lot stronger, but now he was the only one. His strength made Miduel's heart beat faster. Soon they could expect a formidable landing party of specialists from the Royal Academy, the Orten School of Magic and the Center for Magical Arts of the Rauu Foothill Principality. It simply wasn't realistic to think they could keep an event like this a secret. They would come after the boy with all they had. It was foolish to think the mages wouldn't put two and two together, and it seemed Kerr understood the situation very well. Unbelievable! The boy, cornered by circumstances, wasn't showing any signs of upset, as if he weren't at all interested in magical and semi-magical whoop-de-doo and all their imminent consequences. One got the impression that Kerr thought about his actions one move in advance, and that he had certain raw materials and parts at his disposal. No matter how strange it sounds, the High Prince was nervous about his own complete personal lack or readiness for Kerr's illogical behavior. The pile of papers he'd brought to their meeting suggested that they would become a bargaining chip, but what would they be bargaining for? What could he expect? Miduel was only now realizing his unpreparedness and inability to conduct political discussions and actions with one member of the Lords of the Sky. Kerr, it seemed, was full of surprises: you see a youth in front of you, then you close your eyes—and instead of a youth, there's a grown man. The shapeshifter's quiet voice interrupted the Rauu's train of thought.

"My first question is, why did you want to marry your great great grandson off to Frida? The second one is, what stopped you? Please understand, I don't believe the idle talk that says my presence is what put an end to it, your unwillingness to compromise a possible ally. There's got to be another explanation."

Miduel stood up. Idle talk? A several-hour-long preparation for the conversation? Ha! It was a good question and an excellent answer to what Miduel had asked about refusing to cooperate. The old elf felt as if he'd had the wind knocked out of him. How had Kerr managed to isolate the main component? He had to answer, and tell the truth....

Andy got the impression the years, the elixir of dragon's blood had taken off Miduel, all suddenly came rushing back. His shoulders drooped; the wrinkles on his face got deeper. The High Prince leaned on his cane with all his weight and looked Andy in the eye:

"Because I couldn't... no, not like that. You're right, it's not about you. It's about me. I didn't want to cross the line that separates an ancient Snow Elf from becoming a monster. You've asked me the hardest questions. In part, I can't answer them. I didn't expect that from an eighteen year old boy, or... elf?" Andy shrugged, transforming into a Snow Elf. Miduel smiled sadly, shook his head and went on: "I didn't expect questions with such weighty answers." He sighed heavily, glanced at Andy again, and plopped down into a chair. "Ilanta is dying. The consequences of the war of the dragons and the Forest Elves are beginning to show. Two, maybe three thousand more years and the magic will be gone from this world. Do you know where mana comes from?" Miduel asked, and, not waiting for an answer, went on: "Mana comes from Mellornys, true bloods and dragons. Yes, dragons. They unconsciously draw energy from the astral, giving it away bit by bit. True bloods and the Lords of the Sky are the most magical creatures of all sentient beings that populate this world. Three thousand years ago, they were stripped of a future, their nesting grounds destroyed. In response they cursed the elves, burned the Great Forest, and put an anti-flowering spell on the Mellornys. Since then the trees have not borne fruit. The true bloods were killed even before that; those few who were left alive went to Nelita.... The Woodies are growing new trees by grafting, but it's a drop in the ocean, since those ones won't bear fruit either. A magical tree lives about five thousand years. Do you understand what I'm saying? The last young sapling was planted three thousand years ago. Soon the Forests will start dying out. Their agony will be prolonged. The Forest elves have not yet fully comprehended the catastrophe that awaits them. They hope they can plant millions of seedlings grown from young branches. It won't work. The old trees' death will strongly affect the young saplings. The dying network of roots will disturb the connections between the groves." Miduel paused again and swallowed the lump that had formed in his throat. All was quiet in the tents for a few minutes, then the Rauu leaned towards Andy and looked him in the eyes again. "There's another secret. The Mellornys won't grow without the dragons. The Lords of the Sky and the trees are magically connected and complement one another. I don't know how the bond works, and most likely no one will ever know the answer to that question, but the fact remains. The dragons have kept their secret as sacred and would have taken it to the grave, if you hadn't come along."

"What do you mean?"

"There's an ancient artifact in the Marble Mountains, built to detect splashes of magical energy given off by true bloods. The force of the astral flows through it. Who installed it and why is not important now. The ancient device isolated your magic and your penetrating into the outer layers of the energy field. That's where I ran off too as soon as I could."

"So it turns out you were in the mountains while I was looking for you in the archives."

"Yes, I didn't believe my own senses and decided to make sure my eyes weren't playing tricks on me. The ancients' artifact hadn't been checked in a few hundred years, and how could it have? Only the Rauu princes know where it's located, and there hasn't been any reason to head off to the highlands for a couple thousand years. When I got there with my entourage, I found out that the cave where it's hidden had suffered from an earthquake. The passage on the far end was piled up with debris from a landslide, but another passage had opened. My subordinates studied it in detail and discovered copper plates with runes imprinted on them. After they had cleaned all the dirt off the plates, we were able to read that the ancients had wanted to convey to us. This unexpected find shed a lot of light on things and opened my eyes. The world is at a crossroads. The Woodies are completely unaware that their venture is doomed to failure. When the old trees dry up, a magical recoil effect will hit the whole Forest. It won't allow the young shoots they planted to swallow energy from the astral. Mages all over the world will have no mana and become ordinary people. The Forest Elves won't get off that easily—they'll die along with the Mellornys. The last dragons will go after the Woodies. They live longer and their suffering will last much longer. The Rauu, the vampires, and the Dawn-bringer elf races will be dissolved into the human tribes. But now back to me, you, and Frida. Did her parents tell you anything about the possibility of having children?" Andy shook his head. The old elf's words were filling him with horror. "You can't have children." Seeing how Andy tensed up in his chair at the sound of this, the Rauu lifted his hand reassuringly. "Don't get ahead of yourself. You're not sterile. A simple dragoness or a were-dragoness can become the mother of your children, but never a human, elf, or vampire. But a simple girl who has lived with a were-dragon is capable of giving birth to a fully universal mage by another man."

This time Andy stood up. Something went off in his head.

"A fully universal mage? You were interested in my foster parents and turning children into... into dragons?"

"Yes...," Miduel turned away from Andy's eyes, sparkling with rage. "The responsibility lays on each of us like a heavy load, but I am not willing to and cannot take it upon myself. I don't want to become the monster who sends children to certain death. That's why I canceled the wedding of my great grandson to Frida. I canceled it despite the Prince of the Foothill Principality's wishes and despite the tempting possibility of getting a great, great, great grandchild who's a dragon and, as Targ would have it, a true blood. I canceled it so I would never be tempted ... I canceled it, and that's all. It's possible my decision will push the world one small step closer to the edge, but I don't want to be tormented by my conscience. I've come through a lot, and I'm ready to go through much more, but not that. I had to order the others to act haughty around her so she wouldn't think of marrying another one of the Icicles. Arrogance and conceit are more off-putting than anything else. I feared the burden of being responsible. You can run away from the world—but not from yourself. I'm afraid for all Ilanta. The world does not have any chance left...."

"Not one?"

"Not one," Miduel stood up. "There are practically no more dragons left."

"Yes, if people keep hunting them, the end of the world will come even sooner. It's your fault, partly," Andy said, unable to restrain himself. His face was a mask of indifference, carefully hiding his wrath.

"How so?"

"You left the dragons alone right when they needed your help."

"You don't understand..."

"I understand everything," Andy interrupted the elf. He jumped up from his chair and stood facing the High Prince. "The Lords of the Sky, insane after the attack on the Forest, were horrifying even to themselves. But after special squadrons of Rauu and Woodies killed all the crazy ones, why didn't you forbid dragon hunting? What stopped you from doing that? You could have. I'll tell you what—fear of their great power and the black smoldering ashes where the Great Forest used to be. Even a small portion of the winged beasts was stronger and more horrible than a whole army any of the states that existed at that time could come up with. Humans, elves, and Arians decided to quietly soothe their shameful fears through the hunters' greedy thoughts; by cunning and perfidy destroying the disconnected nests. It's too bad for the dragons that they're so independent and individualistic. There wasn't anyone who could unite them, and the Rauu had lost their trust. It's about trust—the dragons don't trust anyone anymore, including their former allies and creations. That's why you don't have a chance at saving the world. And the dragons can easily survive the death of the forests; they're the ones who planted the first woods in Ilanta. That's where the connection comes from; nothing secret about it. It's just that the Forest Elves would rather forget that fact. They'd rather burn any trace of the Lords of the Sky from their memories. I'm refusing to help you not just because I don't want to, but also because if I did, no one would follow me. The dragons won't accept an elven puppet, no matter what you call it. I can guess what you're planning to offer me."

"What?"

"Two possibilities: protection and security in exchange for mana, or, the other option would be to restore the winged tribe. As for the first—dragons aren't cows to be milked, and as for the second, I saw how you sized up Lanirra, and I learned a lot from the look on your face. If it's possible to do anything, it will be done, without anyone's help. You have to deal with this," Andy slapped his palm down on the pile of papers on the table.

"What's that?" Miduel asked.

"It's the helrats' recordings: their correspondence, accounting books, promissory notes and selections from their archives."

"The helrats?"

"Yes. That monastery to the One God was their base, and in that temple they made sacrifices. The crystals that collect mana are the pieces of their statue of Hel. I had to give those brutes so much mana, they couldn't hold it all. Clean out your Aegean stables," Andy voiced his earlier thought referring to the Greek myth. He thought it was a smart analogy.

Miduel was taken aback:

"What stables?"

"Oh, geez. The manure in your backyard that's built up over the course of centuries. The servants of Hel wove their little nests not only here! I meant it when I said these papers would come in very handy to you and the dwarfs. Make a law that says killing a dragon is punishable by death. You're the only one, besides my parents, who I really trust. You can do that all over—with the Rauu, the humans, the dwarfs.... I understand everything, but when Rauu women start buying blood and extracts made from a dragon's glands... and I won't even say anything about the Woodies. It's all here, in these documents. Promise me you'll investigate it without bias."

"What do you want for these papers? As I understand it, you've got a reason for collecting them."

"A portal."

"What?"

"I want a portal. I want your mages to build a portal today. I myself will give it the finishing touch. Soon there'll be so many investigators and mages here, you'll have to elbow your way through the crowd. There'll be freeloaders from different guilds, and I have absolutely no desire to be here when they show up. I don't want to become an object of research. I'll get away somehow... can you make up some excuse for me?"

"I can. What else have you got here?"

"Bank account numbers in Imperial banks, enormous sums, saved up over hundreds of years, and empty checkbooks—carte blanche for the bearer." Miduel instantly caught his drift. The Rauu's squinting eyes gave away his brain's frenzied work. "If you take all the debt bills of the Empire stored in the treasuries of the Rauu principalities and Tantre, it's enough money to collapse the banking system of Pat and devalue the imperial.[13] In a state of financial crisis, the Empire can't wage a war. It's long since fallen under the heels of the big money bags from the banking houses."

"How old are you?" Miduel said finally said after a long silence.

"In half a year, I'll be nineteen."

"Impossible! Tell me where you're getting all this from?" Miduel spread his hands helplessly. His gaze shifted from object to object. For a brief moment, it rested on Andy, who had read an unspoken question in his eyes, then moved to the scandalous papers lying on the table, and again returned to the were-dragon.

"From Alo Troi." Andy sat down in the chair and turned away from the Rauu. "It was difficult for him to remember the Rimm dungeons and the cage, but keeping it all inside was even harder. The fortress of self-control can't always hold one's emotions. His conversation with Miduel thoroughly shook his foundations."

"I remember him. A capable youth, a strong sharp-wit, the best analyst you could ask for. Alo worked in the archives quite often," the High Prince said, taking up the other seat.

"He'd been there. He died right in front of me, teaching me Alat. Along with the language, I practically swallowed his personality. A part of his knowledge that was lying on the surface was transferred to me. Now does your behavior model make sense?"

"Not yet, and it won't. Alo was never known for the logical nature of his actions. Sharp-wits are always a little out of this world." Miduel stood up. "When should we build the portal?"

"This evening, by eight o'clock."

"Alright. Do you want to jump right home?"

---

[13] Imperial—the unit of currency used in the Patskoi Empire.

"Yes, you're very observant, as always." Andy bowed and walked out of the tent.

Andy glanced pensively at Timur, who was shifting his weight from side to side, and Ilnyrgu, who was clutching the head of her sword. He rubbed his hair back and, wiping the sweat off his forehead, said:

"Well, we had a nice chat. Il, let's get packed. In four hours, the mages will build a portal."

***

"When are you leaving?" Andy asked.

Timur straightened his flight jacket and looked at Frida, who was holding Kerr by the elbow. It was sad: they were both suffering. Ice again. Would they remain separated from one another like that, by a spell that freezes feelings?

"In an hour. Just before you guys. The mages are opening the portal to Orten."

"To Orten? You're not going back to your unit?" Frida asked, surprised.

"No, by a royal order all mages, including students who haven't completed their studies, are to be sent to training as combat mages. While you were sharing secrets with the High Prince, the squadron second-in-command from the griffon wing got in touch with the commander of my unit and made sure I was alive and relatively healthy. I won't describe the gross-dert's joy when he found 'cause the only normal word he used was my name. The rest of 'em, in a civilized society, you can get called to a duel for. But it still made me glad: the guys and the commander were really very worried about me."

"Did you..." Andy began.

"I didn't tell them where I was. The second-in-command of the High Prince's griffons asked me not to go into detail."

"And Rigaud? Any word from him?" Andy really missed the blabbermouth. Rigaud, despite his disorganized lifestyle and the out-of-character (for him) jealousy that reared its ugly head on the last day of lessons at Berg's school, was the cement that held the young men together despite their differences and made them true friends.

"Rigaud's already in Orten. We'll see each other there. True, I'll have to go to the commandant's office to get my orders, but after a couple of hours I'm sure I'll turn back around."

"Give him our best, from me and Frida. And…," Andy put his hand in his pocket, "and this is for you." A couple crystals lay on his open palm, glowing neon. They were just like the ones the mages were collecting on their hands and knees in the destroyed temple, but with one difference: these were as big as a nickel.

"I can't accept that. Do you know how much an energy accumulator like that costs?"

"Yes, I do." Andy looked at Frida guiltily, removed her hand from his arm and hugged Timur. "I know, Timur: they're not worth more than my life. Take 'em. The mages that arrived with Master Miduel are now gathering up the shards from that statue. I charged them with mana." Timur's jaw dropped. "Yes, now you know my other secret and you can imagine why the High Prince was looking for me. As for the stones—I'll have more peace of mind knowing you and Rigaud have some extra mana reserves at your disposal. I don't have very many true friends, and I don't want to lose them because their internal reserves run dry at the wrong time. If you want, I can charge you ten more like this." With these words, he put the crystals in Timur's hand and tightly closed his fist around them. It turns out the "icy silence" didn't stamp out all traces of emotion. Andy's heart was now filling up with sadness. He missed the old days as students, which had turned out to be some of the best in his life. With every fiber of his soul, he wished his friends would find their happiness and not perish in the fires of the approaching war.

"Thank you…," Timur said, swallowing a lump in his throat. Frida smiled as she felt Timur's sincere gratitude, childish joy, and the giddiness of a school boy who's found a treasure. She winked at Andy and took a small bundle from her breast pocket.

"And this is for your girlfriend," the vampire handed the amazed big kid one more shining trinket. The shard was in the shape of a heart. "I know someone who might be a good candidate, and if you act a bit bolder and more stubborn, Lubayel will turn her shield towards the winner." Timur blushed. "She's an icicle on the outside, but inside... she likes you." She uttered these last three words in a conspiratorial whisper into the crimson ear.

Frida kissed Timur on the cheek and, grabbing Andy's elbow again, pulled him towards the orcs, who were packing up the tents on the platform. After a few minutes of standing there, Timur headed towards the Snow Elves' camp with a decisive step.

"?!"

"She really likes him," the vampire answered the question on the were-dragon's face, his eyebrows high. "Lubayel is being sent to Orten. Maybe things will work out for them." Andy nodded. He was wondering if anything would work out for *them*. For the last few hours, he'd been feeling as if he were in a red-hot frying pan. Lani's jealous glares were burning him from one side, and from the other—the quiet hatred and jealousy of the K'Rauu. *Apparently, the purple guy's partial to Frida. Hope he doesn't do anything devious out of unrequited love... but actually, he seems like a pretty good guy, nice and all....*

At the camp, they weren't able to sit around. Right away Ilnyrgu roped both love birds into helping unpack the tents and carrying various baggage here and there. Tyigu and the dragonlings were buzzing around the orcs. Their happy game of tag didn't add to the order or organization, of course, but no one dared chastise the frolicsome children.

Andy packed bales and looked at the group of mages setting up trellises on the portal site. Il mentioned in no uncertain terms that sorcerers can trace from the magic the coordinates of the exit point, and so, if he didn't want the location of his parents' valley to become known to a wide circle of people, he should exit some other place. He had to think. When someone goes through a portal, something called a short track is formed. By studying its intensity at the moment, the passage is closed and the force of the "residual" burst, mages can calculate the distance from the endpoint and the direction thereto. It was too late to change his mind; the spatial coordinates of his home, given to him at some point by Jaga, were firmly fixed in his head. He ought to think of countermeasures ahead of time; he couldn't allow the portal to be opened a second time by using the gate as it faded away. He would send all the others in his group straight to the valley, while he still had a few things to take care of....

The portal to Orten was open in an hour.

"Don't be a stranger." Timur slapped Andy on the shoulder. "Come visit me some time."

"You stay in touch too." His eyes, with their yellow vertical pupils, looked in the direction of the elf Lubayel. A blue glowing shard in the shape of a heart from the statue of Hel hung from her neck in the deep recess between her breasts. "Rigaud taught you well!"

The mage standing near the frame smiled politely.

"It's time. Say your goodbyes quickly, gentlemen!" The operator of the portal arch set an hourglass on the small folding table. "You have three minutes."

"Take care of yourself and Frida." Timur squeezed his friend's hand and stepped through the teleport. After him, Lubayel and a couple of mages with bags full of crystals followed through the haze.

"May the mercy and kindness of the Twins be with you," the elf said in parting.

"We'll now change the portal's destination point," the operator announced. "Should be ready for transport in half an hour. Please do not delay in providing the exit point."

***

Thirty minutes later, the portal was so crowded, no one had any elbow room. Fifteen mages were crammed onto the little platform, greedily looking at the saddlebag hanging on the back of the hass Slaisa was leading by the bridle. Even through the thick leather, the power of the large chunks of the former statue shone through. Andy shifted his weight from one paw to the other and licked his chops—what's in the pocket just in case never seems to take up space. He could still recall many Russian proverbs, and this one seemed to fit the situation. It meant some people had no need for more, but took it just in case. Ilnyrgu promised to place active defense mechanisms along the access roads to the valley. She would need the shards to power them. Miduel stood apart from the mages. In four hours, the elf had managed to get fairly familiar with the helrats' documents, and now the Rauu's face constantly reflected the painful thoughts he was enduring. Melima was supporting her great-great-grandfather by the arm. She and Frida had sat in the High Prince's tent for the last hour. Andy wasn't interested in knowing what they were talking about, but, apparently, the girls had come to a mutual understanding. Both the Rauu and the vampire had red noses and wet eyeballs after their conversation. Two dozen warriors stood around the High Prince, in full battle gear with activated defensive amulets. One got the impression that the dragons were preparing to attack the old elf. The griffon riders came to satisfy their curiosity. The whole crowd was humming loudly, with a few individuals, not shy, speaking at the top of their lungs. The griffons' clucking added to the cacophony.

"Are you coming to the dedication ceremony?" Andy heard Rur's quiet voice from off to the side. He looked with just his right eye at the K'Rauu and the vampire, saying good-bye. At first, he had taken the K'Rauu as a representative of the purple branch of the elven tribe. The suitor gently squeezed Frida's hand between his palms. Andy had to work hard at overcoming his jealousy. "Frai's going to take his maturity exam. He'll be glad to see you there for it."

"Targ, how could I forget? How many days are left?"

"Two weeks." Frida turned to the dragon. Andy nodded, saying that he saw no reason she couldn't go home.

"I'll come."

"Great. I'll tell Frai."

"Kerr." A strong jerk to the tip of his wing made Andy turn away from the extremely interesting conversation. *This Rur guy's hiding something.* Lanirra tugged a second time. "Kerr, the mages are calling you. Everything's ready. They need you to tell them the exit point, or else you'll be hovering in the clouds."

"I'm coming."

Andy went into the weaving of a transfer spell, placing runes one after another along with the exit point coordinates—the big boulder in the village, not far from the cave. Jagirra, back in the day, had made him learn a complex cluster, assuring him that everything you know comes in handy in life. *Well, she was right. It's going to be useful.* Closing his eyes, he connected to the astral and pushed energy into the resulting bodywork structure. At the third second of this, with a quiet clap, the haze of the activated portal appeared between the framework of the arch, sparkling all over.

The first to leave the former monastery were the she-wolves, Tyigu, and Frida. Then Rary and Rury dove through the arch, hurried along by the quiet roar of Lanirra, who was unhappy about something. The dragoness was constantly glancing at Andy and twitching the tips of her wings; she was obviously tortured by some sort of suspicions.

"The letter to my mother is in the back pocket of your knapsack," Andy whispered to Ilnyrgu, who tensed right up at the sound of it.

"You're not..."

"Go on. Don't make that face, everything's fine, calm down. Get Olaf and go through the portal, quickly."

Andy tensed up his wings and paws. Il shoved the red-headed Viking towards the carriage on the portal platform and slapped the last hass on the hindquarters. The animal's eyes were covered with special shields to blind it, as on horses when they pull carriages. It roared and in one leap jumped into the haze, dragging behind it the orc and the Norseman. It was time. Andy suddenly lifted off the ground, his giant wings flapping fast. A short bolt of lightning flew from the dragon's right paw and demolished the trellises. The portal clapped shut. Now it would be impossible to determine the exit coordinates. Having made a sharp turn, the dragon, hugging the ground, disappeared behind the wall of the former monastery. A few minutes later a dark shadow crossed the ridge and disappeared behind the tops of the giant pine trees.

***

"The bird flew the coup and left the Tantrian mages in the lurch. Are you certain your guys from the royal Guild wanted to follow wherever your winged protege might go?" Beriem uncorked a bottle of wine and poured the amber beverage into the crystal glasses. The grandson looked at his grandfather inquisitively, expecting him to answer and continue narrating, but the old Rauu cut his speech short. If someone had randomly walked into the tent just then, he probably would not have been able to tell the two elves apart. That elixir of dragon's blood the High Prince had imbibed gave him a short (by elvish standards) period of rejuvenated youth, changing his hundred-year-old appearance into that of a healthy man of about sixty. Miduel could easily get along without his cane, but suddenly quitting habits formed over centuries was easier said than done. The old elf, tapping the stick against his hip, was walking in circles around the little stool. Beriem watched his grandfather and wondered what he (Beriem) was doing here. What did the old elf need of him? Miduel was so authoritative in his demands, he had had to leave his unfinished inquiries in Orten and, with a brigade of bloodhounds from Tantre's Secret Chancellery, grabbing Drang, the head of the royal knights of the cloak, and dagger as company, build a portal to a former monastery of the One God. Grandfather had asked Drang to come because it was a matter of importance to the State. The Duke of Ruma was now, along with the Informants, investigating the cold basements and disemboweled laboratory, while the grandson was immediately brought to the High Prince's tent.

"We wanted to, don't doubt it," Miduel said, picking up his glass of the fizzy beverage. He sat down in the wicker chair. The wine, surrounded by the shining crystal, emitted gas in little bubbles like champagne and a tempting sweet scent. One bottle of the "Snow bubbly" cost ten golden pounds beyond the borders of the kingdom of the Rauu. Only the Tiron red was more expensive. The elves kept the recipes for preparing the sparkling wines a strictly guarded secret. The winery that produced the effervescent treasury income source was guarded no better or worse than the vault of gold. "Do you think your..." the High Prince accented the word *your*, "friend Drang, the Duke of Ruma, left the royal mages clear instructions? I didn't stop them.... One of the weaknesses of an alliance like that is the need to share information. But that's a strength too. What were they able to discover from the corpses of the 'knives' in the woods?"

"Didn't your friend tell you that?" the grandson quipped back.

"Knowing much leads to much anguish. The boy would rather stay silent regarding his adventures." Beriem snorted. "I think you can shed some light on certain circumstances that made him take the orcs in."

"You're going to be extremely surprised at these circumstances."

"I'm afraid I no longer can be surprised by anything. Pour me some more," Miduel held out his glass.

"How can I put this..." Beriem stood up. "How can I put this," he repeated, pouring the wine.

"Spit it out!" the grandfather hurried him along. He was dying of anticipation.

"The royal killers of the Steppe were hunting a certain half-orc and his daughter...." Beriem began and took a sip. The High Prince cleared his throat demandingly. His grandson looked at him and decided not to test fate by keeping silent any longer. A storm was raging inside the old elf underneath his imperturbable appearance, the echoes of which were reflected in the colorful flashes in his aura and the play of the fingers on the knob of the carved cane. Any minute now he might throw the cane aside and tear into his grandson with a good tongue-lashing... when was this? Two thousand years ago, or a bit longer? No, more recently, but it definitely happened. Beriem had had the carelessness of getting caught riding a griffon. Everything would have been fine if it weren't for the fact that there were no seatbelts on the saddle or anywhere. His grandfather unexpectedly gently chided his grandson, and then, taking him into the stables asked him to choose a whip made of a birch branch. The young elf did not suspect his grandfather's intentions and chose the strongest. How badly his rear end hurt afterward! The human method of discipline was now in the reckless rider's head for future use. He never again forgot to strap in, and he looked at the birch branch with fear for a long time afterward. Now his grandfather's aura was sparkling with the same colors in the same way as it had two thousand years ago. "Little Beri's" rear end began to ache, asking him to forgo dredging up those... um, vivid memories and not to call new problems down upon it. What if grandfather suddenly decided to repeat the lesson and go after his backside with the cane? As luck would have it, there's no birch branch handy in the tent!

"What is it? Are you recalling the episode with the birch branch?" Miduel creaked. "I have one, under the makeshift bed." He laughed a loud, rolling laugh, and in a couple of seconds, Beriem joined him. "There. We've had a good laugh," the granddad said, wiping a tear away from one eye. "Don't take it too far, or I'll order the guard to pick the leaves off the branch, and I'll remember my youth."

"Yes, even now I remember it." Beriem rubbed his bottom. "Ok, now to business. In Orten, my agents uncovered an interesting fact. It turns out our hero used to attend the school of Berg the half-orc under supremely interesting circumstances. The half-orc's former governess told us that Berg met a certain young man when he saved his daughter's life. During a walk, the girl became the victim of an accident. A carriage went running wild, and it hit the corner of the building. A piece of the spring mechanism flew out and pierced the girl's chest and lung. The young man in a student's jacket made her drink a strange elixir—and in an hour, there were no traces of her wounds. The girl ate fried beef liver like a horse after that. The strange elixir seems to have the effect of a potion with dragon's blood. The half-orc, grateful for having saved his daughter's life, invited the bookworm to study at his fencing school. I became very interested in the fact that an unknown mix got permission to open a business. Drang's bloodhounds turned the magistrate upside-down and interrogated all the clerks who were still alive after the revolt was put down. The civil servants did not hide the fact that the permission was bought for a bribe of three thousand golden pounds, which were brought to the magistrate's cash register. The half-orc was obligated to provide a month-long course every six months to the city guards for free and to make a voluntary contribution of two thousand coins under the table. In five years of doing business in the city, Berg only got good reviews, a good reputation, and a huge success. But what was a master orc swordsman doing in Orten? Our agents in the Steppe got their hands on a portrait of the swordsman and set out to learn something about the master named Berg. How surprised I was when the answer came the next day. My agent informed me that yes—there was a combat master by that name, and not only was he there, but he was very well known in Queen Lagira's court. True, she was a princess at that time. Nobles in the know whispered that Lagira had a good time in the arms of the middle son of the Primary "knee" Prince-Khan. Then the princess suddenly grew cold towards her suitor and isolated herself in a country palace. Eight months later, a wave of inexplicable murders swept through the country. The Uragar clan was practically cut off at the root, and the Primary "knee" Khan fell out of grace with Lagira, who would sit on the throne after the death of her father, Hadar the Third. A week later, the Prince-Khan died. They say it was his heart, but I find that hard to believe. What does the Uragar clan have to do with it? Berg took a wife from that clan. The half-orc himself disappeared soon after."

"And in a year, he turned up on the other end of the continent with a little daughter in his arms. Go on."

Beriem coughed into his fist, took a sip of wine, and went on with his story:

"After that just details. The agent, through a whole regiment of our puppets, gave us a portrait of the young princess of the white orcs." A thin tablet made of yew lay on the table. It displayed a portrait of a very young girl dressed in a beautiful white dress and elegant slippers with little pearls on them. Little Tyigu bore a strong resemblance to her royal mother.

"Does Drang know?"

"No, our official task was to find Kerr. My subordinates have worked very well. Haven't left a trace."

"Good. Take it away, or better yet..." Miduel threw the tablet with the portrait into the brazier. "Burn it. The girl is actually the person with the most right to the Steppe throne, which I'm sure bothers the Queen. The illegitimate daughter could become the center of a plot against her rule or demand the right to the throne after her mother dies. This is veeery interesting," the High Prince grew pensive.

"Does the dragon know about this?"

"Most likely. But what a bugger, huh?" The grandfather snapped out of his thoughts and looked happily at his grandson.

"Who?"

"Kerr. There's a play actor who's even worse than the two of us put together. He bought me off with the priests' papers, while he hid the little princess from curious eyes. Do you know how to hide something like that? In plain sight. The girl was right in front of us the whole time, went gallivanting about the camp with the little dragons, and no one even thought that the tomboy with scraped knees and callused hands from her wooden sword was the offspring of a royal. Wait!" Miduel suddenly fell silent, stopped by some idea which he was now examining from all sides. "Did your rangers manage to remove the information prints in the forest?"

"A small portion of them. It's not possible to reconstruct the entire picture of the battle using just them. It's fortunate they managed to do even that. One more day and the energy would have dissipated entirely, and we could not have gotten any information from the scene or the ground after a heavy rain."

"I don't need the whole picture. Tell me, did the dragon attack the 'knives' right away?"

"No, we know that for sure. There were about ten or fifteen minutes between the time the knives attacked the caravan and the time the dragon got involved. Why are you so interested in the details?"

"Because the girl is a universal mage of all elements! The pause between the time the 'knives' attacked Berg's people and the moment the dragon showed up can be explained by the fact that Kerr was far away. But he could feel the mental call and flew to her aid!"

"What advantage does knowing that give us?"

"It tells me not to recommend making any plans for the girl, or we'll lose all support from the dragons, and maybe make enemies of them, which is extremely undesirable." Beriem carefully listened to his grandfather and said nothing. A mysterious smile on the old elf's lips told him that he still had a few aces up his sleeve. "Come on, tell me what you're not saying."

"It's about Drang and his daughter-in-law—Irma Lei von Bokk. Duke Ruma will be a grandfather six months from now...."

"And what does the duke's family life have to do with our boy?"

"He and the current bride were once close. We were able to obtain that juicy little bit of information from a classmate and former friend of Irma's."

"Of course. Wonders never cease regarding that boy. We're not going to trail the wife of the son of the fourth most important person in the kingdom. But, as soon as the child is born, we must test him for the ability to wield all the elements."

"Should we tell Drang?"

Miduel choked on his wine.

"How hot is it in Orten? Perhaps your brains have been boiled?" he asked his grandson, coughing.

"I just had to ask, that's all. Did you say something about some papers? These ones?" Beriem pointed to the pile of papers lying on a second little table. "Can I take a look?"

The papers, however, remained untouched for a few more minutes. They heard Drang's voice from outside, chastising the blazes out of someone, obviously one of his subordinates. The elves' discussion took place under a double-solid curtain of silence, which had one unique feature—it allowed sound in from the outside. The grandfather and his grandson sat in silence and listened to the foul language. Miduel shook his head judgmentally. In his opinion, a government employee of such a high rank had no right to lower himself to the level of vulgar swearing in front of his subordinates. Beriem had no problem with strong words—he knew Duke Ruma much better, which meant something very serious must have happened to send the usually calm and phlegmatic Drang flying off the handle.

Soon the curtain covering the entrance was moved to the side, revealing before the elves' eyes the enraged head of the Tantrian Chancellery. Drang's face was as red as a beet. His eyes flashed like lightning; his clothes smelled like a hint of yellow lotus pollen. Tantre's leading nark stopped at the entrance, tore his cloak off and threw it on the ground.

"The dolt!" his exclamation flew down after the cloak.

Beriem retrieved a third wine glass from his trunk and gave the angry man some wine. Drang took the cup from the elf's hand, poured the beverage down his throat in one gulp, asked for more, and only then did he make a slight bow in Miduel's direction.

"Please forgive me, Your Highness!"

"What happened? The High Prince creaked.

Drang waved gestured helplessly.

"That… that…" the representative of King Gil just couldn't find the right word. "That snufl[14] spawn was careless enough to drop the suitcase!"

"What suitcase?"

"The one with the drugs made from lotus pollen, confiscated from the helrats' laboratory. A cloud of narcotic dust hung over the entire squadron that was climbing the stairs. Uf." Drang plopped down in a third seat and stretched out his legs with much relish. "I never would have thought I was capable of running like that. True, that brute who dropped the suitcase can run even faster. Now fifteen people are good for absolutely nothing until tomorrow. Four of them are knocked out completely. Three

---

[14] Snufl—a warty toad

have become grown-up babies. They're saying *goo-goo ga-ga* and blowing bubbles. Five of the guards are running around after butterflies, and three more had to be immobilized by magic to prevent them from mauling anyone. They flew into a rage and began attacking anyone in sight." The Rauu glanced at one another. Their faces remained masks of indifference, but their auras were glowing with all colors of the rainbow. "Now imagine what would have happened had I been delayed just one minute. Have you imagined? The head of the Secret Chancellery would be blowing bubbles or picking flowers with a look of euphoria on his face!" Beriem turned around. His shoulders trembled slightly. The High Prince continued listening to the interesting story in his imperturbable mask, and the vein twitching under his right eye was the only clue to contradict his complete indifference. "I almost turned into a baby, without any magic at all…."

Now the reason for his tirade outside was clear. The man who ran away from the narcotic cloud may not have breathed the filth in, but the dust that came into contact with his bare skin seemed to have had the effect of lowering his inhibitions somewhat.

"Were the Informants with you?" Miduel asked.

"Thank the Twins, the bloodhounds had left the catacombs by then. That's what saved the rest. When they heard my cries, the Informants called up a gust of wind and blew the narcotic cloud away from people, saving them from death by overdose."

"That's good. We'll need the Informants today."

"Again something to investigate?" Drang asked, finishing his wine.

"I'm afraid so," Miduel picked up the pile of papers Andy had given him. "Read this and tell me what you both think of it."

"What have we here?"

"Read it," the ancient Rauu leaned back in his chair and closely watched his grandson and the Tantrian with half-closed eyelids.

As the papers were being read, the man's face grew more and more serious. The light stupor left him; wrinkles appeared on Drang's forehead. The old elf saw how the duke sometimes pondered seemingly insignificant, at first glance, data for a long time. Drang's mind, intricate in intrigues, analyzed every word and paragraph. Sometimes the head of the special services set aside one sheet and frantically began to look for another, and when he found it, compared what was written on another sheet and put the finds aside. An hour later, when it was completely dark outside, Drang read the last document.

"There's a map missing here," he said, massaging his temples. "There are plenty of references to it in the text, but I could not find it with the papers. A few sheets indicating certain people who are important links in the helrat chain are missing also. And another discrepancy: certain extracts are obviously taken from other document folders. They're fragments and incomplete or totally not connected to the general topic, and a few of them contain references to archival folders. I'm afraid to guess what's there—probably it's compromising material. But compromising for whom? I'm one hundred percent sure they're somebody's dirty laundry. The Servants of Death were afraid of their own archives because the mention of them was so veiled that if I didn't have experience as an investigator, I wouldn't have noticed them."

"That's correct. I too came to just the same conclusion. I'm only afraid that we'll never see that map, and we'll learn of the deaths of the people noted in the missing papers from official obituaries," Miduel said. "The dragon took the map and the papers. For some reason, I doubt he'll be having any conversations with the dragon killers."

"I don't know what the dragon will do, but all my bloodhounds are immediately heading out to search for the secret sheets," the duke grabbed a few sheets that deviated from the general context. "So, we can take energy traces from these papers and check the geocaches of the residual background. They should lead us to the archives."

Drang called two mages into the tent. The Guild members, using instruments, measured and recorded the traces from the papers and, once they'd been assigned their task, set out.

"Now we just have to wait for the results of the search," Beriem summed up the situation.

The search went on all night. The next morning, another squadron of bloodhounds was discharged from Kion, which had undergone special trace tracking courses and training in localizing the geocaches on the residual magical and energy background.

Drang wanted to go back to the capital already when the mages found what they were looking for. It was three in the afternoon, and the duke and the pair of royal Rauu were dining on Kiki birds baked in a clay oven. In violation of all written and unwritten protocols, three Snow Elves entered the tent and put several boxes of numbered folders at Miduel's feet.

"Shall we read?" the old elf asked the other two.

"I've suspected for a long time that the Imperial higher-ups were consorting with 'ghouls,' but I didn't think they were doing it so often and with so many common interests involved. The dirt here can't be wiped away before Hel's court," the duke lovingly stroked the archival Talmud. "With a treasure like this in our hands, we can seriously spoil the relationship of the Church to the Patskoi Empire, bring down important figures of the highest circles of the Imperial Court, and present the Emperor in the worst possible light. It's very likely that the Patron can be forced to convene a local council of Cardinals or prepare a conclave, and then the head of the hierarchy of the One God will roll. I propose not opening the second and third boxes here, but waiting until we get to Kion...."

The Valley of a Thousand Streams. Karegar and Jagirra. Two weeks and five days ago...

"Charda!" Jaga looked at her pupil and shook her head judgmentally. "Charda, how many times do I have to tell you that your hair should be tied up in a handkerchief when you're sorting the harvest into bags? Not a single hair can fall into the herbs—not one!"

The girl looked down guiltily. She was ashamed, but what could she do with that mop growing on her head? No kerchief could hold her wild red locks. She pulled her hair back into tight braids and tied two scarves around her head, but it was all in vain. Single strands first escaped from the braids, and then somehow got out of the scarves. The Mistress had it easy: her hair didn't have a life of its own. They were tightly bound in a beautiful thick braid that hung below the waist. Shining like pure mountain snow, it did not at all resemble the red serpent that had taken up residence behind Charda's back.

"Sorry, Mistress."

Her mentor sighed, then immediately smiled, and set a small chopped block of wood up vertically. It seemed a bone comb appeared out of nowhere in the Rauu's hand.

"Come here," Jagirra called the girl over. "Sit down." The elf's finger poked the small block of wood. Charda obediently sat down on the surface Jagirra indicated.

Singing a long drawn-out ditty in some unknown language, Jagirra re-braided her student's hair. Charda listened to her pretty, well-trained voice. The curly red mop became soft and workable under the elf's exacting fingers. Overflowing with a copper sheen, they were twisted into thin braids, whimsically intertwined with one another, and the five flowing brooks flowed into one braid, gathered by a wide green ribbon. The comb in the old herbalist's hand did not poke into her scalp, tearing hairs out from the roots, but gently combed along them, which made Charda squeeze her eyes shut tightly. She felt like a house cat ready to start purring at any moment under her Mistress's warm hands.

"Now that's better," Jaga said, rubbing her palm over Charda's head and throwing a handkerchief around her shoulders. "

"Tie it up. Tell me what the "Sial" recipe is used for and why hair can't get in it?"

"For creating love spells, Mistress."

"Mmm-hmm, and what else?" the elf prompted the girl.

"If any contaminants or foreign matter gets into the mix, such as a hair, then the owner of the hair might fall under the magical recoil of the spell that's cast to activate the herbs," she said quietly and blushed.

"That's correct, and then you'll be suffering from unrequited love from some unknown person, or hate him with all your heart, depending on what kind of potion it is. Now you understand why it's so important to be vigilant and careful about the components?" Charda nodded. "Even in herbs, every detail matters! Now that you understand that, go back to work and try not to let your hair get in the herb mix," she said, smiling.

"Thank you, Mistress," Charda said, tying the kerchief on her head.

Charda went back to the dried herbs laid out under an awning. She once again checked the paper packets containing the crushed leaves. She couldn't find a single hair or contaminant in any of the packets. Sighing in relief, she picked up a knife and placed tiny, thin weights on a special scale. Working under the shade of the awning, she periodically glanced at her mentor. The Rauu brought a few trunks out of the house and was airing out and folding the clothes in them. In between every heap of aired-out laundry, she placed bunches of fragrant red leaves which maintained the freshness of the material and did not allow ants, moths, or other insects into the trunk. Then the elf opened a new trunk, took out a man's shirt and sat motionless for a long time, looking at the intricate design embroidered on the collar. Smoothing the folds of the shirt, Jaga hung it on a clothesline, next to a pair of canvas pants. Quietly humming the "Song of the Sky," which was sung in temples to the Twins as a prayer of blessing on family and loved ones, the elf sat back on the stump Charda had been sitting on just twenty minutes ago. The herbalist's right hand rubbed her left shoulder, where, under the thin material of her modest summer house dress, the skin bore a tattoo of a little dragon surrounded by runes. Jagirra had drawn the exact same tattoo on Kerr a week before his departure to Orten. Charda turned away. It wasn't nice to watch her mentor when her soul was missing her son. The girl knew that the elf had not carried Kerr under her heart or given birth to him, but the thin plaque with his name on it in the "ancestors' corner" told her so much.

Jagirra was aware of the pupil's careful gaze but didn't turn around. A few seconds later, the feeling of being watched subsided. She stood up from the stump and walked over to the shirt. She'd been tormented with worry for her adopted son for ten whole days already. The tattoo worn by Kerr on his shoulder, besides being beautiful and a sign of his heritage, had one more quality that the boy never suspected. Through the dragon and the runes, which were magically connected to their copy on Jaga's shoulder, she could know whether the recipient of the other tattoo were dead or alive at any moment. The elf looked at the enchanted shirt she'd made for Kerr and couldn't stand it. Ten days ago, she'd felt a sharp pain pierce her whole being. She was flying on Karegar at the time, and she almost fell off. That is, she did fall, but the dragon darted downward and caught the herbalist in his front paws. Going unconscious from the pain, she couldn't activate a levitation spell and, if it hadn't been for Karegar, she would have certainly fallen the four leagues to her death. Managing to tell the dragon to fly her home, she asked him to leave her be and walked up to the entrance with a heavy step. She waved at her winged husband, so he would fly away and not trample the lawn, slammed the door behind her, and without any strength, slid down the wall to the floor.

Charda jumped over and caught her mentor, then dragged her to her bed, and sat up all night with the suffering elf, who was tormented by nightmares in a restless sleep. That night Jaga dreamt of wings torn to shreds, a wide river, and the drone of a hard rain. Blurry vague images flashed before her, but she could not understand a single one.

In the morning she had a serious conversation with Karegar. The dragon had not flown away, but laid under the huge oak tree the whole time. The black monster interrogated her passionately. The dragon nervously twitched the tips of his wings and inquired scrupulously about her fall from his neck. He wouldn't hear a word of her excuses, saying she simply got tired out and dozed off. She had to tell him the truth that she suddenly felt very ill, and then she let out some excuse. She tactfully and cunningly avoided telling him why exactly she felt so bad. Karegar did not know about the tattoo. He hadn't paid attention to the herbalist's shoulder in three thousand years; he wasn't about to start now. But even if he had, he wouldn't have seen anything. Jaga had the ability to hide the tattoo on her skin from others' eyes. Charda knew about it. She had noticed it on her mentor's shoulder when they were bathing in a bathhouse located at the hot springs that flowed from underground half a league from Jaga's house. The elf forgot to control it, relaxing in the hot water, and realized something was up when she felt her student's eyes on her. What was "up" showed up on her shoulder and grew bright with various colors. Charda got strict orders not to tell anyone what she had seen and promised to keep quiet about it, even if threatened with death. The actual image of the dragon wasn't that rare, but the intricate pattern of runes around it and the colorful background would have stirred up a lot of questions with anyone well-versed in ancient heraldry. Karegar, for one. The tailed dad hadn't seen the artwork on his son's shoulder either, as Kerr got the same instructions not to show it to his father until Jaga gave him the go-ahead. She had no time to teach Kerr how to hide the tattoo as she could, but the herbalist hoped that by the time he came back from his studies, she would have found the courage to tell her de-facto husband the whole truth. Jagirra knew that the ancient secrets would come to light sooner or later and that when they did, it would not be good. Enira had warned her about this in the letter she wrote before her passing.

"I'm done," she heard Charda say from the awning.

Charda deftly stacked the packets of herbs into a basket. The apothecary scales she used to measure the weight of the herbs were neatly folded into a special box.

"Great job, hon."

Jagirra walked up to the girl and helped her tie up the unused herbs into packets, after which she hung them under the awning roof. It was true, she'd found a great apprentice. The deceased Larga was a good judge of character. She could very easily see into a person's soul. Charda's soul and thoughts were pure.

Enira had selected the red-haired young lady in a village that had been devastated by "greenies." The orcs attacked a border human settlement, killed all the adults, and taken the children as prisoners. The girl was five at the time, and she had been lucky: her mother, before dying by the non-humans' swords, managed to hide her daughter in the basement. The ambulance wagon arrived at the outskirts of the settlement three hours after the last orc left. The "greenies" didn't burn houses—smoke was fine signal to the royal guards and could possibly let them know which direction to organize the chase. The Larga walked along the streets filled with blood and looked at the bodies with true vision—what if someone was still alive and needed help? No one was around. Enira passed between the houses and in one of them noticed the slight glow of an aura. Soon she heard a child crying. That's how Charda met her "grandmother."

When she got to the valley, the girl was truly worried how her granny would fare without her. When she asked to go to the city, Jagirra said no and told her that Enira was no longer alive. She offered her shelter at her house. Jaga had not once regretted that decision. The girl remembered each herb from the first time she was shown it. Jaga never had to explain what each one was for ten times over. Charda also did an excellent job at memorizing the best gathering times, conservation methods, and preparation techniques for each one. If things kept up like this, in a year, Jaga would have nothing more to teach.

The red-headed beauty truly came into her own during the course of the months she had lived in the valley. She blossomed like a rose in the morning. The village inhabitants began to visit the herbalist's house quite often for various drugs. Especially the young men. It seemed they'd been struck with the plague. Jagirra, smiling on the inside, asked her pupil to give patients this or that medicine.

The "malady" infected Dita worse than anyone else, the son of the leather-tanner, who had a cough one week and a bruise the next. A week ago, the invalid's father, Duke, paid a visit to Jagirra. The big healthy guy timidly called Jaga aside and bowing low, began to discuss the fact that the source of his son's illnesses was residing in her home, and if the Mistress didn't object, then for the sake of his offspring's spiritual recovery, he would send matchmakers. The Mistress had no objection, of course. She could see very well that Dita's "malady" was contagious, that Charda had caught it too, that she looked at the hunky guy with goo-goo eyes. Let the matchmakers come, but wait at least half a year. When Charda turned eighteen, they would be welcome at our doorstep. But for now, she lived under Karegar and Jagirra's roof. There was one other condition as well: Dita's beloved must not give up her studies or herbalism either before or after the wedding. The tanner nodded slightly in agreement to the elf's terms, whistled to Gmar who was hiding behind the bushes thinking the Mistress didn't see him and headed off to the village with the good news. When she found out about the subject of their conversation, the pupil fell down at the Mistress's feet and tried to kiss her hand, for which she was punished and sent to gather clover. Barely able to contain her joy at the punishment selected, the girl immediately recovered her dignity and went out to the woods where a certain helper joined her. Jaga was glad that the orphan's fate was turning out so well. She went on worrying about her adopted son.

"Mistress, will Kerr come back to the valley before my wedding?" Charda asked, smashing the elf's whirling thoughts into shards.

"He should," Jaga answered. "Why do you care about that, honey?"

"Dita and I want him to walk us up to the Twins' hands," she said, smiling.

Jagirra smiled too. They were getting ahead of themselves—thought of everything already—who would walk them to the Twins, and how to ask Gorn for his blessing.

Interrupting that vital conversation for every bride, the sound of beating wings rang out in the sky. Raising a small cloud of dust from the earth with the stream of air, Karegar landed in the field. The elf left Charda under the awning and went to meet the dragon.

She hadn't yet taken two steps when she felt a strange discomfort. First, the tattoo on her shoulder began to itch incredibly, and then a wave of inexplicable heat swept over the herbalist. Mana gushed like a river into her inner storage space. Karegar also felt something was off. He saw the magic overflowing around the elf and sensed its influx into himself as well. He hadn't felt anything like that in a long time.

The flow of mana was getting greater and greater. The image on her shoulder began to glow like fire. Jaga felt a high and an increase in strength in the first moments, but now she was experiencing fear instead—what if the influx of external energy didn't end? Her fear became the pain. The energy was beating at her with the force of a battering ram. Unable to contain herself, the elf shouted in pain. The powerful flow of someone else's energy demolished all her inner barriers and didn't show signs of slowing down.

"What's happening to you?" Karegar's voice came to her as if through a thick layer of insulation. The snout of the dragon leaning over her was swimming in a red haze. "You're burning up!"

The fire overtook the elf's clothing. Her summer dress and homespun woolen skirt were reduced to black tatters, but, as strange as it seemed, not a single hair on her body was burned. Jagirra felt the strings of an ancient spell breaking, one after another, under the force of the mana. She dashed off to the woods: something was happening….

"Stop!" Karegar turned about on the spot awkwardly and took off after her. "Jaga, what's happening to you??"

She ran on, paying no heed to the branches and twigs barring her path and flinging back in her face. Stumps, sticks, and ditches didn't stop her. She was flying fast as if she had wings. Fear and pain chased her onward. The insane flow of energy Jaga was experiencing for the first time in her long life was destroying the shackles that were placed on her three thousand years ago. Behind her, forgetting that he had wings and breaking down trees with his body, Karegar made his way through the thickets.

There was a bright flash in her head. The last string snapped. The shackles disintegrated. Jagirra was flung down on the ground and arched her back. The elf lost control of herself as if she were having an epileptic seizure. Tearing a couple young maples trees out by the roots and trampling a hazelnut tree down in the mud, Karegar burst onto the scene and tried to pick Jaga up in his paws, but the elf turned away and crawled away.

"No, don't look, don't touch me," she cried, feeling the flow of mana go down to a small trickle and then dry up completely. She knew she was too weak to stop the transformation at this point. "Don't look!"

It was no use. Karegar, frozen on the spot like a black sculpture, stared at the crystal dragon sprawled out on the grass where the elf used to be.

***

"Why, Jaga, why?" It seemed the old dragon had forgotten all other words, repeating "why, why" like a mantra. His neck was as straight as a pole, but he shook his head from side to side. Karegar stood on the edge of the field and quietly whispered this one word. Jaga, how could she? Why hadn't she told him? Why had she kept silent about it these past two thousand years? Why? Did she truly not trust him enough to be afraid to tell him? He felt, he knew—a simple Snow Elf couldn't smell like a dragon, but why had she hidden her essence from him? Two thousand years—TWO THOUSAND! Would he not have understood? He accepted her as an elf. He was prepared to share his life with her... why? It was so painful... he felt so empty inside, and he felt so nasty from the lack of trust. It was disgusting that she, the one he trusted more than his own self, had spit on the trust in their relationship. Did she really feel that rotten ancient secrets were more important than he was? Why? Jagirra was a dragon. He ought to jump for joy—but his reaction was the exact opposite. He felt horrible inside. He looked at the crystal dragoness, shining with golden scales with green vine-like designs on her sides, and thought that he did not know Jaga at all. All this time he'd been living with a ghost.

"Karegar...," the dragoness stood up on her wobbly legs. Karegar flinched and took a step back from the sound of his name coming from her lips.

"No," he said and paced back in small steps along the hole cut out ten minutes ago by his body. "Don't say my name."

"Karegar. Forgive me, I..." Jagirra took a step towards her de facto husband.

"No, don't come near me. I trusted you. I thought I knew you. I was wrong." Karegar pushed off the ground with all four paws and flew away. "You can forget the way to my cave, got it?"

Jagirra, watching the black spot in the sky get smaller and smaller, fell to the ground in a heap. Her legs couldn't hold her up. The uncontrolled transformation had zapped her of all strength. She wasn't surprised that after three thousand years of life without wings, her true nature immediately took its toll as soon as it was freed from its fetters. She would have to sleep outside. If she changed her hypostasis in her sleep, her house would simply burst. *What timing. Enira, why didn't you warn me that it would be like this? How can I be seen by the one I truly love and who I pushed away with my secrets? Should I tell him the truth and push him away forever? Or should I not tell.... All powerful goddesses, why don't you give me a choice? No matter which way I look, there's only rapids and whitewater....*

Jagirra's thoughts swirled around Karegar. Right now she couldn't think about anything else. How could she tell him that she couldn't transform? He could sense that she wasn't like an ordinary Rauu! What should she do and what could she do? Now she could find words and get him back, but what would happen when he found out who she really was? Jaga had long ago forbidden herself to think about the past. She buried it in an abyss of oblivion and stopped calling herself a Lady of the Sky.... Who was she fooling? She forgot, she buried it, she stopped... but every day the sky called to her. For three thousand years she dreamed of wings, and her pillow, wet with tears, did not let her forget what was lost in the darkness of ages.

A branch snapped in the ditch Karegar had made on his way there. Jaga lifted her head and was face to face with Charda.

"M-mistress?" the girl's voice trembled from worry and fear.

"Yes, my child," the dragoness answered in a serious tone.

"I-is that really you?"

"Charda, now's not the time for stupid questions. Go, run home please, and bring me the long shirt I hung out to dry on the clothesline, and don't forget the sash."

"Yes, ma'am. I'll be right back!"

The girl's actions were true to her words. Soon a light, quick pitter-patter of feet running towards her informed Jaga the girl had returned with the things she ordered. Jaga changed hypostasis. Charda gasped in amazement and bit her fist. The student's eyes were as big as saucers. With the fist still in her mouth, Charda watched as her mentor donned the man's shirt. Jaga activated a "staying" spell. Now the enchanted shirt would disappear at the moment she took on the winged hypostasis and reappear when she again took on elf form. For now, she had to borrow her son's clothes; later she would enchant a couple of dresses for herself.

"Mistress, the house is that way," Charda said, overcoming her fear. Jagirra, after she took a couple of steps towards the woods, stopped and looked over her shoulder:

"But Karegar's cave is that way!"

Neither Charda nor her mentor, upset by recent events and weighed down by sad thoughts, noticed a human figure on the edge of the clearing.

Maruna, Duke the tanner's wife, was gathering mushrooms in the oak grove. The wicker basket was half full when the Mistress ran by in her birthday suit, twenty paces away. Jagirra was acting like she was being chased by a herd of long-maned wolves. She did not notice anything around her and the Snow Elf's beautiful face was distorted with suffering. Upon hearing the guttural cry of a dragon and the crackling of trees being trampled down, Maruna squeezed herself between two thick roots of a thousand-year-old oak and, pressed against the ground, looked on in horror as Karegar chased after her. Trying to calm down her heart that was beating like hunted hare's, she ran after them, staying hidden behind trees and crouched down to the ground. Her curiosity turned out to be greater than her fear.

"Merciful Hel!" the curious country peasant whispered, crawling through the bushes, getting her clothes all dirty and losing the mushrooms in her basket. "The Mistress is a dragon! What will happen now, what??" The woman hid from the old were-dragon in a deep ditch and lay there a long time, not moving. What she had seen frightened her to the core. Karegar had flown away a while ago already. Charda ran into the clearing where the dragoness was from the direction of Jaga's house, and then back in that direction again. But Maruna decidedly stayed put. She wasn't about to leave her relatively safe spot. "I have to tell the others," she decided finally. Carefully, trying not to step on any dry twigs, she made her way towards the village.

***

"Go away!" the strong roar drowned out the sound of the water droplets and the noise of the waterfalls spread out over the lake.

"No!" the answer came loud and clear.

A long blast of fire came from the mouth of the cave.

"I won't leave."

"Then I will!" The lake water seemed to ripple from the force of this angry cry.

"... you... I won't let you."

"What's that?" Gmar darted back ten feet from the slight touch to the shoulder and whisper in his ear.

"Duke!" the dwarf's hair barely sparkled, he was so afraid. "You nearly frightened me to Hel's court!"

"What?"

"Chicken butt! They're fighting, can't you hear?" Gmar squatted down near a fat pine and turned his head towards the dragon's cave.

"All powerful Twins, who could have thought!" Duke said to no one in particular. The forms of the curious village ladies continually flashed and disappeared behind the bushes. "What do you want?" the tanner snapped.

The branches on the edge of the field began to flutter. The muffled voices of the gawking busybodies and the pitter-patter of many feet could be heard. The women were either running off to the woods or changing their position—probably the latter.

"What do ya think, will they make up, or no?" the tanner asked, spitting on the ground near the dwarf.

"I wish they would," Gmar answered, scratching his scalp as its bright color flared. "We won't be able to live if they don't bury the hatchet. I don't want to leave the valley."

"And what's he so mad at her about? Just think...."

"Quiiiiet!" Gmar held up his hand.

Something flashed blindingly on the overhang at the mouth of the dragon's cave. There was an outraged roar. A fireball smashed into the cliff near some rainbows from the waterfalls. Stone debris flew in all directions, whistling and knocking down the tops and branches of giant pines. The dragon appeared at the edge of the mountain platform.

"Stop!" The golden dragoness threw herself onto the black giant's back. Karegar tried to free himself from her grip with his claws. He didn't hold back, and both dragons, in a death grip, plummeted into the creek that led to the lake directly underneath the overhang.

"Bug-eyed Targ…," Duke said, slack-jawed.

"Let's get out of here!" Gmar grabbed his friend by the sleeve and pulled him into the forest. Up ahead, branches crackled under the village women's feet, who had realized before the men had that it's better to stay as far away as possible from a pair of fighting dragons. Safer if one values one's health and life….

***

"Alright," Jagirra said, climbing onto the shore and lying flat on the hot stones. "I'll go. I can't get used to it," she added quietly.

Karegar said nothing. He stood over the former elf and looked at the light playing on her golden scales.

"Answer me. Why?" he asked, flicking blood from his right front paw.

Jaga looked guiltily at what her claws had done. She'd ripped a few large scales from her de facto husband's forequarter. She turned away.

"Would you have believed me?" she said dully, looking at the dark lake water. "Or could you have helped me get rid of the spell?" Karegar didn't answer. "What do you know about 'snares'?"

"I'm not an expert in transplantology and polymorphic magic," he responded quietly. The old dragon didn't know what to do with himself. It seemed he'd overdone it, giving in to frenzy and hurt feelings and pride.

Jagirra apparently wanted to say something in response, but thought twice about it. A translucent membrane fell over the dragon's eyes. For a few minutes she lay there motionless. Only the periodic twitching of the tips of her wings and tail gave away her agitation. From that same pose, not turning her head and not opening the membrane lids on her eyes, she said:

"I was only one hundred and fifty years old, just a snot-nosed kid, when I got the idea into my head of wanting a second hypostasis. It was so popular. All my friends and the older dragons had two hypostases. The girls had their circles and their secrets. They would sneak off to elves and humans, and only I was different. I wasn't interesting. No one wanted to talk to me. What could you talk about with a dragon who knew nothing of clothes and had never kissed a man? At university the talk was all such-and-such a dragon had picked up another 'victim' from the simple mortals. Now I understand that they were subtly and carefully pushing me towards that decision, through my friends and so-called girlfriends, but then, in order to 'come into my own,' I decided to undergo the Ritual. The magical changes didn't hurt at all. It was so interesting and unusual to not have wings, to get an attractive human face, hands and feet instead of a tail, paws and wings. At night my girlfriends and I used to change hypostasis and run off to the human city—it was so exciting and enchanting. The cavaliers and the knights, the balls, getting invited to parties and men's attention, and how I loved it when mortal women would despise me, and their powerlessness before a Lady of the Sky! Life was so full of adventure... idiot! For a whole year I went on living this double life, and then my father died. I think the dragons took too much from the elves and the humans. I think my father was 'helped' when he went to meet Hel. Before that day I didn't know I had enemies. It turns out I was very sadly mistaken. A few attempts on my life made me ask for help from my uncle, who was appointed the leader until a certain dumb young dragoness came of age. I was stupid enough to believe him and agreed to live in the mountains until everything blew over. If only I'd known my worst enemy was hiding behind my uncle's resplendent smile and kind eyes, my uncle, who was patting my head as I was in elf hypostasis and crying my eyes out. I flew to the mountains hoping for peace and quiet, naive girl that I was. The place became a prison. I don't remember how many days I sat in that notrium cell without food or water, but as soon as my strength left me...," Jagirra sobbed and covered her head with her wing. "... my uncle himself cast the 'snare' spell on me. The scoundrel, he couldn't kill a dragon, but the death of a lowly orphaned elf would pass unnoticed. I found aid in escaping. Hiding from my uncle's spies, I made my way to Ilanta. War was raging around me. The lone Snow Elf turned out to be no good to anyone except thieves and rapists. The dragons were far away, could they come to my aid? Answer me! You say nothing…. In order to survive, I had to kill rapists and thieves, and not only them. Elves, humans and dwarfs… I can't count how many people died at my hands. After a month, the way back was closed to me forever. The last true bloods went to Nelita and sealed the portals. If I had known that this was only the beginning," the dragon stood up from the stone and plopped into the lake, stomach first. Karegar looked on mesmerized at the ripples on the surface of the lake from the tears falling from the dragon's cheeks. "Six months later the pain started. My body was trying to turn back into its natural form. I tried to fight the magical shackles, but it was no use. I'll tell you without trying to feign modesty—I'm a strong mage, even though I never finished my studies; and, nevertheless, all my magic was not enough to remove the spell. No one was that strong. Only a blood relative could break the spell. Pain, hundreds of years of pain I felt every day, the involuntary transformations, when all of a sudden my elf body was covered in scales or the fangs would grow back in my mouth, and I was doubled over. The caves of the Berit Mountains became my home. I hid there from prying eyes. Then, it was easy—there were no humans or elves for hundreds of leagues around. The rare bands of dwarf prospectors were happy to share old clothes and news with the Spirit of the mountains. The pain went away little by little. My body stopped fighting, it and I went out among people and began to learn and sell herbs. Two thousand years ago, I met Enira—the White Larga, who immediately recognized me as a dragon. She's the one who led me to you."

Karegar stepped into the water and stood alongside Jagirra. He remembered the old witch well. The fortune teller came to the valley once and stayed there for three months. The black dragon didn't touch the lonely woman. On the contrary, he seldom brought her a portion of his game in exchange for stories from the outside world. One fine day the zavis' cart wasn't where she usually parked it. It had disappeared as if it had never been there.

"Enira said," Jaga went on, "that she would take me to my destiny. When I saw you, I realized the Larga was right. You are my destiny. No matter that I couldn't fly with you on a wedding flight. I could just live near you. I forbade myself to think about wings and remember the sky, but I couldn't keep that rule. I'm probably a weak person. I can't count how many times I tried to get out of here, so as not to see a dragon soaring into the blue heights, to no longer thrown my hands up and scream into my pillow at night from the awfulness of it… but I couldn't. I wanted to tell you many times, to reveal my truth, but what would it have changed? Then you too would have suffered from the helplessness and impossibility of breaking the spell. For two to bear that burden—would have been too much."

"How do you explain your Incarnation today?" Karegar carefully touched Jagirra's wing.

"A blood relative."

"A blood relative?"

"Kerr. He's my and your blood relative. I can't know what made him plunge into the astral, and how he sent that energy to me, but you're looking at the results. The monstrous influx of mana broke down the internal shackles and broke the 'snare' spell."

Karegar was a sorry sight. He looked so helpless. The old dragon turned his head incredulously. His wide-open eyes devoured the sight of the speaker. The lower tips of his wings dipped into the water.

"But how? Kerr, he's... really," Karegar's face became pensive. The same calm, collected member of the winged tribe was before Jagirra once again. "He takes after me in his looks, and in his personality, he takes after you. If that's true, then...."

"That's right. You were never a strong life mage. Nine thousand years ago at the university, they didn't teach polymorphism structures and causes, but there are two beginnings to everything that exists: the masculine and the feminine. You need two dragons to do the Ritual."

"And you risked it?"

"I risked it, and now I'm shaking every day—how is he, and what's happening to him? The astral blow made me worry even more. I know that he's alive, but that doesn't make it any easier." Neither dragon said anything. The Lords of the Sky were thinking their lives over. Each of them had had a life much longer than that of an ordinary human or elf. On the whole planet, only one Rauu could say he was older than the crystal dragon, but that's only a detail."

Karegar moved towards Jaga and covered her with his wing:

"I'm sorry. Forgive me for hurting you and almost making a mess of things and losing the one thing I care about most."

"I haven't told you the whole truth yet."

"You'll tell me when you're ready. I lived without it for two thousand years and I can do it for two thousand more if necessary." Jaga guiltily lowered her head, letting him nibble at her and thereby admitting his dominance, as animals do. "Let's go home," Karegar went on. "We'll have to calm the villagers down because you and I have put on quite a show. Don't forget to put a binding spell on Kerr. If you feel anything go wrong, I'll fly to him."

The Valley of a Thousand Streams. Karegar and Jagirra...

The second day, Jagirra couldn't manage to calm down. Last night she and her spouse woke up from a strong astral blow. Karegar jumped up from the stone bench and dashed out onto the platform in front of the cave, then for several minutes he ran around and craned his neck looking up. The dragon's aura sparkled and flashed brightly, then slowly calmed back down as if it weren't an ethereal substance but indeed its own living organism.

"I thought Kerr was nearby, and I was hearing the sound of wings," the dragon said, walking back into the cave. Jagirra stopped and listened to her internal voice. Her family totem, covered by her scales, responded familiarly with warmth, and she detected the connection. The warmth flowing from the magical channel told her that Kerr was alive. Karegar waited for the nod, turned 'round and 'round in a circle a few times and laid down on the sleeping spot, not forgetting to cover his wife with his wing.

Jaga couldn't get back to sleep. Judging by the slight movements of the whiskers on the tip of his snout and the heavy sighs from time to time, Karegar too was far from the kingdom of dreams. As soon as the dawn painted the tops of the mountains in a pink color, the old dragon got up and flew off to meet Gmar, who was on his way back from the market in Gornbuld. The dwarf was to bring a file of newspapers and, as always, the latest gossip and news from the big outside world, as Jagirra had ordered.

In recent weeks, the inhabitants of the forbidden valley had made their peace with the fact that a dragoness was running the place. Nothing really changed for them: so Jagirra had become a dragon, so what? She was still Jagirra. The countryside village people were simple people, solid hosts with practical skills. The slow-paced way of life didn't change, which meant there was nothing to worry about. The valley dwellers put their heads together and again reached for drugs and other help at a small house, located in the middle of the forest three leagues from the village. A few of them became even more proud of their herbalist. Dita, the tanner's son, went about all puffed-up and proud of the fact that his sweetheart was not just the pupil of some village sorceress, but the Dragon Mistress herself. Soon people became fed up at the proud peacock, and a few of the menfolk decided to beat some humility into the arrogant guy, but they didn't count on the size of their opponent's fists. Dita cracked his knuckles and clenched his fists, next to which shovels look like children's toy trowels, and went to meet his offenders. An hour later, a wagon with a draft hass brought the beaten village peasants and Dita himself to the dragon's taiga house. Dita had gotten it in no small measure from his father Duke. Dorit, a former watchman and a mage who was brought to the valley by Kerr, was in her third month of pregnancy, and according to the dwarfs' unwritten law, she was forbidden to practice magic before giving birth. Therefore, the fighting cocks were brought to the dragoness. The whole gang of fist fighters gasped, groaned and compared bruises in a spirit of camaraderie. Jaga, who was lying near the entrance, changed hypostasis and began to treat the sick fighters with tinctures and cast healing spells. The herbalist drove Dita out of sight and forbade the apprentice to approach her fiancé until she learned the lesson. The leather tanner's son was, by nature, not a stupid guy. After wandering through the thickets, he returned to Jaga with a drooping head and sworn to the Mistress that the excess would not happen again. Charda enthusiastically supported her groom and promised to personally look after her over fist-happy chosen one.

On the second day after the happy occurrence of being rid of the spell, Jaga, for the first time in a few thousand years, tasted fresh meat. She was catching up on her sleep after the long sleepless night when Karegar returned from the hunt and brought half a deer to the cave. She was still ashamed of herself and acted as if she'd never eaten fresh meat in her whole life. Catching the sweet and savory scent of blood, the dragoness pushed her husband aside, grabbed the remaining carcass, and stole it away to the other end of the cave.

"How's the deer?" the male dragon asked with a merry spark in his voice. The question went unanswered. Only the crunching and grinding of bones told him that it was tasty. "Do you remember that you got so mad at me about that moose?" The crunching stopped for a moment. The dragoness growled and went back to her feasting. "I hadn't hunted for three days at that time…," a light roar and a sudden stomp of the tail was the response to the tirade. "Targ, who am I talking to—can you hear me?" Jaga didn't react. "And who was it that wanted to give our boy the business for one little ram?" Karegar said, jerking his wings, and walked out of the cave.

Joking is all fine and good, but behind the old dragon's demonstrative banter once again, the question "why" was peeking out. An iceberg had taken up residence in the personal relations of the Masters of the valley—it was like a river and the shore, separated in winter from water by the fragile edge of the coasts, but as soon as frost starts pouring in, as the ice begins to grow stronger. Now a narrow facet of fragile fall ice lay between the two dragons. All Jagirra's attempts to bring back the old Karegar failed. She, like all women, felt very keenly everything that went on with her mate and worried very much that the changes taking place in him lay on herself as a heavy burden of guilt. The poison of betrayed trust continued to eat away at their relationship, like rust eating at iron. Karegar had given his word to wait and wasn't rushing the moment, not once mentioning in word or deed that he wanted to hear the rest of the story, for which Jaga was grateful to him. And yet she sometimes caught careful glances directed at her, which resounded with the pain of a deep emotional wound. Feeling those glances on her turned out to be hardest of all to bear. It's hard to know that you won't be touched nor asked to tell the truth, but that someone's waiting impatiently for you to be bold enough to reveal it. The old dragon forgave her with his mind, but a resentment had taken up residence in his heart, which gave rise to a feeling of alienation. Two weeks later, the dragoness could no longer hold back:

"As soon as Kerr gets here, I'll tell you everything," she told him one evening. "And then, que sera sera," she added, just audibly, mostly mouthing the phrase and lying down. She would not give up; she would defy the circumstances and fight for her happiness.

***

Karegar showed up near evening time and dropped Dorit off, who was holding onto a large bag with a file full of newspapers from the last month. Gmar, as was his habit, had decided to go the rest of the way on his own two feet. Flights on a dragon's back by no means attracted the merry fellow. Truth be told, he was afraid of flying. The sight of the earth far beneath his feet made him tremble. If the dragon should do a pirouette or any maneuver in the air, his teeth would chatter.

Dorit wanted to bow, but was stopped by Jaga:

"No, it's not worth it. I believe your respect for dragons is quite evident. Don't bend your back."

Karegar was very different from his usual self. Without turning in circles first, he plopped down on the platform and rested his head on the warm stone.

"What news from the outside world?"

"War," the dragon answered instead of the yellow-haired dwarf. A film covered his eyes. While he was flying his rider, she managed to tell him the main news and gossip she heard in the city. "The world's gone crazy. I think this is only the beginning."

"War?" Jagirra asked in disbelief. The dwarf nodded. "Tell me."

The news was scary and disquieting. The alliance between Tantre and the Forest was kaput. The Forest Lordships had become thick as thieves with the Patskoi Empire and had formed a military block against the northern kingdoms. In response Gil accepted the gray orcs, settling them in the north of the country and along the coast.

"Strange how the lords allowed such a blatant disregard for their rights?" Jagirra mumbled pensively.

"There are no more lords." Dorit pulled the newspapers out of the sack. Digging through the file, she opened to a certain page and pointed at the headline: "There. The lords and the pro-elf members of the Free Mages' Guild revolted. The army got the order to destroy the revolutionaries. The lords' lands were taken to the treasury, the castles were leveled to the ground. Vikings who had taken on the citizenship of the kingdom supported the army. The last centers of the uprising were suppressed in three days. The ones who put up a fight were wiped out along with the castles."

"Gil decided not to complicate life for his descendants," the dragon said. "Apparently he'd long since been thinking of pulling out the infection by the roots, once and for all."

"And the Forest, and Pat?" Jaga asked.

"The Empire has been taken out of the game for a long time," Dorit explained, her yellow hair flashing. She opened the last page of the newspaper "Kion Times" and began to read the article with the headline in large, bold print so that it jumped off the page. "As a result of excellent military planning and operations, the griffons and the drag wings of the Northern Alliance dealt a blow to the legions of the Patskoi Empire, concentrated in the region of the city of Ronmir. The result of the mass bombardment was the destruction of the hundred-and-fifty-thousand-strong army of the Empire," the dwarf looked up from the text. "The Northern Alliance is what they're calling the union of Tantre and the Rauu principalities. Now the wings are headed out to bomb the border areas of the Woodies' army bases."

Jaga changed hypostasis, rolled a stump stool up and settled herself next to the girl. The news was something to think about. Enira, in her letter, had written about a big war. If she threw all conjectures aside, it seemed that this latest flare-up was the harbinger of something much bigger. The king of Tantre wouldn't invite orcs and Vikings onto his territory just like that. By following the elementary logic, she arrived at the conclusion that the northerners would not leave their homes just for kicks. Jaga leafed through the yellowed pages and thought hard. Karegar looked like a giant clump of anthracite. Only his tail's twitching from time to time gave him away as a living being. Dorit quietly observed the Mistress's frantic leafing through the pages. She was afraid to disturb the silence that reigned or interrupt the dragons' trains of thought. She could tell intuitively that the Lords of the Sky would come to some conclusion which would reveal the big picture, which, for her, remained a well-guarded secret. At some point, the Mistress, who had found something interesting, stopped rustling the pages.

"Arians," Karegar's bass resounded as he opened his eyes and also lifted the translucent membrane from them. "The orcs and the Norsemen are fleeing Arians," the old dragon put the puzzle pieces together.

Jagirra did not react at all to what her husband said. The herbalist stood up from the stump, staring into space. The folder of newspapers fell to the floor, showing the article she'd been reading.

"Carnage in Orten—what are the authorities hiding?" the dwarf read the headline.

"Karegar," the elf's chest was fluttering as if she'd just run several leagues. Her eyes, now very keen, shone.

"We need to fly to Orten." Without finishing speaking, she listened to something and turned to the village. Dorit followed the Mistress's gaze and quietly gasped. Over the forest, at the far village outskirts, an incomprehensible glow erupted. "A portal! Karegar, someone's opening a portal into the valley! Dorit, quickly!"

The dwarf hardly had time to react when she found herself on the dragon's back, who immediately plunged down through the air from the overhang.

"Come in from the side of the sunlight," Jagirra cried, holding onto his mane. "Dorit, hold on to me!"

***

Flashing brightly in all colors of the rainbow, the portal opened up its belly, expelling a variegated group out into the locality. There were members of different races and… a female dragon with two dragonlings. The last guest barely had time to step through the hazy border when the three-dimensional window behind her slammed shut.

"I don't sense danger," Jagirra said, looking at the red-scaled member of the winged tribe, covering her young with her wings and feeling jealousy towards her unexpected competition. "Karegar, sit at the edge of the field. Dorit, now's not the time to follow custom. Better be on your guard, just in case. Who knows what to expect from this interesting group…."

The dragoness had only just touched her paws to the ground when Jagirra put up a passive magical shield and slid off Karegar's neck. Dorit darted into the bushes. The shield was a good idea—the two women's auras and that of the red dragon gave them away as mages.

The group was indeed interesting. There was a red-headed Norseman, three orcs, and a vampire, all decked out in weapons from head to toe. A few draft hasses were stepping along next to the warriors. The red dragoness added color to the visitors, from under whose wings two curious snouts were peeking out. Jagirra was mistaken: there were three children. A small girl came out from underneath her right wing and hid behind the ruddy Norseman's back. One of the orcs, the leader, judging by her behavior, stepped forward, took off her satchel, and bowed low to the elf. The herbalist breathed in—a familiar smell. The visitors smelled like dragon, especially the vampire and the little orc girl. The main orc woman took a piece of paper from the pocket of her sack which was folded in quarters.

"Mistress, Kerr asked me to give you this letter," the leader extended the paper to Jagirra.

"You know him?" she asked, taking the message. Her heart was beating fast, and she was becoming flushed.

"Yes."

"Why didn't he come himself?"

"In order to prevent the mages from determining the finish point of the portal."

"Makes sense. What does the letter say?"

"I don't know, Mistress. Kerr didn't say anything about the letter until the last minute, on the portal platform. Also, there's a spell on it that allows only you to open it."

Jagirra, barely containing her excitement, took a couple of steps back and opened the paper. Karegar's head hovered over her shoulder.

"How about that!" the dragon cried, having finished reading. "I have to count the cave in the Southern Slopes. I think our son will do what he writes he will." He too then looked at the guests, his gaze lingering on the dragoness and the vampire. He chuckled and laid down on the ground.

"Let's go—we ought not to make the village dwellers nervous with all this uncertainty," Jagirra said and was the first to set foot on the path that led to the settlement. As silently as a ghost, and not at all from where she was expected, Dorit appeared on the field. "Karegar, are you going to keep lying there?"

***

Frida, stepping carefully along the creaking floorboards, headed towards her bed and, not even getting undressed, plopped down onto the cozy mattress. The young warrior's shoulders were trembling slightly. She cursed herself heartily. Why? Why had she listened in? *Wanted to find out other people's secrets, did you? Well now you know, don't you?* The vampire wiped away tears and stared through the foggy window, lit brightly by the light of Nelita... *curse it all....*

Soon they will have been here for two whole weeks. Tomorrow Lanirra would take her to the enclave. Frai would have his maturity exam, and she'd promised her brother she'd be there. She always kept her promises.

Frida looked at the sleeping Ilnyrgu and smiled. The orc stayed true to herself. There was a bare blade at the head of the bed and the handle of a combat knife was sticking out from under the pillow. She wore a chain around her neck that bore a glowing stone—a fragment of the statue of Hel. The Wolf was prepared to go into battle at any moment. The vampire overcame the pain in her back and pulled her boots off. She had never run through the mountains in her life so much as she had here. Il put the large statue fragments to good use and set up active guard perimeters and traps in all dangerous directions, using the stones charged with mana as the power source for the magical weaving. The ever-busy orc included everyone in the work, even Tyigu. After they had been jogging about the steep slopes for a couple of days, she procured the aid of a few guys from the village to help carry stuff and called upon Lanirra to fly them around. The red dragoness pitched a fit at first, but one glance from the elf was enough to make Lani obediently lower her head and let herself be used instead of a hass. She was afraid to argue with Kerr's mother. The elf could show her who was boss.

The very first night, after she had fed and given drink to all the guests, Jagirra asked them to tell her all the details. Settling down near the open fire kindled near the guest house, the dragon and the elf carefully listened to the refugees' story. Ilnyrgu began from the beginning, holding Tyigu tightly as she did. She told the story of Master Berg and the reasons for fleeing the Steppe, then switched to all that had happened in Orten and the half-orc's acquaintance with Kerr. The girls showed the tiny scars on her chest. Il's story continued seamlessly on to the battle in the woods, went on swimmingly to the battle at Ortag, and then came to the events at the former monastery.

"I've never seen anything like it," the orc said with fervor. "A simple mortal cannot overcome a spell like that. Kerr not only broke the spell, he completely destroyed it and slayed the priests. When High Prince Miduel's entourage flew into the monastery, the mages accompanying him were in shock. The level of mana was off the charts, beyond all possible reckoning."

"Miduel?" Karegar interrupted. The orc nodded. "That old shrimp's still alive?"

"He's not such a shrimp any more," Frida spoke up for the Rauu. "The High Prince drank an elixir of dragon's blood and looks quite well. I wouldn't think he looks three thousand years old at all."

"Yes," Il confirmed the vampire's words. "Miduel looks about as old as his grandson. But I'd like to go on. We found the helrats' papers and Kerr used them as a bargaining chip to get the mages to build a portal. He kept a map and a couple of sheets with data on the heads of sectarian cells."

The dragon closed his eyelids in thought, and Jagirra got out a letter. Their adopted son flew home through the nests marked on the map....

When it was Frida's turn to speak, she was quiet for a long time at first, staring into the fire and watching the greedy flames lick at the dry logs. The Forest elves' red fireball flashed before her eyes.

"My story is simple and straightforward," she began. Lanirra quietly scoffed. Frida, ignoring the jealous dragoness, recounted her tale. The girl offered up dry summaries of the events that had taken place. While she was busy telling her story, she failed to notice Jagirra reposition herself next to her. The elf asked her to close her eyes and not pay attention to anything at all.

A quiet whisper enveloped Frida as if she were floating on ocean waves. She did not see what the elf was doing, but the headache that had been tormenting her for the last two weeks slowly faded until it was completely gone.

"Well, how's that? Better?" Jagirra asked. The vampire gave her the thumbs up. She didn't feel like speaking anymore. Lanirra's eyes glinted meanly in annoyance, or was she just imagining things?

Not everything was peaceful in the quiet tucked-away corner of the world. On the second day, there was a conflict between Lani and Jaga. The dragoness got an earful for flirting with Karegar. Upon hearing the angry tirade, the dragoness asked the Mistress of the Valley not to interfere in the affairs of the Lords of the Sky. Jaga, enraged, removed her will shields, changed hypostasis and held her competition's head to the ground. Shocked to the core at the appearance of a fellow clan member, Lani didn't even resist.

"Just think about waving your tail in front of Karegar, and I'll cut it right off to your very bottom!" Jagirra whispered, changing back. The shamed dragoness ran away.

Not counting this conversation, nothing serious happened any of the days they were there.

Frida was coming back from the mountain pass where Il had been working out a few flaws in the magical signaling systems when she came upon the two female dragons having a discussion. She dropped down behind two fallen birch trees lying the underbrush and threw all possible curtains up around herself. She masked her aura and listened. She was curious as to what these dragonesses might be talking about. They were talking about her.

"Kerr should choose for himself," Jagirra said. "Frida is a good girl, even if she is a vampire. I won't help you, but I won't stand in your way."

"It's a dry branch," Lanirra drawled, contempt and a note of superiority in her voice.

"You mean children?"

"I mean them. Why didn't you tell Kerr ordinary women can't bear him offspring?"

At these words, Frida winced. She had always dreamed of a big family with a lot of kids running around.

"Never had a reason to."

"And now? Will you tell him now? Kerr doesn't think of me as a wife, but he took my children under his wing. Karegar happily plays with them, brings them tasty morsels. Rary and Rury call him grandpa…."

Frida closed her eyes and grit her teeth until it hurt. The red dragoness was trickier than she thought. Lanirra was acting through her children. The dragonlings were spending nights in Karegar's cave. The old dragon and the Mistress played with them at length, and Tyigu did not get any less hugs, tumbles or tickles than the winged babies. The winged live wires had somehow broken the ice between the Masters of the Valley and made them grow closer to one another. Lanirra always found time to be near Kerr's parents. She, Frida, was dead to the world in the evenings. After a bit over one week, Jaga forgot about her enmity towards Lani, who wasn't much younger than herself, and stopped feeling jealous of her potential advances towards her husband. Lanirra felt the change and began to carefully gain ground. Frida could only quietly freak out over her own helplessness and wait until the person responsible for her troubles appeared. Only he could make things right. The vampire could feel Kerr's mother's emotions towards her: warmth, well-wishing, and a slight perplexity, which told her Kerr might not choose her. Other things being equal, the elf would accept her into her family, but she would be happier to have Lanirra. As for the old dragon, nothing doing. He honestly could not comprehend what his son saw in the little humanoid, when there was such a lady dragon right here? All the stranger since she, the dragoness, had shown him that she was capable of bearing strong offspring. While the vampire girl was a "dry branch."

"I'll tell him, but I think he already knows. The High Prince of the elves' interest in my son's girlfriend didn't go unnoticed. There are a few lines in the letter asking us to take care of the girl. Miduel ought to know about that specific quality of mixed marriages, humans and were-dragons. The High Prince was married to a Lady of the Sky. I'll let you in on a little secret—Kerr was born a human and underwent the Ritual at sixteen years old. That's why he might prefer Frida. By that age humans form certain sexual predilections; the boys' blood is boiling."

"I hope your son makes the right choice."

"Me too. Frida is a wonderful girl, but she's not one of us. I'm willing to accept her, but I want grandkids already." A tear slid down the vampire's face. So that's what would prove her worth. "Tell me, Lani, did you know about the 'blood cleansing ritual?' To cure the girl's headache?"

"Yes."

"Then why didn't you say anything?"

"Why would I? It kept her at bay."

The dragonesses crossed over to the other side of the field. Frida crawled deep into the forest, dropping a trail of bitter tears as she went. It's okay. A few days' rest in her hometown and she'd be good as new. Let other people's secrets remain secret. Her relationship with Kerr was in danger of breaking up.

***

The next morning, Lanirra flew her to the border of the enclave. The dragoness was literally glowing with happiness at being able to get rid of her two-legged problem. Temporarily, true, but a lot could happen in a short time…. Lani gave the vampire a beacon and told her how to use it. Barely holding back her urge to spit, Frida looked at the self-satisfied beast as she flew away and started off along the well-worn path towards her town.

The girl mounted a small hill and stopped, taking in the view. What a beautiful sight! The white, clean little houses were drowned in the green of the gardens. Hundreds of rainbows were shimmering in colorful hues over a waterfall. The banners of the clans were flapping over the house of the Council. It wasn't long ago at all that the vampire was planning not to come back home, but the Twins had something else in store. Frida made her way down the easy slope and smiled sadly. Evidently, her father's house did not want to let her go just like that. Literally sliding over the ground, she hadn't noticed she upset a strange guard perimeter. There were less than two leagues left to the town. The road wound into a narrow cleft. Constantly glancing from side to side, she carefully walked between the cliffs. Something strange was happening to her. She'd walked that cleft a hundred times, but it had never before been dangerous. Or was she just being overcautious because of the events of yesterday evening? She switched to true vision and looked around—no one was there. She straightened the band across her chest which held her sword and took a step forward. Something snapped under her right foot, and Frida was suddenly enveloped in a cloud of black lotus. The world narrowed to a small bright spot, and it too soon faded. In a minute a horse-drawn cart came around the bend. Someone dressed all in black clothing picked Frida up and put her in the wagon....

Tantre. Orten...

"Well! Turn around, sonny!" The old veteran from the recruiting office, where Timur had stopped along the way to the central commandant, could barely recognize that wet new recruit in this fine brave young officer. "You look good! Oh, very good! Excuse me, ler, for speaking to you that way." Timur, a bit choked up by the encounter, waved his hand. The commandant got up from behind his desk and in a loud voice barked at the whole establishment: "Have a look, you maggots! The army makes a man!" A few new recruits who were loitering in the corner of the large room stared at the loud-mouthed pair with bulging eyes. "Ho ho! You've seen some action?" the commandant's callused finger touched the ribbon sewn on Timur's uniform. "Where'd you end up?"

"First we put down the lords, and then—at Ronmir," Timur said.

The old veteran shook his head. "How long has it been? Just over a month? And you've been grounded, ler?"

"No, sent for retraining at the School of Magic."

The commandant nodded. He was more familiar than most with the royal order. The war was only beginning; soon they would need a lot of mages. It was sad that boys like this went into battle and died. That's why he was lucky to be alive, but, judging by the slight scars on his face which the commandant didn't remember having seen the first time they met, the guy had seen his share of horror. The young man had really felt the effects of war, and he would again. Something terrible was coming, everyone and his brother was rowing into the army, special patrols were catching various rabble, and they were increasing recruitment from the villages. All mages were sent to retrain as combat mages....

"Good luck to you, ler!" The commandant stood bolt upright and saluted the officer. The gray-haired veteran's eyes didn't show a drop of humor or irony, only respect, sprinkled with a substantial portion of the sadness of someone who has seen Hel—pun intended. Timur clicked his heels at the same time.

"You too, ler," the young man said, flinging his hand up to his forehead.

The central commandant's office met him with much ado. Clerks of every stripe were bustling about from one floor to another, officers were swearing, and in the central gathering room, some shady individuals were hugging the walls. They looked like the types you might otherwise meet at the market with a sharpened coin in hand, cutting people's purses in order to swipe the coins. The extra guards at the doors and gates on the windows cut off any possible escape route for the conscripts (forced "volunteers"). After training, these unfortunate soldiers were subject to wearing a bracelet on their right ankles, as an extra guarantee of loyalty. With a bracelet like that, the prisoners would stop thinking of desertion. You can't run far on one leg—if you tried to run, the bracelet would blow up and take your leg with it. New recruits who had come voluntarily, not been brought in by force by the mage's patrol, queued at certain windows.

Timur went up to the second floor. The clerk on duty examined his documents and led him to the right office. That clerk, who was thin as a sliver, issued him a document that said he was to go to the School of Mages and then sent him to the treasury. If one were to believe the news, he should receive a proper thousand golden pounds. That wasn't bad at all—even quite good. The hefty treasurer at first wanted to give him banknotes only, but Timur became quite obstinate, digging his heels in like a donkey, and insisted he give him equal amounts of paper money and gold coins. After fifteen minutes of protesting vulgarly, the clerk gave in.

"Ler, allow me to speak to you!" After he left the treasury, Timur went to the assistant commandant in the rank of infantry alert.

"You may. What is it?"

"Ler, I was wondering if you could clear something up for me. Roidert Rigaud Pront von Trand was sent from our wing to retraining. May I be informed as to whether he showed up in the commandant's office or not?"

The alert's face darkened.

"He did. I worked up his documents myself."

"Ler, is everything alright?"

"Roi-dert, you'd do better to see for yourself. Your friend is staying in the officer's temporary quarters near the commandant. Room one-oh-five."

"Third floor, fourth door on the right," the officers' quarters watch on duty informed Timur a few minutes later.

Timur went up to the third floor. *Hm, nice place.* Carpets, magical lanterns, stucco molding on the walls and ceilings, flowers in the reception room and sturdy curtains on the windows in the halls.

"One hundred and five…, one-oh-five…. There it is." He knocked.

"Go to Targ!" he heard from inside the room, instead of a "come in."

"What, is he drunk?" Timur knocked a second time.

"I SAID, go to Targ!"

"Rigaud, open up. It's me, Timur!"

"Timur?" The door flung open. The room smelled of wine vapors and fumes. Looking at his friend, Timur shivered. The right half of Rigaud's face was distorted with thick scars like worms, "healed," not very well, in the field hospital by the Life mages.

"Hi Tim."

"Hello, Rigaud."

***

"Can I come in, or are you going to keep me at bay?" Timur asked.

"Come on in," Rigaud stared dumbly at the floor. "Close the door. Want some wine?" He turned away from the door jamb and, dragging his right leg, walked to the table. "Too bad there's no grub left. I've got wine, but no food."

Timur carefully closed the door, moved aside the boot Rigaud used to kick out uninvited guests, and leaned his back against the door jamb. The person standing in front of him now did not at all resemble indefatigable smart-alec he'd said good-bye to less than a week ago. The word "grub" sounded unpleasant and unusual to his ears; the old Rigaud would not have used it. He would have said something like "something to eat," "have a bite," maybe even "grab a mouthful," but not "no grub left." It was painful to look at him: he wore a dead, lost expression on his disfigured face and carried a sense of burden. Timur realized why the commandant's assistant hadn't wanted to discuss it with him. His wounds had broken the young man, who was frightfully embarrassed by the disfigurement he'd earned in battle. For now, they had broken him, but if he continued in this same vein, it wouldn't be long until he became a bum. Timur slid his hand into the inner pocket of his service jacket and felt the vials, which were worth ten times more than the salary they'd paid him in the commandant's office.

Timur fondled the vials and remembered how Lanirra had made Kerr destroy the laboratory, incinerate the crushed scales and the potion the helrats had made from her blood. After thinking for a minute, his friend Kerr had agreed to the red dragoness' requirements but asked if he could leave a few vials for his friends. Lani looked at Timur for a long time, gazed intently at the female warriors and the elf who'd been released from prison, caught the scent of the orcs, mixed with the smelly vinegar odor of the red-headed Norseman's boots, and allowed Kerr to give one vial to each of them. Timur, apparently for his intercession and handsome eyes, was allowed four.

"Don't worry, it won't fall," a wheezy voice interrupted Timur's memories.

"What won't?"

"'What won't?'! The wall! Go to the table, no sense holding the wall up." Rigaud set about a little unpretentious tidying up, wiping empty bottles from the flat surface standing on four legs, and placing a few full ones on it. "Take the cup."

"Maybe we shouldn't..."

"Take the cup!!"

Timur decided not to argue with his friend, who had just about gone wild, and obediently took the glass full of amber liquid he handed to him. Rigaud, just like Lanirra, looked at the wine, constantly and unblinking, immersed in his own thoughts. The tangles of scars on his face twitched unpleasantly in time with the twitch of his right cheek. The young man's expression gradually lost meaning and fell into nothingness.

"To the ones whom Hel took under her roof, may they have a light afterlife," Rigaud said flatly, snapping out of the vortex of his thoughts and gulping the glass's contents down in one gulp.

Taking a tiny sip, Timur set the cup down. The wine didn't hit the spot. Targ, what was Rigaud turning into?! Chugging at least a half a bottle of wine in one fell swoop, he got drunk right in front of Timur's eyes.

"Rigaud, what happened to you?" Timur asked in perplexity.

"What happened to me? What happened to me?!" His friend's eyes flashed with madness. "I've been grounded! No more flying! I'm no use to anyone." Rigaud tore off his shirt. "Look, what are you turning away for?!" he cried when Timur closed his eyes at the sight. The entire right half of his friend's body was covered in thick, rough scars from burns. "It's called 'the wax flame' because whoever falls under the spell burns and melts like wax. They burned like moths in a flame. I can still hear their screams and the griffons' wails as they burned alive. Intelligence let us down—like lambs to the slaughter, Tim. Lambs to the slaughter," Rigaud's forehead hit the table and an angry tear slid down his nose onto the polished surface of the table. "Units of battle mages guarded the Imperial mana accumulators for 'puncturing.' If it hadn't been for our tubes of landmines, no one would have made it out of there. The commander and a quarter of the wing burnt up in the first instant. Alert-dert Nois took command upon himself. We took out the guard with grenades and let the landing party down. So many great guys never made it back. Tim, they told us Imperialists are cowards: it's not true, Tim, not true! They fought like lions and suls. They threw themselves at the sword in just their underwear. By the time I made it to the accumulators—oh Twins—only half the wing was left."

"I know."

"What do you know? You dropped your bombs and went through the portal."

"Nimir blew up the arsenal. We had to take the warehouses by storm," Timur said, but Rigaud wasn't listening.

"I got hit by the spell as I was flying," he said quietly, walked over to the window and with his large hand pushed the heavy portière aside. The room was filled with bright light. Against the background of the window and the merry, bright sunshine through the glass "watering" the world with its rays, the stooped figure of the young man looked like a black foreign body. It upset the harmony of the world. "Blackie flew me to the interim camp, all by himself. No one ever could have thought that a griffon would drag its rider in its claws, while the rider's holding on for dear life to the bag with the crystal accumulator. It would have been better if I died, rather than be like this. The Life mages pulled me back out of Hel's judgment, patched me up and sent me to Orten with a 'white ticket.' To get rid of the scars, I'll need twenty thousand gold pounds. The army doesn't have extra spending money, and they don't need cripples in the ranks." Turning away from the window, Rigaud opened the second bottle of wine and filled his glass to the very top.

Timur didn't say anything. He understood that his friend needed to let it all out, share his grief with someone. It was scary when someone who's started to feel like part of something, a part of a whole, who's found a place in life, suddenly finds himself on the fringe and doesn't have enough means to live on. The money the treasury of the commandant's office had given him would last six months, a year at most if he were barely skimping by. Plus, he would have to spend a pretty penny on clothing and painkillers. No one could stay in a trance 24/7. Rigaud had been retired. His "white ticket" meant that he was grounded due to his health. It meant basically getting fired from active duty. Fifteen golden pounds was the maximum monthly pension for veterans leaving active duty at the rank of roi-dert. No, the army hadn't forgotten about its former officer, who'd been given orders to train as a combat mage. In the future, it was possible the state would need the services of a burnt cripple, but for now, he was retired military with only a tiny hope of ever becoming a full-fledged mage and someday restore his health. Stronger men than Rigaud had been broken from the experience, let alone the boy from yesterday.

Having said his piece, Rigaud stood up near the open window and sadly looked out at the street. The party of life was no longer meant for him. Wine was the only joy he had left. Looking at his cup, he didn't notice Timur approach him. A slight blow to the head sent the drunken retiree into unconsciousness.

"Here we go," his attacker mumbled, pulling the guy's pants off and taking the vial of dragon's blood from his pockets. "Sorry, but I don't have time or any desire for conversation. The first thing I have to do is rub you down…."

A few minutes later, the rubbing phase was finished. Timur took out a second vial and poured exactly half of it, to the drop, into the patient's mouth. The other half he generously wiped over his friend's face and neck.

"You look like a twig, but man, is that deceptive!" the "doctor" grunted from the strain of lifting the involuntarily patient from the floor. "To bed with you. Sleep, so you know, is the best medicine," he went on, turning Rigaud's faint into a deep sleep with a simple spell.

The path to the bedroom was strewn with various obstacles in the form of fruit rinds and empty wine bottles. Near the bed, the "porter" almost dove headlong onto the floor together with his load; only the fact that the crumpled bed with the stale laundry was next to him saved them. Snoring, the object of care fell on the bed. The "object" yawned, stretched his whole body and turned to his left side, the youth's snoring made the walls quake.

The "doctor" stood by the bedside for a few minutes watching whole sheets of dead skin come off the patient's right side. The elixir of dragon's blood took its effect. Timur felt a slight tingling in the pads of his fingers and palms. He'd been wiped down with it too—the skin on his hands was peeling off and becoming soft and pink, like a baby's. That wasn't good... Next time he had to be more careful, or else.... One had to be super careful with dragon's blood. In small doses, it facilitated the healing of deep wounds and cured the most inconceivable ailments. But, like any medicine, it had a downside. As soon as you overdosed, the miraculously powerful medicine became a miraculously powerful poison. Drinking of this "spring" more than two or three times would be fatal. Each use left its mark in the form of a building-up of this very poison. At some point, enough became too much, and the person would die. Everything came with a price. Timur rubbed his palms and was glad that the side effect wasn't very big. He wouldn't like to make a date with Hel at the very beginning of his life. He really should listen to Lanirra's advice and instructions. The dragoness was very serious when she described the uses of the blood serum, all the while glancing sideways at Frida. The winged "donor" just couldn't understand why the vampire girl hadn't died? The amount of dragon's blood she received was enough to make two or three full-grown barls lower their trunks for good.

"I have to get some groceries," Timur thought, recalling the insane hunger the former prisoner felt after taking the miraculous elixir. It had twisted his insides into a tight ball. More than likely, this "retiree," once he woke up, would want to eat, no less than a hungry sul. Timur covered the loudly snoring man and went into the hallway. "Call the maid," he told the man on duty.

"One moment," he said, looking at the junior officer and calling the maid by way of a communicator amulet.

Two young ladies answered the call.

"Tidy up, take the trash out, mop the floors. Don't touch the officer. He'll be sleeping for about three hours yet. Don't be alarmed. The roidert's been treated with a magical serum for burns that removes the old skin. It's normal. Please get a set of clean sheets and blankets and air the room out. Iron the quilt. The room should be sparkling like a polished egg by the time I get back. Is that clear?" Timur gave his instructions in choppy phrases. The girls both nodded. "Let's get to it!" With that, two gold coins worth three pounds each fell on the table. Yes, it was a lot, but now he could be sure that the maids would fulfill the task with all zeal and then some.

***

Marika sat down on the bench located at the far end of the school park and, by the peaceful sound of the fountains, flipped through the pages of her textbook. "Life Magic—Main Uses" was written on the cover in a pretty font. The pages quietly rustled under her thin fingers and softly laid down one on top of another. The occasional drop of waterborne on the wind from the fountains kissed the paper and, like tears, left a blurry imprint on it. The lonely fair-haired witch wasn't crying. The days of squeezing her tear-stained pillow until her hands hurt were done.

The past month, which had flown by like an angry steppe hurricane, hadn't brought anything pleasant. A battle on the School shooting range, her arrest and unending questioning in the School dungeon. The feigned politesse of the Informants and the punishing mages, the ostentatious participation in her fate, the investigators' cold, soulless eyes. The tiny damp cell with disgusting spiders in the corners, which became her home for a whole week. The mysterious disappearance of Rigaud and Timur, which gave rise to a wave of gossip and rumors. The revolt and bloody massacre by the Norsemen rebels. The battles at the School and the seniors fighting the punishers. She had lost her only friend this past month, turned away from her and hid behind her fiancé and his father. Not once did Irma pay her a visit. Her former gal pal didn't fit in with the new social group.

She looked like a dumb backwoods lassy compared to the highborn society.

On the other hand, new visits from the investigators followed, and a whole delegation from the Rauu principalities, and hundreds of questions, which she'd had no choice but to answer. Questions that turned her soul inside-out. Questions about Kerr, the orc, the vampire and again about Kerr. Artful, loaded questions, designed to throw her a curveball. Questions about habits, tastes, boudoir preferences…! How the heck could she know what the dragon preferred in bed if he'd slept with the vampire and with Irma?! No, she didn't know anything else! Perhaps he'd slept with someone else too? Maybe so. But she had no idea. The Rauu made themselves scare, and Rector Etran's trusted associates took over, had at her, and the questions began all over again. Who had Marika dated, who had Rigaud seen, what girls were seen most often in the company of Rigaud and Kerr, had they had any romances? Once Marika couldn't take it anymore and went hysterical. The dragon hadn't had any romances except Frida, she screamed at Etran's investigator. What romances could there have been if he came back to the dorm after midnight, practiced and fell into bed? After that little outburst, they eased up a bit. But for how long?

The girl clapped the book shut and looked at the strings of falling water, sparkling brightly like a clear crystal in the sun. This past month she'd learned to live alone and rely only on herself.

"Marika, there you are. I've been looking for you everywhere," Rita plopped down on the bench next to her. She was the sophomore they'd assigned to the empty dorm room next door after the Snow Elves had left. "I have a surprise for you!"

"What is it?" Marika didn't like her neighbor, always sticking her nose where it didn't belong.

"Mmm, a good one. Half the dorm's already sauntering past your surprise, hehe."

"What do you mean? Why are they sauntering?"

"Marika," Rita capriciously blew up her cheeks with air, "do I have to spell it out for you? Well, come on, some military guy on duty's waiting for you! Good looking, too!" the neighbor demonstratively licked her lips.

"Hello Marika," as soon as Marika entered the hall, the officer jumped up from his chair. A gaggle of young pretty flirts hanging about the military man smoothly moved aside, but not one of them left the hall. Each was positively burning with curiosity....

"Timur?!" The book slipped out of her weakened hands and fell to the floor, landing open.

"What, don't you recognize me?" From his sad smile, the white strips of small scars on the young man's face formed into little facial rays, making the guest ten years older.

"Where's Rigaud? Is he alive?"

"He's alive." A weight lifted from Marika's heart. "Pack your things. I'll tell you everything on the way."

She grabbed the fallen book and ran to her room:

"I'll just be a minute!" she called back.

The beauties at the far end of the hall, which included a few of Timur's former groupmates, whispered to one another. They couldn't believe that this stately officer and the bookworm who'd disappeared just over a month ago were one and the same. A uniform really changes a person. And he looks good in a brush cut....

***

"Move your hands."

"..."

"As if I've never seen you naked before. Turn around, not this way! That way. Turn. Stop."

"..."

"Mischief maker. You'd even be shy in front of Timur. Move your hands, now stop!"

"What am I to you, a stallion? And you're spurring me on...."

"You're a shameless gigolo, not a stallion. Don't twist...."

Timur, closing his eyes, was lounging in a comfy chair nestled in the corner of the room. The old black armchair didn't go at all with the rest of the room's décor, which was neutrals, but was so comfortable that no one lifted a finger to change it or throw it away. Timur was grateful now more than ever for the staff's laziness. From the bathroom, where Rigaud and Marika had gone to get the last of Rigaud's dry skin off, he could hear muffled laughs. Let them laugh. Better than gorging themselves on wine. At least Rigaud's back to his old self again....

"Turn your back towards me. I have to rinse off the soap root. You know, these scars are becoming on you, especially the ones on your face. They give you a sort of manly charm."

Timur smiled. *Good job, girl.* It seemed she knew better than he did how to raise their burned friend's self-esteem. The elixir had helped: Rigaud's right arm and leg bent and unbent as they had before he was wounded. Only the biggest ugly worms of scars remained, which had turned into thin white lines. Four parallel scars, like the trail of a predator's claws, crossed the guy's face, about two centimeters apart from one another. The first started at his temple; the second crossed the outer corner of his right eye, which made it look like the young man was constantly squinting. The third scar went from his cheek to his ear, cutting into his hairline behind the upper lobe in a deep furrow. The fourth started at his chin, ran a bit crooked, "cut off" the tip of his earlobe, and sharply turned down onto his neck, where a few more healed ropes descended along his side and back as branching roots. It was entirely possible that the potion could have been more effective, but the amateur doctor was afraid to really rub the stuff into Rigaud's face. All he could do now was to pray to the Twins and thank them for letting him meet Kerr and not letting Marika see the ugliness of his friend before he had used the dragon's blood.

By the time they moved from the dorm into the military housing unit, the maids had imposed ideal cleanliness and order in the room. They had earned their gold twice over. The floors were clean and waxed, the dust was gone, his uniform was washed, dried, pressed, and put away in the closet. There wasn't a trace of the bottles or the smell of wine. A large bouquet of flowers in a malachite vase made the whole place smell like a meadow. The girls had managed to change the bedding from under the sleeping Rigaud. They hadn't forgotten to provide a change of bedding either, although, after the job they'd done, there really wasn't any need. *However*, Timur smiled and scoffed to himself, *he'll probably need it, judging by the mood he's in. They might tear the old ones in a fit of passion....*

***

"Nice," Marika spoke up, swimming into the room in a dignified manner and gratefully nodding at Timur, who held the door for her.

"Yes, not bad," he confirmed.

"What's on the agenda?"

"First up: get someone who's fallen into a deep, dark depression back on his feet."

"Oh, and what's happened to him?" she said, pointing at the black blotches on the sleeping Rigaud's face.

"It's trace of the elixir."

"Well now that I get it, why we wake our hero up?"

By their combined effort, Rigaud was awakened, completely undressed and taken to the shower. Before that he tried to shout, protesting this violation of his rights, but upon seeing his girlfriend's stern expression, he stopped, then straightened his right arm at the elbow, and froze for a while. The "retiree's" brain couldn't accept the miraculous healing without a good explanation.

"Dragon's blood," Timur answered his friend's pressing look.

"Where'd you get it?"

"It's a long story."

"I've got time."

"Go wash up first. Marika, will you help him? Otherwise ... um...." Timur hesitated. The young woman batted her eyes at Rigaud smiling flirtatiously and nodded. Timur didn't have to explain anything to her; she understood the situation for herself, whether by woman's intuition or aggravated feminine flair. The "patient" blushed to the tips of his ears. Well well, one might think that no one knew about the secret visits to the women's dorm and adroit entrances through the second-floor window that Marika had forgotten to shut. No, something else was going on here:

Rigaud was ashamed of himself, of having forgotten about his friends and simply abandoned himself to drowning his sorrows in wine bottles, for falling off the radar. It wasn't becoming of a man and a warrior. "Go on already."

"You promised to tell me," Timur heard from behind the closed bathroom door. "Don't even think about trying to avoid it!"

"I won't," Timur answered, falling into the embrace of the black leather armchair.

To the peaceful sound of the running water, Timur almost fell asleep. He wasn't bothered by the giggling or the loud exclamations of the bathers. Finally, the flow of water stopped, the door burst open, and the robed love-birds came out.

"Do tell," Rigaud said, completely ignoring the delicious spread on the table and sitting down on the bed. Marika sat down beside him. Just one word, a disdainful look at the food, and all of a sudden Timur could believe the former smart-alec had returned, who valued information above all, even a full stomach. "I know you stormed the arsenal. There were a couple of guys in the hospital from our wing. I'm sorry, Tim, for what I said. Why don't you tell me where the portal took you and where you can get your hands on some dragon's blood. And tell me who's kind enough to share some...."

"A kind lady, her name is Lanirra."

"Interesting name," Marika said. "You met a girl?" At that, Timur had a hard time maintaining his inscrutability. Although, Lanirra would have approved of the comparison.

"I did meet a girl, a little later on. Lanirra is a red dragoness. We were jailed in neighboring cells in a helrat's prison. Kerr broke us out."

"Whaaat?" the listeners said simultaneously. Marika's eyes got big and round, the scars on Rigaud's face turned red; he leaned forward resting his elbows on his knees and stared at Timur unblinking.

"Tell me everything," he said in a voice that was hoarse from emotion, but at the same time firm, as if he weren't willing to hear any arguments.

***

"Yeees," Rigaud drawled, "you really had a good time. Can't hold a candle to you." Marika tactfully said nothing. "You said something about a girl? Well? You met a girl?"

Timur stood up from his chair, tugged his jacket downward and walked across the room.

"The young lady will be here to study in a couple weeks... I'll introduce you then."

"Oh wow, what secrets you have!" Rigaud laughed. "I'm interested! Is she cute?"

"She's cute," Timur answered calmly, managing not to blush. No one said a word about Frida, and no one mentioned Lubayel, either. "I'm going to go get settled. It'll be night soon, and I haven't gotten settled into my room yet." Timur stopped at the door: "Remember, tomorrow you're going to have to be bright-eyed and bushy-tailed."

"What for?" Marika asked instead of Rigaud.

"Rigaud, don't you want to get back on duty?" He nodded. "Tomorrow morning let's go to the commandant's office!" Timur said finally and slid out the door.

***

"I'm not going to the commandant's office," Rigaud said, the scars on his neck becoming engorged with blood like veins on an arm squeezed in a tourniquet. Something flashed in his friend's eyes, sending shivers down Timur's spine. And then he understood the now former griffon rider's decision.

"Alright," he mumbled trying not to show the oncoming bitterness and went to the window.

"Timur…,"

"It's okay," he said, stopping the unnecessary words with a gesture of his hand. "I get it."

"You always were the most understanding, you man of few words." Rigaud stood up next to his friend and rested his palm on his shoulder. They looked at the city in complete silence, a city wrapped in a shawl of morning fog: a white fog near the Ort and a pink one, tinted by the rising sun, near the rooftops of the Plain. In a little while, the new day would break the milky covering into small patches like rags and make the fog evaporate. But for now, the city was catching its last, sweetest dreams, tucked in under the white blanket.

Through the open window, they heard the clicking of heels against the pavement. Marika slid out the hotel's front door and sat down in a carriage awaiting clients. The sleepy driver, covering his yawn with his left hand, bowed at the girl, listened to the address, nodded and took up the reigns. A few minutes later, the fog swallowed up the carriage carrying the bookworm as she hurried off to class.

"I… I don't know how to say this…," Rigaud finally broke the extended silence.

"You're afraid!" The answer was a fierce look and despair, splashing in the depths of Rigaud's eyes. "What of?"

Squeezing his hands into trembling fists, Rigaud turned away from his friend. The man of few words was right. He was afraid that the pain would return. He didn't want to be helpless before the circumstances and again be left alone with them, one on one. What had he accomplished in his life? What would he leave behind him? The war had reared its ugly head and showed its toothy grin. Victories are won by pain and suffering, the easiest place of all to lose one's self. There's no room in the war for childish games. He'd recently almost remained under the enemy citadel as a cold dead body. The dragon's blood healed his wounds—what a shame it couldn't heal his emotional scars. One real battle changed him entirely. No matter what anyone thought, he would go back to the army, but this time come not as a snot-nosed boy, but a fully trained combat mage, capable of defending himself from enemy curses and defending others from them, too. The Imperials owed him, big time. Scary thought—dying without leaving one's mark. Today he made a decision. It wasn't easy; it tore his soul in two, but his path was chosen. Timur might think it base, but he didn't want to be grig, that is, cannon fodder, or an army's bargaining chip. It would be stupid to mess up his second chance, given to him by the man of few words, Kerr, and an unknown dragoness.

"I'm going to the rector. I hope she'll send me back to School. I think that after just a month and a half I can still catch up on my studies. I want to become a real mage." Timur didn't say anything. He had learned to hide his feelings very well. His face remained impassive. His aura didn't betray a single flash. Whatever was going on in his head and in his soul remained a mystery. He could see that Rigaud wanted to say something else, probably something important. Something that would explain or shed some light on his decision, but some internal battle didn't allow him to speak up.

"Let's go then."

"Where?"

"To the School! Where else?! You go see the rector, and I'll go with my orders to the chancellery. You head downstairs already; I've got to go to my room and get the documents."

"What the heck do you need the papers for?"

"On the way, we'll stop at the bank. I left something there in a safety box. It's scary carrying something like that on you."

"?"

"Go on now. Half that scariness belongs to you."

***

Casting penetrating glances at Rigaud Pront von Trand, who was standing at attention, Rector Etran rubbed the Life mages' official conclusion from the hospital on the front in her hand for a long time. The funny little paper didn't at all correspond to the healthy look of the former bookworm. Either that or... never mind. The hospital mages wouldn't write total nonsense. They had grounded the guy for good reason—with wounds like that you can't fly anymore. It would have all made sense, except that the young man standing in front of her didn't look at all like an "invalid." An invalid like that could take on ten Imperial soldiers by himself.

"I'm listening," the three-dimensional illusion of a portly lady lit up over the desk.

"Verona, would you be so kind as to prepare an order to send Mr. Rigaud Pront von Trand to his previous group with the obligation to make up the work he missed in the next three months? Also, please write an order to the chancellery to settle the bookworm in the dormitory, perhaps in his former room." She turned to Rigaud: "Are you satisfied?" Rigaud smiled. "Don't over-stretch yourself, you're not on the parade marching grounds. And please, if you would be so kind as to explain this to me?" The rector's finger tapped the hospital mages' conclusion. Master Valett, who was sitting in an armchair in the opposite corner of the office, scoffed. The head of the School punishing mages still bore traces of his burns on his face and arms. The guild agents who had infiltrated the security service hadn't wanted to give up without a fight and had upped the carnage. The smile on the new student's face faded away like last year's snow. "Roidert, cat got your tongue?" the rector said, not waiting for a response. "Judging by the army's Life mages' conclusion, the entire right half of your body should look like one big scar. My eyes are telling me a different story. Were the mages mistaken?"

"No ma'am, Madam Rector!"

"And I don't think they had any reason to lie, did they?" Rigaud didn't answer. "If you'd rather not share your secret, that's your right," the rector drummed her fingers over the table. She looked pensively at the diagnosis and then looked up at Rigaud: "I don't dare keep you any longer. Pick up your orders and dorm room assignment from Verona. Don't forget to familiarize yourself with the current course schedule and pay the punishers a visit to retrieve the things you left upon fleeing."

When the door had closed behind the student, Etran turned to the head of security:

"What do you think?"

"Nothing out of the ordinary."

"Really? Just explain it to me, then!"

"Etran, you're surprising me!"

"Alright, alright, you've got me. My brain isn't working at all."

"I know just one potion that can heal severe wounds in such a short time…."

"Dragon's blood!" the rector realized. "Very interesting. Set a couple of your guys on the young man and order external surveillance. It wouldn't hurt to get in touch with the Secret Chancellery."

"Already done. They told me not to step on their toes. Valett's last words made the rector think, and think, and think. It was worth listening to the wishes of Duke Drang's subordinates.

"No need for external surveillance. Better not tease the Secret Chancellery."

***

"Well, how'd it go?" Timur darted over to his friend, who had long ago finished his business and had been milling about the rector's doors for a good hour. Rigaud held the order, sealed with a stamp, under his nose. "Congrats!"

"No occasion for that," Rigaud grumbled, gloomy as a rain cloud. "Let's go for a walk in the park. I'll tell you along the way." He took his friend by the elbow and pulled him away from the administration. "It's not a school; it's a nest of vipers!" Rigaud said, finishing his story and spitting into the fountain. "The rector won't back off. She'll send her watchdog. I should have listened to Marika."

Timur, pulling off his jacket and shirt, sat down on the parapet and rested his back under the cool streams of rushing water.

"Don't let 'em get to you. No one will touch you. For better or for worse, we're friends of a were-dragon, and there's such a tangled knot of politics tied around him that they'll be afraid to touch us, at least the rector certainly won't. I told you about the High Prince, learn to draw your own conclusions."

"You think so?"

"I know so! Let's go to the dorm. I've been given an order to move back into my old apartment, but they warned me I'll have to evict the new lodger myself. The Targ's henchmen!"

"Timur."

"What?" Throwing his shirt back on, he turned towards his friend. The skinny guy rubbed at the yellow sand of the path with the toe of his boot and with the expression of a battered dog, looked at the sparkling glints of water in the bowl of the fountain.

"Will you be my witness?"

"WHAT??" With a "woosh" a button flew from his shirt and hit the granite bench.

"Don't let your mouth hang open like that," Rigaud joked sadly. "I'm asking: will you be my best man?"

"Uhhhh..." Timur had fallen into a stupor and couldn't utter anything intelligible.

"I proposed to Marika."

"Targ! So that's why you decided to go back to the School! Is that the reason?"

"She's pregnant. Two months. The Life mage said it'll be a boy."

"Almighty Twins! Who's the father?" Timur asked and immediately realized he'd just put his foot in his mouth. The friends looked at one another for a few minutes and then started laughing, louder and louder, to the peaceful sound of the fountain. The bookworms relaxing in the park after class turned and looked with surprise at the military men laughing and patting one another on the back. What was with these grown men? No one could have guessed that these happy twenty-five-year-olds had just turned seventeen. War....

Tantre. Orten. Lailat...

"Your Highness, I can't offer you a cogent explanation of why the Arians stopped destroying the spy birds thrown onto their lands," the mage from the army intelligence department who'd been invited to the meeting mumbled.

His Highness Gil II, the Soft Spoken, according to his ingrained habit, stood at a wide panoramic window and admired the city. From the height of the summer royal residence, a stunning picture opened before him. The Middle and the Plain, intersected by the arrows of the avenues and covered with patches of parks, looked as if they'd fit in the palm of your hand. The colored tiled roofs of the buildings ran to the river, stumbled over the main city wall and once again crowded to the very channels that were heading north. The mighty Ort rounded the city smoothly and rushed towards the sea, taking the waters of dozens of streams and tributaries, flowing down from the southern foothills, and giving precious moisture to several wide canals, dug by dwarf masters three centuries ago. The white, yellow, and pink rectangles of the blossoming gardens went up to the horizon. There wasn't a single cloud in the bright blue endless sky. Instead he saw three combat griffons with riders on their backs. Three dozen half-birds kept a constant guard over the airspace above Lailat. Gil, with regret, turned away from the window and looked at the mage:

"So, you can't give me a cogent answer. And who can? What have you come to the palace for? To admire my collection of ancient tapestries? The northern mages quit catching your birds, and you were glad. Drang, what do your analysts suggest?" The head of the Secret Chancellery glared at the representative of the competing office, stood up, and reported heartily:

"Sire, the analysts suggest that the Arians have finished a certain stage of their activities or what it is they're preparing. They no longer need to keep it quiet. Any attempt on our part to use counter-sanctions against them would be pointless. In order to clarify whether that's so, I've sanctioned a batch of new feathered spies. General Olmar," he bowed in the direction of the elderly warrior. It wasn't worth chastising the man for the slovenliness of his subordinates. The general himself would feed these imbeciles with the rod. "... suggests increasing the grouping of golems on the northern coast. After considering a bit, the external intelligence service, jointly with the 'shadow dwellers' of the Rauu principalities created a batch for shipment. Next week seventeen gulls will be released from the islands of the Wolf archipelago onto the coast."

"Well well," His Highness took up the "warm" spot by the window. "Everyone except the members of the Royal Council is dismissed." After waiting for those in question to leave the room, the king opened a small secret door hidden in the wall near the bar and retrieved a couple of bottles of wine from behind it. "Would anyone like some invigohol?" A clever servant arranged cups with the hot drink and plates of biscuits on the table.

Olmar gratefully nodded to his monarch, who was well acquainted with the general's tastes. The largest cup of the refreshing beverage was placed near him. "Gentlemen, I ask you to speak frankly. The games in front of the public are over; no need to covertly struggle against one another."

"I'll go out on a limb and suggest," Garad, the first chancellor and a friend of Gil's since childhood, stood up from behind his desk, not touching the wine or the invigorating broth. "… that we ought to consider reducing the timing of the Arian invasion we adopted three months ago. We don't have three years. We don't know how long the Twins have in store for Tantre to remain, but it's certainly no more than a year. It would be foolish to hope the northerners don't have any spies here in our lands; the efficacy and effects of their actions in taking over the islands tell us to the contrary. Here the Arians undoubtedly have the advantage. They know everything about us; we're feeling out our way in the dark. Now we have a unique chance to land our army on the continent. We, and the Rauu, are fighting a war on two fronts. Meriya is not a threat: the old king died, and his sons are tearing the state apart. No one will come to the aid of the gray orcs, and then it will be too late to resist. We should unobtrusively speed up peaceful negotiations with the Empire. Yesterday I was informed that an Imperialist diplomat had sought a meeting with our ambassador in Rimm. The point of the Imperialist's movements was to secure the peace as soon as possible. The Empire's been put in a difficult position. The northern legions, as a result of our efforts, no longer exist. In the east, the 'belt' Steppe khans have taken the Tarkel region and landed their aircraft on the Tiger islands. The information about the Emperor's lack of reserves, leaked by the white orcs through the Ilit sultanate, has yielded its first fruits. The Emperor is prepared to make some concessions and pay out incentives. It's time to end the war in the south. We don't have the right to thin out our forces."

"You haven't given the meeting any new information, Garad. According to the latest data from our knights behind the scenes, the Emperor used the Ronmir defeat to the full extent. Yes yes, don't look at me like that. My fellow monarch, during the ensuing chaos, arranged a mass purge of the dissatisfied elements. All the opposition leaders fell under the executioner's ax. Until the felling of the dissatisfied is finished, there will be no negotiations, and at the border, the status quo will remain. We can bomb the border territories as much as we like, but as soon as our army moves away from the operational bases, the Woodies will immediately strike at our back. Our attacks on the Forest bases and bombing of those long-eared filth's army camps have been like a mosquito bite to a barl. Any peaceful initiative on our part will be seen by Pat and by the Forest as a sign of weakness—all will incur all the consequences thereof. That's why I say we continue to grow our strength and teach the mages. Drang, your thoughts? What can you tell us about the High Prince and the orcish princess?"

"I'll begin with the girl," the principal spy began after swallowing his invigohol. "My people sniffed out the girl before the agents of the High Prince's grandson did. The Rauu's scornful attitude towards humans played right into our hand. The spectacle wherein my men pretended to be thick-skulled simpletons came off swimmingly. Our allies still don't suspect that their secrets are no longer secret. We got a message from trustworthy sources that the High Prince has forbidden anyone to touch the orc girl. If we are planning to restore relations with the Lords of the Sky, we should do the same. The princess has come under the wing of our protege."

"The boy's that serious?"

"More so! One's blood curdles from the thought of the were-dragon's power. The High Prince had good reason to ask you for carte blanche in order to find him. The young and still quite ambitious dragon played Miduel for a fool and removed the map from the last bit of the helrats' archives. If everything goes as we were saying, the crown will be missing several of its subjects, and a new enclave will be formed in the Marble Mountains. We need to prepare ourselves for the possible loss of a small chunk of our territory and attempt to tie the were-dragon to ourselves."

"How?" the monarch said, surprised.

"It's not possible to do that directly, but we can get his friends on our side since they are now under the dense hood of the Secret Chancellery. The kids turned out to be nimble creatures indeed—befitting for friends of that formidable creature—and managed to hide for a while on our dear General Olmar's homestead." The old warrior lifted one eyebrow skeptically. "The young men signed two-year contracts. It's somewhat difficult to root out fugitives in the army. The army counterespionage service really doesn't appreciate anyone meddling in its affairs. They both showed up at the storming of Ronmir and earned the rank of officers."

"What do we get out of it?" Olmar spoke up.

"The dragons are molting, which means we can bargain for their scales and blood, just what the helrats were getting by killing them, we, with the right approach and organization, can get from the live lizards and willingly. I hope I don't need to explain to anyone just how valuable the dragon's blood is? And the firepower of one dragon mage? What our boy did in Ortag and the surrounding areas is simply indescribable."

"I don't understand why the lord of the Icicles attaches such importance to the were-dragon?" asked the chancellor.

"The were-drag is capable of pumping mana from the astral plain. The level of mana in the former monastery after he destroyed the Servants of Death was over fifteen bell!"

At that, the chancellor whistled quietly.

"How do you plan to recruit the dragon's friends?" he asked.

"Heavens, no! No recruiting."

"The chancellor asked the right question," the king put in.

"The young men manifested miraculous heroism during the battles. Why not write a small article about this in the newspapers? First give the general facts, then out sly journalists will plump up the facts—and then the newspapers with their portraits will come out. The crown appreciates the merits of young people; the heroes will receive rewards from the hands of His Majesty. For the sake of such a thing, you can sacrifice a couple of confiscated estates from Lailat. The country needs heroes, young people need an example to follow: and here is a living example, more precisely, two examples! This way we kill two suls with one stone: we'll one-up the Rauu, and raise patriotic sentiments in the youth environment."

His Highness poured himself some wine and paced back and forth in front of the window. He didn't like the fact that instead of affairs of state, he had to attend to covert intrigues within the country and between their allies. The ancient elf had impressed Gil, essentially taking the reins of government in the Rauu principalities into his own hands. Miduel never mixed professional and personal. The old elf was known as a notorious schemer, but he never directed intrigues against his allies. His ban on any activity involving the orc's daughter was a sign of his character. With her help, they could pull countless tricks on the Steppe! Instead of that, the old elf decided to keep the peace with the were-dragon. It was a strange decision. Clearly the High Prince's interest in the winged boy was hiding something else.

"I approve the newspaper campaign. Let's return to the subject of the Arians. What are we to do?"

General Olmar stood up. Examining all present with his eagle eye, the old commander rested his palms on the countertop:

"I suggest turning all the information we have over to the king of the dwarfs and the Great Prince of Mesaniya. It's time for them to build some fortifications for themselves."

Tantre. Orten...

"Hey there, could you give me a paper, please." Timur summoned the street vendor boy over with a hand gesture. The boy caught the small coin on his way there, darted to his customer, and slipped him the latest copy of "The Times."

"Dragon Insanity! Flying Beasts Destroy Third Castle! Herds of Dragons Attack Humans!" the distributor of the press shouted at the top his lungs, waving the newspaper, and, scratching his dirty heel and adjusting his cowlick, rushed into the crowd.

Slipping the paper under his arm, Timur stepped towards the barracks of the training regiment quartered in the Middle. He'd have something to read this evening. Crazy dragons. Hm. If he wasn't mistaken, Kerr had reached his fellow tribesmen's nests, and now the angry Lords of the Sky were destroying the helrats' lairs. It was a worthy job, pleasing to the Twins.

The commandant's errand boy, who appeared at the School three hours after class began, handed roi-dert Soto an order, according to which he was to appear in person in front of the commander of the training regiment. Rigaud, for the sake of some company, was offered a one-month contract. The brand new newlywed was wearing a fat husband's bracelet on his wrist. He glanced at Timur and waved the paper.

"It's more fun if we're in it together!" the skinny guy grinned gleefully.

"Tell that to Marika."

"It's okay, she'll understand. We could use some extra money," Rigaud answered and touched the crystal Kerr had given him. "I want to buy a house in the Middle, and I have no desire whatsoever to bargain with Kerr's stones. I've got a feeling down in my heart that we'll need them; boy, will they come in handy. The rector can do with one tiny chip!"

***

Oh Nel, intercessor, oh how my hands hurt. It feels like they're going to fall off. Timur, not undressing, collapsed onto the bed. I wonder where the volunteer offices found those dolts? Stupid villagers, incapable of putting a couple words together, and they're making them second-in-saddles! Probably be better off with the rat-like guys from the dock-side areas. You can bet your bottom pound the cunning company used to earn their bread through robbery or were members of a thief guild. The tattooed recruits' lack of magic bracelets on their ankles was not an indicator of security. At least I wouldn't turn my back on them in a dark alley. Although it's disgusting to stand in front of these rats too—they're home-grown thugs, they're muddy the water in the wing, but it's okay, he'll beat the idiocy out of them or drive them into the grave; otherwise, they'll drive him to the grave.

For over a week now, he and Rigaud had been acting as instructors, training the new recruits of the newly formed wing, which consisted of griffons caught around Ronmir and volunteers picked up in the outskirts of Orten. The skinny guy was having a great time. The commander was using him as civilian personnel. A flexible schedule, payment at the going rate, no jerks hovering over his head and behind his back. Awesome! He should have such a life. But what a life he did have! An officer of His Majesty's army should be an example for others to follow, and punctuality not the least of his admirable qualities. The wing's commander, alert-dert Togo, could not care less that his subordinate was studying in the School of Magic. His order stated: be there at five, which meant at five o'clock and not a second later. Move your feet, officer. It was an exhausting regime: first, they squeezed the juice out of him in school, then they hung him out to dry at the regiment. Thanks to the commandant, kind soul. He didn't forget the guys. Apparently, he thought that the participants of the storming of the enemy citadel would not be hampered by some extra money since the allowance granted didn't cover the bookworms' costs. He decided to contribute to the financial issue. The bosses weren't aware that the sale to Rector Etran of one fragment of the statue of Hel, donated by Kerr, enabled the friends to retrieve five thousand weighty round coins of a tender yellow color.

The commandant, to speak frankly, didn't give a pile of griffon dung about the wetbacks that had donned military uniforms, but a strange guy from army intelligence, nodding from behind the back of a no-less-strange scout, and a pencil-pusher from the Secret Chancellery urged him to assign the designated persons to the training regiment. He wasn't able to discover the reasons for the secret service's interest in the young men. Moving his eyebrows to the center of his face, the clerk from the Secret Chancellery advised him not to get involved in the ruinous swamp of politics, because he'd come across dozens of people who, in the prime of their life, because of idle curiosity, were sent to the halls of the Twins. Please don't repeat their fate. Not a single muscle on the commandant's face moved, but his palms started sweating. Competing offices rarely collaborated. Now he was observing more than collaboration…. Members of different departments were, in good friendship, blowing on the same bagpipes. A joint game was possible in one case only: Duke Drang and Marshal Olmar, who had received the coveted title just two days ago, agreed to join forces. Or, His Majesty had clocked them both on the head, stuck their faces in the mud….

"To Targ with their secrets, I've only got one backside," the commandant decided. "Putting my butt on the line isn't worth the effort. And the request, what's a request to me? It won't cost me anything to wave a couple of orders around and ask the objects of interest of the secret service to serve the Motherland."

Stretching his whole body, Timur took the newspaper from his pocket. The letters jumped around before his eyes. He was so tired, his eyes were crossed. Setting the crumpled "Times" aside, he threw off his boots and uniform and got in the shower. Standing under the icy water, his forehead resting against the wall, he thought about Lubayel. The Snow Elf had sent him a letter saying that the Rauu would arrive in a week. The princes were sending two mage regiments to Orten and Kion. Soon the School would be crawling with Icicles. If only it would be sooner…. Rigaud and Marika would probably be surprised. That thought put a smile on his face.

Timur turned the water off, got out of the shower cabin, put clean shorts on his wet hips, and sat down on the edge of the bed. *What's happening in the world? Hm, the province of Atral. The third castle's been destroyed by a flock of dragons in the foothills of the mountains. The winged killers did not leave a single person alive. Baron von Strog died along with all his household members, servants, and guests in the mountain monastery. As for the monastery, by the way, not a single stone left on stone....* Looking up from the article, Timur looked at the map of the kingdom hanging on the wall. There were more than half a thousand leagues from the Baron von Strog's castle of to the first one, Larno's, destroyed a week ago. Kerr was far away.

Timur turned the page. There was an article in the center spread about the storming of Ronmir. He didn't bother to read any further. The newspapers lie anyway....

***

The letters were blurring, dissolving, swimming, dancing around in a circle. The paragraphs lined up in even rectangles and attacked one another. Sparks from the explosions of large fortress chuckers flashed on the surface of the newspaper sheet. A morning fog ascended to the sky from all the blasts. The walls of Ronmir appeared before his eyes, breaking up the white cloud. There was fire everywhere, people rushing about among the charred ruins. Griffins, lined up in attacking formations, were plowing through the camp to their cawing, which was magically increased in volume for effect. Bits of the walls were flying from the fortress in every direction; tiles were whistling as they flew by, the heavy ceiling beams were hammering the pavement and the surviving rooftops. In a second, the fortress walls were overcome by an all-consuming flame. The red tongues of fire formed into a human-shaped figure. He knew this fire-person. The fire couldn't change Nimir's facial features. The first-in-saddle smiled sadly, extended his hand, and touched Timur on the shoulder:

"Timur, stop dozing!" he said, in Rigaud's voice for some reason. "Wake up!"

Timur opened his eyes and stared at the voluntary "alarm clock," uncomprehending. His heart was pounding, and his whole body was covered in a sticky sweat from the nightmare.

"Come on, it's okay, wake up." Marika then came into his line of sight. A thin, cool hand lay on his forehead. "It's okay, it was just a dream." Her spouse stood beside her, looking at his friend with a worried expression.

"What is it?" Timur asked. "You guys look so worried, I'm starting to worry too. What happened?"

"Your door wasn't locked...," Rigaud said, fidgeting with his bracelet. Apparently, it had become a new habit of his. "You never showed up this morning for training in the park. I didn't know what to think. You're always so punctual, and then you went missing...."

"Rigaud came running from the park, said you were missing. Well, we decided to pay you a visit, sorry we're uninvited," Marika continued instead of her husband. "The door wasn't locked." The young woman fell silent and looked cautiously at her host. Her nervous little fingers pulled at the skirt of her flowered dress. "You were just really groaning in your sleep and grinding your teeth, and I actually got the shivers at the sound of it."

"Ronmir?" Rigaud asked quietly.

"Yes," Timur answered. The two fellows glanced at one another with understanding and nodded. "Wait five minutes. I'll hose off, and we'll go get breakfast together."

***

Marika was the first to notice something strange.

"Honey, what's wrong? You're as white as a sheet," Rigaud said, hugging his wife around the waist and kissing her cheek.

"They hate me. They hate my guts," Marika answered, shooting her eyes towards the company of girls located at the fountain. "But I can't tell why."

"Ahem…," Timur coughed, following Marika's gaze. He was met with the come-hither smiles of the school beauties. "Let's beat it. I don't like that kind of attention."

When they reached the catering establishment, the friends occupied a table in the corner of the hall and called for the waitress. The rosy-cheeked girl who answered the call in a starched apron and cap rounded her eyes, gasped, and with lightning speed disappeared into the back room.

"Perhaps we should leave?" Marika whispered.

They didn't have time to leave. The boss of the School cafeteria darted out from the back room and, waxing eloquent, started rushing around their table.

At his third lap, the odd fellow was caught by his wide belt by Timur, who had stood up from his chair.

"Sir, I'm getting dizzy from your running already," he hissed angrily. Being the object of attention can be very psychologically distressing, especially when you don't know why everyone is making a fuss over you. Timur wanted to say something else, but he suddenly held his tongue, letting go of the heavy cafe owner's belt and going to a nearby stand on which a newspaper was lying. Picking it up, in complete silence, he skimmed the text, went back to the corner of the room, and threw the newspaper down on the table. Half the page of the "Kion Post" was filled with giant portraits of himself and Rigaud.

"Young heroes of Ronmir," Marika read the headline. She grabbed the paper and dove into reading the article. "Boys," she said after finishing, "you've been awarded the order of the 'purple flame on a golden ribbon.'" The newspaper slid off the table and hit the floor. The fat cafe owner retreated into the kitchen, not turning his back on the honored guests. The "heroes of Ronmir," shocked by the news, sat there slack-jawed, straight-backed as if they'd each just swallowed a short crowbar.

The Purple Flame Order was the second-highest and most democratic distinction of the kingdom, and it was awarded only for military exploits and merits. A member of any class could receive the Order—the army doesn't divide people up by their origin—only they awarded them very rarely. The Golden Ribbon gave the recipient the right to inherit the title of count, along with all the ensuing consequences….

"Dear," Rigaud said, smiling, the stupid expression still on his face, "you married a poor baron, are you also going to love a poor count?"

"Clown." Her thin fingers lovingly touched the scars on the ribbon-bearer's face.

"It can't be, Rigaud, it can't be!" Deep furrows appeared on Timur's forehead.

"What are you talking about?"

"About this!" he tapped the newspaper with the toe of his boot.

"Timur, you shouldn't be so distrustful!"

"Really? Just think. Really think. Rack your brains and put the facts together, what I told you. Has our news guy really stopped being able to analyze?"

"Targ!" Rigaud spit on the floor. "You really know how to rain on a guy's parade. What'll happen to us now?"

"I don't know. Welcome to politics, my friend. We're now bargaining chips, and I can't say what kind of a little—or big—prize they're going to trade us for."

"You jerk," Rigaud said without anger. In just those few minutes he had rather grown to like the Order and the title of count.

"Yep. But I can put you in a better mood: our food will be free today," Timur answered, turning to the owner coming out of the kitchen. The girls who were going after the owner were dragging a mountain of snacks on trays. For breakfast, the company of heroes didn't pay a jang....

Their portraits in the paper, a free breakfast, increased attention from women, the quiet envy of men... the goodies just kept coming. At the beginning of the third lesson, where a lecture was being given for the entire first year and the mages sent to the School to finish their studies, a man entered the artifactory magic hall in the uniform of a royal messenger, accompanied by the rector. Rigaud got an awful feeling in the pit of his stomach. Timur frowned and nudged his friend with his elbow:

"I'll bet you anything that messenger's here for our souls."

"Oh yeah. I won't take that bet—I'll lose my money."

"You're so greedy!"

"I am what I am."

Timur was right. The boy was a helpless pawn in the service of the chancellery of His Royal Highness. In a perfectly delivered speech, he called the "heroes" to the blackboard. Accompanied by the sound of the lengthy standing ovation from the bookworms and audience members, and the broad smiles by Etran and the artifact professor, master grall Toro, Rigaud and Timur received two sealed envelopes containing invitations to the royal summer residence for the welcome party upon the occasion of the arrival of High Prince Miduel, Lord of the Rauu, in Orten. The event would take place in two days. There, at the same party, the young officers would receive their awards from the hands of King Gil II himself. They should wear their dress uniforms. Rigaud could show up in his civilian's suit, but it would be preferable for him to put on his army jacket with all its patches and regalia. It was a military award, after all, and even though the roi-dert had been grounded, it would still be a sign of respect to wear the uniform. They were allowed to invite one guest each to the welcome party. They had permission to miss their duties in the training regiments. Upon concluding his speech, the messenger once again congratulated the young men on the awards they had earned and made his exit.

"Who are you going to invite?" Rigaud asked, looking at the invitation and check for a thousand pounds. His Highness had taken care to see that the invitees to the fête would be dressed in their best and could buy dresses and jewelry for their guests. It wasn't every day you got to attend a state reception.

"No one," Timur snapped. "Sorry, Marika," he bowed courteously to the girl, threw a notebook with notes into his bag, and went to the door.

"Hey...," grall Toro interrupted him. "The lecture's not over yet."

"I have an order to appear immediately at the unit, from the general," Timur lied, showing the master his coveted envelope.

"Alright," the bewildered professor answered, "you're free to go." Toro was no mentalist, a trait many bookworms took advantage of.

***

Half the day he wandered aimlessly about the city. He didn't feel like going back to the School. Being famous has a bitter aftertaste. Fake smiles, ingratiating glances, girls ready for anything with their looks like hungry predators having laid their traps.... It was really great that Marika was wearing a large pendant with a chunk of the statue of Hel and constant protection; otherwise, she would have given in to the curses and envy long ago. How'd she managed to catch such a stallion? Rigaud used to be on the prowl for female attention, and now how she's magically pruned him, the lousy girl. One word and he's at her beck and call.

Finding himself starting to go weak in the knees, Timur remembered that he had to sew his dress uniform and polish his boots. Wandering here and there about the little side streets, he found a tailor shop. "Danast— master tailor," the signage read. "Not a cheap establishment," Timur thought to himself examining the fancy dress in the window. He stood outside the strong oak door for a few seconds, then he crossed the threshold.

"Hello. What can I do for you, sir?" the shop worker came out of the back, greeted him politely and respectfully bowed his head.

"Hello," Timur stopped near the mannequin, which was dressed in a chic ballroom gown. "I'd like to order a job from master Danast—sewing my dress uniform."

"I'm sorry, the master doesn't work with military uniforms," the shop worker said glancing at the young officer. He wasn't their kind of client—his boots were worn, and his jacket was crumpled. They wouldn't make any money off this man. The client noticed the shop worker looking at him through the reflection in the window. He chuckled: he's judging me by my clothes. You're in for a surprise, tailor scum.

"You've misunderstood me. I need a dress uniform made from the very best fabric. I'll be grateful to your establishment if you could correct my shoes to match the uniform."

A curtain wiggled behind the shop worker. Someone was taking interest in the conversation.

"That does change things. The senior assistant can take your order. As I said, the master doesn't sew uniforms."

"What a shame. Apparently, I'll have to go to another master. I can't show up at a royal welcoming party in clothes made by a senior assistant.

Sorry for taking your time." Timur clicked his heels and turned his back on the shop worker.

"Two hundred golden pounds," he heard a cracked voice from behind him.

"Two hundred pounds is an insane price for a suit, a total rip-off," Timur thought, turned around, and met the gaze of a maroon-haired dwarf. "Final offer," the short-stack announced.

"Let's shake on it," said the guy getting ripped off. He turned to the counter and shook the master's large hand. No need to be thrifty; he was spending the king's money. The deal was sealed. "You must complete my order by tomorrow evening—or I'll turn my chucker on you."

The mountain-dweller's hair flashed and sparkled blindingly.

"That's not possible!" the dwarf jumped up in alarm.

"You named your price. You said no bargaining. I agreed to your conditions, and now you're saying it's impossible to complete my order? Are you going back on our deal?"

"No," the dwarf answered dismally. The client had trapped him Going back on a deal already made would mean losing his good reputation, and reputation was something one couldn't restore later on. His clients would find another tailor. No one would want their garments sewn by ashamed master. And he looks like just a kid….

"Sit down, I'll take your measurements."

"I asked about boots."

"One hundred pounds."

"Fine. You understand, of course, that the order must be done to a T and ready when the suit is."

The dwarf gnashed his teeth.

Thirty minutes later, full of "free" invigohol, and having lightened his purse by three hundred pounds, Timur left the hospitable establishment. They had promised to deliver the uniform and boots right to the dormitory. It was worth a little extra effort for the price he paid. It was crazy—simple peasants thought of twenty pounds as a huge amount of money, and he had given up ten times more, just for some clothes, cloth he would probably wear very seldom. What was the world coming to?

In the meantime, the evening had come. The magical lanterns that lined the avenues and park trails lit up. It seemed the city had put on its dress uniform. Timur sat for a while in the summer restoration on the shore of the man-made lake, listened to the music and enjoyed the exquisite cuisine. The waiters clamored around the promising customer. The women at the neighboring tables shot him glances, but the young officer remained indifferent to their feminine charms. *Let them think what they want. I don't care. It's a nice night. I think I'll walk back to the dorm....*

***

The park was empty. What idiot would run around the trails with lead weights on his feet and a heavy bag on his shoulders in a dank fog? It was morning—the time for the last dreams, not for senseless running around. Rigaud stopped Timur and tossed him the training sword made of raw iron:

"Here. We'll work on our low stances, and then you'll show what you're made of on the attack. Move!" The skinny guy and Marika did not ask any questions about where he'd been all day yesterday. A man sometimes needs to be alone. His friends perfectly understood his mood.

"That's enough," Rigaud stopped the practice. "If you stick your leg out, your leg's going to get it. If you lean forward, you lose balance and might take a slanting blow. Don't take your hand to the side; we're not working with shields, so the left side is open to attack by the enemy. A quick puncture—and there'll be one more dead person. Do you want to become a zombie? No? En guard!"

Skinny and toned with lean muscle all over, Rigaud wasn't cutting his friend any slack. Their practices were as rough as can be. Mistakes were immediately punished by would-be fatal punctures and strikes, after which you wouldn't get up again in a real battle. Every day the former second-in-saddle committed fewer and fewer goof-ups, but he still had a very long way to go to become a real swordsman.

"That's it," Rigaud spit out. "Let's get off the field."

They gathered their equipment and went to the dorm. Timur didn't take off his heavy anklets and belt. He would take them off at home.

About a hundred yards from their building, a dozen figures stepped out from the fog with traveling bags on their shoulders. The closer the friends got to the figures, the clearer it became that the Rauu had arrived at the School. Apparently, the guests from the Marble Mountains had arrived through the School portal, since there was still more than half an hour before the gates would open. The elves looked the young humans up and down. Their eyes showed sincere respect. They saw the weights hung all over their bodies. The men had obviously been training for over an hour. Not everyone could force himself to get up at such an early hour and go out in the cold fog. Timur suddenly threw his equipment down on the ground and butted into the group of female elves.

"Ow, watch where you're stepping!" one beauty piped up. He had accidentally stepped on her toe.

"Lubayel!"

One of the girls turned around, dropped her bag from her shoulder, and ran to meet him.

"Timur!" she squeaked, wrapping her arms around his neck and kissing him on the lips.

The Icicle spectators smiled at the scene. Rigaud shook his head and whistled subtly. *Wow, the man of few words, you've really caught me by surprise!*

Tantre. Orten. Lailat...

His Highness bowed to the chancellor and quietly asked:

"What do you think of our dragon friend's fellows?"

"Interesting young men. They've got some talent. It would be worth paying them some mind. Drang wasn't exaggerating when he told us about them," Garad answered, watching the handsome pair, a human and an elf woman momentarily frozen in the dance step. "Count Soto's escapades never cease to amaze. And where did he get a uniform of that caliber and such a beautiful partner? Olmar can take offense if he likes, but next to the young man's, his uniform just doesn't measure up, or it looks like a poor relative's tunic!" The king laughed.

"That's not what I'm talking about."

"I realize what you're talking about. I don't think the elf girl is here on assignment from Miduel. You can just tell by the way their eyes sparkle when they look at one another. And I'll tell you something else: the guys have done a great job rising to the occasion. I was watching them during the award ceremony, and I observed the looks they gave you and Miduel. Soto's aura was even and calm, which means he has extreme self-control. When you began speaking about their heroism, a little glint ran over it, as if he'd mentally made a wry face. He's indifferent to rewards and gifted estates in Lailat. They don't want to become pawns in a political game."

"They're still just boys!"

"If you could see the illusiogram of the second medal recipient after the battle of Ronmir, you wouldn't be so dismissive."

Gil II leaned back on the throne, which was mounted on a low platform, and thought. Was he playing games? Yes. The whole of life is a game. Children have toys and games that are small. Older people play games in the yard and outside. For people with power, the playground grows to the size of the city, province, and country. In the hands of people with great power, the world itself is the toy. It seems that the world was sick of being played with like a doll. He decided to play the role of a doll-maker and play with people's fates for a bit. After games like that cities were reduced to ashes....

"Your Majesty! Targ take it! Get Garad over here," violating all norms, Drang's voice came from the communicator amulet sewn into His Highness' collar, which did not signal anything pleasant for Garad.

Not turning his head, the king directed his eyes only towards the darkened niche on the right of the room. There stood the main state spy. Gil looked at the chancellor and closed his eyes. Garad walked away from the throne, crossed a third of the room slowly in a laid-back manner, loitered among the courtiers for three or four minutes, and then came to a stop beside the head of the Secret Chancellery.

"Calm down, Gil, it's okay. Smile, smile, Targ take you," the monarch mentally soothed himself. The pallor on the chancellor's face as he returned was not reassuring. *What now?* Judging by Garad's confused expression, nothing good. The old elf too began to fidget on his throne. *What, not a comfy pillow?* Or had he too been informed of something through a whisper from the amulet? The High Prince's grandson approached the throne. The relatives were conversing earnestly about something, and Beriem slipped unnoticed from the room. This was getting interesting.

"Code 'double,'" the tiny magical amulet piped up.

It was as if someone had pulled the very core out of the king. It seemed to him he was moving down the steps of the platform, and the throne was crumbling into dust. The fun of the official reception faded as if covered with a dark veil. This was bad.

Shaking his head, hiding the worry that had taken hold of him behind a wide, cordial smile, His Majesty stood up from the throne and descended the platform. A crowd of nobles immediately descended on him. The monarch had finally deigned to socialize with his subjects!

Curtsies, bows, nude, powdered shoulders, deep décolletés, ingratiating (and not very) glances. A couple of times he sensed hatred directed at his back. Mm-hmm. I have to remember to remind Drang to have his people shake information out of everyone here. His Highness was not a mage, but that spark of a "whisperer" which was discovered in him by his tutors was developed through long and rigorous training. Someone hated him with all his (or her) heart and soul, but who? He mustn't leave survivors or revenge-hungry relatives of those who were supposed to be executed for participation in the revolt. If he let his guard down even a little, he could be sent to the Twins' court. It might be poison in his wine. The King snickered. Drang would have his work cut out for him.

Snapping out of his gloomy train of thought, the king scanned the room and all those in it. He saw the ladies' intricate hairstyles and revealing dresses and the men's austere suits, mixed with frequent spots of military uniforms, the glitter of decorations and jewelry; people fussing about. Gil never liked noisy gatherings. From his earliest childhood, the future monarch preferred quiet pastimes with a book in hand. But whoever asked a king what he preferred? Preferences were one thing, but the life of the heir to the throne was something else entirely.

***

His Highness, Olmed the I, Olmed the Swift, king of Tantre, kept his son close, ruling over him with an iron fist. At ten years old, the king's son was sent incognito to be raised in the Army Infantry Corps for sons of the nobility. "We'll see what you make of yourself," his father had said, pressing his lips into a thin line. "Don't even think of blabbing about your origin, or else...." The monarch's dark brown eyes flashed with rage.

The prince didn't answer, no matter how hard it was to keep silent. Kitchen duty and a lashing for minor transgressions, and a cold lock-up for serious misconduct.

The teachers and teaching style at the Corps were most strict. Right from the start, the young page had no time for anything at all except class and homework. He didn't complain when his father asked him about his studies during the short scheduled vacation. With a helping he had from the old king, people started calling Gil "Soft Spoken" when out of earshot. What was there to tell if the Corps was flooded with members of the secret service and detailed daily reports of the young cadet's life were placed on the king's desk? Gil was never stupid or naive. Excellent grades for time management and mastery of the martial arts made the strict father glad. Gil met Garad during their time in the Corps. The active and mischievous Garad was a kind of pole, pulling the cadets towards him. A storyteller and a brawler, he took the quiet man under his wing. Often they fought back to back. The Corps leaders always looked the other way when it came to fights between the cadets, as long as they didn't involve magic or steel. The young men needed to let off steam, so let them. As long as they didn't maim on another. On the other hand, who took whom under his wing was a serious question. The mischief they made together....

Gil turned eighteen, but no one celebrated his birthday. A week before the holiday, Olmed I the Swift died. It was a stupid way to die, no other way to put it. His father rode out to the shooting range where the military alchemists were testing some sort of non-magical explosives. The power of the blow exceeded all expectations. The magical shields instantly dissolved and the stone bunkers were blown apart like straw houses, burying the alchemists, the king, the generals, and the entire crowd gathered there that day under the rubble. Personal defense amulets saved no one. Rockslides up in the mountains resulted from the quaking of the earth from the blast. The riverbed of the river flowing through the shooting range overflowed. The people covered by the stones choked out their last breaths....

As per tradition, the crown was laid upon the young king's brow in the central Temple of the Twins one month after the old monarch's funeral. Along with the crown, Gil inherited a huge pit of vipers at the throne. His father's confidants and simply the richest people of the kingdom thought that they could control the Soft Spoken.... He gave them the illusion that this was indeed the case. The inexperienced king nodded to one, smiled at another, and with a smart look listened to the advice of a third. He hated most of his father's courtiers with every fiber of his being. They had become vultures, tearing the country apart and increasing their personal gain. Those who were truly sorry and cared about the state were pushed back into the last rows and defamed backwards, forwards and sideways. He played the puppet. And, in complete secrecy, the seemingly cast-off friends of the former page boy, under the leadership of Garad and the slippery fifth-year student of the Kion Academy of Magic, Drang, were surreptitiously placing anonymous letters among the dissenting camps and spreading various rumors. The young pages were recruiting newcomers to the party of the king from among the nobles, the former strongmen of this world who had fallen into disgrace, who'd been pushed to the background of politics.

The poison-pen letters and rumors were effective. The friendly choir of the highest of the high-born stopped singing in unison. Squabbling broke out among the dignitaries vested with enormous power. In the struggle among the families, the king was forgotten. Who needed the pup—a mere shadow of his once-great father? As long as he didn't get in the way. Busy with their own quarrels, the nobility let Gil go into a marriage with an unknown noblewoman from an ancient, albeit poverty-stricken family. The wedding did not bring the monarch any blessings and did not affect the alignment of forces of the political camps. The dukes and the lords were wrapped up in the intrigues against one another and forgot about the king. To their chagrin, the king did not forget about them. One fine day, they suddenly saw the light, but it was too late....

The Soft Spoken, like a thief in the night, had gradually and unnoticeably appointed his own people to all the major positions. The Kion garrison was led by Colonel Olmar. Getting the upper hand over the noblemen (who had recovered from their bickering), fifty army soldiers showed up at their doors, reinforced by five mages. Some of them even got several hundred soldiers and dozens of magicians sent to seize them. In one night, the real power passed into the hands of Gil and his supporters. The people and the simple noblemen remained unaware of the events that had taken place. Some former strongmen of this world lost their heads in dark dungeon cells. Some fled their posts and paid huge fines, rejoicing that they did not repeat the fate of the former. Some left Kion and the country for good. The Soft Spoken had confirmed his nickname, pulling off a huge task in secret, without letting on to the numerous spies and frienemies.

After that came long years of consolidating his royal power and strengthening the country. The army underwent radical reform. Like mushrooms after a rainfall, griffon breeding plants sprung up in the mountains. The system of material maintenance of parts changed. The number of combat mages who could not only conjure but also hold a weapon increased by an order of magnitude. In the depth of the Southern Rocky Ridge, dozens of secret laboratories were engaged in various military investigations, often completely illegal. Gil realized that the boil of human-elf relations that had come about after the siege of Orten four hundred years ago was beginning to come to a head with new strength and would, at some point, burst. He would have to take measures to heal the boil in advance. As it turned out, he had good cause for concern twenty years ago. The boil burst, as always, at the worst possible moment....

The former allies became foes. The north and south were on the brink of war. He was forced to hold balls and receptions for the amusement of traglomps. Politics could go to Targ for all he cared. How disgusting it had become for him to look at the ugly mugs of the leeches, sucking up to the throne, trying to procure favors from the crown and boasting of their nobility and proximity to His Majesty!

Garad and Drang escaped the fate of being crushed by the vices of power, but their children should not be allowed to approach the feeding trough. The gray mass that couldn't smudge the parents corrupted the offspring. Since the times of Olmed, nothing had changed. And what of it? You haven't got long left. The Arians would beat all the nonsense out of your heads. Recent events made many fear the king and had shown people who was really in charge of the country. And things would get even worse—Gil looked at the joyful faces and thought that he would have to introduce a strict dictatorship. The nervous faces of Garad and Drang just shouted about the need for this step. In the meantime, we'll still smile….

Exchanging a couple of meaningless words with those hungry for communication and making some happy with some compliments, Gil walked around the hall. Immediately behind the monarch, as if from under the ground, three bodyguards sprang up. The custodians of the monarch's body kept a certain distance, but no one was deceived by their feigned relaxation. Looking at the trained guardsmen, one wanted to get rid not only of one's weapons but also of any seditious thoughts. Mage-killing mages struck an unconscious sense of fear into people and elves.

The king walked around the courtiers for twenty minutes, then lingered a little near a group of decorated military officers. Now the main burden of strengthening the country rested on the army. Hm, of all these officers showered with lofty favor, the two youngest seem to be missing. The young heroes and their dates preferred to retreat to the dancing part of the hall, which was separated from the banquet portion by a curtain of silence.

The king looked at the dancing young men and again sank into unpleasant thoughts. Garad and Drang were wrong. He wasn't thinking of getting an edge over the Rauu and Miduel. He had other plans for the dragon's friends. The guys were good at making friends. The chancellor was right. They couldn't care less about awards and estates, and they didn't want power. The dragon really had a knack for selecting his friends! These people would never betray their country or their crown and would take a fireball for their friend. The dark shields around Count Soto's aura made one think twice when speaking to him and have an attitude of respect. Rait, who was in his second year at the Orten School of Magic studying under a false name, like the heroes of Ronmir, had just turned seventeen. Rector Etran should subtly unite the young people. Her son needed real friends and comrades-in-arms. The young count wouldn't ever give him away under the pressure of circumstance. He wasn't that kind.

Causing him to start, the pea of the communicator amulet vibrated. The double is ready, and you must leave unnoticed and make a beautiful exit. The royal Mages' Guild will have to work a piece of bread and butter. The room is full of magicians; none should notice the substitution.

Cunning flashed in the king's eyes. The corners of his lips twitched in a slight smile—this is exactly what no one expects of him. Stepping over the curtain, Gil plunged into the sounds of the orchestra.

"Your Highness," Count Soto bowed his head. The elf woman curtsied.

"May I invite your friend to a dance?" the king smiled and practically choked from the youth's penetrating and slightly glacial look. And they called the Rauu "Icicles!" The roi-dert seemed a likely candidate for the title at the moment, not his blushing lady friend. Truly, the elf had found a kindred spirit. The count bowed elegantly, stepped aside, from the encouraging smile he gave the elf, the white scars on his face formed into rays reaching from the corner of his left eye. The ice in the glance melted, giving the girl a wave of warmth and giving himself confidence. *Garad is right, a thousand times right: there's nothing fake going on here. How they look at each other….*

Gil took the girl in his arms and spun her around in time to the music.

The music stopped. Taking the girl by the arm, the king, to the whispers of the courtiers, invited guests, and elves, led her back to her cavalier.

"Don't forget to invite me to the wedding," he whispered to the austere young count. And where was his imperturbability?

The guy's shields dissolved. His aura shone with all colors of the rainbow. His eyes grew round.

Satisfied with his little trick, the monarch left the dancing half of the hall. It was time! While most of the courtiers would be discussing the king's escapade and busy examining the girl, he wedged himself into the center of the group of guardsmen, from which point they all accompanied him to the throne. No one paid any heed to the fact that this solid group of guards subsequently made its way to the hall's side door.

***

"Drang, may Targ invade your liver! What on Ilanta??" the king swore, walking through the secret passages under the palace.

"Your Majesty, let's go to the operator's room," the duke said tiredly.

"Tell me—cat got your tongue? There's a whole hall full of guests, foreign ambassadors, and the head of the Rauu up there. What is the meaning of this circus?"

"The High Prince will be joining us any minute now. You'd better see for yourself. It's hard to explain. If I had to sum it up in one word…,"

"Well?"

"Arians."

"Mother of…," the monarch hiss between his teeth.

"Mother of…," he said again in the operating room, examining the panoramic illusion. The elderly High Prince came up beside him.

The ground was far below. From the height of the bird's flight, they could see the thousand-fold armies lining up in ranks for battle. There were at least a hundred thousand warriors and mages on each side.

"Drang, the Arians are already on the continent?"

"Yes, sire. The Shanyu was lying in wait for them, but the gray orcs missed the landing of the army's first wave too, and did not have time to sink them."

"So there's the second wave too?"

"Yes. Truvor, show him," the head of the Secret Chancellery asked one of his workers.

"Mother of…," the king sighed a third time.

A thousand ships—from simple drekkars to enormous leviathans, next to which the combat galleons of the Dawn Bringer elves looked like puny minnows—were beating the waves with their stems, leaving trails of white foam, which were immediately sailed over by other vessels. As far as the eye could see, the sea was covered with sails.

Grabbing his head in his hands, one of the operators fell off her chair. A tiny stream of blood trickled from the mage's nose. The Rauu who was controlling an owl fell into convulsions. The view of the army in preparation went dark. Life mages rushed in; the operators who lost consciousness were carried off on stretchers.

"What happened?" Garad asked. "What's wrong with the operators? Why did we lose visualization?"

"The Arians attacked the large mana absorbers. The birds are dead. The death of the animal is always felt by the operator!" Beriem answered instead of Drang. "Well, there you have it. The northerners have left the shamans and themselves magic-less. You can't win a battle with just personal defense amulets. Steel will decide the outcome. Whoever kills more of the other's mages first will win. The absorbers can't work for too long, three or four hours at best, then they'll blow up and let all that they've collected out, and their functionality radius is limited."

"Drang, do we have anything we can replace the birds with?"

"We'll try to cast off some gulls and golems from the shore, but it'll take at least three hours to get everything ready."

"Go!" Gil turned to Miduel: "What are we going to do?"

"Wait."

Northern Alatar. Peninsula of Kanyr. Ulus Kirn...

"Noino,[15] what was that? Yljag asked, clenching his spear. A strange wave of cold ran over the orc's whole body. The other warriors around him glanced at one another, baffled, barked and squatted on the warg's hind legs.

"Shaman stuff," the uncle spit on the tangled grass. "Don't be a wuss, stay near me, hold your shield, and everything will be alright. Don't go getting ahead of me. Get your bow ready. I've no desire to meddle with these newcomers. It's better to shower them from afar with arrows."

"They're not newcomers—they're Arians."

"Shushug dung all the same. I'll put their heads on a stake, maybe that'll add brains to their heads It'll teach them to trespass on our land. We need to cut them up, before they cut us up. If we don't stop them now, it'll

---

[15] Uncle (*Orcish*)

be too late later on. Look at the island orcs—where are their islands? No islands! Where are the redbeards[16]? No redbeards! They've gone begging. Who else wants to become a beggar?" the old gray-haired veteran yelled loudly and looked at the frozen line-up. A dozen of eyes was looking at him from under their helmets. No one wanted to leave their ancestral territory. They'd been working this land for thousands of years. "No one? What are you silent for?! Your mouths stuffed? Do you think the old fart's lost his mind? My fangs fell out, that means my mind's gone too? There, beyond the hill—there's your enemy! A true foe! This old fart's not a crow, he's not gunna caw and croak worthless words! The Arian freaks pushed the Vikings and the island-dwelling orcs off the islands. We're all the same to them. Fight, Hygyn's degenerate trash, or we'll be chased out of here with mares' tails! They're not here to plunder! This spawn of the accursed gods needs land and slaves!

"Look!" someone in the line cried. A few orcs were pointing at the neighboring hill, from behind the top of which the smooth ranks of the enemy infantry were coming out on the gentle slopes. Banners were fluttering and colored flags flapping on long peaks.

"Why's the Shanyu taking so long?! We have to strike while they're still getting into formation!" Ilyag heard.

"Knock off the conversation!" yelled the commander of fifty soldiers, whipping the nearest back. "Shut your pie holes! What are you afraid of? The 'greenies' and our ancestors drove the Arians out like street rats. Do you think there's any force that can stop orcs? These pikemen— the hand gripping the whip pointed in the direction of the Arians—are just blind puppies against 'white shields!'" Dozens of heads simultaneously turned towards the rows of phalanges bristling with spears. The rows of orc infantry looked much more imposing.

The heart of every Steppe warrior filled with pride of their army. There was no force in the world capable of defeating the Shanyu's baturs and nökürs. They could annihilate any barrier! No troop formation could withstand a joint attack from a phalanx of "white shields!" The cavalry charge was like a rockslide or a steppe wildfire—it wiped out everything in its path! Why was the chief dragging his feet? Give the order, Big Steppe Wind! Oi-lo, hhhrrraaa-hrrra! Your warriors will sweep the wretched freaks off the face of the planet and stuff sacks with enemy heads! Hrrrraa! We'll have a great plunder! Lots of loot! Hrrra-hrrraaa! Our blood is

[16] Orcs' nickname for Norsemen.

boiling, our horses wheezing, our wargs, sensing the adrenaline and upcoming battle, are roaring. What was the Shanyu waiting for? Did he doubt his nökürs?

***

When the warriors began to grumble, and the expectation reached its pinnacle, the regiment drums sounded, and the roar of dozens of horns announced the start of the fight. The Shanyu had given the order. "HHHRRRR-RAA! HRR-HRR-HRRR!!! HRRR-RAA!" rang out over the field. The gray orcs' war cry would make anyone's blood freeze in their veins. There was something ancient and primal in the cries of the children of the Steppe.

The loud yet muffled cry of the enormous gongs resounded, curdling blood and setting hearts fluttering. The warg units of the right flank flooded the hill in descent. Huge wolves galloped in long strides, speeding over the ground. The cavalry dashed forward behind the wargs. A large squadron of Arians on horseback drove out to meet them. Thousands of arrows soared into the sky, pelting both sides with fatal rain. Bright flashes made Yljag cover his eyes. Blinking from the "flies," he looked at the battlefield. The magical charges were not finishing the enemy cavalry off. The enchanted arrows clapped down upon their targets powerlessly, pouring their killing power out in the form of the bright flashes. Their magic turned out to be no match for honest iron. It became clear what the cold feeling was some while ago that had made the warriors shiver. The Arians' shields were sucking up mana. This time, the riders reached for their good old "whistlers[17]." A penetrating whistle accompanied the new cloud of spiky death. These arrows ripped through the heavenly blue and fell on the Arians, who covered themselves with their shields, killing and wounding, knocking the unlucky from the saddle.

The Shanyu, surrounded by his advisers, khans, and generals, observed the battle from the top of a hill. His experience as a warrior and commander's intuition told him that the northerners had prepared some dangerous and unpleasant surprises for them. The orcs weren't used to

[17] Whistling arrows.

fighting in the hills; the cavalry charge needed room to make a broad sweep. The battle had just begun, but he knew they would not get the upper hand if they couldn't push the enemy back onto the flat plateau located right behind the Arians. No wonder they stood on the hills. They were not fools. They understood that in a limited space it's more difficult to enact a large-scale strike. The cavalry's and infantry's actions would not be effective. The Shanyu leaned toward his messenger.

The squadrons collided like two opposing waves. Yljag raised himself up in the stirrups. His sharp steppe vision allowed him to see swords and scimitars clashing with fiery flashes, spears flying, horses and wargs lying on the ground, the riders of which immediately fell under the hooves and claws of the animals. They fell like sacks from the saddles, cut down or stabbed by spears. The Arians effectively wedged themselves deep into the cavalry ranks but were stopped by the warg units. The wargs pounced at the enemy with the wrath of Khirud the lightning-armed. Smelling blood, the animals jumped right over the heads of the first few rows in giant leaps and wrecked havoc among the enemy. The toothy beasts that were stripped of their riders did not remain on the sidelines. They threw themselves at their enemy along with their fellow wargs. The Arians could no longer withstand the pressure and fled. The second wave of orcs darted from the hills in obedience to the thunderous rumble of the drums.

The follow-up strike was terrible. The cavalry charge in pursuit of the fleeing cavalry plunged into the infantry ranks, messed up the military order of their opponent's front-line regiment, and swept it into pieces. The lassos then immediately whistled, and there was no protection or salvation from them. They pulled the Arians' horses down along with their riders, who were then crushed by the weight of the horses. The wargs ripped human flesh apart. The lasso-throwers, in sight of the enemy troops, dragged the soldiers they'd caught through the whole field along the ground behind their horses, ripping up their flesh on sharp stones. A dense shower of arrows shot from the hill over the heads of those standing in front could not stop the offensive onslaught of the thousands who had flown into a rage. The Arian army's left wing began to back away.

The Shanyu waved his hand. The trumpets sounded. The troops, in a united wave, rushed forward. Thousands of feet pounded the ground all at once. Like a shining silver ingot, the phalanx, bristling with thousands of spears, set out in search of glory.

An insane carnage took place at the Arians' front-line regiment. Fighting broke out all along the front and spread like wildfire from there. The large boulders on the slopes of the hills at the Arians' right flank didn't leave the cavalry a fighting chance. The joint strike was broken up into separate pokes of out-spread fingers, but it didn't allow the northerners to relax, either. The archers were sent to the front lines and contributed to the turmoil in the orderly rows of enemy infantry. Yljag snatched his bow from the quiver and fired arrows at the enemy at high speed. Khirud protected him from taking any "gifts" in return, which had already sent more than one valiant orc to his ancestors. The unit spun in an endless circle dance in front of the Arian Pikemen, covered by their wide shields and bristling with long spears. Breaches would occasionally pop up here and there in the joint ranks. If a shield fell and another warrior fell to the ground, the empty space was immediately filled by the next shield-bearer. The long black arrows of the Arian archers whistled, sent in a canopy from behind the back rows, completing the mutual exchange of lives.

The combined roar of the phalanx troops as they cut into the center of the enemy formation rang out over the battlefield, drowning out the other sounds of the ongoing combat. A massacre most bloody ensued. The huge orcs chased their enemy away. The front line slowly arched into a curve. The horse and warg units descended upon the left flank, which was continuing to retreat before the cavalry charge's constant attacks. For over an hour, the Shanyu's nökürs couldn't put down the defenses of the fiercely resisting foe. At some point, the heavily armored horse units sensed the weakness at the junction of the Arian regiments and attacked this spot. A wide gap formed in the ranks of the enemy troops. At the command of the drums, plowing people into the ground and toppling the ranks of northerners who had tried to resist the pressure of the archers striking at point-blank range, three tumens[18] plunged into the gap. The orcs escaping to the highlands saw before them the regiments of the second line. Behind the enemies' backs towered the poles of the absorber, shining like gems.

Hrr-ra! Hrrr-rra! Hrr, hrrr! Calling and ululating, the units plunged at the enemy, killing and cutting into their backs as they fled, impaling the crazies who imagined themselves capable of defeating a Shanyu's daring

---

[18] The largest organizational tactical unit of the orc army, the number of which was usually ten thousand horsemen.

horsemen on their long cavalry pikes. The tumens, spreading over the highlands like a river that broke through a dam, lined up in an offensive cavalry charge formation. The tumens' unit struck at the backs of the newcomers' defensive screen regiments. More and more units of soldiers kept filing into the gap. The right wing was the first to ram against the unseen barrier. Myriads of stakes and forked sticks concealed by the long grass stopped the oncoming attack, and the horses ran straight into them at full speed. The wargs pierced the pads of their paws and rolled along the ground, mutilating and killing their riders. The riders flew over the heads of their animals, flung from the saddles. The rear units, unable to stop in time, also fell prey to the hidden stakes. A victory cry turned into cries of pain and the awful scream of the horses with broken legs. At some point, a silence fell over the battlefield. The chaos and clanking of the combat quieted down, only to explode with new screams of pain from the left-flank cavalry charge, who fell into the traps in turn. The "spoons" of dozens of catapults arranged in front of the enemy army then flung their contents with a dull thwack. Hundreds of pots of earth oil broke among the stalled horde, followed by burning arrows. The inhuman wailing of orcs and animals burned alive drown out all sounds of battle.

The attack sputtered to a stop. The Arians' defensive screen regiments, which had escaped the cavalry charge and were responding with the myriad of arrows, opening the attack vector to the second-line regiments, moved back and to the right in an organized fashion.

"Horns, call the 'white shields' back, now!!" the Shanyu commanded. Oh, Khirud! Why? Why have you turned away from your faithful sons? Mother Steppe, why have you allowed your children to be led into a trap? Why have you covered my eyes with the ghost of an easy victory? "Command the tumens to retreat!"

The Arian generals, like cheese in a mousetrap, sacrificed a few regiments in order to destroy the entire enemy army. The heroic resistance of those doomed to the slaughter lulled the vigilance of the experienced steppe dwellers....

The horns sounded. It was too late. Three enemy columns were closing in on the phalanx, covered with body-length shields. The first rows of Arians dropped to the ground, the second few got on their knees, and the third few lifted their loaded crossbows to eye level. Their commander gave the signal....

The heavy crossbow bolts pierced a multitude of holes in the wall of shields. A second discharge increased the number of wounded and fallen. The archers ran up and jam-packed the alleys between the attacking columns, their long arrows immediately starting to stick like skewers into the crevices. Like an avalanche, the enemies fell upon the phalanx of the "white shields."

Cutting off the retreat path, the northerners' warg units struck at the tumens, who had fallen right into their trap, from behind the hill. The Arians released hundreds of armor-clad woolly rhinos in their frontal attack on the orcs' cavalry.

A bloody chaotic "porridge" was cooking in the enormous "pot" of the flat plateau. Rhinoceroses wiped away the weak screen barrier in their path and cut into the bulk of the cavalry. The Shanyu turned away. A tear rolled down the old orc's cleanly shaven cheek.

The Arians had won, but the battle wasn't over yet. Forty thousand nökürs were in the reserves, but any human or orc that was not blind could see their fate was already decided. The Shanyu could see. The enemy had declined the use of magic and had deprived the orc shamans of it. They had counted on it, and their calculations turned out to be correct. Without magical support, not used to fighting with only iron and steel, the troops were doomed.

This wasn't the end. The Shanyu summoned Tyrba.

"Yes, my commander!" the khan bowed.

"We're retreating. Organize cover."

"But…," the poles of the "absorber" came crashing down, cutting off the khan's words. Getting the upper hand over the shamans, the Arian mages entered the battle. Magic returned to the battlefield, but it didn't help the orcs. Most of the sorcerers were killed in the very first moments of the magical battle. The Steppe army fled….

The Shanyu marched the surviving tumens off to the south after the massacre.

Tantre. Orten. Lailat….

"Your Highness!"

"What?" The king hadn't noticed that he'd nodded off in the soft armchair.

"Duke Drang says the birds are on their way," the messenger bowed before his monarch.

"Let's go," Gil nodded to the High Prince.

"I'm so tired of waiting. I've spent half my life waiting," the old Rauu squeaked, following the king of Tantre into the operator's room.

***

"What's the news?"

The head of the secret service shook his head dejectedly at the monarch's innocent question. The king got more information from Drang's hopeless expression than he would have liked to know.

The panoramic illusion confirmed their gloomiest predictions. The birds were too late. Black patches on the ground were like a footprint of the combat spells that had been used. They could see deep craters, containing some charred remains of what used to be a warg, an orc, or a human.

The blood-stained field, tens of thousands of corpses, flocks of crows and small striped griffons circling above…. As soon as the men will finish off the wounded and collect trophies, it'll be their time—time for a feast.

On the sidelines, the horse units were rounding up thousands of prisoners. Hundreds of mages were hanging collars on captured orcs. The gentry would be dealt with separately.

The "white shields" had given their all, to the very last orc. They stood like a stone ridge in the middle of a river, the raging waters rushing against it. Their powerful defense amulets deflected many magical attacks. The phalanx did not retreat, restraining the furious attack of armored columns and collecting a rich harvest. The professional warriors, who had been training with the sword since they were five years old, could fight as a formation and as individuals. They gave the army the chance to retreat, flee southward, saving a few tumens with their lives.

"The second wave has reached the shore," Drang broke the heavy silence.

The king didn't say anything. He waved at the operator. The illusion went dark.

"We have to make peace with the Empire," Gil uttered. The High Prince closed his eyes in consent.

"And the Forest?" the first adviser asked.

"Soon the Forest will have bigger problems than us. The Woodies are out of the game for a while, for the same reason we're entering it," the monarch answered. "Drang, keep me posted on all developments," he added, leaving the room.

***

"Your Majesty," interrupting his discussion with the rector of the Orten School of Magic, the illusion of Gil II's personal secretary appeared above the wide black wooden table.

"Octavius, I asked not to be disturbed," the monarch frowned.

"Sire, please forgive me, but Duke Drang was very insistent," the secretary said, embarrassed. The king chuckled. Yes, Targ invade his liver. When necessary, Drang indeed knew how to insist.

Leaning back against the back of his chair, the king looked at Rector Etran. They would have to postpone their conversation, all the more so since the head of the School could not boast of success in the field of matchmaking. She hadn't been successful yet, but some progress had been made. The business should be fixed so that the initiative comes from the people themselves and they won't ever suspect that their actions are being directed by somebody. It was an excruciatingly difficult task, Targ take it. They didn't have much time left. In a week, according to the royal decree, Etran had to exchange her post as rector for that of the governess. She would take on a few more headaches and would not have time to deal with certain delicate issues.

"Show him in."

Recently, the duke, like a Hel's raven, had been bringing only the blackest of tidings.

"The duke asked me to tell you that they're waiting for you in the operator's room." The illusion disappeared.

"Targ," the king swore. "Let's go, Etran. It's time for you to dip your toes into affairs of state. Who do you suggest for the post of captain of the city and the province guards?" he asked cordially, stepping into the hall.

"I think Hag Tur Seaman would be a wonderful fit for that post. The Viking's show what he can do, and it's most impressive. He's got a great education, he's diplomatic, both with the warriors and with the merchants, and he understands the customs of the common people."

The monarch gave a meager grin:

"It's no surprise the Viking was a student of Beriem's."

The rector's eyebrows flew up high.

"You didn't know? I'll have them send you the detailed file, but, in general, I approve. Talk to the Norseman yourself."

"Hm," the rector grunted.

"Sire!" The guards, reinforced with a mage, went on duty.

Nodding to the guards, Gil stepped into the operator's room. Uh-oh! Someone was going to get it today, bad. This "someone" lowered his eyes guiltily.

"Sire, I decided it wasn't necessary for the secretary to know, but the High Prince is in the palace," Drang said.

"Targ's conspirator!" the king barked, and greeted Miduel without a drop of ceremony.

"Show me what you have," he ordered the duke, sitting in the soft chair next to the elderly Snow Elf. "Has Beriem met with the Great Prince?"

"Yesterday," the elf answered. "The Shanyu's ambassadors arrived in Mesaniya."

"How about that...," the king drawled, watching the crystals installed in their stands from the corner of his eye.

"Alekhaner Mesanskii knows about the battle. The orcs have suggested an alliance."

"And what does the prince think?"

"He agreed. The orcs will march their tumens south, they're packing up their nomad camps. The Shanyu will not maintain the defense of Tartus, the grays' cities are not designed to withstand a siege. The prince will get, by the most conservative estimates, an army of forty or fifty thousand. After the latest defeat, most of the nomad settlements have peacefully rejected the Shanyu. The khans are actively making friends with the 'greenies.' Soon the Arians will force this gang of swindlers on Meriya and the Forest. Taiir will take it very badly. The kingdom of Mestair has died before it was born."

"Cannon fodder."

"Yes, but without the orcs we don't stand a chance. They can sit behind the walls of their fortresses. The Shanyu is trying to preserve his people. He's got nothing else left; the Gray Horde is gone. In Mesaniya, they're hurrying to repair the mountain citadels and build barrier fields by paving them with explosion-stones, on the trails to the border they're installing magical traps."

"We can cross Meriya off the list. The princes have been fighting for the throne and are very unlikely to come to an agreement. The 'greenies' will trample them beneath their feet without any effort. I'd like to know, will the Arians head south or content themselves with the lands of the gray orcs?" Gil thought for a moment. "Drang, tell me, why have you gathered us here?"

"We found the reason for the Arians' exodus." The king felt a wave of tension flowing from the High Prince. "The sea is swallowing Aria. That's why they attacked Alatar."

"Their exodus?"

"Please, take a look." An image appeared over the crystal stands.

A bird was flying high over the water. Over the foamy waves, here and there an occasional island with temples built on them could be seen.

Strange, why build temples in the middle of the sea? The king didn't have time to think about that. The wind stopped pushing the waves, and the seagull flew in lower. Under the blue water, they could see houses. The bird made a circle. There could be no mistake about it—a large city had been buried beneath the mass of seawater. Soon they could see the shore. The sea's waves lazily beat upon the smooth stones of the pavement of a street drowning in the watery depths. The seagull, turning south, flew along the shore.

The image changed. Now, instead of the smooth surface of the sea, under the winged spy they could make out enormous trees, decorated with yellowish leaves. Gusts of winds went by and carried the foliage off in large quantities, scattering it below and carpeting the earth with them.

"Once we had determined the coordinates, we set a couple owls on Aria," the duke explained.

"What are those trees?" the king asked, struck by the forest residents' giant proportions.

"Mellornys," Miduel whispered.

"Mellornys?!" everyone in the room exclaimed in unison. Their shock was endless.

"It's begun," the ancient elf uttered with just his lips.

Soon the forest was left far behind. The bird approached some city. They could see clear, even streets and buildings below the feathered belly.

"Let's see the long view, please. Yep, just there. Stop right there!" Drang ordered the mage controlling the illusion.

It wasn't a city. For many leagues around there were warehouses and sheds. Huge animals with red and black hair, powerful tusks and funny trunks like barls were dragging numerous trolleys along the rails laid between the warehouses, around which dozens of people were bustling about. The owl the operator was controlling made a few circles and flew along the main line, from which the side-tracks branched out. The rails of the central road led to a cyclopean portal. The mages of the kingdom built a similar construction for the relocation of orcs from the islands.

The feathered spy, flying around the giant portal arch, headed towards some cupola-shaped buildings, rising to the sky on the nearest hill. The rays of the setting sun lit up an enormous temple and the snow-white walls of the buildings of a large city located near the foot of the hill.

Flying over to the place of worship, the owl landed on the branch of a sprawling tree and hid in the dense foliage. The square in front of the temple was crowded with people. Everyone was waiting for something.

The sun gradually set behind the horizon. Darkness fell over the city. The edge of the shade went up and up along the golden cupolas of the temple. Finally, the last ray broke away from the high spire and died away completely. The sea of people that had filled the square staggered backwards and rushed away from the opening gates of the temple.

In total darkness, one small flame lit up inside the temple. Next to it one more, then more and more. From the open gates, a river of flames flowed out onto the street. Thousands of people in long white robes belted with either sashes or wide belts were carrying torches. In the very center of the column of people, eight shirtless beefcakes were carrying some sort of palanquin on their shoulders. Behind the palanquin, tapping the pavement with the ends of their staffs, priests, and mages with long beards followed. The people in the square extended their arms towards the procession and lit their torches, already in hand, from those that were already burning. Each new flame immediately got into the procession at the end of the line. There was no end in sight to the river of fire; it encompassed thousands of luminous dots. Myriads of sparks ascended into the black sky from the torches. From the view in the operator's room, it looked as if a giant flock of fireflies was hovering over the procession.

"Almighty Twins!" someone in the hall mumbled when the owl switched branches.

The torches that were half-way burnt were flung to the ground; they were immediately replaced with new ones. Soon the whole road was strewn with red-hot coals, along which the Arians continued to walk calmly with their bare feet. No one in the procession had shoes.

The torch procession went to the city, where new rivers of fire met up and merged with it. The road, straight as an arrow, brought the living river to the wide square in front of the portal arch. As soon as the first torch-bearer crossed the invisible barrier, magical lanterns lit up on the poles surrounding the square. A bright light lit up the surrounding area. The blanket of darkness, having been burnt up on the sparks from man-made fireflies, receded. The owl, with an eerie, quiet hoot, flew to the frame of the arch, where it hid in the thick shadows. The human river spread across the square.

The palanquin, covered with a veil, was met with a roar like thunder. The image quivered. Apparently, the frightened bird wanted to fly away, but the will of the controlling mage held the feathered creature in place.

Carrying the palanquin onto a high platform in the center of the square, the bearers retrieved long narrow blades from their scabbards and froze like statues.

The long-bearded old guys ascended to the platform. The main guy stepped forward. Raising his golden staff, he started saying something. It was impossible to tell what he was talking about—the bird's hearing brought only a creaking sound, the whistle of the wind, and the hum of the crowd to the listeners' ears.

The old priest finished his speech and pulled the cloth from the palanquin. The crowd went wild. Obeying some sort of signal or impulse, the right hands of all those crowded onto the square shot up into the air. Every fist contained a long curved knife. Their eyes sparkled with a fanatical gleam. The old guys moved away from the palanquin.

Miduel jumped up from his chair.

"It can't be," he whispered with his pale lips, looking at the skull and front legs of the dragon, between which lay a thick book and a large medallion with a blood-red stone in the center, shining with a dull yellow gleam. "The Book of the Guardians... The key... It can't be...."

Miduel turned and looked at the others. The elf's eyes were glowing with a crazy gleam. His jaw was quaking.

"They won't stop with the orc lands. They'll go all the way to Kion and Rovinthal in the Rauu Foothill Principality. The Arians won't make any deals with anyone. Nothing will stop them."

"Why?" Gil asked dumbfoundedly.

"The Arian priests have the Key and the Book of the Guardians."

"What?" the King of Tantre asked again not understanding a word.

"The second guard, he flew north. Two thousand years ago, a large Imperial navy sank him, not the northerners' mages! He had the Key! The Arians want to open portals between the planets and bring dragons back to Ilanta! And they have everything they need to do this—EVERYTHING! The Treir cemetery, south of Kion, is the central portal. The Rovinthal hill is the first cargo point. The Torin walls are the third. The Arians just need one of them. The true bloods sealed the portals three thousand years ago. The Book of the Guardians contains the passwords, and the Key opens the portal gates."

"You've always wanted the dragons to return to our world. Why are you so upset now?" Beriem spoke up. No one knew he was there or how he got into the room.

"The fact that the medicine can be worse than the illness. The true bloods never came back. In three thousand years, they could have somehow gotten in touch, but they never did. The Mellornys on Aria are dying, the northern mages are losing mana and can't stop the sea from swallowing up the land. It seems like the Arian elite has come to an agreement. The priests decided to break the seals of the inter-world portals, and the powerful would get their profit. War. They've been preparing for war for decades now. Only war can hold back their power...."

Beriem raised one eyebrow skeptically.

"Oi, weren't you the one who told me that breaking the seals would require a simply insane amount of mana? Tell me where the Arians will get it."

"Pup!" Miduel blew his top. "Don't you understand anything? Look at those people!"

Beriem detached himself from the wall and walked over to the illusion. The grandson's cheeks turned red.

"Save us, Hel," Rector Etran was paler than death. She could guess what the curved blades in the Arians' hands were for. "It's a pledge! These people—they're a pledge!"

Gil the Soft Spoken, Garad and Drang all gasped in unison. The operator mages froze in horrified silence. A pledge: it was a short and terrible word that encompassed the lives of thousands of people, people who are ready to willingly sacrifice themselves or happily lay down on the altar. Thousands of sources of mana. The Arians would break the seals. They would crush them to dust!

"The stone in the center of the Key is glowing," Beriem glanced at his grandfather.

"I noticed," the High Prince said. "Someone's charged it with mana. Eh, if only we could find the second Key."

"The time for thinking things over is up," His Highness Gil II the Soft Spoken pronounced decidedly, standing up from his chair. Chancellor Garad followed as if he'd been doused with boiling water, then the head of the secret chancellery Drang and all the others followed suit. "Garad, starting tomorrow morning there will be a dictatorship in this country. Universal mobilization shall be declared. Take care of the newspapers, copy the crystals, and show on the central squares of all major cities outtakes from the landing of the second wave and portions from the Kanyr massacre. Marshall Olmar, prepare camps for the mobilized; you have two months maximum to train them. Drang, increase security measures. You're responsible for the rations program. Etran, our plans are canceled. The prince is being transferred to Kion; you're taking up your post henceforth. The Royal Council will convene in an hour in the large reception hall. The representatives of the United Rauu Principalities are invited to the meeting. Your Highness, who is your delegate?" he asked the High Prince.

"I'll be there myself," Miduel creaked.

"Excellent. I'll expect you in one hour," His Majesty turned around sharply and left the operator's room.

"Grandson," Miduel said to Beriem.

"Yes?"

"Give the order for three air regiments to scour the mountains. Find our boy. I need to talk to him. Be careful and extremely cautious in all you do. Don't go looking for trouble."

"Why do you need the were-dragon?"

"The boy has to decide whose side he's on."

The Marble Mountains. Andy...

His right wing ached. The old dragon, driven completely mad, almost tore him to pieces. The poor old dragon. Andy turned away from the messy cave. This was the second dragon he'd killed.

The seven dragons he'd gathered did not judge him. Dragons understood very well. Perhaps they'd done the same thing before, but he judged himself. Seven samurai, and he was the eighth. They were few and far between.

"Where will you go now?" Gray lowered himself down onto the mouth of the cave, flapping his wings loudly. He was an ancient dragon of a black color, like daddy Karegar, with scales that had turned whitish with age, and crests on his back.

"Home! I'll go home now."

"Don't think about anything. You couldn't have helped him."

"I'm not thinking about anything," Andy twitched his wing. "It's just I feel lousy. I can't wrap my head around it—what have you done to yourselves? How did it come to this?"

Gray, creaking like an old man, laid down on the warm sun-lit stones. Now he really reminded Andy of the boa constrictor Kaa from the story about Mowgli. His Adam's apple, covered with thick plates, jerked on his powerful neck. The red-hot embers of his eyes hid under a translucent film, his bushy eyebrows froze motionlessly. Even the thick whiskers, twisted from vibrissae, ceased to move in time with his breath at the tip of his muzzle.

"It's sad to realize it, but you're right, we're the ones who've done this to ourselves," the dragon let a bluish cloud of smoke from his nostrils. His brows shot sharply upward; his red eyes flashed violently. "What did you feel when the old crazy dragon threw himself at you?"

Andy tried to remember the emotions that overtook him at the moment of the short attack.

"Rage. An all-consuming rage."

The fire in his friend's eyes slowly went out. Gray looked at their six companions bathing in the lake.

"Rage, rage…. Imagine a V-formation of hundreds of dragons, overcome with hatred and thirst for wood-elves' blood. What was their rage like? It was such a rage, controlling us, that many of us began to go into a state of combative insanity. It's a terrible thing once it takes over empaths who've lost touch with reality. They were the first to lose it; the empathic wave destroyed the rest. Some of them experienced a weakened control over their minds, went mad. We didn't want to burn the forest. Those still in control of themselves put up a fight, but…," Gray fell silent. The memories stirred up the thousand-year-old pain in his soul. "Kerr, it's horrible: to see your loved ones sacrificing themselves to a spell cast by one of the insane ones. The fireball pumped with the force of the dragons was brighter than a thousand suns. The flame wiped the ancient Mellornys out like toothpicks. The 'latch spell' stripped the Mellorny forests of any fruits. We doomed the Woodies to a slow death."

It was an entire Apocalypse on a single, separate plot of land. Andy's imagination drew a picture of an atomic bomb—that's how closely Gray's descriptions aligned with a "nuclear" bombardment. It became painfully clear why the dragons couldn't unite after the war.

No one came back to the nests destroyed by the Woodies. The growing young (there were isolated cases) hidden in the mountains were left unattended. Not everyone was lucky, Lanirra for example. Most of the Lords of the Sky were mad and attacked the others at the slightest sign of aggression or any action at all that might be mistaken for aggression. Sometimes, even without any provocation, the insane ones would try to destroy everyone in sight, which they could do. There were attempts to unite them, but they all fell apart due to the young dragons' inability to comprehend and the mad dragons' wrath. It's difficult to reason effectively when your audience is spitting fire at you and casting spells. The young left unattended by their parents degenerated into half-wit predators who brought no less trouble than the hunting parties. A unique situation resulted when the Rauu, united with their former enemies, were forced to kill the insane individuals…. The concoction that spilled out of the pot of war when it boiled over scalded everyone—those involved and those not involved. And somewhere far away, beyond the horizon, the shadow of the creator of the slaughterhouse loomed.

Gray spoke for a long time. The old dragon was stating his version of events. In many places the narrative converged with what his adopted parents had once told him; sometimes it was different; in some places, it did not correspond to the initial version. The ending interested Andy most of all. Pouring out his soul, veiling the story's action, Gray stopped at the forest elves' conspiracy. It just wasn't possible that the children of the Forest had arranged their trap in a castle! If that were the case, what prompted them, and who planned the massacre? Then Gray was quiet for a long time. Apparently, it was hard for him to share his view of things. Andy, folding his wings, laid down next to the ancient dragon.

"The slaughterhouse was set up by one of the true bloods. He was the one who led the elves to the nesting grounds," the ancient dragon said, or rather, spit, and in one adroit motion flew off.

**

Gray's cave was the fourth he'd visited, following the little x's and detailed descriptions on the parchment paper. At the first, Fate once again decided to test Andy's strength and endurance, tossing him an unpleasant surprise in the form of wild dragons unwilling to have civil conversations. The dragons from the first nest met him with all the kindness of their toothy, fire-breathing souls. A bit more and the entire effort would have been cut short, a total fiasco.

He found the large nest marked on the helrats' map at the place where the Servants of Death brought him. Making a sharp turn, Andy began to descend in circles to a rocky ledge convenient for landing. He was saved by the fact that the attackers hadn't considered the position of the sun, and the victim was warned by the sight of two fractured shadows on the cliff wall overtaking a third—his. He was able to avoid coming under the fiery ejaculations thanks to a sharp transition from smooth soaring to a steep dive. The burning bursts singed only the fork of his tail. The attackers synchronously turned around and sent a few orange balls at the crystal dragon, who was booking it to the ground. The unwelcome stranger didn't go splat on the ground—he opened his wings at one hundred yards from the surface and cast a speed spell. These allowed him to come out of the dive and avoid meeting the orange balls with fatal force. There was a thunderous crash. The magical shield covering his posterior hemisphere saved the young yo-yo from fragments of shrapnel. If it weren't for the defense, his wings would probably have been torn to shreds. Andy somehow realized immediately that they weren't happy to see him, and no one was planning on talking to him. After the warm welcome perpetrated by the hosting party, he began to share their lack of desire for discussion. He decided it was necessary to high-tail it out of there.

And as luck would have it, the hosts decided to accompany him to the door. The kindhearted pair, with the tenacity of a jackhammer, chased him up until the cultivated peasant fields. The game of "catch me if you can, fireball" was very exhausting. In order to answer the angry hosts in a worthy manner, he had to stop, but he certainly couldn't do that, which was why he would just have to beat his wings as fast as he could and put up his shields. Attempts to increase altitude were immediately thwarted by direct machine-gun fire: his chasers were not stupid. They weren't planning on giving their prey the high ground by letting him ascend. Andy flew in zig-zags and cursed daddy Karegar something fierce for skipping the subject of air combat basics in his young dragon's school.

The mountain lake visible in a narrow valley was met by a grateful prayer. Practically backed into a corner by his pursuers, hugging the ground as he flew, the dragon folded his wings and dove into the water. A naked man ran out of the lake and onto the shore, covered by thick trees, and instantly disappeared among the foliage. The dense tree crowns gave the naked boy a few instants, which he needed so very badly just then, to hide himself under every possible curtain. The two angry beasts, who differed from the "diver" only in the color of their scales and their slightly smaller dimensions, circled the narrow valley for thirty minutes and then went home.

Andy, arms open wide, lay on the moist earth, overgrown with dense low-leafed grass. Unite-shmunite. Got pummeled, didn't you? Did you think they'd meet you with open arms and a nice fresh piece of meat? They met you alright—and you escaped by the skin of your teeth. Oh, my hands are shaking so bad. Interesting, why are my arms and legs trembling when I was hammering my wings. It's a mystery of nature. The main thing is, I'm still alive. What conclusions can I make after a performance like that?

First: relax! Second: it'd be worth having a few interweaves I keep ready for activation and three, no, better four, passive shields. As experience has shown, no one's going to give me time to weave anything fantastic. Third: don't just approach nests indiscriminately. Better do some recon first. Fourth: no sense in going back there. They're not happy to see me. The idea of a united flock of dragons will not be met with understanding by the local beau monde. Fifth, and most important: I suck at air combat. What's to be done? Which leads us to the sixth conclusion: I have to study dragon's arts. But that begs the question: where can I find a teacher for a short term, just during the planned operation?

If I get a chance, I should find out who these dragons were and why they attacked without warning. Behavior like that seems more appropriate for… predators defending their territory. The guess was an unpleasant new entry in his mind, a bitter and disappointing idea. That would mean his plan was futile, doomed to failure before it began. Andy punched the ground. No, not yet, I won't turn off this path!

Changing hypostasis, he dove into the cold water of the mountain lake....

***

As Gray later told him, he knew Natigar, owner of the second cave he visited. The emerald dragon, in the prime of his life, survived the destruction of the Forest, but it was better to keep away from him. The young dragon had suffered mentally. He kept enough of his will to leave the attacking V-formation, but that's all. Luck left him after that. No one knew what would come into his head at any moment....

The emerald dragon was saved from the hunting parties by the sheer cliffs and a fifty-year nap. He carried on for three thousand years in this manner. He slept, woke up for five years or so, and again fell into unconscious oblivion for another three or four. This existence could have gone on for the Twins know how long, if it hadn't been interrupted by the self-declared benefactor. The meeting of the two dragons ended in the death of the master of the cave. If it hadn't been for the security measures taken by the guest, he could have lost his head. The emerald dragon was the first and, Andy hoped, the last dragon he would have to kill.

For a long time, Andy studied the approaches to the cave and outlined retreat routes. Who knew what to expect? *Fool me once, shame on you. Fool me twice....* Dozens of automatic guard modules reoriented towards collecting information, circled around the mountains with the nests.

The master of the cave was home. The large dragon, with scales of a bright emerald color, was cleaning dirt and bones from the cave. The waste and bones were caught up in little tornadoes and taken out by the whirlwinds to a rushing river a league from the nest, where they were chucked into the water. Not a bad way to clean away the traces of one's stay.

Andy thought for a long time. What approach should he take? It turned out he was totally clueless about the winged tribe's mentalities. Karegar didn't get hung up on things like that. Jagirra taught him magic, but she didn't pay much mind to the toothy beasts' psychology either. Which meant that, in fact, he was equating dragon behavior to human behavior, projecting features of humans' character onto the winged race. Just how far off he was became frightfully clear when the above-mentioned crystal dragon, out of pure ignorance and good will, almost became the husband of a certain scaly beauty. What was natural as air to them remained a well-kept secret for him, a mystery beyond all telling. He had no idea how to go about approaching his emerald-colored tribesman. *Maybe there were certain rituals that need to be performed? Targ only knows!*

No matter how he racked his brains, he couldn't find a solution. But he would have to communicate somehow. No one had crossed out good old trial and error. Andy, priming several defense and attack interweaves, flew out to meet his fate.

Two leagues out from the nest, the thin latticework construction of a signal cupola flashed in the sky. The emerald dragon had received notice of the guest's arrival. Andy waited for the host's reaction. The dragon remained standing on the platform near his cave. The guard modules his guest hadn't forgotten about this time controlled his upper and posterior hemispheres. He couldn't see any dangerous surprises or local residents angry over the intrusion. The situation gave some preliminary confidence.

Flying over to the platform, Andy extended his front paws forward and beat his wings quickly. Following a sudden hunch, he looked at the emerald dragon. Targ, insanity danced in the yellow eyes that met his. The instantly activated shield swallowed the "icy arrow" sent at his belly, which was vulnerable during landing. Andy folded his wings, crashing down from above onto the madman. A punishing blow threw him against the cliff wall. The emerald dragon wasn't planning on sticking his neck out under Andy's fangs. Turning, he waved his tail. Golden scales flew in all directions. A dark stripe of blood decorated the crystal dragon's right side. A hot blast of flames pounded his defense shield. A second wave of the tail sliced the air. Andy, jumping aside, charged at the host with the "press" spell. The air became thick and threw his opponent to the mouth of the cave. The "stone knives" spell, which ripped open the cliff, broke through the shields and, like a butterfly, skewered the dragon on a spike. There was a bright flash. Once he had started his attack sequence, Andy simply couldn't stop: a whistle of the "axes" interweave and the headless body twitching on the stone needles went limp. Next to it, stunned by the sudden and brief fight, lay the "benefactor."

No thoughts at all. The platform, covered in blood, beat back any attempt at putting together rational thoughts. Bringing down the cave vaults with a powerful fireball, Andy flew to the river.

Targ! Horned devil and other hellish beasts! What was that?! Whose tail have I stepped on or hoof have I crushed? Why? Why are Fate or the Twins playing with me like this? Someone has too wild an imagination. I'd like to knock the guy's horns off. At first, he wanted to forget his quest and book it home. As in, he hadn't done anything to deserve this! But... how could he then look the others in the eyes? Frida, Lanirra, the kids, his parents.... What would he tell them?

After washing away his and his opponent's blood in the icy lake water, Andy immersed himself in settage. His trance allowed him to get his thoughts in order and restore his energy channels. The short melding with the astral spurred the regeneration of the fibers.

There were so many absurdities in the fight with the emerald dragon. Now, in a state of settage, Andy could say he had met a child. Yes, the "icy arrow" looked threatening, but it didn't harm his shield. The combat version would have broken the shield to smithereens. The large child did not understand what the strange guy was coming at him for. And the "strange guy," jacked up on a huge portion of adrenaline, saw this game as an attack. On the other hand, the game and the toys weren't so harmless. A dragon who'd reverted to childhood could rip a "visiting butterfly's" wings or head off, without grasping the fact that this would harm the "butterfly."

He felt nauseated from his own discovery. The fight and its consequences burned up yet another little piece of his soul, which was already becoming more and more hardened every day. He had no pity. Andy understood that pity was useless in the current situation. The questions "why" and "what did I do wrong" were no longer asked. "Wrong" happened three thousand years ago. Now he would have to clear up the consequences of those ancient and cobweb-covered events.

"I'm sorry," Andy whispered, flying to the landing platform in front of the former entrance to the cave.

The third "x" was a dead end. If at some point dragons had lived here, it was ancient history. Neither the modules or Andy's aero-reconnaissance brought any results. Not only did the mountain indicated not smell of dragons, but not a trace was found for ten leagues around that could point to the nearby presence of a Lord of the Sky. Maybe the dragon or dragons living in the mountains of the Lard province had become masters of disguise, but if so, Andy did not have the time to sniff them out. After going through three spots suitable for nesting with a fine-tooth comb, just to satisfy his conscience, Andy flew north.

He had to get out of the province as fast as he could. The last thing he needed was the authorities hunting him down for destroying Baron von Larno's castle catching up with him. The dragon-made lake of magma swallowed the castle of the helrats' henchmen. Along with the baron, twenty people, servants and guards at the castle, were sent to Hel's judgment. The servants and guards were well aware of the master's evil-doing. Andy, changing hypostasis, spent the night in the walls of the castle. Larno's turned out to be a grateful listener, happy to hear the Rauu-mage's stories all evening. He wasn't a baron, just a soul, with the minus being that his castle basement stunk of black lily powder. Andy was glad that the austere owner did not keep small kitchen servants within the walls of his residence or other child servants. He wouldn't have wanted to take the sin of child killing on his soul. There was already so much blood on it, it could not be washed clean in a century.

***

"How much?" Andy subtly placed a golden coin in his palm worth ten pounds. The sketchy guy's gaze fixated on the golden circle and stayed there. "Name your price for your information."

A roadside tavern turned out to be a great place for collecting info. The establishment bore a significant name, which one could guess, looking at the oversized signboard depicting three minnows.

The fourth "x" did not have a clear geographical reference. The parchment indicated that on the outskirts of the mountain village of Olzhi a black dragon was seen a few times; people saw the remains of his feasting much more often. The hunting party sent by the abbot came back empty handed. Or rather, half the members of the expedition came back. The rest wound up dead in the clever traps the dragon set in the mountain trails. The capture of the elusive dragon was considered more trouble than it was worth, but they made a mark on the map. Who knew, maybe it would come in handy someday? Thank you, it sure did.

A few leagues away from the village, Andy landed in a wide clearing in a forest and changed hypostasis. His search for the elusive mountain resident had to begin with gathering information from the locals, and that would be easier for a human to do than a dragon. In a few minutes, a "hunter," dusty from a long journey, walked into the tavern "The Three Minnows."

"Sir, I really don't know," the short guy said, swallowing his spit and wiping his sweaty palms on his pants. Andy found the guy very unpleasant. He reminded him of a burbot. He had an inexpressive face, whitish, empty eyes, greasy hair combed back, and a wide mouth with bloodless lips. He was more like a necromancer's dream than a man. His countenance just begged to be used in experiments on the repose and raising of the dead.

"Who does know?" the coin flew up to the white ceiling and returned to his wide palm.

"I... I can get you a meeting with the guy, s-sir." The "burbot" was so afraid of the wandering hunter his knees were knocking. He thought those blue eyes with no whites could see right through him and knew his every thought, but greed for an easy pay-out made him sit there at the same table with this monster in human form. The hunter radiated incredible power. At first glance, there was nothing special about him, but as soon as you looked into those bottomless eyes, hidden by his wide-brimmed hat, it became clear that tracking down and overtaking a dragon all by himself was nothing to the guy. A curse on Trog the tavern owner for glancing at the promising client, suggesting pulling the wool over his eyes. The client might be the one who gets the better of them; guys like that don't forgive lies and offenses....

"Do it," a two-pound coin hit the counter. "It's a down payment. You'll get the rest after the meeting."

"Y-y-yes, sir. I'll be qu-qu-quick about it. Don't worry."

"You're the one who should be worrying," the hunter's lips spread into an ill-boding smile. His sharp fangs flashed. The "burbot" grew legs and touched the floor. "Go on!" The go-between jumped from his place as if he'd been kicked. "Hey, let's have some ale!"

The crowd that had filled the room followed the twerp and lost all interest in the hunter. Hudd-burbot, (Andy made up a nickname for the guy), clearly feared this man, whoever it would be. And the self-preservation instinct of a well-known panderer and go-between was always first and foremost, which meant it wasn't worth picking a fight with him. Well, Targ take him. It's day yet; there'll be time to find someone else for a good fight.

"Get out of my sight," Andy snapped at the go-between, tossing him ten pounds. "If what this sleazebag says is true, you can tell me where the dragon's nest is located," he said to the man the "burbot" had summoned. "How much for your service?"

The new character was a lot nicer to look at and commanded respect. By the look of him, his mannerisms and gestures, the man was an experienced tracker and hunter. There was something else about him, something painfully familiar, but the spark of recognition was buried under a whole chain-full of defense amulets.

"You don't speak very kindly of others," he said, ignoring Andy's question.

"If you mean that go-between, he doesn't deserve any other title. Calling a cockroach a cockroach wouldn't offend you, would it? I called a sleazebag a sleazebag, and no one can convince me I'm wrong about that. So…?"

"Perhaps you're right. I don't know where the nest is, but I can point you to the spot where the dragon likes to spend time after hunting."

"It's not the nest, but beggars can't be choosy."

"Well said."

"Use it," Andy waved his hand. "How do I get to the dragon's relaxation spot?"   "Rela-what?" the tracker did not understand.

"The place where the winged beast likes to unwind, spend his free time?"

"Two hundred pounds. I'll take you there myself." The hunter leaned towards Andy. "Payment up front."

"I don't think that's what we agreed on…," Andy began.

"We haven't agreed at all yet," the hunter interrupted him. "Take it or leave it. I'm not bargaining."

"You're quite the businessman," Andy smiled. His purse clanked dully against the tabletop. "You've got a deal!"

"We'll leave at the crack of dawn," the hunter said, taking the money. "See you tomorrow."

"Goodbye," Andy answered, looking at his guide's wide back as he walked away. *Now that's a serious guy. Seems trustworthy. It'll be a shame to kill him.*

***

"Lar, what are you going to do with this?" Nide kicked at the cocoon of a heavy-duty trap containing the subdued foreign hunter, wrapped up in invisible fetters.

The old dragon, grunting, laid down on the ground.

"Same as always—burn him to a crisp, or maybe I'll leave him out under the sun. He'll croak in a couple of days. Was he alone?"

"Yes, which is why I offered to bring him here."

"Thanks, Nide."

"You don't owe me any thanks. I'll owe you till the day I die."

"Stop it, we've been over this. You don't owe me anything."

"Whatever. Ilona and Bugger say hi. The wife's worried about you—maybe you should relocate? Guys like these won't back off." Naid indicated the cocoon. "That's the third slimeball in the last six months, and those squadrons before him? What if someday I'm not around?"

"Are you worried?" the dragon said, letting the lecture in one ear and out the other.

"Yes."

"Has Booger made another prophecy?"

"No, just ramblings."

"Spit it out."

"My girl said your time has come, and you'll fly away."

"Your daughter isn't exactly wrong," someone said from the cocoon. The dragon dashed onto all four paws. Nide snatched his wide cleaver from its sheath. Unbeknownst to them, the strange hunter had somehow gotten out of the fetters and was standing behind the conversing pair with an independent air. "Please forgive me, Nide, sir, I had the very worst opinion of you. Please, don't do anything stupid." The stranger lifted his hands in a gesture of peace-making.

"Your aura," the dragon whispered, the ghostly shine of an attack interweave spreading around him. Andy did not know the spell. It looked beautiful, but he had absolutely no desire to find out how deadly it was.

"My aura is fine; will you permit me?" A multi-layered magical shield formed between Andy and the dragon/human pair. The ancient dragon turned out to be a true virtuoso of magical interweaves. Another strange construction grew up behind the formerly fettered man. Judging by the tension of the nodes, it was an attack pattern.

Andy slowly undressed in front of the dragon's and hunter's stunned eyes.

"What's the meaning of this?" Nide asked. The dragon didn't say anything. His gaze was fixed on the golden tattoo on the naked guy's shoulder.

"One second," Andy said and changed hypostasis.

The black dragon and the hunter both went into shock. Bulging eyes, dropped jaws—they looked like twins.

"Well I never!" Nide exhaled.

"Who gave you that coat of arms?" the dragon asked, shaking his head. He came out of his stunned state much faster than his friend.

Andy was taken aback. The tattoo was a coat of arms? Then again… he had long-since suspected that Jagirra wasn't a simple elf.

"My mother," he answered, briefly but very significantly. There was no sense in lying. Andy had long ago made the connection between the Rauu hypostasis and the Ritual. It wouldn't have been possible without Jagirra's blood.

"Your moooother…," the dragon said in surprise. The shield and the attack interweave disappeared. "Your mother?" he asked again.

"Yes."

"Such a twist of fate! Have you come for me?"

"Yes," Andy repeated, wound up.

"What use could anyone have for an old sick dragon?"

"It's a long story."

"I don't have anywhere to be and I would be glad to hear it."

They flew out at first light. Gray, the old dragon himself asked to be called that, carefully listened to Andy's story. He was most interested in the were-dragon's incentives and motivations for going wild. Considering them relatively well-founded, he agreed to fly with the crystal dragon and even took upon himself the difficult burden of negotiating with other potential fellow travelers and comrades-in-arms. No one desperately tried to persuade him otherwise, but a certain individual's satisfied mug spoke for itself.

"You wanted to ask me something?" the old dragon looked at Andy, who was shifting his weight from leg to leg.

"I need a teacher. Your heavy-duty trap made me suffer, and…,"

"Don't pour honey on sugar," Gray interrupted him. "I'll help you as much as I can."

"Thank you."

Andy changed hypostasis and walked up to the hunter.

"Goodbye, Nide. Who would have thought? For the first time in my life, I'm glad I was wrong about somebody!"

"The feeling is mutual!" the hunter smiled. He had a large hand and a good firm handshake. "Take care of our old man."

Two weeks of searching melded into a kaleidoscope. In the time that was left, they visited five more nests as marked on the map. Two were abandoned; three were home to dragons. The second, sixth overall, was the most successful. Through Gray's ambitious efforts, the winged company immediately gained three male dragons and two dragonesses. The last one to join their group was a young, five-hundred-year-old male. He had lost his parents to the helrats twenty years ago. It was a rare sight, the wrath with which Velitarr doused the Servants of Death's castles and warehouses in the fire. The dragons later decimated every stone of Baron von Strog's castle....

At the seventh "x," there was a misfire. They had only just landed on the cliff platform when the master of the cave attacked. As Murphy's law would have it, Andy was the first to land. The short battle ended in a natural outcome. The old dragon was no match for youth and strength....

***

"So are we flying or not?" Sonirra asked Gray, smacking her lips ravenously.

The dragoness had eaten her fill of half the bull's body. That morning Andy had purchased three bulls in the village. The poor cattle could sense its fate and did not want to leave its former owners. The Rauu that had paid insane money for the horned meal—thirty pounds, asked them to leave the doomed animals in the pasture. The peasants did just that. Ten minutes later the bulls were gone, disappeared who knows where. Everyone knows that Icicles are, without exception, ingenious mages.

"Let's fly," Andy flew over to the lake.

"Where to?" Velitarr's head popped out of the water.

"Home."

***

"What, she hasn't come back?" Andy hovered over Lanirra.

"No, she hasn't come back," the dragoness snorted. "I left her a beacon, but she never gave the signal."

"Targ!" Andy growled.

He beat his wings all night. The flock he'd gathered reached its new home only when dawn was breaking. But they were already waiting for them. Daddy, it turns out, knew Gray, and volunteered to accompany the newcomers to the caves they had prepared for them. Andy was standing around with nothing to do. He wasn't used to everything happening without him. Circling around his home cave for a while, he flew to Jaga's house, but his adoptive mother wasn't there. Strange. And the mysteries didn't stop there.

The grass near the house distinctly smelled of a female, a mature, attractive female. The scent did not belong to the red dragoness; Lanirra had a different scent. After waiting for over an hour, Andy flew to Lani. In response to his innocent question—where's Jagirra?—the dragoness lowered her head to the ground and answered that Jaga was gathering herbs and had asked not to be disturbed until evening. As in, she wanted to talk to him herself that evening, and before that, there was no way.

What Targ-some herbs could they be? What was she up to? What kind of herbalist would be gathering herbs now? Andy pressed his would-be wife, but couldn't get another word out of her on the topic. The dragoness simply kept insisting that she was gathering wild herbs. The orc women who happened to be nearby were no better. It was some kind of conspiracy! Andy, spitting in a fit of anger, asked where Frida was. The answer was disappointing: not here. A week ago, Lani had flown her to the vampires, and they hadn't heard anything from her since.

"I don't believe for a minute that you didn't cast some sort of spell on her," he said to the dragoness.

"What do I need her for?!"

"Don't lie," he growled. Lanirra took a few steps back. "Tell me!"

"What do you see in her?"

"None of your stinking business! Tell me! I got to know you a little bit. You've got a reason behind everything you do." The dragoness sputtered. "Well?"

"Curse her!" Lani cried in Eddy. "You have me, what else do you need?"

"Hold your tongue," Andy answered. "You're not my wife."

"Idiot!"

"I'm tired of arguing," Andy unexpectedly calmed down. "What tracking spell did you put on Frida?"

"I didn't," Lanirra said quietly. And just then, a small handkerchief blew his way: "I hope you choke on it. Her blood is on the kerchief. Find her yourself." The dragoness lifted straight up off the ground and flew into the sky like a firework.

"Il, will you help me?" he asked the warrior.

"I'll help. Give me the handkerchief."

***

Andy was flying toward Rimm for the third hour now. Ilnyrgu had cast a tracking spell on Frida's blood and assembled something like a compass. She glued an arrow to the small bit of fabric with the dried drop of Frida's blood, the sharp end of which pointed in her direction.

"That's it?" Andy was surprised at how simple the device was.

"That's it," the orc said.

"Hm," Andy snorted skeptically. How does a device like that work?"

"Follow the arrow. It'll point directly to the vampire. If you can wait three or four hours, I can make a map."

"We don't have time."

"Well, sorry."

Forgetting to take off his clothes, Andy changed hypostasis. Bone buttons flew in every direction.

"Targ!" he swore. He regretted losing the outfit. He grabbed the "compass" and repeated Lanirra's maneuver.

The "compass" pointed in the opposite direction of the vampires' enclave. *The wonders of this crazy day never cease.*

Below, the age-old taiga drifted by, along with white clouds, scratching the tops of a giant sequoia. Rare villages and towns flashed here and there; the yellow road crawled on as an infinite serpent. Becoming pensive about the upheaval that was walloping him from all sides, he overtook a merchant caravan stretched across a village. Diving into a cloud, Andy looked at the compass. The arrow turned one hundred and eighty degrees. The caravan!!!

***

"Archers, prepare your bows!" R'ron cried. Frida grabbed her bow from her quiver, twisting, rested one end against the saddle, pressed the string-less weapon against her shoulder and began to put the string on. Once she had assembled her bow, she straightened her quiver and ran her fingers over the arrows' feathers. She was ready.

What in Ilanta? The young woman switched to true vision and examined the woods abutting the road. Not a single speck of human aura for two hundred feet around.

"Halt!" Obeying the command, the carts began to come to a stop. The merchants and servants quickly installed large shields along the sides. *So suspicious. Then again, they've been there, many times.* Swords rustled as they came out of their sheaths.

"What is it?" Rur asked, running up from the tail of the caravan. His father was going to give it to him good for leaving his post.

"I don't know," Frida answered.

"My father's being an idiot."

"I don't think so...." Frida never got a chance to finish her sentence. The communicator amulet on her neck began to vibrate.

"Frida, come to the head of the column," R'ron's voice came through the artifact.

The vampire spurred her hass. Consumed with curiosity, she galloped past the wagons and upset people. Twenty yards before she reached the head of the caravan, she suddenly felt a terrible pinch in her temples. *Nel intercessor....* How quickly her arms went limp and her heart began to pound! Over the lead wagon, hovering in the air, tied up tight with magical fetters, was the caravan boss. Fat Merdus was jerking his legs; his eyes, nearly popping out of his head, turned this way and that. Fifteen feet away from Rur's father stood Kerr.

    ***

"Frida!" Andy cried with joy. Then he immediately went on his guard. The girl went pale as a morning fog. What was wrong with her? He got the feeling she wasn't happy to see him. "Hello!"

"Fly away, Kerr," she said, jumping down from her hass and walking up to him, then stopping about a meter away.

Well, that's a nice "hello" for you!

"?!!"

"Go away, Kerr."

"What are you saying? Fri..."

"Listen to me," his girlfriend interrupted him. "Leave me alone."

Another hass stopped behind her. The saddle creaked quietly.

"You?" Andy's eyebrows slid upwards. A crack appeared in his stony self-control.

"Yes, me," Rur answered and stood next to Frida.

"I thought you would be trouble from the start. Is this your doing?"

"Yes, it is," the red-eyed half-blood smiled.

"We're married, Kerr." Frida lifted up her sleeve, showing the spousal bracelet. "Rur's my husband."

"Why?" The were-dragon's surprise knew no bounds. "Why??"

"I'm a 'dry branch,' haven't they told you?" Frida started to cry. Rur tried to hug his wife, but she pushed him away.

"A 'dry branch.' It's better this way than watching Lanirra take care of you. You're a dragon, and what am I? A free-loader? How long could I last with you? One hundred, two hundred years? Go away, Kerr. Leave me."

"But..."

"LEAVE ME! If you love me, leave me alone. Please."

"Alright." The yellow pupils appeared in his blue eyes. An evil smile came across the were-dragon's face. Frida got startled.

"Please, don't touch Rur! Promise me. I won't ask you anything else."

"Alright, I promise."

Andy turned away. When he again turned to the girl, her face was pale as death. There wasn't a drop of blood behind it. It was a frightening face. A cloud of strength billowed around the were-dragon. If he had his way—nothing would be left of the entire caravan.

"If I wanted to, I would have killed your wretched little husband and the head of the guards a long time ago."

"The commander of the guards is my husband's father. His name is R'ron."

"They call him 'davur.' Remember me?" Andy said to the tall vampire, who shook his head. "Maybe you remember a double notrium cage with an old orc shaman woman and a boy? I see you do. Tell your son and his bride that you were transporting prey. Thank Frida that you're still alive! And you," an invisible grip brought the numb Rur right up to Andy's face. Two magical arrows fired by someone in the guards clapped powerlessly against the defensive cupola he'd erected. "If you hurt her, you'll curse the day you were born. Got it?"

Andy threw Rur down and walked up to the vampire.

"Be happy. I know why you agreed to marry him, no matter how funny it sounds."

"Why?"

"This boy reminds you of me! Goodbye!"

Andy changed hypostasis right in front of the entire caravan and shot into the sky. The caravan boss, free from the fetters, collapsed to the ground.

The Marble Mountains. The Valley of a Thousand Streams...

Kerrovitarr appeared seven hours after his departure. The celestial body had already risen long past midday. The members of the small band had managed to rest and take a nap after the long, sleepless night.

Gray, who had never yet laid on his side, and Sonirra, a green dragoness, were busy checking out the caves prepared for the newcomers, which were located on the southern side of the Bowing slope. The ancient dragon often came running out to the rocky ledge. He felt troubled. His unexpected student, of whom he'd grown quite fond over the last week, might do something stupid. Or maybe he was wrong to worry, just getting all bent out of shape over nothing…. In old age, you become overly suspicious about everything, but Kerr's skirmish with the red dragoness did not bode well. Lanirra was a beautiful girl. Gray, busy with examining the cave and cleaning out the remaining debris, could not ask the Master of the valley to clarify what connected the two. The old dragon made a mental note: he needed to talk to Karegar as soon as possible to clarify the disposition. Something was wrong and something wrong was happening in their new home. He could feel in his gut that things weren't as rosy as Kerr had described. A certain tension was hanging in the air.

Larigar did not like the way Lanirra was acting. She was demonstratively presenting her rights to his student. Without a prick of conscience, the red dragon was taking advantage of Kerr's ignorance of the dragons' customs. On the other hand, it's his own fault. He shouldn't have taken her children under his wing and given the mother hope—or was he hoping that she would like one of the recently arrived males? It was a logical thought. The boy was more cunning than some people thought. If he was counting on her taking a shine to one of the new males, then his scheming would be one hundred percent justified. Vitgar and Romugar walked in front of Lanirra, who was helping to clean out the cave, like puffed-up peacocks. They arched their necks and lifted the crests of their wings; everything short of cooing like doves. He was afraid they might start fighting. Didn't the red lady have any restraint?

Gray once again went outside, opened his wings and lifted himself up a bit on his hind legs. A dark shadow covered the old dragon for a split second. His belly almost touching the tips of the pines, Kerr flew over the slope. His student, without stopping, rounded a small hill and disappeared behind the tops of the trees. When she saw the sparkles of the crystal dragon's wings, got ready to fly off, but Gray stopped her.

"It's not worth it. Wait a bit."

The dragoness hissed.

"Alright, whatever you say," Gray said softly, "but I would definitely not recommend approaching him right now."

Lanirra roared and laid her head down in resignation. She could admit that the old dragon was right and was her senior. She managed to catch a glimpse of her beloved's uncovered aura, which was flashing with bright red, clearly the red of a rage. The dragoness twitched her tail happily. The little human had really made him mad. The two-legged girl had lost. Lanirra hadn't left her half a chance. Folding her wings sweetly, she went into the cave.

Gray, following the self-satisfied woman with his eyes, thought hard. She was wrong to try and hope....

***

With a total lack of concern for decorum and for the village ladies whispering in the dense bushes, his hands folded behind his back, Andy, like a pendulum, paced along the wide sandy beach near the place where the streams that originated in the hot geothermal springs fell into the lake. Thirty steps to the streams, thirty steps to the black boulder, and back again

It's all cursed! Everything! Three times cursed! Four!!! The giant boulder caught by magical fetters flew a hundred yards and disappeared into the depths of the lake. Slight ripples ran all the way to the shore from the spot where the innocent stone had fallen into the water. They helplessly licked the golden sand of the beach and disappeared into the still surface. Small branches cracked under the feet of the beautiful girls as they took to their heels. Following the fading auras with his eyes as they ran off, Andy sat his bare buttocks on the warm sand and hugged his knees.

What rotten luck. Unlucky in love! What can a guy do to get a good death or a good relationship around here?

He was certainly unlucky in love. Polana, Irma, now Frida... who else? Lanirra, nothing but problems there, too, but that's a different story. More like she was the one brokenhearted for him.

Frida.... Andy jumped to his feet and, for the hundredth time, paced the well-beaten path. Stream, turn, a hole, what was left of the black boulder. What hole was left in his soul from this, and how many were there in all? Did he love the vampire? Probably... or no? If he loved her, why then did he leave her with that black-haired jerk? Frida was fine, but.... The fire of love died on the School shooting range. All that was warm and stunning, all that was between them, was preserved in the form of bright, unforgettable memories. Miduel, why did you bring us together again? Seeing her again was more like an attempt to rekindle a dying fire—ash flying everywhere from the burnt up logs and feelings, the coals crackling, but not giving off any heat. It wasn't love; it was a zombie raised by a necromancer. Frida felt this. Her fire was still burning bright. It was a shame that he was just a "painted fireplace," so to speak. And it wasn't her fault. He couldn't give Frida what she deserved. He had too much going on, and Lani did everything she could to end their mutual journey.

He did not suffer from the same incredible passion for Frida that he had for Polana. He didn't feel puppy-dog joy from the very sight of her, but he did feel the warmth of being at home. He did….

A "dry branch." The dragoness had probably enlightened her on the details of the were-dragon's reproductive potential and was rude to her about it. Karegar and Jagirra were possibly brought into the discussion. He was almost sure that Lanirra had reminded her of his adopted parents and picked on Frida every day, wearing her down like a stone made smooth from water.

Andy stopped and dug into the sand with his foot. What was wrong about his last meeting with her? On the road, he didn't pay attention to the obvious signs; now they were impossible to miss.

False. Frida was lying. He didn't have her sharply developed empath abilities, but he could catch tones of bile and the unpleasant aftertaste of a lie. The vampire did not love the red-eyed half-blood. She didn't love him, but she preferred to be with him. What made her do that? A duty to her family or her clan? She was convinced of what she was saying; you can't force someone to speak with conviction. She went to him because the boy reminded her of him. Had she decided to replace him with a substitute and forget? It was hard to believe, too obvious. There was something else, something imperceptible, that was hiding the former Frida, keeping her from him. It was in the conversation. Strange that her head wasn't hurting. Who was behind that? He hadn't put up any shields, and he was overflowing with feelings… Lanirra and Jagirra, who had a hand in this? Is that why Jagirra disappeared the first day of his return? To give him a chance to blow some steam? Then her son, once he'd cooled off, wouldn't be tossing accusations right and left. It was just like Jaga to do something like that. His adoptive mother was always acting wisely.

Andy chuckled. He would surprise the elf. He could only hope that no one, not the she-wolves or Lanirra, would blab about his third hypostasis. It should be a pleasant surprise.

Andy sat on the sand and stayed there for a long time, disconnected from the world, not thinking about anything.

He had to let off steam, cool off, and then understand himself and everything that was piling up on him. On the other hand, he obviously did not need the girl anymore. She had talked about her duty to her family and clan a long time ago. What an interesting boomerang! He'd created his clan with his own hands and wings, and he couldn't disregard their best interests. His duty to his winged tribesmen was crushing him to the state of a stingray or flounder. Whoever wrote that song about kings being all-powerful was truly wise. They are, except when it comes to love. Amour wasn't for them. Kings couldn't deal with pink lovey-dovey and romantic reflections. Real kings, anyway.

Well isn't this just a witches' shindig! Enough shedding tears over what might have been. He was way too busy for that—his to-do list was a mile long! He had to begin and to finish. Soon they would be expecting guests in the valley, welcome and not very welcome. Are all those hundreds of griffons scouring the mountains for nothing? The Rauu had decided to violate the status-quo. Andy had to put forth a lot of effort to maintain the "sliding" curtain of invisibility when they flew over the pairs and threesomes of air trackers. With a search group like that, the discovery of a hidden valley flows from a hypothetical question into the practical plane. *In the final analysis, there's still time. How soon will we be discovered? The Icicles will not leave the dragons alone. The High Prince will try to enlist the support of the Lords of the Sky, and given that the war with the Arians is not far off, the iron-clad arguments in favor of the Northern Alliance will come into play. Targ take you! There will be no dragons on any side!*

A foreboding smile spread across the blue-eyed were-dragon's lips. Such a crazy life. Irina, at seventeen years old, would go to the meadow and dance about like a goat in an "elvish" dress, thinking only about cavaliers, and he was being dragged into politics against his will. Remembering his original home did not especially upset him. *Time heals all wounds. Where is my home? Hm? What would I be THERE, if I get back to my home world? A human, a dragon, or some sort of chimera? The object of study, a juicy titbit for some secret laboratory? This is my home world, now! But I can't forget about the promises I made to myself—to send news. Maybe I should work on that while no one's bothering me? I'm ashamed to say it, but in four weeks I haven't gotten around to dealing with the papers I obtained in Ortag. It's a disgrace. If my memory serves me, there was something in there about building portals.* Andy activated the "beacons" and got the worn-out pages out of his "pocket."

"… Building any portal means having an exact knowledge of the exit coordinates. In order to enact the 'puncture,' its position in three-dimensional space must be defined. For this purpose, a 'cube model' is used…."

After that, nothing. Half the text on the page disappeared without a trace. What now? Andy turned the old tattered page over.

"… There are ways to construct passageways without coordinates. In this case, a 'beacon' is used. Special artifacts act as beacons, through which the operator mages can set up the output coordinates.

"Besides the methods described above, there are also so-called 'hard' or 'fiducial' points on the surface of a planet, hereinafter 'F.P.' The F.P. are tied to a certain spot and can be described by a simple Tagar-Liarra equation. The nature and pattern of the formation of the F.P. on the planet surface are still unknown, which does not prevent us from actively using empirically derived formulas. When building stationary portals, the second method is used: the placement of arches at the fiducial points. This combination allows us to guarantee the exact settings and eliminate malfunctioning.

"See an example of the calculations below…."

Where are the formulas? What a crock—missing pages, and no formulas. What did I pay you for? A total scam, like showing a kid some candy and then hiding it again. And what's this? On the last page of the outtake, there was a model of some sort of interweave.

"… This is the Tagar-Liarra equation with settings for a hard point exit in the mountains of Lidar, reduced to the rune scheme of the magical interweaves and the determination of the coordinates. As you can see from the schemes, seventy percent of the interweave is a repeat of the previously proposed 'beacon' puncture scheme. The main differences are the addition of the coordinates and the introduction of the direction vector into the scheme. The runes are activated from left to right, in the order of the rows…."

Interesting. Andy repeated the scheme on the ancient outtake in his head. The runes arranged in strict order looked like the facets of a crystal changed from raw crystallized carbon into a stunning diamond. For the sake of an experiment, he activated the first rune. The power nodules lit up with a blue flash, and the facets began to twinkle....

In the center of his chest, just like a volcano erupting, the medallion with the red stone tore its way to the surface, breaking his skin. The runes engraved on the yellow circle started to move around the surface in a strange circle dance. It seemed to Andy that he was being pricked with thousands of hot needles, drinking up mana from his internal stores. He wanted to cry out, but instead of a cry, a muffled wheeze came from his throat. His body went numb. The stone in the center of the medallion let off a red ray of light. The runes that appeared on his creation glowed brighter than the sun.

"Nooo!" A dragoness with beautiful golden scales landed on the edge of the beach. From the direction of the Bowing slope, a few more dots were approaching as well, emerged from the eye of the portal, surrounded by an iridescent glow.

The last thing Andy saw before an inexplicable force took hold of him and cast him into oblivion was Karegar and Gray flying out from behind the tops of the pine trees.

Orten. The governor's residence...

"How are you enjoying your new position? Up to your eyeballs in worries?"

"You can't imagine how right you are, Your Highness!" Etran smiled, bowing politely to Miduel.

"Oh, cut it out, just call me Master. I'm more used to that. Since this is an unofficial visit, let's not make a big hullabaloo over a V.I.P. throughout the whole residence." The Rauu made a subtle gesture with his hand to the "star" of the bodyguards. The well-trained fighters, no less strong than combat mages, checked the hallway. Two elves glanced into the office, after which they let the High Prince in. The bodyguards wanted to follow him, but, obeying their boss' stern glance, remained outside. "I'm so sick of those guys!" Miduel said contritely, lowering himself into the embrace of the soft armchair. "I can't even go to the latrine without three oafs surrounding me."

Governess Etran lifted her hands understandingly.

"One of the cons of being in a position of power. You, Master, better than anyone, ought to know that those in power are not their own."

"Listen to yourself! But actually, you're right," Miduel folded his hands on the head of his carved cane and stared at the former rector of the School of Magic. It seemed unfounded, but she suddenly began to feel uncomfortable. "You're surely wondering why I left His Majesty Gil in Ortag and am sticking to you?"

"It had crossed my mind."

"I need your help."

"What kind?"

"I need a portal to the Marble Mountains. It would be great if the order came from you. Gil's already given his approval in this matter. The exit point will have to be in the air, which can't be done without "veil" accumulators. I'm afraid it won't be possible to get to the valley on foot without stepping on cutting stones or other fatal surprises."

"In the Marble Mountains?"

The Rauu nodded. Etran squinted.

"Your agents have found our boy's nest?" she guessed.

"Don't go blabbing. We found it. We received the intelligence an hour ago."

"The portal's not a problem. It'll be done, but on one small condition...." Miduel smiled.

"Consider it agreed. I've already ordered a griffon to be prepared for you." Etran knocked on the tabletop. She wasn't used to having people predict her behavior before she herself could.

The Marble Mountains. The Valley of a Thousand Streams...

No one was minding the approaching griffons. So much for traps at every step....

Miduel looked around. Not a bad place. Karegar had found himself a nice little nook! Just then, a bright flash on the shore of the lake below caught the Snow Elf's attention. Dragons' forms appeared as dark shadows, rushing towards the unknown magical event.

"Straight to the lake," the High Prince ordered to his first-in-saddle, who nodded in response and pulled on the reigns. The golden griffon made a sharp turn. Copying the leader's move, three half-birds steered after him in his wake.

***

"Nooo!" But it was too late. Kerr was pulled into the portal's open jaws. Jagirra threw herself after him, but was too late. With a loud clap, the spatial window slapped shut. A gust of wind ripped the yellowed papers from her son's hands.

Jaga changed hypostasis and made a "snaring net." In a few seconds, the wandering pages were in her hands.

"What was that?" Karegar rumbled, landing next to Jagirra. She didn't say anything. The answer came in the form of a quiet rustle as she frantically leafed through the selected pages.

The ground quaked. Gray came down with a thud next to Karegar; Lanirra folded her wings behind the ancient dragon. Riding griffons appeared from some unknown source, bearing the High Prince's standards. Lanirra and Gray prepared attack spells.

"Are you deaf?" Karegar roared at the elf. "What was that?"

"A portal…," Jaga fell to her knees. A tattered page fell from the elf's hands and, caught up by wind, flew to the High Prince, who had dismounted. The dragons, it seemed, weren't paying the uninvited guests any attention.

"A portal? To where?" Karegar kept interrogating her.

"To Nelita," she whispered.

"What?" several people exclaimed at once.

"He can't go to Nelita, Karegar! He can't." Jaga covered her face with her hands. "How did he get the Key? Karegar, he has the Key!"

"Why can't he go to Nelita?" the dragon persisted, ignoring her lamentations.

Jagirra tore her dress off:

"Look!" The elf's shoulder was decorated with a tattoo in the form of a little golden dragon surrounded by a complex garland of runes. "Kerr has the same tattoo. I put my family coat of arms totem on him. My uncle will kill him!"

"You," the black dragon sputtered in a rage, looking at the tattoo. "You! It's all your fault! YOOOOU! I'll kill you!" A fireball burst forth from Karegar's front paws. The magical discharge did not hit the kneeling elf, who did not make a move to defend herself. The ball flew apart with fiery splashes in all directions upon striking Lanirra's shield. The dragon stared at his right paw in shock. What was going on? When had his magic returned? He didn't have long to sit there in surprise—a powerful blow from a tail knocked him to the ground. The red dragoness threw herself on his chest.

"Don't you dare. DON'T YOU DARE!"

Casting Lanirra off of him, Karegar quickly dashed to his feet, rocketed into the sky, and flew towards the mountains.

"I remember you," Gray's enormous snout hovered over Miduel. "You've aged, Reemiko's husband."

The Rauu crumpled the ill-gotten page in his fist. The past had stepped out of the shadows and dealt him a cruel blow.

"But how could he have opened a portal?" Lani asked Jaga, who had gone into a trance, shaking the sand off herself.

"Kerr had the Key to the portals."

"The second Key's been found," Miduel uttered in sheer amazement.

"Lani, fly to the caves. Tell Vitgar and Romugar to find Karegar. It would be best if everyone joined in the search for him, and if you find him, hold him until I get there."

The red dragoness lowered her head to the ground, took a few steps away from the elves and humans, and flew away.

"Don't even think of flying away. We need to talk a lot of things over," Gray turned to Miduel, grabbed Jagirra with his front paws, and flew after the dragoness. "I'll be right back," they heard him call from the sky.

"Did you know about the tattoo?" the High Prince asked Etran.

"Yes, what about it? Oh!" The former rector took a step back from the Rauu's obvious desire to slap her. He maintained his self-control.

"You are a youngster," the Rauu hissed, "and a presumptuous turkey."

"But what does it mean?" Etran asked, wary.

"It means that we're up Targ's backside! We mustn't let the Arians have access to the portals! Whoever arranged that carnage three thousand years ago will come back to finish off his victims!"

The foothill principality of the Rauu. Rovinthal. One week later...

"How did you find the Arians' secret agents?" Beriem, lying on a sofa, asked the head of the department of external operations of the Rauu intelligence service.

"We had to arrange a leak," the "shadow-dweller" coughed in his fist.

"And you, it turns out, are a very reckless elf." Beriem peered at the elf very closely. "So just a leak?"

"Not only that. I risked adding an extra person to the party and manipulating things through him from behind the scenes."

"And did they fall for it?"

"As you can see."

"And how did the Arian agent influence the vampires?"

"Oh!" the intelligence officer put his pointer finger up. "I've never seen that method before. The mental effect was enacted through a weapon." He rang a bell to call for someone.

Two elves entered the room. An entire pile of blades and weapons (besides firing weapons) lay on the table in front of Beriem.

The "shadow-dweller" grabbed a sword.

"This is R'ron's sword. At first glance, it seems no different from any other, but that's where looks can be deceiving. A small passive artifact is hidden under this decorative knob. Same for all of these knives, swords, and shields. You know very well how much vampires suffer from a maniacal desire to have the biggest collection of sharp objects. Thanks to the bogus information we arranged to be consistently dished out regarding the were-dragon, data about him reached the interested parties. Naturally, my agents kept all approaches to the girl under a tight lid; they tracked her friends and acquaintances. R'ron came under our surveillance purely by chance. If he hadn't shown an interest in the dragon and his girlfriend, we wouldn't have noticed him. Then—more. The dad took it upon himself to help his son Rur, who was suffering from unrequited love, with a certain problem. What's interesting is that during the preparation to kidnap the girl, they became friends, not as father and son, but as two bosom buddies of the same age would. That's when our surveillance officers made their first conclusion: that the vampire isn't working for the Woodies, but for some other structure. His style is much different from the Woody exploits. It wasn't hard to figure out that he was under some sort of mental influence; the son came under it too. We decided to continue the operation and find out who the puppet master was. I should tell you that the operation almost went belly-up when our observation of the abducted girl was temporarily lost due to some annoying mishaps. Presumably, at that moment, when she was under the effects of black lily powder, they processed her a little. They tinkered with her brains, because at all other times the agents didn't let her out of their sight, and they didn't observe any direct effect. At the same time, we discovered that they were affecting their targets through the weapons. The scheme is stunning for its simplicity and the sheer genius with which it was carried out. Each individual amulet cannot create much effect by itself, but the Arians used an accord scheme, wherein the independent amulets start working as a united whole. You just have to give the command to the lead artifact. The human, elf, or vampire will have no idea whatsoever that they're under the mental influence. They'll feel like they're giving themselves advice, very good advice, which allows them to benefit from any scenario. So, here too 'light' thoughts came into the vampires' heads."

"How did the vampire get her hands on the weapons containing the artifacts?"

"Her betrothed shared with her."

"Well yes, how could I have not guessed. When did you discover the Arian?"

"Hm, we almost lost him entirely. The were-dragon was so upset he almost suffocated the scoundrel. Then he decided to get even rougher, and we were able to establish for certain the fact that the caravan boss wasn't who he was pretending to be, and caught him red-handed. The brain-busters uncovered his memories. The Arian did not have time to hide them. Once we got all those footholds, and after relaying the information to Tantre's Secret Chancellery, it wasn't difficult to put the pieces together."

"Praiseworthy, but you know what?"

"What?"

"Cut any mention of the vampire girl out of the report you're preparing for the High Prince. It's not worth teasing a rabid sul. Admit it: in the circumstances we're dealing with, that wouldn't bring you anything good."

"What should we do with the girl?"

"Are you having some problems?"

"Not yet, but the mental influence on the vampires has disappeared, and what will happen when the dragon comes back?" Beriem chuckled sadly.

"If he comes back. Leave everything as it is and forget you had anything to do with it."

GLOSSARY

Geography

Alatar—the largest continent on the planet of *Ilanta*.

Aria—a continent located north of Alatar.

Empire of Alatar—a state existing two thousand years ago that pursued an aggressive policy of conquest. Approximately sixty percent of the total area of the continent of Alatar was subject to the Empire. The continent itself was named in honor of the Empire. Northern kingdoms such as Tantrc, Mesaniya, Meriya, and Rimm were at one time secluded barbarian provinces of the Empire. As a result of civil war, the Empire of Alatar was broken into separate states and ceased to exist.

Ilanta—a planet.

Kingdom of Mestair—a legendary human kingdom located on the territory of modern-day Taiir and the Great Principality of Mesaniya, which existed three thousand years ago during the age of the dragons. As an independent state, it was destroyed by the dragons and their allies during the war with the Forest Elves and few human states that had joined them.

The Light Forest—the state of the Forest Elves, limited to the growth area of the Mellornys.

The Marble Mountains—a large mountain range crossing the northern part of Alatar from north to south. From the north, the range is bordered by the North Sea, and from the south, by the Southern Rocky Ridge and the Long sea.

Mesaniya—A Great Principality located north of the kingdom of Tantre.

Nelita—The second planet in a triple solar system: Ilanta, Nelita, and Helita. Nelita is considered the dragons' native land; it was named in honor of the goddess of life, Nel. The literal translation is "eye of the goddess of life."

Ort—the largest river in the north of Alatar, flows across the territory of the kingdom of Tantre.

Patskoi Empire—a human state with the capital at the city of Pat. The Emperors of Pat consider themselves the heirs of the Empire of Alatar.

Rimm—a human kingdom located east of the Marble Mountains.

Steppe—the self-designation of the kingdom of the white orcs. Located in the east of Alatar.

Taiir—a dukedom

Tantre—a large kingdom, second largest after the Patskoi Empire, located in the central part of north-western Alatar. Geographically limited by the Marble Mountains and the Northern and Southern Rocky Ridges.

Has access to the Eastern Ocean and the Long Sea. Its capital is the city of Kion.

Miscellaneous

Alert-dert—a military rank corresponding to that of captain.

Asgard—in Scandinavian mythology, the heavenly city is the abode of the Aesir gods.

Book of the Guardians—a book in which the dragons recorded the password spells to the interplanetary portals. The guardians are the dragons (true blood mages), who stayed on Ilanta to guard the portals. At the time the events described herein took place, all guardians are thought to be deceased.

Chucker—a magical artifact that allows its user to throw balls of capsulized spells.

Drag—a flying lizard that can be saddled and ridden.

Feather—a junior military group of twelve to fifteen rideable animals.

The Goddesses' Eyes are what people call the planets Nelita and Helita. Helita, Nelita, and Ilanta make up the system of planets that revolve around their sun.

The Gray Horde—the collective name for all the "gray" orcs residing in the northern coastal steppes; the strongest khanate of the "gray" orcs was also called the Gray Horde.

Gross-dert (gross- leading, dert- wing)—a military rank in the air units of Tantre's army, corresponding to that of colonel.

Hel—mistress of the world of the dead.

Khirud—the main god in the pantheon of the "white" orcs. Khirud the lightning-armed is the god of warriors and daredevils.

"Knee" Prince-Khan—that is, one who is bent at the knee, living in total vassal dependence on the king, unlike a "belt" prince or khan, that is, one who bows at the waist. Belt khans have a high level of autonomy, can mint silver and copper coins, and maintain personal militias, some of which are comparable to an army. They collect their own taxes independently on their lands, sending one twelfth to the king's treasury. In the event of war, "belt" princes are obligated to present one third of their troops to the king's army. "Knee" khans, most likely, are hereditary governors of the lands and take an oath of fidelity to the king.

Loki—the Scandinavian god of mischief

The Lynx clan, the Dragon clan—the strongest clans of the island Norsemen.

Nökürs - elite warriors and bodyguards.

The Northern Alliance—an alliance of Tantre, the Rauu Principalities, and the dwarf kingdoms.

Odin—a Norse deity.

Pound, jang—the currency of the kingdom of Tantre. Pounds come in silver and gold; jangs are a small copper coin.

Rauu—Snow Elves. The first artificial race created by the dragons for battles against the orcs.

Roi-dert—a junior officer's rank, corresponds to that of lieutenant.

Rune Keys—used for opening portals.

Second-in-saddle—the second rider on a large golden griffon. Usually armed with a bow, rarely with a magical chucker.

Servants of Death—helrats, priests of a cult forbidden in all countries which perverts the very name of the goddess Hel. Hunted dragons and actively promoted human sacrifice.

Severan—a cold northern wind.

Taili-Mother—The deity of the "white" orcs, representing the feminine, analogue of the goddess Nel.

Targ—the dwarf god whose name took on a negative connotation in almost all countries. Occupies the niche of mischief-maker and prankster, analogous to *Loki* in some sense.

Teg—the polite form of address of a nobleman; *grall*—to a mage. *Teg grall*—the form of address of a noble mage. *Tain, taina*—titles for high-borns, male and female, respectively. Professor/master/mistress [first name] Teg grall (tain/taina) [last name].

True blood—a mage who, unlike others, can work directly with the astral and consciously take mana from it. Other mages can extract mana only from the planet's magical field.

Snekkja—a row/sailboat of the Scandinavian peoples in the twelfth-fourteenth centuries. Predominantly used for raids. Held up to one hundred people.

Valhalla—a heavenly palace in Asgard for the fallen in battle, a paradise for the valiant warriors.

Wing—a regiment of griffons or drags consisting of one-hundred-twenty to one-hundred-fifty rideable animals.

BOOK RECOMMENDATIONS:

Thank you for reading this book. Please consider leaving a review and joining our Facebook page 'The Dragon Inside' and remember you can contact Alex on Facebook or our website.

Fayroll by Andrey Vasilyev is an exciting adventure story about Harriton Nikiforov, a journalist forced to write a story about the newest online craze 'Fayroll'. Along the way he meets a variety of interesting characters and finds a life changing epic quest that will change his life forever. This series was a best seller in Russia when first published. Find Fayroll on Amazon.

Hello, dear readers! Our digital publishing house's mission is to find new gems of the modern fantasy literature. We've given you many series that have been thoroughly enjoyed, especially by our male audience, but we would like you to know that we keep all of our readers in mind. With that being said, we're glad to introduce you the book of Lina J. Potter, a romantic fantasy series named "Medieval tale"! We hope that all readers will enjoy our new female heroine and her adventures! The first book from the series is now available for order.

I also want to recommend Realm of Arkon, a great series written by a friend of mine: G. Akella. He is one of the most popular and best-selling LitRPG authors in Russia. Book one is currently available for free until the end of the month on Amazon.

Made in the USA
Monee, IL
17 September 2020